SAILOR
STORY

Kurt Burke

ISBN 978-1-0980-1002-7 (paperback)
ISBN 978-1-0980-3388-0 (hardcover)
ISBN 978-1-0980-1003-4 (digital)

Christian Faith Publishing, Inc.
832 Park Avenue
Meadville, PA 16335
www.christianfaithpublishing.com

Printed in the United States of America

There is a fundamental difference between a sailor's story and a fairy tale, one begins with "Once upon a time," the other with "This ain't no shit."

—J. A. Carlile

ACKNOWLEDGMENTS

For my mother who imbued me with a sense of history, for my father, an unending source of information, nautical and otherwise. And to Rhonda who is always there for me.

This is a work of fiction and the stories portrayed in this book are imaginary versions of factual events, although many of the characters were real. I certainly apologize if anyone feels I disparaged the character of someone now-dead more than a hundred years. If anything, I hope I brought to light the importance they brought to the history of the nation and the subsequent impact on its development. Any resemblance to real people in the fictional characters I portray is unintentional, just my effort to make the story interesting, amusing, and believable.

KB

The *Mary Eleanore*, built 1824, Robert Craig & Sons, Philadelphia
Sunk August 1865, off Cape Fear, North Carolina.

CSS *Alabama*, built 1862, John Laird & Son, Liverpool, as *Enrica*
Sunk June 1864, off Cherbourg, France.

Cunard Line RMS *Karnak*, built 1853, Liverpool
Sunk April 1862, off Nassau Harbor

CSS *Tuscaloosa*, built 1850, Philadelphia
Turned over to the US Navy in 1865.

PROLOGUE

May 20, 1861

Night was falling when Captain Thomas Carlile gave the order to change course to larboard, toward the Virginia coast, the move further concealed by the drizzling rain which had been falling all day. The man with the glass in the foretop confirmed that no stray sail on the horizon would witness the maneuver. After entering the waters of the Chesapeake in the morning, they had cleared the naval squadron at Hampton Roads earlier in the afternoon without a challenge. Carlile mused that the navy had bigger fish to fry trying to prevent the plethora of merchant activity out of Newport News and Norfolk along with persistent rumors of the development of an ironclad being built by the new Confederate Navy. Besides they were clearly inbound toward their home port of Baltimore. The *Mary Eleanore* responded like the champ she was, changing tack with almost no loss of speed. She was a brigantine of 120 tons, 90 feet of waterline but with a draft of less than 10, a hermaphrodite brig with fore and aft rigged main mast, making her nimble and giving her the ability to lie quite close to the wind when necessary. She was ideal for the coastal trade but sturdy enough to weather the Atlantic crossing. A true asset to the family business.

Standing at the quarterdeck railing, Carlile shifted his gaze forward as his nephew and Second Officer Arthur rigged a tackle hoist above the open main hatch and heard cursing from below as the men there trundled barrels of Bordeaux wine aside to gain access to the hidden compartment on the orlop deck. Quickly the three cases marked *Westley Richards & Co., Birmingham* were hoisted to the deck in preparation. Each case contained mercury fulminate caps designed for the '53 Enfield infantry rifle. A small and dangerous cargo, but his brother James had negotiated $1,000 in gold coin for the transaction, almost half of which was straight profit. The crew would remain quiet as well, in part due to their sympathy with the cause and in bigger part due to the bonus they would receive for this night's work. Carlile had more concern for his nephew who vocally made his politics known and was considering joining the Confederate Navy. Arthur already had a life full of loss and an unsympathetic father stuck on the values from their Quaker ancestry. If he enlisted, it would be a hard blow for the family business as Arthur had not only proven adept at handling ship and crew but was equally sound negotiating deals for cargo. He seemed to have a true sense for what would fetch top dollar on both sides of the Atlantic as well as a great memory for inventory details. Arthur had also proven, on occasion, to be a passable ship's surgeon which further endeared him to the crew. Their legitimate cargo of French Bordeaux would be most welcome in the Washington City backrooms, bars, and government offices that were already rapidly expanding in response to the war effort. *Money to be made*, Carlile thought.

The drizzle abated as the *Mary Eleanore* eased past New Point and on up along the sandbank. There were only subtle shades of contrast between the black of the sea, land, and sky. The offshore breeze was still thick with low hanging mist, and it was inky-dark by now. A single shuttered lantern in the stern was all that marked the location of the ship, slit open on the landward side to provide a beacon. As the *Mary Eleanore* reached the rendezvous point, Carlile brought her into the wind and backed the foretopsail, already double-reefed. The mainsail started to luff in the light air, and the *Mary Eleanore* began to roll slightly in the current as she came to a stop. *A milk run.* Already Carlile could hear the slap and creak of oars as a boat approached along with some sharp but unintelligible command from across the water.

Carlile heard Arthur call out a challenge, "Sic semper tyrannis," and the confirming reply, "Death to tyrants." He mused for a second on the incorrect translation then heard the thump of the boat coming alongside with the rattle of the chain, securing it to the ringbolt on the side of the ship below the mainmast shrouds. Within a minute, Arthur and Maller, the bos'n, had the crates hoisted up into the air in a cargo net, then over the side and into waiting hands in the boat below. Maller was a stump of a man with huge hairy arms. He was useful in any sort of altercation, just his presence enough to make potential opponents nervous. He handled the heavy cases with the ease of a man accustomed to such tasks as indeed he was, timing the motion of the ship to assist his pull on the rope. Carlile caught a glimpse of a gray uniform kepi with black brim and CSA emblem on the man in the stern of the boat, a navy officer. Transfer complete, the boat unlatched and began to pull hard for shore.

"Put your helm over," Carlile called over to the helmsman at the wheel. "Shake the reefs out of that tops'l if you please."

The *Mary Eleanore* broke into a turmoil of activity, feet padding across the deck and sailors jumping to the rigging to trim sail. She spun slowly in place, then heeled slightly as the wind came around to her quarter, gathering speed in one smooth motion. *A milk run.* Arthur was at his side then, radiating exuberant release of tension and sense of accomplishment.

"You have the helm, sir," Carlile told him then turned and strode aft to the companionway ladder. As he stepped behind the binnacle, the mist seemed to thicken almost imperceptibly around the *Mary Eleanore*; and as he left the deck into the confined space below, Carlile noted that it was raining again.

S ome men are defined by the events of which they become a part. I on the other hand have been pushed and pulled through the events of history by others welding far more control than me until I find myself toward the end of my days, reduced to the role of a traveling physician, still eking out a living on the riverboats and rough frontier boomtowns of the American West. Long ago, I gave up my inheritance, family, and identity, believed to be dead. The alternative would be a noose, and I have no notion of being sacrificed to the legacy of an evil man who became beloved by the nation simply from having died at the hand of a misguided egomaniac in the name of a dying cause. My only solace is in the ability to visit occasionally with my daughter, a true lady—even if I despise the Yankee she married. He is no gentleman and sharpens saws for a living, but Nell seems happy with her lot and this has to be enough for an old father to wish for.

So I embark on a poor sailor story. I set the truth to paper because others cannot or will not, either through fear of their own demise or because it would result in the rack and ruin of political and financial careers they have developed reaching into top government positions. Some men have the enviable ability to bury their past secrets and turn disaster into success regardless of the toll taken on their fellows.

I was born John Arthur Carlile in Baltimore. My father, James Carlile, had moved there from Philadelphia in 1829 after the untimely death of my grandfather and turned his inheritance into a small mercantile and liquor store on Forest Street in the north end. He had his younger brother and ward, Thomas, in tow and together, they made a huge success of the business. He married well to Caroline Welsh, the daughter of a local merchant and importer. By the time I came along, they had moved the grocery to a large corner location on busy Orleans Street across from what was then the Baltimore Mall. I grew up in the store, back alleys, waterfront, and in the home of my Uncle Thomas on East Baltimore Street.

I have many fond memories of growing up in Baltimore. The brick row houses come to mind with the brick inevitably crumbling away but the doorsteps done in impeccable marble. I recall the shopkeepers and tradesmen in their leather aprons, worn not just to save their clothing but as an iconic symbol of status. Letting the world know they possessed honest skill. The smell of blue crab steaming in salt, beer, and bay seasoning is etched into my consciousness, my aunt serving wonderfully-delicate crab cakes on crackers. Some of my earliest memories are of earning pennies for an afternoon, watching over the drying racks full of *lake trout* for the fishermen, using a stick to ward off the marauding gulls. I think I was about four when I finally realized my name was not "hon," that it was just a term of endearment that all the women used.

My father and Uncle Thomas had acquired a merchant vessel and named it after my uncle's wife, Mary Eleanore. Thomas was referred to as Cap'n Carlile by all as far back as I can remember. He dressed the part too. Black wool greatcoat and seaboots even in the summer, a yard of checkered shirt and a bicorn cocked hat that, along with the curly black beard and twinkle in his eye, made him appear to be an adventurer from bygone days. My childhood friends persisted in the notion that he was a pirate of the first order; this rumor was further spread by the belief that our family business had been founded on selling bootleg liquor. Indeed I knew this to be more than a half-truth as I was allowed aboard ship on occasions that involved little risk of our smuggling activities being discovered. For an active boy, romping about on the spars and rigging was not unlike a trip to a carnival and the crew were objects of awe with their stories of adventure in places I had only read about in books.

My Uncle Thomas married Mary Eleanore Semmes of Carroll County, widely considered to be the most beautiful belle in the entire city. Her family claimed decent from Huguenot royalty, from Henry of Navarre, and had settled in Maryland early on. I always wondered what kept my uncle away at sea when clearly he had the sweetest and prettiest lady in the world right there at home. Certainly I was smitten in love with her my entire childhood and spent an inordinate amount of time at her home, jumping at the opportunity to do chores or otherwise ease her burdens. Her home overlooked the harbor then, although taller structures obscured the view later. I always felt pulled toward the ships and their activity and was very much at ease even then with the riff-raff that accumulated, as always, along the taverns, brothels, wharves, and quays surrounding the basin and northeast branch that was the entire Baltimore harbor at the time. I was sad to hear later that the old house had perished in the big fire of February '04.

My father had other plans for me and sent me to school. He was always quick to remind me of the error of my ways and kept a maple wood cane as a reminder to me of my family's place in the world whenever I was truant or came home with a tear in my pants after sticking up for my integrity or later on in rescuing my stepmother's reputation. I hated him at the time for never seeing my side of a story; but later, I recognized in him a profound sadness with the illness, then death, of my mother and found some peace with him, if not quite an understanding.

My mother passed when I was five but birthed my brother Jimmy before her death. They called her illness consumption of the liver back then. Unfortunately she passed her illness along to my brother at birth and Jimmy was always sickly. I believe the doctors' inability to diagnose or treat the illness made me angry as only can be done by something beyond one's control. I would somewhat conquer this later by studying medicine; but in my younger days, it left me with plenty of opportunity to be less than sympathetic of others' inadequacies. To top it off, my father then married Ms. Mary West just nine months after my mother's death.

My new stepmother was a twenty-year-old girl who had lived with her parents around the block from the store and she was a regular customer. She had little control attempting to parent me. My father was quite a bit older. Consequently those who already disliked me were quick to point out that my father was easing his grief with her even before my mother's passing, and I was quick in attempts to put those words back in the mouths of the accusers. I wasn't a large youth, but I had no notion of quitting. After the worst fights with the largest kids, I was grudgingly accepted which just meant I was an angry youth with a bad attitude and large friends. I have to admit that it was not always larger kids that I fought with; I had just as little patience with my younger peers as the older youths had with my antics. My father had been busy with the grocery and import shop along with my stepmother's first two pregnancies, so I was left primarily to my own devices. I didn't see him much unless negative reports of my activities became known. By the time I was thirteen, he decided enough was enough, I was packed up, sent to Richmond, Virginia, and enrolled in school at the Maymont Military Institute.

M aymont was pretty much what I expected. We drilled, marched, ran, stood post, attended class, and polished everything. The school was located just outside the west city limit near the waterworks, above and overlooking the Kanawha Canal and James River. On arrival, I was issued the uniform that had been purchased for me, light gray broadcloth tunic, brass buttons stamped with the school insignia, and black high collar. Two pairs of white linen trousers and crossbelts to which leather pouch and bayonet were attached. A felt shako with brass insignia and black pom-pom and model 1809 Prussian smoothbore musket completed the ensemble. I signed a gentleman's code of conduct, swore an oath to uphold it, and was told I would be held to a high standard of personal dress. My appearance and demeanor apparently now reflected upon the institution.

I was assigned to a dormitory room and met my roommate. If Maymont was what I expected, Eugene Parish was not. Eugene was tall, slightly stooped, and awkward. He could not keep his feet in time during drill and in spite of every effort to the contrary, his appearance was permanently rumpled. Eugene was from somewhere in Western Georgia and had the thick accent that immediately reminded one of a country bumpkin. He was an extremely popular target for the upperclassmen who were tasked to run the day-to-day operation of the unit; they would get within an inch of his face, insulting his parentage at the top of their lungs, at which point, inevitably from the back rank, could be heard a call, "Wal gaawly, caydet sergeant!"

If Eugene was a terrible example of a soldier, he made up for it in other ways. He could calculate trigonometric functions in his head and taught me to use pictures to elicit answers to complex mathematics and engineering equations. I heard that Eugene's parents had arranged his academy appointment to escape some argument over his gambling winnings that perhaps exceeded lawful bounds. I, on the other hand, kept Eugene from accumulating demerits for inspections that he would have otherwise failed along with convincing peers not to apply physical means to coerce him into a more military bearing. Upper-class hazing was the norm in the beginning but subsided on into the term as even the cadet sergeants were dependent on the plebes high-functioning level to score their own marks with the staff.

The cadet company was divided into four platoons of four squads each; platoons and squads were housed in dormitory sections which in turn were divided by sides of the long hallways. School faculty commanded the company and platoons while platoons and squads were presided over by the upperclassmen who commanded sections. There were always more first and second-year cadets as the older boys who were not successful enough to obtain a command billet would usually leave the school to specialize in alternate pursuits. Due to my inability to keep my mouth shut and my other endeavors in self-amusement, I found myself a bit of a target for the cadet sergeants who not only needed assistance keeping their weapons and equipment in top condition but also were in consistent need of sand buckets on the third floor to be used as fire retardant. It also appeared that I was a top candidate when our platoon was up for watch, especially last duty of the night or during the heavy thunderstorms that frequent that part of the country. Still I managed high marks in most areas and avoided discipline from the faculty.

The barracks hall was a three-story I-shaped stone building on the north side of the quadrant, the four corners being occupied by stairwells. Latrines were in the basement, a great refinement at the time, but there was no running water and part of duty was to haul water to fill the keg used to promote sanitation for washing the drains in the floor trough. Rooms contained pairs of box beds, writing tables, hardback chairs, an oil lamp, and washbasins. Each room had a corner fireplace for warmth in the winter, although they really provided little heat and firewood was always a scant commodity.

The main school building faced the main drive and parade ground from the west side with entry foyer, grand hall and kitchens on the ground floor, all faced by an arched stone veranda the complete length of the front. Classrooms and staff offices occupied the upstairs floors accessed by a grand staircase, starting in the center of the foyer. The grand hall was used for dining and any other formal meeting or ball sponsored by the institute. It featured three sets of enormous French doors that opened directly onto the veranda. To the west, behind and uphill from the main building, were the stables and a low chicken-coop style building that housed the servants.

On the south side, overlooking the James River, were three substantial two-story residences. The center home was set back slightly and was occupied by the superintendent, the other two were for the staff and their families. There were splendid private gardens behind these homes extending down the hill. In the center of all this was a long looping drive. On the east side apex, where the drive divided, was the entry gate, flagpole, and two no-longer-functional six-pounder brass howitzers that, although ornamental only, were kept in gleaming condition.

The food was surprisingly good and plentiful. Black servants in school livery cooked and served meals that were all-you-can-eat—in the fifteen minutes you had for mess. In addition, eating was done at seated attention with eyes front and back straight at all times. Deviation from this policy resulted in clearing your place early and an apology to the faculty member charged with oversight of the mess for the day. Consequently there was little conversation in the dining hall.

In addition to classwork instruction, we learned to drill as units, both on foot and on horseback. The school kept a stable of superbly-trained mounts. We also had instruction in gentlemanly pursuits such as social niceties, dancing, and fencing. We were occupied with this and chores, from reveille to tattoo Monday through Friday. Constant and contradictory orders bellowed by the upperclassmen contributed to a sense of exhaustion, especially when accompanied by affirmation that you were hopelessly unable to get anything even close to correct. Colonel Phillips, our superintendent, was a religious man so Sunday was spent first in church, then confined to barracks for introspection and study if we didn't draw watch duty.

Sunday was also mail call, looked forward to by a bunch of homesick boys. Perfume-scented letters from girls at home were passed around the group accompanied by catcalls and off-color humor. Packages were the most prized as they contained baked goods and other sought after treats. These were opened and generally shared by the group. We had a particular plebe Jimmy Rhea in my squad who must have communicated this to his family as on a particularly warm May Sunday, he received a small sealed wood box from his brothers at home in Philadelphia. The platoon crowded around expectantly to see what could be so special. When the lid was unsealed, a horrific odor spread through the room. Seems his brothers all defecated into the box, sealed it up, and mailed it to him. Jimmy was always the prankster of the squad, and this made me wonder what his family life had to be like. Our cadet platoon Sergeant Richard Schuab was tall, well-muscled and sported a permanent scowl. Even he snorted out a half-laugh at this turn of events.

Saturday was the best day of the week. It began with inspection of persons and quarters then proceeded to parade of the student company. This became more elaborate as we became more proficient with the drill manual. We often had dignitaries come to view the spectacle, especially the fourth Saturday of the month when the school hosted a gala ball. In mild weather, young ladies flocked to the school in fine calico dresses, undoubtedly looking to attract the affections of the older students; the institute tuition was steep, and the cadets all came from upscale homes. After midday dinner, we were given leave until 8 o'clock and we took that opportunity to explore the city and environs unless we had to be present for duty or to prepare for a school event.

Cadets and platoons were subject to weekly assessments from the staff that often resulted in demerits that needed to be worked off. This spiraled into more disaster as when reporting to the duty officer, he was bound to find something wrong with uniform or equipment which resulted in additional demerit. No doubt this was all part of the program, and the result was that platoons and squads became tight-knit organizations that were self-supporting for survival. Our twelve-member squad became inseparable—eating together, studying together, and cleaning equipment together. We were the fourth squad of the fourth platoon and began referring to ourselves jokingly as the forty-fourth death squad.

Our platoon commander was Captain Giles, an ex-army officer who had served with General Jackson in 1814 at New Orleans and was held in high regard by the other staff members. He had white hair that swept back from a high forehead, reminding one of biblical pictures of God. He had a solid build even at his age and could be formidable in an argument. I recall once when Eugene Parish was called to his office to be questioned as to his opinion regarding poor peer ratings he was receiving. His answer was apparently not what was expected, and Giles's response could be heard clear across the quad for approximately ten minutes. When Eugene reappeared, his eyes looked like a deer who has already been downed and is waiting for the coup de gras. I seemed to have better luck.

One night, when third platoon had the watch, there was a particular boy who had a habit of sleeping on duty. Eugene and I sneaked out and painted his shoes zebra-patterned with the chalk that we used to keep our belts white. This was observed by all when falling out for reveille in the morning and caused quite a spectacle. The next night, we were confronted by Cadet Robert Miller and two of his mates. Miller was from Ohio, a pain-in-the-backside spit-and-polish self-styled leader of the third. He said that sons of liquor merchants were not gentlemen and should not be accepted to fine institutions like Maymont. He raised his fists in fine marquis of Queensbury style. I grabbed his wrist and dropped him to the ground, street-style. It was over before it began. A guy has to have a good ground game; he looked very foolish. The story must have spread quickly because the next morning, I was called out of class to see Giles in his office. He asked me if I had a problem with Miller.

I told him, "Not anymore."

He responded with a hmm, appraised me with one bushy white eyebrow raised for about five seconds, then said, "Dismissed." Once he even told me that his impression was that I would make a passable officer.

Giles was also our history professor and combined the classwork with tactics and evaluation of the battle reports coming out of Mexico at the time. The whole school followed with interest the exploits of Zach Taylor and the progress of General Scott's march from Vera Cruz to Mexico City, along with the treachery of Santa Ana in making agreements with the United States to pursue peace then attacking Taylor at Buena Vista. Taylor's order to Braxton Bragg to "Give 'em a little more grapeshot" was the saying of the day. Comparisons were made to Napoleon's campaigns as he was regarded as the military genius of the age—even above and beyond Alexander, Hannibal, Caesar, Gustavus Adolphus, or Frederick the Great. The news of the capture and occupation of Mexico City came that fall, but the celebrations were rapidly followed by dissent over what dispositions should be made. Although slavery was illegal in Mexico, our boys from the north were against acquiring too much territory in proximity to Texas. Our boys from the south, for the most part, thought the complete annex of Mexico was the most favorable solution. The nation had followed President Polk's manifest destiny policy all the way to war, only to be bitterly divided by the success of that war. The generous terms of the Treaty of Guadalupe Hidalgo in February 1848, came as a pleasant surprise but in the long term did nothing to resolve these issues.

I, of course, was a Polk supporter, being both from Maryland and the offspring of a merchant family. Polk's replacement of the Black Tariffs had made immediate lucrative prospects available for the import of luxury products from Europe, the quality of which could not be matched by what was being manufactured in the United States at that time. In addition, I was bemused by attitudes toward slavery. My father had acquired Maddie to cook and clean when my mother had fallen ill. My Uncle Thomas had voiced his displeasure with this at the time, but Maddie had rapidly become an integral part of the household and that was that. At school, I discovered others had an almost religious pro or antislavery fervor, although I noted that nobody had any objection to eating meals prepared and served by the school servants. The students all came from affluent backgrounds and were accustomed to being catered to whether the help was hired or owned. All the better-class homes, to my knowledge, had servants regardless of their politics. At my young age and urban background, I had little experience in the difference between household servants and field hands along with no thought of the concept of what it meant to be owned. For me, the whole question was what the government should be able to tell me about what I could and could not do.

Beginning in the spring of 1848, I began to look more and more forward to the monthly academy ball. My father's cousin, John Snyder Carlile, was a representative to the Virginia General Assembly in the house of delegates from the western portion of the state. As such, he maintained residence in Richmond when the assembly was in session. He often came on Saturdays as he was a big supporter of the institute, and his young wife, Mary Ellen, would accompany him with her entourage of female friends and relatives. That is how I came to meet Ms. Mary McDowell.

3

Mary McDowell first accompanied my Uncle John's party to the Maymont Academy Ball in April 1848, and we were introduced. She was a relative of his wife; her mother had sent her to a finishing school in Richmond and had encouraged her attachment to Mrs. Carlile's household for the social exposure. Her father owned a small farm in Caroline County, along the Mattaponi River near Bowling Green, which had been in the family since about 1700.

We connected immediately, we were both just fourteen-year-olds in a city away from home. I was struck by her bright-blue eyes that could alternately sparkle with mischief or make you take a step back when she was not quite pleased with your opinion on a topic. Unlike most girls I had met, she would let you know what she was thinking rather than defer coquettishly as was normal in those days. She was medium height, slender build, and had blond hair tinged with a light-reddish-brown that started straight at the top of her head but ended wavy on her shoulders. The tightly-curled coif, so popular at the time, would only last her a short time before strands would begin to stray from their appointed locations. She had just the slightest suggestion of freckles on a rather small nose.

I began to visit my Uncle John's town house on Saturdays when I could get leave, sometimes bringing Eugene Parish along as for some odd reason, my uncle developed a favorable opinion of Eugene. They would argue the engineering feasibility of continuing to build the Kanawha Canal to support the economic growth of Virginia to the west. Mary McDowell had a friend, Betsy, and the four of us would walk the city spending time in the market, parks, and admiring the architecture of the government buildings and manors up on the hills. Occasionally my Aunt Mary Ellen would take us for a carriage ride in the countryside when she felt she ought to be chaperoning. Although my Uncle John was close to forty, Aunt Mary Ellen was only a twenty-year-old, so she was sympathetic to our budding friendship.

I spent that summer break working in the warehouse that my father and uncle used to store goods being shipped in and out of the country. I quickly learned that not all our cargo was declared to the harbormaster and assessor, the remaining portion being moved in and out of the warehouse quietly at night. I knew that some money changed hands to smooth this process; and at times, an especially nice vintage bottle of wine or liquor was delivered to private residences in town. Once I assisted delivering a finely-crafted French armoire to a large home in the west end.

The presidential election was in full swing, and my father was a Democrat and Cass supporter once it was confirmed that Polk would not seek reelection, citing that he had accomplished the goals he had set and developing health issues. Rumors cited his increased alcohol consumption as the basis for his health problems; this may have been more or less medicinal. The Whigs had been steadily losing popularity and support over the past decade, even Van Buren had defected and was busy garnering support for a new party. To everyone's surprise, Zach Taylor threw in his hat with the Whigs, rejuvenating the party. Taylor was wildly popular with the masses as the hero of the Mexican War. The election, all of a sudden, became a hotly-debated contest.

I returned to Maymont in the beginning of September and resumed my routine. As a second year, I was treated as more of a crony of the upperclassmen who now had new boys to break in. Even Eugene Parish was more or less left alone in spite of his continued inability to learn martial skills. The academy had a policy of keeping the boys on property for the first four weeks of term to acclimate them to the rigors of the school schedule. The end of September, Saturday, ball marked the end of confinement. In October, leave resumed and I began to see Mary McDowell again; we seemed to pick up right where we had left off and were best of friends.

The presidential election that November was not as close as it appeared on paper. It was the first national election to have everyone in every state vote on the same day, making for a gala event. Taylor won the majority of the populous eastern states, making the outcome a certainty before the returns from the western states began to be counted up. The West went for Cass almost entirely.

Christmas break came and went, the busy routine made time pass rapidly. I was really looking forward to the Saturday outings with Mary when I could share anecdotes of the happenings at the academy and just have her as my companion in our explorations of the city. At about that time, I was given cadet corporal stripes and additional responsibilities within my squad, an honor for a second-year student.

January 1849, began with a cold snap. It was clear, but the temperatures remained in the twenties for two solid weeks. Standing watch at the institute became arduous, and my new responsibilities included making the rounds of the post to ensure due diligence and attentiveness. Posts were relieved at two-hour intervals and were performed at attention or at present arms whenever there was an approach to the post. Especially at night, this could become a tedious task, and the freezing weather made things downright painful. It was useful instruction for the first years showing them how to avoid locking their knees to prevent collapse before their rotation was accomplished.

I was a novice at romance, and although I was not unfamiliar with the ways of the world, I had no clue regarding the motivations and thinking of women. Indeed I believe I was convinced that my best romantic play was to comport myself in a most courteous and gentlemanly manner, even when my thoughts strayed elsewhere and my eyes would admire the way her hips swayed when she walked, the small amount of breast that she allowed to show in her décolletage and that soft place where her neck met her shoulder. There were a couple of events that suggested Mary had other plans for our relationship.

On a Saturday leave, my aunt and uncle decided to pick me up for a carriage ride and Mary came along to provide me with company. We had plenty of scarves, and the carriage was piled with thick blankets to thwart the cold wind. We drove to a spot overlooking the James River Falls, spectacular with the sun shining on icicles hanging from the rocks and trees where the rising mist from the falls froze fast. My uncle and I were having a lively discussion about his efforts to get funding to complete the canal between the James and Kanawha Rivers. His constituency was from the western portion of the state, and he was pushing for means to transport coal, timber, and the increasing agricultural output of the western region to markets in the east. The canal would enrich Virginia as a whole without having to resort to the Potomac River routes which would be controlled by Washington. I was more for steam power and railroads, citing this as the wave of the future and avoiding costly upkeep of waterways due to the seasonal flooding of the rivers. Mary was having an intense discussion with my aunt over some household matter, I felt her move in close under the blankets for additional warmth from the physical contact. I was immediately aroused. Somehow her hand brushed across my lap, and I heard her breath intake softly. I turned to look down at her, my eyes pleading an apology, but she was smiling and she rubbed my bicep with her shoulder under the blankets. I must have blushed, my uncle gave me an appraising look and after the outing told me to be very careful, that her father was not known to be an understanding man.

On another instance, we accompanied Uncle John and Aunt Mary Ellen to the Richmond Theater, a grand four-story opera house of the old style. We had a booth toward the front as befitted my uncle's prominence. We saw Edwin Forrest do Shakespeare; I thought the acting to be overdone, but Mary was enthralled. I'm not sure who was more animated, Mr. Forrest or Mary McDowell, but I know I enjoyed watching her range of emotion through the performance along with her fairly constant grasping of my hand or forearm when Forrest hyperbolized lines for emphasis.

With the coming of March, the weather warmed and spring came early. Inauguration in those days was March 4, but it was postponed until March 5, at Zach Taylor's insistence as the fourth fell on a Sunday. Heady events were in progress; reports from California territory regarding gold strikes were arriving daily and talk of making California a state were rife as were the rumors that the federal government was to outlaw slavery in the new territories won from Mexico. Southerners were incensed, Texas continued to stand on the claim that much of the new lands were part of their state so slavery was legal even in the portions claimed by Texas north of the Missouri compromise line. Tempers flared.

Mary and I were chaperoned more effectively that spring by my aunt—no doubt at the behest of my Uncle John—in an effort to avoid trouble. Most of our meetings took place at my uncle's home in Richmond and had taken on a much more formal feel, no longer like best friends romping about the city on adventures and sharing stories about school events. Therefore, I was taken completely by surprise when Mary took matters into her own hands.

On an early June afternoon, we had escaped and were exploring on the east side of the city, along the river near the base of Chimborazo Hill, when we discovered a partially-hidden cave leading into the base of the cliffside. Popular culture said these caves had been used in bygone days to brew and store beer; but now, the hill was a common where boys went to play and livestock grazed. It was not yet really a part of the city. The weather was unseasonably warm and a thunderstorm came up, quickly accompanied by a deluge of rain. We had been talking of going home for the summer and plans we had for the school vacation when the rain began to fall. We started laughing, pushing aside the brush that partially blocked the entrance to the cave in an effort to get to shelter. As we entered, Mary suddenly tripped and I caught her in my arms to steady her. I looked into her eyes and saw a combination of mischievousness, amusement, and passion. I suddenly understood that her tripping was not accidental. We kissed. My hand moved up tentatively to touch her breast, fully expecting her to stop me right there, but there was no resistance and I could feel her nipple already hardened through the fabric of her summer dress. We continued to kiss, our tongues touching, and I could smell jasmine.

I would like to tell you that I threw her to the ground and made a satisfied woman of her, but that was not the truth. Fact is she pushed me to the ground. She straddled me, unbuttoning my pants, and took me into her. It was fast and messy, but afterward, we leisurely kissed and held each other for about a half an hour until we realized that we had better get moving before there were questions asked. On the way back to my uncle's townhouse, I asked her if she was all right. She stopped, turned toward me, and looked me straight in the eye. "I got what I wanted," she said.

That was the last time I saw Mary McDowell for several years. When I went to my Uncle John's the next Saturday, she had left for home. She had left me a note with her address, telling me to write her over the summer and that she would see me again in September, but she never returned to school for the new term. At the year-end graduation ceremony, I was promoted to cadet sergeant for the coming term and billeted as guide for the fourth platoon. My father was quite proud.

4

Summer was a busy time at home in Baltimore, although I hardly felt it to be home anymore. With the success of the mercantile, my father had purchased a large new home on Aisquith Street and this was ruled over by my stepmother with the assistance of Maddie, our girl. My brother, Jimmy, was now a ten-year-old but pretty much confined to the house as his illness had progressed. He was very thin and pale but had the best sense of humor. His ability to make situational observations and turn them into a laugh was amazing, but I wasn't laughing when I saw how his ribs stood out and his arms and legs were just skin and bone.

My mathematics education made me a natural to assist with keeping the ledgers, although my father employed a bookkeeper along with buyers, clerks, a butcher, a tailor, and a shoemaker. My father had been a journeyman cordwainer, or shoemaker back in Philadelphia, and considered this as his specialty—he was a founding member of the Baltimore guild. My half-brother Thomas followed in the family tradition and apprenticed with the shoemaker, although he was showing an interest in women's fashions as a whole. My half-brother Alfred was a rambunctious toddler and kept Maddie busy being underfoot. My stepmother was with child once again and, during the hot summer days, had little patience for his antics. I decided early on to occupy one of the attic rooms over the store rather than stay in the home and, although it was sweltering and stagnant during the day, it provided me with a quiet space of my own to retire to in the evenings.

Our operation was as complex as it was simple. Our buyers scoured the countryside for deals, purchasing flour, tobacco, vegetables, fruit, meat, beer, and distilled liquor. Sometimes when the market was right, we even bought timber or kegs of nails and other hardware. We had these goods shipped by train on the B & O Line or by wagon through a freight company where we got excellent rates for regular runs. These purchases flowed into our warehouse where they were processed, then sold at wholesale to our store for resale or to our shipping company to put aboard the *Mary Eleanore* for movement to other locations. A section of the warehouse was reserved for meat packing and processing of other perishables. The shipping company of Thomas Carlile, which was the *Mary Eleanore,* made about three trips per year traveling first to either the Carolinas, Georgia or Nassau, Cuba or Haiti, selling part or all of the initial cargo there, then loading up primarily with cotton, tobacco and/or sugar for shipment across the Atlantic to England or France. We then loaded manufactured goods or specialized commodities such as wine, liquor, or quality textiles for shipment to Baltimore. These were then sold back to our warehouse for redistribution. We often carried a mail bag for private individuals or contracted with government entities for this service. We would always make special arrangements with people or companies to take on additional loads and as we had a reputation for keeping business matters confidential, some of what we shipped needed to escape the attention of the government officials. This was also easy for us due to my father's friendship with George Kane, who was assessor and collector for the port, then even more so when my father sold the grocery and took over the assessor position himself. Since our family was a major player and employer in the city of Baltimore, we had access to the highest level of society and were in a position to grant or get favors from not only the city fathers but within the Maryland legislature as well.

Then of course, there were the extracurricular activities which included the purchase of liquor from undeclared makers both in Maryland and Virginia, homemade stuff that was possibly better quality than what the legitimate producers made. As time went on, we began to import clandestine shipments of firearms from overseas.

This cargo never even entered a port but would be transferred at night to a fishing boat or small craft along an unpopulated stretch of shoreline.

As the summer progressed, I became much more involved in purchasing, especially with regard to products such as linen and wool cloth, furniture, tobacco, foodstuffs, metal hardware, and other manufactured goods arriving by ship and rail, both from overseas and domestic locations. Our warehouse just off Lombard Street provided easy access to both the docks and the Baltimore and Washington rail depot at Camden Yards. This provided a headquarters for my daily activities. We were most noted as a distributor of beer, wine, and liquor. This was a rough business, so my father provided me with a hired man, Gayle, to see to my safety. Gayle was short of stature, wide of shoulders, universally unshaven, and with the largest hands I've ever seen. He had a stray eye that caused most folks to underestimate his sharp intelligence. He carried a Bowie knife that he used as a tool for all occasions—even meals. I heard that he had a very nice and very tiny wife at home that no one ever met. One time, I was going over paperwork in one of the many watering holes that prevail along the basin, I saw Gayle approach from across the road with two of his cronies, laughing over some mischief they had perpetrated. As they approached the door, I heard one man say, "Let's get Gayle!" I heard a thud, thud.

Gayle came through the door, popped up on a barstool, and called out, "Whiskey, and follow it with a beer, my good man." When I looked out the window, I saw both of his friends sprawled out in the street.

We had a competitor in the liquor business, Patrick Martin. He ran a business similar to ours as he was a ship captain as well, although my Uncle Thomas referred to him as a lubber. I was to come to know Martin much better later. Once, a purchasing deal became tense between Martin's agent and myself over a batch of local beer. He was overbidding me, hoping to take advantage of my inexperience. When I let him have the product for a bit over the market value, he became angry and began cursing me loudly. Gayle solved the problem by picking the man up bodily, stuffing him into an empty keg half-full of garbage, and rolling him down the street. I wasn't as impressed by the action itself as I was by the look of pure enjoyment on Gayle's face when he was about to pounce.

Often after dark, we would have to move product into or out of the warehouse on a secret basis. When our ship, the *Mary Eleanore*, was in port, we would take excursions across the bay to Kent County. There was a distiller there who provided us with malt whiskey off the books. These bottles were labeled "Strathisla," a popular single-malt scotch whiskey, and a comparison of the label with the real scotch indicated the presence of an engraver with talent. We sold this mostly to politicians in Washington at a premium price or used it as a bribe for the local tax assessors and the police commissioner, George Kane.

George Kane was an interesting man and a great friend of my father's. They had started as competitors in the grocery business, but George Kane branched off into the state militia and politics, becoming a self-styled colonel then leveraged this into becoming an assessor and collector after which, he convinced the mayor into making him chief of the police. Kane was a short burley man of Irish decent with dark curly hair and a bushy beard. He had hard-blue eyes that could instill fear, and he did not back down from anyone, making him both friends and enemies. He wore military-style double-breasted coats, leaving the middle button undone so he could insert his hand to emulate Napoleon. He was admired by most unless you happened to get in his way, a decision you would then regret.

Baltimore of the time was plagued by street gangs, the largest being the Plug-Uglies. Having to pay protection money was just a part of doing business. Kane brought in his own men then organized and operated the police force in a military fashion. His men were armed with revolvers and soon brought the gang violence under better control, unless it happened to be nearing election time. A business tax was assessed to pay for law enforcement, so basically protection money was legitimized. The city was a safer place for the average citizen though.

Kane, my father, and other members of the city establishment would get together for coffee, and whiskey at times, in the afternoons to argue politics and terrorize waitresses; Kane was a staunch Whig while my father adamantly went Democrat. They were friends enough that my father could get away with calling him Mick to his face while Kane would refer to my father as Gravy. This friendship must have been effective as we never ran into any trouble with our extracurricular activities. In fact, quite the opposite as my father was invited to most of the upscale summer parties and had connections within the city, county, and federal governments. I was introduced around at these events, although I was clearly second fiddle to my father's influence. Still I was noted as up-and-coming in the business and even managed to catch the eye of some of the young ladies present.

I most enjoyed the expeditions in the *Mary Eleanore* as I admired my Uncle Thomas who was the captain. He was in his element on the water, and it was obvious that he ran a tight ship. Orders were obeyed instantly, and the crew asserted that he was he was an extraordinarily competent and fair master. It no doubt helped that bonuses for out of the ordinary duty solidified the crew as a family and kept mouths closed when on shore leave in the city. Uncle Thomas had a great understanding of military history and on these trips, we would debate strategy and tactics of bygone battles and wars. He would always tell me to ask myself who benefited financially from a war to discover the truth regarding the motivations of the heroes and rulers. I was far closer to my uncle than to my father.

Looking back, I can see my father was grooming me to take over the family business in spite of our frequent disagreements, although I was making choices favoring my own independence rather than following in his footsteps. I can see, in retrospect, that he had my best interests in mind and no little concern that my attitude and behavior would result in my coming to a bad end, but he had little ability to express affection toward me and I no doubt inherited this quality from him, so we were constantly at odds. I was effective within the business, however, and my father ensured that my wardrobe reflected my place within the establishment.

I wrote Mary McDowell several letters over the course of the summer but never received a reply. By the end of August, I was looking forward to resuming my life in Richmond and especially anxious to see Mary again.

The school year had a disappointing beginning for me; of our original squad, only myself, Bob Smith, and Jimmy Rhea remained at the academy. Bob had always been a natural and was now in the second as platoon sergeant. Eugene Parish had not returned, which was not surprising, and Jimmy Rhea now had the old fourth squad; it was only natural that we became roommates. With his nature, Jimmy became the main source of angst for the new plebes and as I had little patience for them either, I often amused myself at their expense as well. As a cost-saving measure, the barracks hall beds were wood boxes, solid on five sides, but the bottom had just a slat in the middle to hold the whole together. We would flip these over, replacing the straw mattress and bedding so that when the unsuspecting cadet returned to his room, exhausted from a difficult day and plopped himself down on his bed, he would fall straight through to the floor. On another occasion, there was a plebe, John Hoffman, who had an inordinately high opinion of himself. Jimmy and I went in and removed all his belongings, stacking them neatly in Captain Giles's office. Jimmy trumped up a story that food had been stolen from the kitchen and that his squad was suspect. As part of the code of conduct, stealing would result, of course, in expulsion. Young Mr. Hoffman returned to find his belongings cleaned out and a note to report to the captain immediately. Mr. Hoffman then had to do some quick thinking to explain to Giles why his belongings were there in the office and why he had come to get them. Jimmy and his corporal, a second year named Oakley, would sneak out after taps, enter a plebe's room, grab him by his ankles, and jerk him out of bed.

Usually screaming. Although these hazing measures were prohibited, this was difficult to enforce.

In spite of these antics, I missed the camaraderie of the old squad. In addition, I soon found out that Mary McDowell had not returned to Richmond for the school year. I was rather lonely, and I buried myself in my studies to compensate. I know my compatriots had some concerns regarding my demeanor as I was once more quick to anger and expressed little joy in daily events. I had one small perk as befitting my administrative duties as platoon guide—I had a small desk in the anteroom of Captain Giles's office. The office had a coal stove and subsequently was far better heated than the barracks hall rooms. Giles would regale me with his stories fighting Indians with Generals Severe and Jackson in Alabama, shocking tales of savagery and bravery of the bygone soldiers he had served with. Mrs. Giles would sometimes stop by the office and would transfix me with her disapproving glare when she caught him storytelling; apparently the captain was prone to nightmares after musing over the past. Like it was my fault.

At the beginning of December, I was summoned home due to the death of my brother, Jimmy. Although the news should not have been surprising, it still came as a blow. I was granted leave and given a ticket for the Richmond coach. This was also disruptive to my plans. I had saved to rent a horse for the trip home for Christmas break, planning to use the freedom of action to stop and see Mary McDowell on the way. It was not much of a detour to take the old road at Carmel Church to Bowling Green, then rejoin the pike at Fredericksburg.

Let me tell you about the coach in those days. It was typically overbooked, eight or nine inside the cab, and sometimes even an extra on top with the luggage and driver. The coach was pulled by four horses and had little to no springs, either by design or because they were worn out. Potholes in the road caused tooth-jarring thuds; I often wondered if the driver took perverse pleasure in aiming for instead of avoiding them.

In the summer, it was sweltering and odorous, unless you could manage a window, the stench of sweat mixed with an unhealthy variety of other body odors and perfumes. In the winter, other bodies were the only source of heat as the coach had no widow dressings and the wind would whip through the coach unobstructed. As a young man, I often had to relinquish my seat and sit on the floor or on top with the driver. There was always a lively conversation, usually with an undercurrent of hostility as the number of men to women was usually two to one; and even women accompanied by their husbands were subjected to the subtle competition from the rogues in the carriage. Being the south, of course, this was done with a veneer of exaggerated courtesy in the name of gallant behavior. It was a two-day trip if there were no maintenance issues, including the change at Washington for the final leg north to Baltimore. There were two stops for change of horses and meals; the first at Fredericksburg before going over the good bridge on the Rappahannock. The road deteriorated further north to Quantico where it met the Potomac and followed that river to Washington. Quantico is a quaint little mostly-one-street town that exists primarily due to an enviable location.

Jimmy's funeral was a huge affair held at the First Presbyterian Church downtown, presided over by the Reverend Williams. The church was later moved to Franklin Street but then, it was an enormous brick structure with twin steeples and a landmark of the city. It was well-attended by the notables of the town and was followed by a procession to the Loudon Park Cemetery. Extended family and others gathered for a wake at the Asquith Street house; there were perhaps three dozen and more visitors in attendance.

I can still remember that night distinctly. Maddie had set up hors d'oeuvres and punch in the dining room, guests gathered there and in the large drawing room that opened just off of it. There was a fire in the fireplace, and that, along with the number of bodies in the room, made it quite warm. Aunt Mary Eleanore was the reigning belle, her complexion beautiful in her black dress and her brother, Raphael Semmes, was engaging the guests with tales of valor. Semmes was a navy lieutenant stationed in Washington, on duty to evaluate and repair lighthouses along the coast. He was medium height and thin with light wavy hair, sporting a mustache and goatee. He cut quite the dashing figure in his officer's uniform with sword and sash and was attracting much attention with his storytelling. He was as handsome a man as his sister was a beautiful woman, and he especially was captivating to the ladies present. Lizzie West, a young cousin to my stepmother and who was slightly older than myself, was especially hanging on his every word. Semmes had been decorated for bravery during the Mexican War, saving many of his crew after the ship he commanded was lost in a storm. He and his remaining crew then marched with Winfield Scott to Mexico City. The navy needed a war hero and he fit the bill. He had been given much attention in the newspapers for his actions.

My Uncle Thomas was standing by the fire and looking disgusted. The temperature in the room overwhelmed me a bit, and I was feeling sad and lonely so I stepped outside the front door into the chilly evening air for a few minutes, then re-entered the foyer and climbed about halfway up the oak staircase where I could sit and have a good view into the drawing room through the banisters. I saw my father go into his study with another naval officer, James Bulloch. I knew from helping with the business that we were involved with shipping cotton for Bulloch to England from his plantation in Georgia. The study was across the hall from the drawing room and was situated under the staircase, further back. They closed the door and I could not overhear their conversation in spite of my attempts.

Suddenly above the conversation, clinking of glasses and cutlery emanating from the party, I heard angry voices coming from the kitchen in the back of the house. Just then, Lizzy West came running down the hall, looking distraught and mussed, sobbing as she raced out the front door. I jumped down from the stairs and strode back to the kitchen to see what all the fuss was about. I entered the kitchen to see my Uncle Thomas and Raphael Semmes facing each other almost nose to nose, color up in both their faces. Just then, Semmes said, "So what? It's not your business. I don't know what my sister sees in you, you're nothing but a crook."

Semmes noticed me then; I saw his eyes shift to me just as Thomas punched him square in the face, knocking him back against the wall. Before Semmes could respond, Thomas turned on his heel, brushed by me, and stomped out of the kitchen while hissing venomously, "How can you be a hero when you lost your ship and a quarter of your crew?"

Semmes yelled after him, "You weren't there!" But Uncle Thomas was already gone. Semmes then looked at me, the back of his hand pressed to his nose to stem the trickle of blood beginning to form there and said softly but with venom, "What are you looking at, boy?"

I left the party and wandered the streets for a couple of hours, thinking about Jimmy and mulling over what I had heard. It was cold that night; I increased my pace to generate warmth. My hands were jammed into the pockets of my pea coat, my chin firmly in my scarf, knotted in front to keep my coat collar up. The moon was up and almost full so the clouds from my breath were clearly visible in the night. Baltimore had not yet installed gaslight all around so the moon was my only guide.

I finally returned to the store on Orleans Street and my attic room above it. The store was long closed for the night, and my lantern gave off little heat so it was nearly as cold inside as it was out. I was palpably lonely and missed my former friends, to say nothing about my feelings for Mary McDowell whom I had not seen in over six months. She increasingly occupied my thoughts, wondering if I had been just an amusement for her. I had received no response to any of the correspondence I had sent. I was tired and angry over Jimmy's passing along with this recent defamation of my uncle whom I thought to be my only real family that I could hold in high esteem. Fact was, I was feeling sorry for myself and wanted an adventure instead of responsibility.

The *Mary Eleanore* was due to sail the next morning on the tide, so I packed a bedroll and warm clothes along with some biscuits to tide me over. In the predawn that morning, I went down to the wharf, quietly boarded the ship, and hid myself below in the fo'c'sle forward, careful to avoid the crew sleeping in their hammocks. I was not quite sixteen years old and determined to run off to sea.

It turned out the biscuits were a bad idea. I woke up face-to-face with a rat, the size of a cat, almost choking on a chunk of the bread. When I sat up abruptly and began waving my hands, he didn't even flinch, just stopped eating and showed me pointy sharp teeth while making a threatening noise. Then there was a rustling in my bag next to my hand that was propping me up, and a second rat came out of the bag, dragging half of a biscuit in his teeth. If anything, the second critter was larger than the first. I propelled myself on hands and feet backward, away from my belongings, over some coiled rope, then smacked the back of my head into something hard. It turned out the obstruction to my flight was the foremast between decks and I pushed my back up against it, sitting there for a second, watching as my rations were consumed.

Just then, I was grabbed roughly from behind and suspended in the air by the back of my coat, hanging by my armpits with just my toes touching the deck. I heard a deep growl.

"Vell, vat have vee here?" I recognized the voice of Maller the bos'n of the *Mary Eleanore.* I must have emitted some kind of noise in my alarm that alerted him to my presence or else he heard my head smack against the mast. "Vot is the cap'n gonna say!"

He turned, swinging me with him, then gave me a push that sent me stumbling toward the ladder leading to the upper deck. He pretty much hefted me ahead of him up through the hatch and into the morning light, somehow using the roll of the ship to add to my flight trajectory perfectly. On my end, I was not prepared for the accompanying rise of the ship's bow and ended up in a heap on the foredeck to the accompaniment of snickers from two sailors at the shrouds. Maller grabbed me once again by the back of my coat and dragged me indecorously to the quarterdeck, presenting me to my Uncle Thomas as I finally found my feet.

"Stowaway, cap'n," he said.

My uncle gave me a hard look, straight in the eye, but I didn't flinch. There was a pregnant pause, as if he hadn't seen me being hauled all the way to him, then cleared his throat with a "Harumph" as I was accustomed to seeing him do when weighing a decision. "Your papa is gonna skin you, boy," he said.

I straightened up and said, "I'll deal with that when I see him."

I saw his face redden, and I knew I had made a mistake. He bellowed at me, "On board this ship, when I say something, when I give an order, *when I even make an observation*, you *will* respond with 'Aye aye, sir,' or 'Yes, captain,' and nothing else." Out of the corner of my eye, I could see an evil grin on Maller's face. Uncle Thomas continued, this time becoming more dispassionate. "The sea is a hard mistress, no lie. You'll be regretting this choice. When you are given an order, you will obey instantly, or I'll be finding out why, understand, *Mr. Carlile?*"

"Aye aye, sir!" I said.

He turned to Maller and said, "Sign him on, put him on the starboard watch, and keep him out from underfoot. He can help the cook, then turn him over to Mr. Jones to learn some skill."

"Aye, sir, we can't jus drop him zomevhere?" Maller responded.

"We'd lose the wind and a whole day," said the captain. "We'll get a note back home when we pass an inbound ship."

And so I began my career as a sailor. I had been aboard quite a bit and knew the basics of the ship, but that didn't nearly prepare me for life at sea. As I was no kind of hand, I was berthed in the steerage with the ship's boy, Otto. Otto kept the pantry, served the officers, and otherwise ran errands for the captain, living on his table scraps. I think he was also tasked to keep an eye on me. The regular workday began at noon with all hands and was to 8:00 p.m., the starboard watch taking over at that time under the direction of Mr. Jones, the first officer, or mate as he was called. Larboard watch took over at midnight under Mr. Thompson, the second officer, and we again replaced them from 4:00 a.m. to 8:00 a.m. before breakfast.

When not on active watch or sleeping, we were still engaged in maintenance of the ship which was never-ending. I started by scrubbing pots, hauling coal for the fire and water, along with broaching casks and cutting meat and vegetables that were packed in salt. I then reported to Mr. Jones where I learned to reef, furl, and splice in the foretop, some fifty feet above the pitching deck. I had some trouble with seasickness at first, waves of nausea, especially when confronted with the smell of the bilges in the steerage. I have to say, I stood to my duty nonetheless and earned some grudging respect from the crew as a result.

To the crew, I was an odd entity, and they didn't know exactly what to do with me. They knew who I was from earlier trips; so on one hand, they didn't play many of the usual tricks on the new hand. On the other hand, they really wanted the captain's good opinion so didn't coddle me in my duties. Certainly no one knew how to be friendly with the owner's son who talked like an educated man. So for the most part, they ignored me when we were in a group and that let them have a sense of normality.

The cook was an older man, thin-faced and with receding greasy blond hair. He was missing his left eye and had a patch that he used intermittently to cover an ugly and scarred empty socket. He was known to all as One-Eye Dick and every now and then, the older crew members would remark that meals were cooked by a penis. Dick had an irreverent sense of humor, and he was likely to return these comments with musings around what the food really consisted of or what he did to add special flavors to his concoctions. Hot meals were served at the change of watch, so breakfast at seven bells in the morning watch and supper at eight bells in the evening; although, of course, the entire crew was on call for any emergent activity. A midday meal of cold meat and bread was picked up between duty assignments and a cup of beer or brandy went with it. Hot meals typically consisted of a stew thickened with flour or roasted fish when a significant catch could be made.

Sundays were task-free, other than the general handling of the ship, and were spent leisurely repair of personal belongings, or the endless quantity of rope used in running the ship. A pudding came with Sunday supper. This was just ship's bread crumbled and soaked in seawater, to which was added molasses and dried plums or raisins, then baked. It was surprisingly tasty, and the crew looked forward to the treat. Workdays were spent sluicing, tarring, cleaning, painting, or repairing and replacing any wear and tear in the spars, rigging, or makeup of the ship. The officers were very good at keeping the crew members moving at all times. The cooking fire was kept lit unless a storm threatened, and the galley area amidships was a popular spot to hang out when off duty, especially in the cold weather. The sailors would carve, repair belongings, and tell far-fetched tales of their journeys and the wonders they had beheld on the sea or in exotic foreign ports. It was an unwritten code that these stories went unchallenged, and further, they were accentuated by another man not only agreeing but adding detail to further verify these events. Not that anyone was naive enough to believe all that was said, it was more of a guideline. After all, the difference between a fairy tale and a sea story is that one begins with "Once upon a time," the other with "This ain't no shit."

Now sailors are notoriously reputed to be evil, that care must be taken so as not to have your belongings scammed from you and your women deflowered. I must agree that there is some truth to these rumors, although this can only happen to a man who is not smart enough to recognize when he is being played or with women who are willing, to at least, some degree. Sailing men tend to be in a high degree of physical fitness, and animal magnetism does have an effect. Among a tight-knit crew, there is a code of honor that is not to be broken; too many dangers exist with just occupational hazards without adding the ire of your fellows. Even when in port, the crew will continue to act as a unit.

On the morning of the second day out, we rounded Cape Charles and entered the rougher waters of the Atlantic shortly after sighting a sail inbound. Sailing ships at sea are a beautiful sight, and as a sailor, evaluation of the sailing qualities of other vessels makes for fine conversation. We stood in to pass close, discovering that she was the *Envoy*, a Cooke Line vessel that had been blown south in a gale, and was headed north to Delaware Bay en route to Philadelphia. My uncle's thoughts of getting a letter through to my father regarding my presence aboard were changed when we were still a half-mile off; we were downwind, and the stench emitting from the *Envoy* made me lose the contents of my stomach. She was a passenger ship carrying Irish immigrants. I had witnessed this to a degree in my time on the docks, but Baltimore was not a usual point of entry for these ships. The immigrants put up a fee for their passage and were packed below decks, often having to provide their own food for the journey. The more tickets that could be sold, the better profit for the ship owner; and the people were not allowed on deck but were left to wallow in their own filth in the little space they had below decks. Often, as was the case with the *Envoy*, extended passage due to storms resulted in the passengers running out of food, starvation, and disease running rampant. Those who died had to be piled in a corner and their decomposing bodies added further stench to an already untenable situation. We stood off to windward to escape then turned south on our course.

Just before daylight on our ninth day out, I heard the call "Land ho, to leeward."

I recall wondering at the time how it was that sailors are so adept at recognizing changes to the horizon at night; but later, with experience, I found that when surrounded by only sea, sky, and stars, one becomes adept at noticing subtle changes. It still requires a keen eye but has also to do with smell because land, or even change in weather, comes with a distinct air. This is a survival skill at sea, detecting shallows or rock outcroppings that cause the surf to break over them as well as being able to identify and skirt dangerous changes in the weather.

Later that morning, we rounded Hilton Head and entered the South Channel of the Savannah River, passing the newly-finished brick Fort Pulaski that occupied Cockspur Island to the north. Although the flag was flying over the fort, it looked to be otherwise unmanned which I thought to be strange. By this time, I was passable in my duties and had taken a liking to romping about in the rigging. So although it was past eight bells and I was no longer on duty by then, I was occupying a spot at the t'gallant masthead to get a clear view of the scenery.

After an hour working up the channel, we arrived at the city, a significant town but considerably smaller than Baltimore. We were expected and warped into a quay that had been reserved for us. The wharf in Savannah is parallel to the river and takes advantage of the natural curve in the stream along an escarpment at the town so that the deepest portion of the channel abuts the harbor. River Street runs along the wharf and is the usual combination of warehouse, mills, market area, and tavern as is found in most shipping ports, although right in the center is a town square and stone-built inn surrounded by more upscale establishments. The afternoon was passed in significant activity, unloading kegs of nails, casks of beer, shoes, and other manufactured goods that were our cargo. Our new load had not yet arrived. I heard from the others that we were to take on cotton to be transported across the Atlantic to England. We were allowed some shore leave, although I had to return by eight in the evening to stand watch. I think my uncle had arranged this to keep me out of trouble.

By midnight, I had been awake more than a full day, so I hit my hammock and slept, not drawing the anchor watch. I seem to remember vivid dreams, but that was common for me when sleeping aboard while in the shelter of port. Normally when at sea, I could just about sleep standing up. It's amazing how one adapts to the movement of the ship at sea and out of the ordinary motion or no motion at all results in fitful sleep.

I was awakened shortly before noon for the workday with a message from Otto to report to the captain and jumped up, jogging aft to the quarterdeck. I took the companionway ladder down in a single hop, using the banister to vault below decks. I approached the cabin through the narrow passage, rapped twice, and entered at his bidding.

"Reporting as ordered, sir!" I announced. I was preparing myself to support not being sent home but was surprised at his next statement.

"We're going on business tomorrow morning," he said, eying me. "Brush out your good suit and be ready at sunup, I'm relieving you from watch tonight."

"Aye, sir," I said, continuing to stand in front of his desk expectantly while he returned to the papers he was studying.

After several seconds, he seemed to realize that I was still standing there and growled, "That's *all!*"

7

At first light, I met my uncle at the sally port and followed him down the gangplank onto the quay. We strode straight across and up to the street where a black man in livery holding two horses became visible through the morning mist. My uncle greeted him, "Morning, Richard, how's the missus?"

"Nevah bettah, Missah Carlile," he responded.

I had never seen my uncle ride before and was impressed with the agility he showed mounting the tall bay provided for him. For my own part, I had been drilled in cavalry practice at the institute; much of the maneuvers being done with stirrups over the saddle and this had honed my skill more than adequately. The black mare I mounted snorted and stamped, ready to go, and I leaned forward, rubbing her up behind the ear. I was immediately impressed by the quality of the horseflesh provided.

The morning was cool; I could see the breath from the horses' nostrils in short puffs. We started at a trot, moving up to Bay Street then turning west toward the outskirts of town. Although Christmas Eve was a Monday, there was little traffic due to the impending holiday and as the city blocks transitioned to farmland after we crossed the canal and bypassed the waterworks, we broke into a canter for a couple of miles. We slowed to a walk as we crested a wooded hill, the sunrise casting long shadows in front of us. The low mist that had covered the surrounding country was clearing, and it promised to be a beautiful day. After another mile or so, the horses turned into a farm lane, seemingly on their own will, giving me an inkling that we were nearing our destination.

A couple of hundred feet further on, we emerged from the trees into an extensive open area with a colonial stone and frame home on top of a gentle rise, wisps of smoke coming from chimneys on both sides, indicating activity inside. As we approached the home, I could see that a small brook skirted the bottom of the hill on the far side, past which stretched a considerable cultivated area that was now harvested brown stubble. The whole was bordered on three sides by trees and a row of massive old oaks lined the drive, leafless due to the advanced season. In the distance, the stream disappeared into the woods, down by the river. For all appearances, this was a modest but successful farm, and I was curious as to the reason for our short trip to the countryside.

The door was answered by our host himself; it turned out to be James Bulloch whom I had recently seen with my father in Baltimore. James was a barrel-chested man with bushy sideburns that came down to his jowls and were connected by his mustaches. He had a manner about him and a look in his eye that immediately impressed upon me that he was a thoughtful and intelligent man. He led us inside to the foyer.

"Glad you could come out," he said to my uncle while ushering us through open French doors into what had to be a study.

The room was paneled and contained several large chairs and a desk, behind which the wall was a bookcase from floor to ceiling. Two tall windows on the eastern exposure allowed sunlight to stream into the room, making it bright and cheery.

"Pardon, but we don't spend much time here anymore since my father built Bulloch Hall up Atlanta way," he said. We sat and were promptly served hot spiced wine by a mulatto girl in a black-and-white maid uniform.

"I'm looking for a shipping partner," Bulloch said. "My father passed last summer. and I'm trying to get things back on track. We've got a cotton gin and a lumber mill, I can get bales and planks down to Savannah cheap by rail." He paused, eying my uncle's reaction to gauge his interest. "Between the export duty, cost to ship across, and the measly price the damned English are willing to pay, I'm not making the kind of money that could be had in old days. With the overseas demand and the rapid rail expansion here in Georgia, I'm doing better selling lumber than cotton."

At this point, I observed aloud that the English were keeping cotton prices low by importing as much as possible from Egypt, an area that they exerted control over in tandem with the French since Turkish power in the region continued to wane. Both men respected my naivety by pausing to light up their pipes, this information obviously not being new to them. They eyed each other with a glint of humor. I then stated that American planters might do much better if only they could combine to develop a syndicate that could regulate prices on exports.

This statement more piqued their interest, but Bulloch responded, "It's a great idea, boy. But getting any cooperation among these gentlemen is an impossible task. They are extremely independent and competitive, someone would sell out on a whim if they needed the money," he said. "The only thing most landowners around here agree on is that the Yankee-controlled federal government is depriving them of their livelihoods and liberties."

I noted that British policy in Europe was allowing Russia to expand its power, and it was only a matter of time before they butted heads. War would increase the need for and price of the raw materials that we could provide. Russia, at that time, had not only defeated the Turks to gain control of the Dardanelles and Bosporus straits, but by sending a large army to the support of the Austrian emperor in crushing the Hungarian Revolution, had established themselves as dominant in Central European affairs. Russian control of the Black Sea and access subsequently to Mediterranean ports was some cause for concern for the English mercantile establishment.

Bulloch responded, by noting darkly, that the United States should be wary of their own policies lest it lead to insurrection within its own borders. I found this an interesting perspective from a navy officer, but we all knew that South Carolina had threatened secession a couple of times over tariff issues and a bitter debate was raging in congress regarding the disposition of the lands acquired in the Mexican War. This political discussion left me with a favorable impression of Bulloch's grasp of affairs, but perhaps that was because he actually listened to me, not dismissing me outright as a youth. I noted also a gleam in Uncle Thomas's eyes under his bushy eyebrows.

My uncle then diffused the mood by saying, "I talked with my brother James regarding a partnership, he said you could fill my ship for overseas voyages."

"That I can," remarked Bulloch.

"The problem is that would lock us in, and we couldn't arrange cargo of opportunity that would net us better profit," stated Uncle Thomas. "What might be better is if you could come up with your own ship. Be great for us if we had access to your Savannah facilities, and we could put our Baltimore warehousing and connections at your disposal, an alliance of sorts. Of course, you would have to come up with the funds for your own vessel," said Thomas. "In the meantime, we're glad to move your merchandise when we're available."

There was a knock and a tall thin young man, not much older than myself, entered the study. "My brother Irvine," Bulloch introduced him. "Family's all coming down to Savannah for the holiday." Bulloch paused, taking a couple of pulls on his pipe. "You drive a hard bargain, Thomas, that's not something we're prepared for just yet," Bulloch said. "My duties with the navy occupy too much of my time." He paused again, then said, "But glad to continue to contract with you to move my cotton."

My uncle reached inside his coat and pulled out a package wrapped in brown paper and tied with twine. He placed it on the desk with his hand still on top. "Prime Maryland pipe blend," he said. "I find it indispensable when I'm stuck thinking over problems."

We all stood then and exchanged hearty handshakes. "We just butchered some geese for Christmas supper," Irvine announced. "Could you do with a couple?"

That is how we were equipped when we arrived back at the *Mary Eleanore*, already loaded and anchored out in the river channel. One-Eye Dick roasted the two fat geese for supper that night, along with dumplings in gravy, potatoes, and a grand plum pudding. He had acquired some roasted peanuts, a new food to me that proved delightful to snack on. The entire crew ate their fill for Christmas

Eve, sitting around the galley fire, telling stories of Christmas past and good cheer was had by all, helped by the effects of brandy to wash it all down. The next morning on Christmas Day, we sailed for England with the tide.

My first cross-Atlantic voyage was fairly uneventful, and I quickly settled into the routine. With the exception of myself, the crew were able-bodied sailors—all and most duties didn't require verbal orders. Most of the sailors enjoyed showing off their skills and participating in my nautical education. I was generally well-treated. Maller, the bos'n, was the exception; he carried a short length of rope with three knots and liked nothing better than to leave a bruise on my backside if I wasn't first up in a task or even if he thought I wore my pants too tight. I learned to keep a wary eye out for him whenever I came up from below, or while on deck, as he had an unnerving way of sneaking up.

We made way up the Irish Sea without making landfall; I could feel the difference once we made our entrance into more sheltered waters. The choppy turmoil of the Atlantic gave way to the long rollers of the Irish Sea. The weather remained mild for the beginning of February, and we took full advantage of the westerly wind to make time. After a day's journey to the northeast, we sighted the coast of Wales off Holyhead in the morning, turning to the east but remaining out of sight of the coast to remain clear of the mudbanks created by the River Dee. Early the next morning, we sighted Black Rock Light, and by sunup, we anchored off North Wall in the Liverpool Channel. After negotiations, we were allotted a slip in the Canada dock then spent the day, with tackle and hoist, unloading our cargo to the pier. After cleaning up, we were paid off a portion of our wages and given shore leave for the evening.

Our crew were veterans in this port and knew just where to go, so I tagged along with this joyful bunch. I had always admired the way sailors walk when on land and busied myself imitating their rolling gait, propping my round tarpaulin hat on the back of my head. We stopped at an old inn and pub off Regent Road, got a table, and began to ply the local beer. The establishment was about half-empty, but in addition to the patrons at the bar or dining at tables along the wall, there were several women near the massive fireplace in the corner along with a gent who was busy plucking and sawing out lively tunes on a violin for pennies. Once it became clear that we were Yanks and had some money to spend, we became a center of attraction.

My shipmates pushed me into a dance with a girl they knew as Polly, and after a second dance, she took me by the hand and led me up the stairs to a chorus of shouts from my fellows. Polly was short and curvaceous with curly light-red hair, smelled a little like ripe potato, but had a great smile, good teeth, and a twinkle of mischief in her bright-blue eyes. She looked older and wiser but was probably not much older than me. We quickly found an empty room, and she pulled me down on top of her. To my surprise, she reached her climax very quickly then continued to educate me in ways of pleasure, both to her and myself. After several very enjoyable hours, I fell fast asleep, exhausted, with her naked in my arms, feeling quite like the king of the world.

I awoke the next morning to three surprises. Polly was long gone, the landlord was pounding on the door, demanding payment for the room, and my purse was empty. I quickly pulled on my pants, grabbed my shirt and coat, opened the window, and jumped to the hard-packed dirt road below. I rolled as I landed, narrowly avoiding being stepped on by a horse pulling a cart on morning deliveries. I ran while pulling on my shirt and coat, looking back to see a man in the window yelling and pointing his finger at me. I made my return to the ship by backstreets and had my hackles up all day, waiting for the authorities to track me down, but nothing ever came of it. When I lamented later about losing my money, I was teased remorselessly by my shipmates but found it added to my bonding with the crew.

For a long time after, whenever I went aloft to reef or furl, someone would always remark, "She's a proper lady, boy. Ya willn't be losin' yer coin while yer with her!"

We took on food and water, and I assisted Dick in the screening process. Provisioning in Liverpool was done on a buyer-beware basis; some casks could contain rotten meat, weevil-infested biscuit, or even rocks and wood in the bottom to make up weight. There were also times when product was surreptitiously unloaded from navy vessels and sold to profit the purser or other officers involved. Being caught with contraband of that caliber could result in difficulty with the port authority to include fines and long delays. In any case, it was important to be thorough. Luckily us Yanks had a reputation for being difficult to bilk and that, along with using reputable sellers, resulted in few problems. In the meantime, the captain went ashore to make arrangements with our agent for a new cargo.

We left dock and anchored in the channel. Life aboard ship in a foreign harbor is easygoing, although much work is done in preparation for the next voyage. Mr. Jones, the first officer, supervised the activity in the absence of the captain and he was an efficient taskmaster. The ship was scrubbed out and repainted where necessary. The hull was scraped of barnacles and weeds along with any necessary caulking that needed attention. The standing rigging was retarred, and slight alterations were made to the trim of the masts and spars in an attempt to get the most possible speed and best handling out of her. The crew took great pride in getting things just so. The majority of the men worked on the first watch, leaving a rotating three-man duty assignment to maintain security for emergencies. The repair and refit activities during the day were done in gangs, so competition and a general holiday spirit prevailed. Limited shore leave was allowed under the understanding that no trouble follows. Still after a couple of weeks of these pursuits, a bit of tension began to ramp up and sailors, in general, were glad to get the new cargo aboard so they can be quit of the land and its attachments.

Finally the captain returned, and the next two days were spent loading our new shipment. The *Mary Eleanore* had been refitted to allow for a compartment that was on the portside and amidships, almost directly in line with the main hatch. It was on the orlop deck above the hold so designed to be safe from any bilge water. It was ingeniously constructed so the panel could not be discerned from the hull and impervious to any search unless you knew exactly how to access it. Among the iron-bearing hubs, intricate carriage lamps, and boxed bolts of cotton, wool and linen cloth were four rectangular unmarked crates about five feet long by three wide and one-and-one-half deep. These were stashed out of sight.

Once loaded to the brim, we sailed on the morning tide. Uncle Thomas liked to make a show of getting under way, especially in English ports as they were snobbish about their seamanship. The gang at the capstan brought the anchor cable up short, and the yards were braced; then at precisely the right moment, gaff sail, foretopsail, and jib were loosed and hauled in tight. The *Mary Eleanore* came to life, swiveling away from the wind as the anchor was brought up and catted. Even heavily laden, she immediately began to make way into the channel, then the huge foresail was set. This made her heel about ten degrees and almost immediately doubled her increasing speed. We would have drawn envious looks from many of the other captains in the harbor and, from my station in the foretop, I could see spyglasses come up and turn to have a glance.

This was my first experience in discovering that the trip west across the Atlantic is typically more difficult than the other way around. The trades run southerly before finally turning west, and as this would take us well out of our way, we were obliged to turn toward America after a few days' voyage south. The North Atlantic is an area of alternating light winds, then gales which, along with the always-choppy seas, require diligence on the part of captain and crew. Still we had a good trip and made Cape Charles in a forty-one-day crossing. Shortly after entering the Chesapeake Bay, we were hailed by a small sloop of about twenty-five feet that approached us from the York River estuary. We hove to and our hidden cargo was transferred to the waiting smaller craft. It was rumored among the crew that these were rifles but if that was the case, their ultimate destination remained a mystery.

We returned to Baltimore Harbor the next afternoon, and I was on edge while doing my duties, anxiously awaiting a confrontation with my father. It never came though. He simply took the path of least resistance and cut me off, so I was obliged to remain aboard ship. After a few days, my Aunt Eleanore put her foot down with Uncle Thomas and I was allowed an attic room in the old house on Baltimore Street where I was made welcome and fed delightfully. So it was that I passed the next couple of weeks until it was time to resume my nautical career.

9

We set out on a warm day in mid-April of 1850, and the spring weather was ideal for sailing. We were back in Savannah, then across to Cherbourg, with a consignment of cotton and timber, arriving on a pleasant early June morning. I came to love the French ports and people; there is always a sense joie de vivre there and none of the puritan values regarding the expression of love that is so prevalent in England or America. Besides that, the French have a special affinity for Americans. We bypassed the outer harbor wall between the forts constructed there, then slipped by the *Jetee des Flamands* to anchor in the commercial harbor area of the *Petite Rade*. The *Rade de Cherbourg* is very impressive, with manmade estuaries built complete with protective forts designed to create a huge harbor space across the north end of the peninsula, leaving just two channels for sea traffic to pass. A further inner wall, or jetee as it is called, then further protects the commercial and military ports, leaving space enough for several hundred ships. It is a busy place. We were assigned a slip by the harbormaster, offloaded our cargo, and began to take on casks of wine for the return voyage. While there, I took my turn on the three-man anchor watch and was surprised when one of my fellows pulled out his pipe and installed himself in the fo'c'sle vent while the other simply crawled in under the longboat cover for a nap, leaving me alone to tend to the bell and lamp. I was further surprised that when Mr. Jones took a turn around the quarterdeck that they were both suddenly attentive to their duty as if they knew in advance what time Mr. Jones would do so.

On the return trip across the Atlantic, I applied to move from my berth in steerage to the fo'c'sle with the other able-bodied hands, and this was granted, making me a regular part of the crew with like pay and privileges. I began taking my turn at the helm with this change as well, a post of honor that was rotated every two hours. It took some practice to keep the ship on a heading, especially in weather and gathering too much leeway would result in a sharp reprimand from the officer on duty. The weather continued to hold fair on into July.

The captain took pains this trip with my further nautical education. I used the sextant to shoot the north star and calculate our latitude along with timing the sunrise on the chronometer to figure our longitudinal progress. I charted these and landmarks, kept the starboard watch log, and learned to use the glass in the binnacle to anticipate changes in weather patterns. The crew found this mostly amusing, especially since it was plain that the captain had no immediate intention of granting me any authority over the working of the ship.

Monday, July 15, dawned eerily. The sky off the stern was flaming-red, tinged greenish around the edges. We were thirty-four days out of Cherbourg and had been looking forward to homecoming less than a week away. The weather had been clear and warm with a consistent breeze out of the southwest, a dream crossing. By breakfast, thin clouds were scudding across the sky and a dark mass began to appear to the southwest. I could see my shipmates casting worried looks in that direction, then surreptitious glances toward the quarterdeck as if hoping for a magic response from Mr. Jones.

The captain had apparently been called, for he appeared on deck from the companionway ladder as I was finishing the shift log. He paused, took a look at the southern horizon, now flashing with lightning, then glanced into the binnacle to check the glass which I had just recorded as thirty and a quarter.

He looked at me and growled, "Let me show you something, boy." He tapped the glass twice with his index finger, and the level fell instantly to twenty-eight. "We're in for a blow," he said.

Maller, the bos'n, appeared as if he had been summoned, and the captain said, "Call all hands and prepare to ware ship. Batten the hatches and tie down anything loose, if you please, Mr. Maller."

"Aye, sir," was the reply. Then Maller put his whistle to his lips and blew the three-tone call that was all hands. "All hands ahoy," was the cry. "Tumble up and take stations." Maller then began thumping on the hatchways to emphasize the point.

The *Mary Eleanore* burst into a flurry of activity as the crew ran to their posts. I myself took off instantly for the foremast ratlines and was aloft before most made it up to the deck.

"Prepare to ware ship," was the call, then, "Loose the gaff."

We had been close hauled on the starboard tack, but now with more pressure on the jibs, the *Mary Eleanore* began a smooth turn away from the wind.

"Shiver the foresail," was my prompt and as the sail was let go from the deck, the four of us on the yard began frantically to furl it up with the tops'l and t'gallant above me changing shape as the wind caught them from a different direction. "Square the foreyards," then, "Steer full and by," were next, at which point, we loosed the foresail, our fellows hauled the gaff tight, and the *Mary Eleanore* took off running from the approaching cloud mass with the wind now on her larboard quarter.

"Set course nor' nor'west." I could hear the captain say to the helmsman.

Not two minutes passed before there was a call from the quarterdeck. "Take in the t'gallant and put a reef in the foresail."

Two of my mates scrambled up the rigging to furl while we released the sheet, then we grabbed the clew lines and hauled away until the sail area was reduced by half, tying them off at the topmast head. No sooner was this done than we were struck by a gust that knocked me off my feet and I was left hanging by my armpits on the yard. I scrambled to get my feet back onto the toe rope where I could hang on safely. Good seamanship by the captain had prevented us from carrying away a yard or worse.

In spite of our efforts to skirt the storm, it overtook us rapidly, turning the day almost as dark as night. The wind whipped the rain sideways and waves began crashing into the ship, pouring over the deck and then draining from the scuppers. By then, we were down to reefed foretopsail and gaff, jib and staysail, and the captain was obliged to resume our tack to head the bow of the ship into the mountainous waves, the tops of which were being cleft off by the roaring wind. After perhaps three hours or so of being battered by the crashing swells, we finally furled all but the staysail and hove to into the wind and waves.

We remained like that, bobbing and twirling like a cork in a maelstrom for the better part of a full day, wind howling and waves crashing over the deck. The helmsman was tied off to prevent being washed overboard, and the pumps were manned continuously. The galley fires were out, so all that could be had for sustenance against the wind and wet was cold salt beef that I could gnaw on until small chunks could be chewed away, along with hard biscuit that was a tooth-breaker unless soaked in seawater for a few minutes. Water everywhere and none to drink, if a barrel had been broached, it would have tipped instantly or filled with seawater anyway and likely caused risk of life or limb to anyone close.

Around mid-morning of the sixteenth, an even weirder event occurred. The wind abated to a strong breeze. The waves, although still high, were not mountainous. The rain stopped, and a tunnel of white cloud formed above our heads. We could not see the sun, but the rays hitting the white cloud walls above made the whole tunnel glow iridescently with just wisps of rainbow effect toward the tops. I had imagined that this was how heaven appeared. This situation lasted perhaps thirty-five minutes before the far side of the tunnel engulfed us with wind and waves, hitting us from the opposite direction.

It felt almost like the ship hit a rock. Our staysail luffed then shredded like paper, and the *Mary Eleanore* began to broach to. The captain instantly ordered the gaff sail double reefed and set to bring her bow around. Two men jumped to the mainmast rigging while others hauled on the halyard, and this dangerous task was accomplished in seconds, the *Mary Eleanore* beginning to turn back into the wind.

Just then, two things happened. An enormous wave hit the ship directly broadside, spilling over the deck and skidding her sideways. Several men were on deck, including myself, and thankfully no one was lost overboard, although it was all I could do to hang on until my head broke the surface and I could breathe again. The masts must have whiplashed, however, because then there was a loud crack and the main topgallant mast broke off above the yardarm, crashing directly down on the two men still aloft before the rigging came up taut and stopped its downward progress. One man was knocked back into the topmast head, but the second, Charlie Watson, was thrown clear, just by luck grabbing on to the sling line where he managed to hang on for a couple of seconds by one hand before losing his grip, his other hand desperately grabbing for the yardarm.

I saw him begin to slip and used the roll of the ship to jump to the mainmast ratlines, stretching out my hand to catch him and haul him in as he fell. Fate had other plans, and the *Mary Eleanore* began her downward roll, changing Charlie's trajectory. His fingertips brushed against mine as he hit the backstays and bounced clear, disappearing instantly into the sea. We never saw a trace of him come back to the surface, he was simply swallowed up whole. To this day, I sometimes wake up at night when there is a storm, seeing Charlie's checked shirt flapping in the wind and the expression on his face changing from hope to despair as he realized I would not be able to reach him in time.

Bill Stevens, the other man struck by the spar, was brought down, and we took him below. He was unconscious and the back of his shirt was ripped, exposing a sixteen-inch gash in his back from his right shoulder across the back of his ribs. It wasn't bleeding badly, but the flesh had begun to swell, causing it to roll away from the cut; and I could see bone under the meat. I called to Dick, the cook, for his sewing kit and a bottle of whiskey. I splashed some liquor onto the cut, causing him to spasm, but the men pinned him down. I cut his shirt away with my knife, then sat on his head, took a slug from the whiskey bottle myself, and proceeded to stitch him up using a whipstitch the sailmaker had taught me.

Funny thing, Bill had a great tattoo of a maiden riding a dolphin on his shoulder and my first thought, when I saw his injury, was that it was such a shame that his tattoo was wrecked. Subsequently and fortunately, Bill's injury did not get infected and he made a full recovery. After that, the crew began to call me doc, and they would come to me for boils, rope burns, splinters, and the like that are a sailor's nemesis.

On the afternoon of the seventeenth, the storm finally calmed to the point that we could resume our progress, and we limped past Fisherman's Island into the Chesapeake on the twenty-fourth. When we reached Baltimore, I was amazed at the destruction there. The whole waterfront had flooded and the wharves were under repair. Ships were aground a considerable way up on the shore. Houses that had been shoddily built had been blown down, roof shingles were to be found in every cranny. Many trees had broken, and there were limbs in the streets everywhere. The telegraph service that had been newly built was down as were most of the poles that carried the wires. Afterward I heard many say that this was the worst hurricane they had ever witnessed, and I can attest that it was the same for me.

10

We were a month ashore in Baltimore, refitting from the storm damage and getting the *Mary Eleanore* shipshape. We had all hoped that Zach Taylor, being a southerner, would be sympathetic to the goals of property owners regarding division of the spoils from the Mexican War, but he had, instead, promoted the Wilmot Proviso, incurring the wrath of his initial supporters. But Taylor had died suddenly in July, leaving his vice president, Millard Fillmore, to take over. Fillmore was from Western New York in the north but was a believer in the compromises being proposed by Henry Clay and Steven Douglas in congress, measures that had been blocked previously by Taylor. There were whispers around that Taylor had been poisoned, assassinated for his political stands, but others said his lifestyle finally caught up with him. He had apparently contracted cholera from a jug of milk and a bowl of cherries, disproving the popular saying about life and bowls of cherries.

When we finally sailed at the beginning of September, we were embarking on a different kind of profit-making venture. We were bound for Key West, loaded down with rifles, shot, gunpowder, food, and other supplies meant to equip a force being formed there for an expedition to Cuba. Many thought that the Spanish colonies in the Caribbean and Central America would be the best means of expansion for slave-holding territories for the United States. In addition, Spain had declined to a third-rate power following the Napoleonic Wars, and it was incumbent on the United States to prevent England and France from scooping up lucrative pieces of the Spanish Empire for their own gain.

Mexico had long since established her independence, even if many thought her efforts at self-government were in vain. More recently, most of South America had rebelled, the naval action at Lake Maracaibo sealing the loss of Spanish supremacy there. It was not uncommon for American *filibusters* as they were called to attempt takeovers of territories then seek to attach their ill-gotten gains to the United States. Although this was illegal, these soldiers of fortune were romanticized publicly, and, certainly, the examples of Texas and then California pointed to the possibility of success in these ventures. In the case of Cuba, a Spanish colonel had allied with certain business interests in the United States, and they were busy raising an army of invasion in Florida. It was widely believed that the Cuban people would flock to their standard in revolt against Spain given a decent opportunity.

At Key West, we discharged our cargo then took on three passengers, an officer and two soldiers, from the force being assembled. The officer was one Javier Gomez-Vallejo, resplendent in a blue uniform with red facings along with a single gold epaulet on his right shoulder, topped with an eight-pointed star, marking him as a comandante or major. He sported a full-brimmed tall hat with red plume. Gorget, hussar boots, and saber completed his outfit. He looked as if he would be more at home at a diplomatic dance party than on the quarterdeck of our vessel.

We made the passage overnight and at first light made landfall, entering a small inlet northwest of a village called Granma. We hove to and launched our longboat, our guests reappearing on deck to depart. The change in their appearance was dramatic, now dressed in torn and dirty-white cotton clothing with wide-brimmed felt hats. They would easily pass for poor Cuban dirt farmers. We were there perhaps an hour before our boat returned and were in the process of bringing it aboard when the lookout cried, "Sail ho, across the headland."

The captain turned to George Thompson, the second mate, and said, "Mr. Thompson, take a glass up and see what you can make of her." He then commanded, "Prepare to make way and get that boat secure."

We set sail and got underway, racing under a full set of canvas to make the western end of the opening before we were cut off by the approaching ship. Thompson was back on the quarterdeck reporting, "She's Spanish, looks like a customs schooner and armed. She's flying her colors and coming fast."

My thought was that obviously, the country must be on alert to be able to respond to our incursion this quickly; either that or just bad luck.

We made the top of the bay as the schooner was rounding the headland on the other side, perhaps a half-mile off. The *Mary Eleanore* was fast and nimble, but the Spanish ship was built for speed and the gap began slowly to narrow, even when we had set our studding sails after clearing the bay.

The captain said, "Run up a tricolor and see how they respond."

A French flag was brought out of the locker and run up at the stern. The Spanish responded by altering course slightly to windward to keep us pinned against the shoreline as best as could be done. Just then, a puff of smoke appeared on the schooner's bow, the boom of the gun echoing across the water. A splash appeared no more than fifty yards off our stern, but the captain remarked, "Not too smart, that will cut their wind some."

The *Mary Eleanore* had two small brass swivel two-pounder guns that could be mounted amidships by the gangways, and the captain ordered these brought up, mounted, and loaded. The wind began to ease off as we left the land behind, and this seemed to affect the speed of the Spaniard more than us as we had the taller masts. Although she presented as a menace, that schooner was a beautifully-built ship. The chase had become a dead heat with the Spanish some seven hundred yards off our stern, slightly to starboard. This went on for an hour and more before the strangest event took place.

A rain shower appeared in front of us like a curtain, complete with a huge rainbow. Instead of moving away as we approached, the colors remained stationary and we sailed right into the middle of the refraction. It was intense, the air glowing with shimmering color all around us. When I looked straight up, I saw the reflection of the *Mary Eleanore* on the cloud around us, complete to myself, staring back down. It was like one of the new photographic images that were being developed. Then we were clear of the squall, if you could even call it that. It was just one cloud, a rainbow, and a downpour of rain.

The Spanish schooner then entered the rainstorm behind us and simply disappeared. I was in the foretop when it happened and had a clear view. One moment she was there, the next she was gone. No sign of wreckage, no sound of an explosion, nothing. Then the rain quit and the cloud began to disperse. At first, we thought it to be some kind of trick, but it was now a clear and beautiful sunny day. After a few minutes, we turned back to see if we could find a clue as to their demise, but they were just gone. At one point, we fished out a two-foot piece of spar, the severed end charred but smooth as if it had been cut off with a hot knife. Nothing else. She had been a sixty-foot vessel, at least, with a crew of perhaps thirty men and had vanished into thin air. Early in the afternoon, we gave up the search and set course back for the Florida coast.

We subsequently picked up a load of cotton, oats, and peaches in Charleston and made the voyage across to Liverpool, arriving back in Baltimore for the Christmas holiday. We must have made exceptional money on the Key West trip, all hands were given a five-dollar bonus entitled hazard pay, the officers double that. We all knew this was also to keep our mouths shut as it was rather illegal to abet the filibusters. I found out later that the Spanish government had issued a complaint but did not get a good identification of the *Mary Eleanore*. We were accused of spying, sinking their customs ship, and murder of the crew; this was ignored by the American government. I heard later that the filibusters we had supported did in fact invade Cuba but failed to rally any support from the local populous. Those who weren't killed in battle were all executed by the Spanish authorities, including American citizens. The US government issued a complaint about barbaric treatment of prisoners which was in turn ignored by the Spanish government.

It turned out impossible to keep everyone on board quiet, and for many years, yarns about the disappearance of the Spanish ship could be heard around the Baltimore harbor, expanding in their improbability with every telling until it seemed we were saved at the last instant from bloodthirsty Spaniards by naked mermaids who sucked their ship into the sea in a whirlpool in order to snack on the flesh of the drowned sailors. Which is possibly as close to the truth of the matter as I can come up with.

In all, I spent three and a half years aboard the *Mary Eleanore* that first time around; but as time went on, I began to feel I was falling behind my peers. In the spring of '52, George Thompson left our crew. As was customary, the captain told the crew they could elect the new second mate. As was also customary, the crew felt honored by the captain's faith in their judgment but could not accept and turned the decision back over to him. I was appointed second mate.

Now second mate is what is known as a "dog's berth." The perks were that you live in the quarterdeck and dine at the captain's table with real silverware. The cons are that you continue to reef and furl with the hands while keeping aloof enough to be able to command them. In addition, any mate that wants to maintain respect must always occupy the hardest and most perilous position in the rigging. I must say I managed this fairly well and was not averse to the double wages this position included. I began to think about attending college, specifically medical school, and began to save most of my wages toward that end.

11

I enrolled at Maryland College, in Baltimore, in September of '53 in the medical program to sate my growing interest in that area. I passed the entrance examinations easily due to my comprehensive previous education at Maymont Academy, and the school was eager to get my tuition money as well. I had been saving steadily over the past three years, not an easy accomplishment on a ship's officer pay of twenty dollars a month. Still there had always been bonus money for extracurricular cargo. My father's residence on Asquith Street was pretty full and busy with my three-year-old half-sister, Caroline, now in addition to the boys; but my Auntie Eleanore had prevailed once again, and I was allotted the back attic room in the Baltimore Street home for accommodation which was snug and convenient as it opened right on to the back stairwell. These stairs ended in the kitchen near the backdoor to the home, so I was able to come and go without much disturbance to the household. My room was originally designed as a maid's quarters but had been used mostly for storage over the past several years, including storage of my own belongings. I earned my keep splitting wood and hauling water for my aunt in the mornings before school, and she typically ensured me breakfast to start my day.

My initial concern was for appropriate wardrobe because although I had a couple of nice suits, I had now reached my full height and even with alterations, they were reaching past the limit of available cloth. My beaver hat and cravat were still fully functional if slightly old in style. Luckily my auntie came through for me once again, and I received a brand-new suit as a Christmas gift that year.

She was the best, and I know she really had little difficulty convincing Uncle Thomas to help me along, but I loved her to pieces for it.

First class in the morning was anatomy and physiology in the medical building on Lombard Street. This was only nine blocks from home, an easy walk away. The medical building was a Greek-style structure with portico and columns gracing the front steps. Anatomy was upstairs, inside the dome of the building. Chemistry and physical philosophy were held in the laboratories downstairs. The remainder of my school day was spent at the law school building across the Greene Street Plaza for composition and debate. It was a great program, especially later into the coursework when we began to do dissections and discover how various afflictions affect the workings of the body. I rounded out my day working two or three hours in the afternoon at a counting house, down off Camden Street, for expense money.

One of the first things I did once established on land again was to write my Uncle John and Aunt Mary Ellen to inquire about Mary McDowell who was Mary Ellen's cousin. I received a response by the end of October, letting me know that she was engaged to be married at Christmas, apparently an arranged situation. Her father had passed away, leaving the farm in considerable debt, and the arrangement would prevent Mary's brother from losing the property that had been in the family for generations. I determined to take the first opportunity to see if I could change her mind.

At Christmas break, I hired a horse and took the trip down to Caroline County, Virginia, leaving before dawn. It was a cold winter that year, and there was snow on the ground all around. I arrived in Bowling Green late in the afternoon and inquired for directions to the McDowell farm. The light was fading when I came to the residence, an old-style colonial farmhouse on what looked to be a pleasant lane. Mary's brother, Isaac McDowell, answered the door, and he appeared to know instantly who I was. I found out later that he had intercepted my correspondence, that Mary had never received it and believed that I didn't care further. Isaac was short and burly with sandy hair, cut short, and hard blue eyes. I noted that he also had just a hint of freckles on his nose. He told me brusquely that Mary was not at home and that I was not welcome in spite of the cold and approaching nightfall. He then slammed the door in my face. As I turned to go, I saw the curtain draw back in an upstairs window, a face peering out. It was Mary. When she saw me, she drew back and the curtain closed.

I rode about a half-mile back down the lane then tethered my horse in a grove of trees, obscuring his presence from the road. It was fully dark by now, but the moon had come up, almost full, and the landscape around was opalescent with the reflection off the snow-covered fields. It was beginning to get quite cold. I made my way back to the road, taking note of the landmarks so I could find my way back, then trudged back down the lane to the McDowell farm.

All was quiet when I arrived, but I took no chances and crept up to the house along a rail fence to the side. There was a trellis on the side of the porch; I carefully and quietly scaled it onto the porch roof then approached the window, now dark, where I had seen Mary earlier. I tapped lightly on the window, waited, then repeated just slightly louder. The curtain parted, and there was Mary. She gasped when she saw me, putting her hand to her mouth. Then she slid up the window with hardly a noise, just a slight hiss.

"You shouldn't be here," she whispered.

She was now eighteen, and her face was lovelier than even I remembered. She was in a robe and nightgown; I could see she had filled out in a good way.

"When I saw you in the window, I couldn't resist," I whispered back.

She frowned hard at that and said flatly, "I'm to be married in three days."

"Can I change your mind?" I asked.

She leaned out the window and very softly kissed me on the lips, her eyes holding mine as she did so. "No, John Arthur Carlile," she said softly with just a hint of a tear appearing in the corner of her eye. "It's very important that I do this, and he is a kind gentleman, he is very good to me. Now go before you make me cry." Then, "Always be a friend to me," she said softly, closing the window and letting the drapes fall shut.

I sat there for a moment, hardly noticing the cold, my heart in my throat. Finally I promised, "I will," aloud to the night and slid slowly back down the porch roof to the trellis, dangling my legs over the edge until I got my feet firmly onto the slats.

I no sooner got my full weight on the trellis than it broke with a huge crack. I grabbed for the trellis and caught the top along with a branch, but these too snapped off in my hands and only served to bounce me backward after my now-stretched-out body smashed full-length into the side of the house. I came tumbling loudly to the ground, landing directly on my backside, knocking the air from my lungs. I sat stunned for only just a second, then jumped up and ran for the road. As I turned the corner, I heard the door burst open and a voice calling out. I didn't look back but ran until I reached my landmark, turning into the copse to fetch my mount. I was breathing hard, listening for sounds of pursuit as I sprang astride into the saddle but heard nothing. Still I took off at a gallop, smacking my steed with the reins while bent hard over his neck and didn't slacken pace until I was halfway back to Bowling Green.

I spent some of my meager funds to stable my horse and get a bed for the night at the inn. They looked askance at my late arrival and disheveled appearance but didn't say much. I had to share the bed with two other fellows, and I didn't say much about that, so I guess we were even. I was up and saddled by dawn, spending another cold day getting back to Baltimore. I recall the cold wind being in my face all the way on the return trip, but maybe it was just worse for having had my hopes dashed so completely.

I met two like-minded gentlemen in debate class, Martin Price and Steven Gardener, and we began to spend some evenings together studying, debating, or just drinking and smoking. As time went by, it became less studying and more carousing. Martin and Steven were both law students and roomed together on Mulberry in the twelfth ward. Both were an inch or two taller than me and well-built, Steven thinner with dark wavy locks and an easygoing smile, Martin a big blond with an eye for the girls and up for any crazy adventure. Martin's father owned a crab boat that operated out of Chaptico Bay, and he had spent much of his life on or around the water. Steven, by contrast, was raised by his stepfather on a tobacco farm on the Maryland side of the border from Leesburg, Virginia. We were as unlikely a trio as could be had but got along famously.

Our favorite haunt was Jack's Tavern down by the train station. Jack's was in a brick commercial building, wedged between other enterprises that seemed to come and go. When coming in the front, there was a long, highly-polished straight bar on the left with a line of stools and a big mirror behind. On the right were eight square wood tables with chairs along a brick wall that had been carved with the names of patrons of the establishment over the past forty years or so. In the back was a door that led to a cardroom that had some pretty constant—and probably illegal—activity, judging from the traffic in and out. At times, some fairly high stakes gaming was done back there, way beyond my limited means. A sign above the door to the establishment read, "Jack's Tavern. Liquor in the Front, Poker in the Rear." It was an amusing place with cheap beer and a constant pall of tobacco and lamp oil smoke from about head level up that left the ceiling beams with a permanent coat of glistening dingy-brown. They would also fill gallon jugs for you from the tap for a ridiculously-low price that you could carry away to create your own party elsewhere.

Steven was interested in politics, especially in utilizing his legal talents to support efforts to tailor laws specific to tobacco exports. He owned a small trap and horse. Sometimes on a Friday, we would make the trip south to Washington City so he could rub elbows with representatives and other lobbyist types. We would all work on finding free lodging or have to spend the night in the buggy under a horse blanket. At the least, we were predatory on the affections of the daughters of the prominent in the city.

Now Baltimore was a rough-and-tumble town, and the unwary could find themselves with a lump on their head and missing their purse or their watch from a pickpocket while visiting certain areas of the city. Washington was—and still is—different, downright dangerous. Murder and mayhem runs rampant in a place where money exchanges hands daily to buy congressional votes and delegates are wined and dined by the privileged to curry favor and influence. The three of us cut a wide swath and were forever coming up with strategies to amuse ourselves. Soirees were held weekly in the downtown hotels and residences; we crashed these functions at will for amusement and to meet people, especially girls.

Steven was a natural in these settings—beautiful damsels took to him like bees to a flower. Martin didn't do badly either, and his devil-may-care attitude attracted the more adventurous, along with the married but bored. I must have been a more serious type. I certainly had my share of girlfriends but most wanted a committed relationship or a marriage proposal.

In April of '54, I was up on Fourteenth Street, returning after midnight from a party to the buggy. I had been told, "I'm saving myself for marriage," by one very pretty Ms. Douglas and was going over sour grapes in my head, not paying full attention to my surroundings when a figure jumped at me from the shadow of a door alcove. He slashed at my throat with a knife and only my fine-tuned sailor's reflexes saved me, the blade cutting my shirt and chest muscle on the left side. I grabbed his arm and used my hip as leverage to throw him to the ground. He landed hard on his head with a hollow sound, like a bowl hitting a floor, falling then on his shoulder and side. I backed off a step and opened my clasp knife to defend myself further. The man just lay there, not moving, then jerked back to consciousness. He began groaning and curled into a fetal position; I saw blood begin to ooze from under him. He continued to remain still and after a minute, I rolled him on his back with my foot, remaining ready in case he decided to resume his attack on me. He had landed on his own knife, and it was protruding from his side between his ribs, in all the way to the hilt. I could see a dark circle of blood spreading from the wound. He began coughing and a trickle of blood came from his mouth, trickling down his chin.

My medical training told me his lung was punctured and he was not going to make it, but I was also hopping mad at having been attacked and the pain of my own wound was starting to register. I bent down and pulled the knife from his side; he groaned in protest. I wiped it off on his coat, then stood and looked around to see what witnesses there might be to the fight. Seeing no one, I examined the man further. He was about my height but thin, cheeks sunk in and oily dark hair that came to his shoulders. His coat was old and dirty, but his boots looked brand-new. He looked up at me as if expecting some assistance, but I was really angry and the wound on my chest was beginning to throb. I knelt down beside him and took his purse and the knife scabbard from his boot top. I hesitated for a second, then took his boots off him as well. They were too big for him and slipped right off, but it turned out they were just my size. When I left him, he was still alive, but I doubt if he lasted the night.

When I got to the livery where the buggy was checked, I was able to take off my coat and shirt to examine my wound in the lamplight. Seemed I'd been pretty lucky, it was a slash about five inches long, just below my collarbone, but only perhaps a half-inch deep. It looked pretty grizzly, there was a lot of blood on my chest and soaked through my shirt and coat, but it had already begun to coagulate. I used my ruined shirt to put pressure on the wound then woke the boy who was looking after the place and told him to run for a pail of water.

His eyes got big when he saw my injury and all the blood and said, "Mister, you need a doctor."

"I am a doctor," I told him. I got my bag from under the buggy seat while he fetched the water then soaked my shirttail to clean up around the wound. I couldn't see very well because the cut was high up on my pectoral, so I had the boy hold a fragment of mirror I found in the office, and I stitched it up backward which hurt like the devil. I did have the advantage of being a fair way toward intoxicated. I fashioned a bandage from the remainder of my shirt, tying it over the shoulder and under the opposite armpit, then made a sling from a piece of horse blanket to immobilize the whole, preventing me from reopening the wound. When I examined the purse I'd taken, it contained seven dollars and change, so I flipped the boy a dime and had a friend for life. I crawled into a pile of hay and went to sleep.

I woke up about an hour before noon the next day, stiff and very sore. Martin and Steven came tumbling in shortly after, in high spirits, laughing and joking. They looked at me, blood-soaked coat, no shirt, bloody bandage and sling, and Martin said, "Johnny boy, where'd ya get the new boots?"

We all busted out laughing which just made my cut ache worse. They had a jolly good time making me laugh the whole ride back to Baltimore.

When I got home, Auntie Eleanore grabbed me by the ear, sat me down, and did a proper bandage. She gave me a ten-minute earful on the topic of my wayward behavior, then kissed me on the forehead, fed me a piece of pie, and sent me off to bed. The seven dollars didn't quite cover replacing my shirt and coat but took the sting out of the loss. The boots and boot knife were fine additions to my wardrobe; I still have the knife.

I first met Janie Marie Engle at her twentieth birthday party in February of '55. Her best friend, Susan, threw the party at her father's house on H Street, just up from the Navy Yard, both girls being daughters of naval officers. The girls were hitting the wine pretty heavy, and Susan was taking every opportunity to grab my arm or engage me in flirtatious conversation. For whatever reason, Susan was not what I had in mind; she was slurring her words and showing other signs of inebriation. My sixth sense told me I'd better get clear of the situation, so when the party began to wind down, I took the opportunity to thank her for her hospitality, collected my coat and hat, and made my way out the front door. I had no sooner stepped down from the front porch when to my surprise, both Susan and Janie came out and began to harangue me verbally for leaving so early. I apologized, saying that I had a family engagement early on the morrow, but they weren't buying my excuse.

At this juncture, Janie told me I was just scared of Susan, so I moved up right in front of Janie, bowed, kissed her hand, and said, "Ma'am, I'm afraid of all women."

When I straightened up, our eyes met and held for just a second; I was instantly intrigued by the way her blue eyes clashed with her black hair. I got the feeling I startled her a bit as well. I turned and walked away, figuring the situation to be way out of my control.

In March, Martin, Steven, and I crashed a party at the Willard Hotel ballroom for Janie's father, Frederick Engle, who had just been promoted to full captain and given command of the USS *Wabash*, one of six new steam frigates authorized by congress the previous

April. Janie attended with her consort, a midshipman attending the new naval academy at Annapolis. Since her young gentleman was busy trying to rub elbows with the officers present and Janie was looking bored, I took the opportunity to approach her. She obviously knew I was not invited but seemed to appreciate my attentions. I found out from her that she was to spend the spring with her friend, Susan, while her father was in Philadelphia, seeing to the fitting out of his new ship. I also found out that Susan's father was responsible for the armament procurement for all six of the new ships, causing him to travel between Boston, New York, Philadelphia, Washington, and Norfolk.

Janie expressed interest in my surname, Carlile, and said that was also her mother's maiden name. Both her mother's family and mine were from Philadelphia, but we could discern no mutual relatives. I told her that I was expecting to graduate Maryland College in June and would attempt to start a medical practice at that time. She was intelligent and articulate and seemed to appreciate that I didn't press my attentions, possibly due to the presence of her date for the occasion. We must have been getting a bit too animated in our conversation, however, because at that point, her midshipman beau came up and made a point of steering her away from me.

Later in the evening, I came upon a disturbing situation. A young lady of my slight acquaintance was trapped in a corner by a large man whom I came to know later as Ward Lamon. Lamon was an attorney and partner with Abraham Lincoln who was then a rising star in Illinois politics. He was a great bull of a man and had this girl trapped with one hand on each wall, penning her in. He had been drinking heavily, and she was looking very nervous, so I came up behind Lamon, putting my hand hard on his shoulder to get his attention. When he turned to see who I was, the girl took the opportunity to slip under his arm and make her escape. Lamon looked at me, then at the young lady making her getaway, then back at me.

Something happened then that was new to my experience. All recognition seemed to leave Lamon's eyes as if there was no longer anyone at home there. He took a big roundhouse swing at me with his fist. Luckily I was ready and ducked it but had to take a couple of steps back to avoid him. He came rushing at me like a bull. By now, my ire was up, I had been drinking as well and was feeling quite courageous, so I stood my ground and hit him twice very quickly. Might have been drops of water in the sea for all I could discern the effect this had on him, and he hit me, a glancing blow on my right cheekbone that just about put me on the ground. That man could hit. Several of the men around both of us got us apart, and I found myself being dragged back by Martin and Steven, all the while kicking and punching. Out of the corner of my eye, I saw Janie Engle giving me an appraising look.

Hotel security had been called, so the three of us fled the hotel before those bully-boys could arrive. We twirled down the street, slapping each other on the back and making jokes. They both told me I was crazy for taking on Lamon, that he was reputed to be a brawler. I was a bit miffed with them both at the time for interfering but later thanked them. If Lamon had got me to the ground, I think he would have killed me with his bare hands or, at least, stomped me into oblivion.

The very next Saturday morning, I hired a horse and took off for Washington, accompanied by my school lab partner, Sam Mudd. Sam was a quiet and serious student, about my height but slender. He was already showing signs of a receding hairline. Sam's father owned a tobacco farm in Carroll County, about thirty miles further south of Washington, rather close to where my Aunt Eleanore's family resided; and he was going home for the weekend. We had been working on pharmacological interventions for dysentery and cholera; on the way south from Baltimore, we were actively discussing the virtues of ginger root. We had been having some success mixing this with salt and molasses for trials on poorer patients who sought out the medical school when unable to afford a doctor, a mutually beneficial relationship as we could then document clinical trials. Lemon, lime, and other ascorbic solutions had been partially successful as well but not in tandem; we were trying to discern why this was so.

Our timing on arrival was impeccable; Janie was alone in the house, Susan having just dashed out to the market. Janie invited us in to the parlor for tea. I introduced Sam, and we all had a lively conversation going. After about fifteen minutes, I gave Sam a hard look, raising my eyebrows. He got the hint immediately and got up to leave, citing that he still had a couple hours' journey to make it home and wanted to be there for supper.

Once Sam had left, Janie turned the conversation to my medical training. When she found out that I was actually seeing patients, she asked how I went about examining females. I had her sit on the piano bench and looked at her ears, nose, and throat in the light from the window, then explained how my stethoscope worked. I told her I had the patient remove the outer garments then listened to the heart, lungs, and abdomen. She stood, reached behind, and unbuttoned her dress, then let it fall to the floor.

"Like this?" she asked.

Well, I'm not too much of a dummy and got the hint immediately. I stepped right up and kissed her. She pulled me in and kissed me back hard, then broke free, grabbed my hand, and led me upstairs. We made love for about an hour before we heard the front door open and Susan's voice calling for Janie. She had seen my horse tethered in front and was wondering who their guest was.

"I'll be down in a minute," Janie called. We laughed, dressed quickly, then came down the stairs together. When Susan saw us together, I could see she knew instantly what had happened and she was not too happy but made no fuss over the situation. The girls went about making supper, and I hung out with them in the kitchen, talking politics and current events. I recall the topics ranging from President Pierce driving drunk and running over a man in the street to the voter fraud scandal in the recent Baltimore mayoral election, then about Hawthorne's newly-published book, *The Scarlet Letter*, that was an instant best seller. By the time we sat down to supper, Susan seemed okay with the way Janie was taking proprietary control over me, hanging onto my arm. We had an excellent meal, after which I excused myself and started back for Baltimore, not wishing to overstay my welcome. I did get a nice good night kiss, and Janie pressed herself nicely against me as I was leaving.

After that day, I took every opportunity to make it back down to Washington. My friends began to remark about my repeated absences, but I didn't care. I was addicted. Janie just plain liked to make love. She didn't want to do it in any exotic way like some of the French girls I'd met in my voyaging, but she did like to be on top. She was not a classic beauty, a little too small on top and a little bit large in the bottom, but she had a very cute face and was smart as a whip. In addition, she had a way of setting her jaw when she didn't get her way that drove me kind of crazy. She would get this smoky look in her blue eyes when she was passionate that would get me going as well, make me want to please her.

Janie had her quirks too. For one thing, I know she was still seeing her beau, from the naval academy, the whole time she was seeing me. I think he just didn't give her enough attention. I believe she had other suitors as well. Another odd thing was that she really liked my scars. She would sit on top of me and trace them lightly with her fingertip. It was like she was cataloging me, asking how I got each one. Just fascinated with them, the knife wound on my chest, a gouge I have on my shoulder from an errant marlin spike, and the old marks on my back from my father's cane. The other thing about her was that she liked my pipe, especially after lovemaking. These days, it's more common to see a woman smoke but not back then. At least not in my experience.

In any case, we got along famously for about two months, until one day in June, just before I was to complete my school exams. We were in Janie's bedroom, with her as usual astride me, her hands planted on my chest, when the door burst open and Susan's father strode in, apparently having just returned from a trip. It seemed that Susan was intent on having her revenge after all and had told her father what was going on.

"Janie, you ought to be ashamed of yourself, what will your father think?" he thundered. That's when the fateful words came out. Janie had instantly rolled off me and gathered the bedspread about her.

"He forced me," she said in a little tiny voice.

I could see that the man was a worldly sort and was convinced that this was not the truth, but he was honor bound to accept this statement from her. "Get dressed," he told me. "You will surrender yourself to me until the constable arrives to arrest you. At the very least, it seems you've abused my hospitality in an ungentlemanly fashion," he shouted at me. "If I were her father, I'd kill you."

I didn't say anything but got up and dressed quickly, mulling over my options in my mind. I was not about to be arrested and go to any jail, much less the infamous city prison over in Judiciary Square. I had a pretty good idea what kind of treatment to expect when it became known that I was there for assaulting a lady; so I maneuvered myself around the bed then rushed him. I hit him square in the chest with my shoulder, and, although I have to give him credit for an older man that I pretty much bounced off him, I moved him enough to get through the door. I turned and gave Janie a hateful look, she was still sitting in the bed, blanket around her and knees under her chin, then dashed out the door and bounded down the stairs.

"Stop!" he bellowed after me, but I was gone out the front door and on my horse in a wink.

I took off at a gallop and didn't slow down until I was clear of the city limits.

A few things happened as a result of this incident. I talked my Uncle Thomas into taking me back aboard the *Mary Eleanore* as an able-bodied hand. We sailed the following Monday. I missed my exams and didn't receive a diploma from Maryland College. I rectified this later by having one engraved for me from a copy of the real thing. I dropped my first name and began to be called by my middle name, Arthur. That is the name that appears on my diploma. I bought a gun. I spent the last of my savings on it but figured it for a good investment. It is a very nice .31 caliber five-shot Colt Dragoon revolver; I still have it although cap and ball weapons have become obsolete.

I heard later that Janie and Susan didn't provide much to the constable in the way of identifying me, just my first name John. As it was, I spent almost two years again at sea before I resumed my career ashore. The same man who did our scotch labels provided me with a diploma for twenty dollars, after which I decided to try going back to Richmond to hang out my shingle. In the meantime, I avoided Washington City like the plague.

Janie had the last laugh though. After about a week at sea, I discovered that it hurt to urinate. By the time we reached France, I had a couple of smallpox. I had to spend precious wages on a hack French physician for a mercury and cauterization treatment. The cure was successful but abominably painful. I wondered for some time after if I would be capable of fathering children.

13

When we returned to Baltimore in September, I found a number of things had changed. My father had sold the mercantile on Orleans Street. His friend George Kane had prevailed upon him to take over the position of assessor and collector for the city. Although Mayor Hinks was American Party and my father a Democrat, the city council elections had returned Democrats to prominence, and my father had many friends among the newly-elected politicians. In any case, he was now a wealthy man, his worth on paper exceeding $10,000. I knew he had thousands more squirreled away for emergencies; he had no trust in the banks. Tax collecting also had its perks; in addition to the salary, there were many opportunities for him to turn his head to imports and line his pockets for his efforts on the behalf of the profits of the merchant community. He ceded full ownership of the *Mary Eleanore* and the warehouse facility to my Uncle Thomas to preclude appearances of impropriety.

I was now more or less on speaking terms with my father, although neither of us went out of our way to do so. I guess he had finally resigned himself to the fact that I was determined to do things my own way; and even if he didn't approve, he understood that he had no ability to affect change over me.

Onboard the *Mary Eleanore*, there was change as well. Mr. Hutchinson, who had replaced me as second officer, had repeatedly earned the disgust of both captain and crew. He was not only too lax toward the men with their duties but also loathe to assume the positions of honor handling the ship. To maintain the respect of the crew, the mate was expected to be end of the yard when reefing and middle position when furling as these were always the most dangerous. The captain paid him off and told him he was through. He left the ship making vague threats under his breath, but the captain just gave him a friendly clap on the back, then a not-so-friendly shove when he got to the gangplank, sending him tumbling down to the wharf where he sprawled out in a most unceremonious manner, his round hat being caught by the breeze and rolling down the street. I found myself promoted back to mate, the captain's announcement on the subject being met with a cheer from the men.

Now as I mentioned before, the second officer has charge of the larboard watch, midnight to four, then eight to noon, when the entire crew comes on for the regular workday. The midnight watch leaves plenty of room for introspection. Anyone who has been to sea can tell you that on a clear night, the stars are so plentiful you can hardly make out the constellations and seem so close you can almost reach out and touch them. There is a quiet that prevails beyond the creak of the timbers and regular whoosh of the water as the prow cuts through the rolling waves. At eight in the morning, the pumps need to be rigged and the decks scrubbed, then everything organized to be ready for the coming workday. The most important task is to have an endless set of chores ready, needing accomplished and a good command of vulgar vocabulary; for although the men may grumble, they are really happier with their hands busy, feeling they are earning their pay. Additionally it is comforting to know that you are a part of a taut ship when it comes to holding the elements at bay. Proper preparation for the weather that will inevitably come ensures the safety of the ship and all hands. A ship at sea is a living, breathing thing and a taut ship has that healthy feel to her. Our captain ran a taut ship.

By 1856, we were actively engaged in smuggling operations. With every trip, we would return with cases of rifles, gunpowder, and other military stores. We had a standard rendezvous off an uninhabited portion of the Virginia shoreline, always at night and always met by men wearing hoods who would row out to meet us. Captain told me, at one point, they were the Knights of the Golden Circle and the weapons were destined for Kansas. He was obviously distasteful of the politics but not the money. Whoever was funding the operation had deep pockets. In addition, I suspected my father of being a member of that organization. He always looked smugly satisfied with our success.

Cotton had gone up in value in Europe due to the Crimean War, France and Britain having thrown in to assist Turkey against Russian expansion to the south and west into the Balkan territories. Uniforms and equipment were in great need. Austria initially welcomed Russian assistance when it came to rebellions in Serbia and Hungary; but as usual, Russian Armies can be too much of a good thing. Most of Europe decided eventually that the Czar had become too big for his britches. At first, there was little action, described famously as the French Army doing nothing and the British forces helping them do it. The whole thing became an ungodly mess with Balaclava and the siege of Sevastopol—with the Russians throwing masses of men against prepared positions. Disease ran rampant and both sides' armies were unprepared for the winter. It was all covered in the newspapers along with photographs. The British and French citizens began complaining of the cost both in lives and tax money. Russia finally caved after the fall of Sevastopol and sued for piece in March of '56, the result of all the killing being Russia was no longer allowed to keep a significant fleet in the Black Sea. For a few years, at least.

Following the end of the war, the need and, subsequently, the price of cotton dropped dramatically. England was in a rut for food-stuff and building materials, so our cargoes began to reflect this. We were shipping flour, corn, wood, and tobacco primarily and returning with high-quality manufactured goods, furniture, wine, and liquor.

The elections of 1856 were interesting affairs, although I was at sea mostly and we only arrived back at port in October. The may-oral race was hotly contested and because of previous violence and corruption during the '54 elections, the city council put pressure on Mayor Hinks to call for General Steuart's militia to maintain order. Hinks issued the order then rescinded it, perhaps feeling his party would lose if the election was fair and supervised. The American Party, or Know Nothings as they were called in Baltimore, were ironically made up mostly of second-generation sons of immigrants, along with the gutter trash living along the basin.

The street gangs had organized, using the volunteer fire departments as a base, each ward with their own organizations. Previous to the elections, it was not uncommon for them to compete over responding to a blaze because they were paid by the call. There had been several instances of the competing firemen engaging in brawls on arrival to a fire, the winning team then getting to extinguish the conflagration. Obviously these irregularities, as they were called, took up much valuable time to the detriment of public safety and property loss.

During the municipal election, serious violence erupted with shots fired and pitched battles raging for several hours. At one point in, the sixth ward artillery was brought out to disperse the mob. Democrats were fighting against Know Nothings, Rip Raps, and Plug Uglies. In all, five people were killed outright with many dozens wounded. My good friend Martin Price was shot in the leg, shattering the bone and requiring amputation. I received news later that his wound became infected and he died just before Christmas. He was just twenty-three years old.

Thomas Swann, the American Party candidate, won the election with claims of voter fraud all around. After the election, Mayor Swann called upon George Kane to reorganize the fire department. As with the police, Kane was the man for the job and by force of will, friendly or unfriendly coercion, and some political wrangling, a new citywide fire department was born. Several years were to pass before he could get all this accomplished. He even managed to get a special tax pushed through to get upgrades to the existing equipment along with rudimentary medical training for the officers. By the time Kane was done getting things on track, Baltimore City Fire Department was the envy of such organizations nationwide.

James Buchanan won the presidential election, returning the Democrats to the White House. Millard Fillmore, the old Whig, ran for the Know Nothings and won only one state, Maryland, to my father's disgust. The surprise was the new Republican Party which had recently come into existence. John Fremont, the ex-soldier of fortune and hero of California in the Mexican War, ran on a straight antislavery ballot and took most of the northern states. The country was obviously polarizing once again and around the issue of slavery—not just states' rights.

Life onboard ship started to feel stagnant once again, and by January of '57, I began to plot what would be next for me. The long night watches gave me plenty of time for planning. I increased the amount I was saving from my earnings instead of spending on entertainment in ports of call and negotiated to have an engraved diploma made during a side trip smuggling whiskey. Sailors typically spend their free time upgrading or repairing their gear or practicing sleight of hand technique with cards or shell game and talking up their next get-rich-quick scheme. I spent some time hand carving a frame for my diploma, and it looked very professional. I was, at that point, actively looking for a sign that I had disappeared from the notice of the authorities.

14

In May of '57, I figured the coast was clear and I felt I had accumulated enough savings to make a start on a medical practice. I picked
Richmond to give it a go, recalling my years there as a youth fondly.
It took me about a month to find just the right place, but it worked
out for the best. I discovered a two-room suite on the north side of
Olive Street, on the second floor above a silversmith shop. It was
a few blocks above Mayo's Bridge, and the Virginia & Central rail
depot right below Shockoe Hill. The front room faced the street and
had two tall windows that allowed plenty of light, although I had
drapes made to block the afternoon heat in the summer. This room
was accessed from the main staircase, and I put a little bell on the
door to warn me when I had a client. The backroom had a single
small window overlooking the alley, a side door with an exterior staircase to the ground, and a big cast-iron woodstove for cooking and
heat. I screened off that side of the room, adding an iron bed and
my sea chest for a living area. It was small but much larger than
the accommodations I was used to onboard ship. The other half of
the room was therefore enclosed; I got an old oak desk and hired a
carpenter to build bookshelves and an examination table to my specifications. With an overstuffed chair and my diploma on the wall, I
had an office.

I worked out a deal with Andrew Gibson, an apothecary on
Pearl Street. I got cost breaks on medications, powders, and balms in
exchange for exclusive referrals for prescriptions from my practice; it
was a lucrative proposition for us both. Andy Gibson was a skinny
old Scotsman with a thick brogue and a twinkle in his eye. We soon

became fast friends and remained so, even later when we didn't track in the same social circles. Andy always had a story with a moral to it that would bring me back to earth when I got too full of myself.

I initially relied on my Uncle John to make referrals for my services to his government contacts, and as word spread of my existence, I had plenty of business. Unlike others, I remained unwilling to do business in trade, and this worked out as well, giving me a better quality clientele; although I was always willing to make a house call for the right people. I charged a dollar per visit and soon had three to four clients a day, giving me an income of perhaps eighty dollars per month. I became very adept at exaggerating the severity of the afflictions I was presented with, then having to make multiple appointments necessary to finally cure conditions that generally resolved on their own. Hysterical women became my specialty, and they not only became repeat customers but were the best gossipers, spreading my growing reputation by word of mouth in their social circles.

This left me with savings and spending money after expenses, so I looked for other opportunities to meet and become noticed by the social elite of the city. Uncle John was instrumental in assisting, he was a wealth of information regarding the right cafes, taverns, and events. He really seemed to enjoy taking me under his wing and creating my image. With his advice, I began to dress, speak, and act quite like a dapper southern gentleman. John Snyder Carlile was an old scammer at heart; he had started his own way in business at an early age, as a young teen, and was proud of what he had been able to achieve with just his wits. Now he had me well on my way to becoming the physician to the city's exclusive.

Richmond, in those days, was still the gay and fun-loving community I remembered from my teen years at Maymont Academy. It was nothing like the rough and ready cities like Baltimore and Washington to the north. Taverns like Bird-in-Hand, Lynch's, Lafayette Saloon, or the Eagle were known all over the country, for not only their wine cellars and liquor stocks but also for their bills of fare, offering the best fresh food from the local farms. Hunting clubs and racetracks in the English tradition provided endless entertainment as did the dozen or so theatrical halls offering a choice of programs. The Metropolitan Hall and Marshall Theatre had performances ranging from Shakespeare to burlesque, along with new American productions featuring rising stars such as Jenny Lind, Edwin Booth, or Joe Jefferson. Fine imported or domestic luxuries could be purchased at Keen, Baldwin & Co. or John Dooley's Hattery and grocers like Pizzini's and Antoni's put the selection we used to have at my father's store to shame. I began to make a weekly pilgrimage to Richardson's Cigar Store, not only for the tobacco but for the educated talk regarding the differences in the available products. All part of my newly-acquired cultural affect.

In December of that year, my fortunes improved even further. I was attending a soiree at the Monumental Hotel when I had a tap on my shoulder. I turned and found myself face to face with Mary McDowell—no—now Mrs. Mary Curry from the news that I'd had. At twenty-two years, she was a picture of loveliness; I swear she became more beautiful every time I saw her, no longer the skinny teen I once played with. She was dressed all in black which suited her complexion, and I soon learned that she was newly widowed.

"John, I'm in a bit of trouble," she told me.

"I'm Arthur now," I chided her. "I left John behind me in Baltimore."

She told me that her husband was a bit older and had died of a coronary while in her arms. His family was contesting her inheritance of his property and had gone as far as to make allegations of foul play on her part to the local sheriff in an attempt to prevail in their lawsuit. She had even been unable to continue living in the home she had shared with her husband. I was most gallant and informed her that in my estimation, he was the luckiest man in the world to have met his demise in such a fashion and with such a lady. I accompanied this statement of fact with a sweeping bow and elicited a smile from her for my trouble. I also told her I would use my newfound connections to see if I could obtain a reputable attorney that would take a chance representing her for payment upon her successful conclusion of the matter.

We sat and talked for an hour, catching up on each other's lives. I did my utmost to enthrall her with tales of my seagoing adventures, and I believe I succeeded in, at least, having her rapt attention. There was a profound sadness about her that I couldn't quite define, but it just added to my proprietary feelings for her. Finally her brother, Isaac, came to collect her and, with an unpleasant look in my direction, whisked her away. I walked away feeling elated—no—on top of the world and resolved that I would never again allow her to get away from me.

The next week, I made arrangements with Will Richardson, Esq., a rising star in the Virginia legal community to take on her case on the basis that she would pay his retainer if he could win and he provided me with a letter for her to that effect. That Sunday, I made the first of many trips up to Bowling Green to see her. At some point, I purchased a horse and tackle as this had become a cheaper alternative to renting each week. I couldn't afford to neglect my practice and so could only make the trip on Sundays; but every once in a while, she would be able to make it to Richmond and we would enjoy supper in town or attend a performance. I was most careful to keep things above board to forestall any negative impact on her legal case. When I was in Bowling Green, we would meet, accompanied by her brother or in public. When in Richmond, we would stick with Uncle John and Aunt Mary Ellen for company. At first, Isaac McDowell disliked me intensely, but once he discovered the caliber of my attire and became more informed as to my stature in the community, he became much more friendly. For my part, I continued to dislike him and never trusted him but kept my opinion to myself as not to cause anything to come between Mary and myself.

In May of '58, Mary's case came before the magistrate and the court ruled in her favor, finding that she had no fault in her husband's death. She was also granted the full estate including their home in Hanover Courthouse, just north of Richmond. I took her to supper to celebrate and at some point on into the meal, found the words to express my undying affection for her.

She just looked at me sadly and asked, "What would you want with an old widow woman like me, John?" She insisted on continuing to call me John even though no one else did so.

"I'm smitten and totally in love with you, always have been since the moment I first saw you," I replied. "I'll pursue you to the ends of the earth if necessary."

In June, at the solstice, I asked her to marry me and she agreed. I skipped the step of asking Isaac McDowell for her hand, but no one appeared to notice. We spent the summer and fall in a whirlwind courtship of rides in the countryside, picnics, shows, then later, Christmas shopping in the city. We were married on New Year's Day at St. Paul's in a grand ceremony with the reception following at Uncle John's residence on Capitol Street. My family came down from Baltimore for the occasion, and it was a gala affair.

Immediately after, I moved in with Mary at the home on the New Bridge Road, just south of the Hanover Road. This was a small estate of about twelve acres, enough to keep two horses, chickens for fresh eggs, and a nice garden for vegetables without truly having the size or workload of a farm. In addition, the location was ideal for me to keep my lucrative practice in Richmond. I had a half-mile walk in the morning to Peake's Station where I could catch the morning train into the city. In all, it took me just over an hour to get to my office in the morning and the same to return home at night. I began to take Saturdays off, in addition to Sundays, unless there were emergencies to attend to, and rarely would I remain in the city overnight for medical necessities, taking advantage of my makeshift bedroom there.

We were as happy as a couple could be, enjoying the bliss of married life, in spite of Mary's occasional bouts of melancholy. And after only a couple of months, she informed me that we were to be parents. I whooped and gathered her up in my arms, then said, "Sorry, I guess I should be more careful."

She smiled, the old gleam of mischief in her eye, and replied, "With child but not fragile!"

So passed the happiest year of my life, managing my medical practice and helping people during the day, then home to the love of my life at night. By September, Mary was already getting exceedingly large, so, with a doctor's curiosity, I checked the baby's heartbeat with my stethoscope and discovered, to my astonishment, two separate heartbeats. It was to be twins without a doubt. I was walking on clouds at this turn of events, Mary maybe not so much. She was having to endure the heat of the Virginia summer in extra-large size. She told me she was perspiring in places that made her feel unladylike which just made me laugh.

As the autumn came on, Mary was less able to keep up around the house, so I hired Sally, a black girl from the owner of a neighboring farm, to tend to things. Mary had some objection to this; she had always been opposed to slavery, but she had to admit that she was in need of the assistance.

Second week of November, Mary was experiencing some discomfort. So as her doctor, I confined her to bed rest. I figured it was still two to three weeks before she was due. I had figured the births would come around the first of December and had planned to take some time away from the practice at that time. I spent the weekend pampering her in every way I could think of. I knew her and surmised that if she called it discomfort, what she really meant was it was painful.

On Monday, the fourteenth, I went to work as normal. Just after midday, I received a telegraph from the office at Peake's Station telling me to come quickly, that the babies were coming. I rushed out and went down to the train station, but it was over two hours before there was a northbound train, and even then it was a freight. Due to the emergency, they allowed me to ride in the caboose with the brakeman, slowing enough at Peake's Junction to allow me to jump to the ground without suffering injury. I ran the half-mile home, arriving to find the house quiet. I called out a haloo and was answered from upstairs. I bounded up and walked into a horror. Thomas Kinney, a local doctor, met me at the bedroom door, preventing me from entering. His wife was seated on a chair by the bed with a bundle in her arms. No sign of the girl, Sally; she had apparently fled. There were bloody sheets, clothing, and rags everywhere. Mary was in the bed, not moving and extremely pale.

"There wasn't much I could do, Arthur," he said. "By the time I got here, the hemorrhage was significant. I opened her up and was just able to stop the bleeding. One child was stillborn, the other, a girl, is still hanging on."

"Mary?" I asked with my heart in my throat.

"Still with us but just barely. She lost too much blood, there is little chance."

I pushed my way past him and got on my knees by the bed, grabbing her hand. She opened her eyes and looked at me with that sad expression I had tried so hard to drive away.

"John," she said. "You've always been so kind to me." Then that mischievous twinkle returned to her eye, and she motioned me close. She smiled and whispered very softly, "You know I killed my first husband. He was a very bad man, he hit me and called me the cruelest things, so I poisoned him."

I was stunned and appalled by this admission, but she just smiled like an angel and closed her eyes. And just like that, she was gone. I put my head down on her shoulder and cried like a baby.

15

I buried her in the McDowell family cemetery up in Caroline County, it is a beautiful spot that occupies corner parts of two properties and several neighboring families have used it since the early 1700s. It sits on the north side of a small valley created by a brook that runs through the bottom lands, a track road going past further up the hillside provides access, the ridge beyond which is densely forested. The cemetery itself is open and grassy right up to the iron fence surrounding the plot. I believe Mary would be happy there with her family.

I named our daughter Mary Eleanore after my favorite aunt, but I had difficulty managing things. She was not a content baby and kept me up nights. Sally, the neighbor's girl came over to help at first; but after she caught me in my chair talking to my deceased wife, she was spooked and refused to come over further. To add insult to injury, she spread gossip about a ghost in the house so none of the other black girls in the area would agree to provide me with any assistance either. My father finally solved my dilemma by sweeping up my daughter and taking her home to Baltimore for Maddie to care for. My half-sister, Caroline, was now a nine-year-old and had been sent to school in Pennsylvania, her vacant bedroom was turned into the nursery.

As I was now alone in my home, the farmhouse became an oppressive place; everything about it reminded me of Mary. I had no energy for the place, and it began to become overgrown with weeds and vines as would befit a haunted house. My neighbors, who had been very supportive at first, began to avoid me and my property. I began to spend most of my time in my Richmond office, so I determined to sell the place as I had little further use for it. Isaac McDowell made a case to the court that the property was owned by his sister prior to our marriage and should rightfully remain in the McDowell family. This proved to be a ridiculous claim, and I ended up selling the place back to the Curry family for almost nothing seeing as they owned it to begin with and still had title to the adjacent fields. That made Isaac McDowell my mortal enemy; but since I never liked him to begin with, I cared little for that outcome. Moot point as it turned out anyway, the house was destroyed by Yankee artillery fire just two years later during the Seven Days.

As the weeks went by, I began to neglect my practice, preferring the company of barkeeps who would agree with me that life was tragic and unfair—as long as I kept paying for drinks. My friends and colleagues, who had been sympathetic toward my plight, began to lose patience, advising me to quit the antics and get back to work. I attempted to see a couple of ladies who had been very flirtatious with me while I was married but found they had lost interest now that I was single again, although my unkempt appearance might have tipped the scale a bit with that. I do find that women are far more competitive than men in reality and without a wife, there was no other woman to compete against. So I found myself to be somewhat of a pariah.

In May of 1860, I made a trip back to Baltimore to see my daughter and family. While I was there, I sounded out Uncle Thomas to see if he would take me back aboard ship once again. He looked me square in the eye, as was his style, and told me no. He said, "You're in no shape to be any good to me or anyone else for that matter. You've got to get yourself straight before you can move on." Of course, I took this advice the wrong way, figuring everyone was just out to get me down.

On the return trip, I took the detour out to Caroline County to visit Mary's grave. I was sitting on the grass, with the sun on my face, telling her how much I missed her and how much our daughter had grown when Isaac McDowell came through the gate and stomped up to me. Someone must have told him I was there; he was bright red in the face and obviously furious. "You have some nerve," he yelled at me. "You have no business here!"

"I have every right to be here, she is my wife!" I said, my lip curling in distaste for the man. I jumped to my feet, beginning to get angry.

"You killed her," he hissed.

So I hit him. He saw it coming and tried to dodge, but I caught him hard on the cheekbone. He was no patsy and came right after me; we stood toe to toe for a couple of seconds, exchanging punches. We each took a step back and glared at each other, breathing hard. Then Isaac laughed but not a nice laugh. He said, "Get the hell off my property. Next time I'll shoot you." He turned and walked back up the hill and through the gate.

At first, I felt like I had won the day; but on the ride back to Richmond, I began to realize that I had just had a fist fight while standing on my wife's grave. That knowledge sat rather awkwardly with me, and I stewed on it all the way there. When I returned to the city, I sold my horse and saddle then packed my bag. I was in such a funk of self-loathing that I didn't even take the time to say goodbye to friends, family, or clients, but I was clearheaded. Only because I'd never been there before, I set out for Norfolk on the train the next day, June 1.

16

I grabbed the southbound train out of Richmond and was soon frustrated by a two-hour delay in Petersburg while they attached additional boxcars for the southeast run to Portsmouth. It was already sweltering in the passenger car, even with the window pulled down, and I had neglected to acquire any reading material to keep me busy during the trip. I mused over some possibilities for the future in my head. I had my savings and $100 from the sale of my horse and rig, so I had some buffer to survive on until I could avail myself of a new opportunity. I was looking forward to a new adventure and chomping at the bit to get moving on it. When we began to move again, I incurred the wrath of some of the ladies seated behind me by not closing my window. I was enjoying the late spring air and didn't respond to their passive attempts to let me know how the wind was rearranging their hats and the hairstyles underneath.

I did note that this was all to the amusement of a particular woman sitting across and one seat behind. She was traveling with a man who was obviously her husband; he was well-dressed in a silk suit and was poring over what appeared to be account ledgers open on his lap. From my angle, I could just see the glint of silver on the head of his stick in spite of the hat perched upon it. She was attired in a fashionable tan dress with minimal décolletage; the color contrasted magnificently with her auburn hair. I could tell she was a bit older than me, perhaps thirty, the twinkle of mischief in the look she gave me in response to the complaining from behind me certainly set me on a firm course of obstinacy. I returned her smile with an evil little grin of my own.

We arrived in Portsmouth toward supper, so I found a quiet tavern for some refreshment and a portion of pork roast and new potatoes from the kitchen. I got directions from the proprietor for the ferry across to Norfolk, then made my way to the harbor. Although by now it was past seven o'clock, the sun was still up due to the advance of the season, and the ferry was taking advantage to accept the additional business. To my surprise, the couple from the train was aboard the ferry as well. I introduced myself and found out that they were Samuel and Priscilla Sutherland. Samuel was the son of one of the largest and most reputable firearms dealers in the south. I had seen their shop on Main Street in Richmond many times in passing. Samuel was thin and balding slightly, impeccably dressed. He remained aloof and glued to his ledgers, but Priscilla was chatty especially after she discovered my profession. She told me they were to take passage on the British and Foreign steamship *Karnak*, due to arrive on the morrow. She told me her husband was checking into items they were importing from England that had hit regulatory snags, and she had come along for the adventure. I could tell she was flirting, although her husband appeared not to notice, and I began to hatch a plan.

I took a room in a boarding house, the usual type that widows run to keep the wolves from the door. The landlady, Mrs. O'Toole, was thin, iron-gray-haired with a stoop and distinct Irish brogue. She was happy to find I was a professional person and happier when she caught a glimpse of the contents of my purse. She gave me a cheery room on the second floor overlooking the street, letting me know she served breakfast at eight and supper at seven, although if I was hungry, she could possibly come up with something. I have to say that during my three days there, meals were hearty and delicious.

I went out that evening, walking the waterfront, searching. I was looking for just the right person to assist me in my plan while being careful to watch my own back. In the third tavern I visited, I found the man I was looking for. He was older, perhaps in his late forties, obviously a sailorman. He was sitting by himself at the corner of the bar with one eye on the door and positioned so none could get behind him. A baggy white-ish shirt concealed his build, but I could see the forearms of a hard man who has worked hard all his life. I could see him appraise me when I walked in, trying to determine if I was what I appeared to be.

After ordering up a beer and scanning the room for some five minutes, I timed my approach with him finishing his beer, walked up and said, "Buy you a drink?"

"Sure," he said. "But what's it gonna cost me?"

"Just a business proposition, cost you nothin' to listen."

He grunted his assent, so I pulled up a stool and ordered another round for us both. After the bartender left, I remarked that I could see he was a hardworking man, that I needed just such a man to facilitate a project. He looked warily at me and just grunted again, this time not so hospitably. "I need to have a man lose his way for two days," I said while looking at him intensely. "I don't want him harmed in any way, just made unavailable."

He gave me another of those appraising looks, then remarked, "I don't think I want to know why you need this done but let's say I'm interested, if the wages sound good."

"How's twenty bucks sound?" I offered. "Meet me here tomorrow morning at seven, and I'll give you a gold eagle up front to cover your expenses, then another when I get word that he's disappeared."

"I can't get the down payment now?" he asked.

"I don't carry money when I don't have to," I replied. Besides, I didn't really trust him not to get stinking drunk on my money and not show for the job. Twenty dollars is two months' wages for a sailor, so I had his attention for two days' work.

"What do I call you?" he asked.

"John," I replied, "John Doe. You?"

"Davvy." Then after a pause, "Davvy Jones," said with a conspiratorial grin.

I stood then, shook his hand, and turned to go. "Till tomorrow."

"Lookin' forward to workin' with ya," was the reply.

I left the establishment and turned left, walking south along the waterfront. After watching the reflections in the shop windows for a few blocks, I confirmed Davvy was following me from a discrete distance, so I took the next street to the left in a nonchalant manner then ran quickly around a half-block until I was back through the alley to Riverfront Street, pausing to catch my breath. Sure enough, it was only twenty seconds before Davvy crossed in front of me, hustling so as not to lose sight of me. As he passed, I struck a match, using it to light my pipe. He jumped back when the match flared, turning toward me as he backpedaled. I took a puff, extinguished the match, and said, "Smoke?"

His expression went from guilty to angry in a flash, and he began to sputter out an excuse, but I cut him off and said, "Look, I appreciate a cautious man, but we have to exercise some trust in this endeavor."

He looked at me and frowned, but I could see he clearly didn't want to lose the payday and realized he had underestimated me. "Night, John," he said and turned and retreated down the street the way he had come.

I finished my smoke, waiting until Davvy was some distance off, then returned to the boarding house where I got a great night's sleep, perhaps for the first time in over six months.

The next morning, I was up at first light. Mrs. O'Toole was kind enough to feed me early, bacon, eggs, and fresh-baked bread. At seven sharp, I arrived at the tavern and was pleased to see Davvy was already there. I shook his hand, pressing a ten-dollar gold eagle into his palm as I did so. I led him to a pier where RS *Karnak* had just been tied off and was preparing to load cargo and mail. *Karnak* was a big, trim three-masted steam ship, passenger cabin amidships in the classic clipper-style. Her bright-red funnel looked freshly-painted and sported three black pinstripes and a black stack-cap. I had done my homework and knew that *Karnak* ran the connecting service from New York to Nassau and Havana, had a mail contract for that, in addition to what passengers and freight she could manage. Norfolk was not a usual stop on her route; I suspected that my acquaintances the Sutherlands had some involvement with this.

I laid out Davvy's part of the scheme for him as we stood there watching. "I need you to go aboard and get a good look at the ship's surgeon, he's your target. *Karnak* sails Monday morning on the tide, and he can't be aboard when she goes." Monday was the fourth, just two days away. "I'll meet you Sunday night, nine o'clock, at the tavern with the other ten dollars when I confirm he's missing."

"What's my excuse for going aboard?" Davvy wanted to know.

"Try asking about employment," I said with a sarcastic tone.

Off he went, and it looked to me like he gained *Karnak's* deck without being stopped, but longshoremen were already flowing onto and off the vessel to assist taking on cargo. For my part, I merged back into the shadows, waiting and watching. Pretty soon, Davvy came back down the gangplank, giving me a nod and a wink to let me know he had accomplished his initial mission. He turned when he reached the street, disappearing into the growing crowd of laborers, sailors, and vendors accumulating along the riverfront.

After about an hour, my patience paid off when a short burly man with graying muttonchop whiskers, wearing a blue uniform coat and beat-up brimmed cap came down the plank, crossed the street and entered a restaurant immediately to my right. I waited a minute and followed him in. My timing was impeccable; he was just returning from the bar to a table with a drink and as he was sitting, I pretended to trip over a chair and catch myself on his table, making sure the impact was sufficient to spill his drink. He bounced immediately to his feet, his face turning red and bushy eyebrows turning down in irritation. He stepped back to keep the liquid from dripping onto his clothes. I immediately feigned embarrassment, apologized, and offered to replace his drink. He looked at me warily, then nodded his assent. I went to the bartender and obtained two shots of his best whiskey, along with two tap beers, returning to the table with hands full. I sat without asking, which peeved him some, but he mellowed on, beginning to sip the whiskey with a sound of approval from his throat.

"Dr. Arthur Carlile," I said, holding out my hand.

He shook my hand then said, "Thomas Brownless," in a hard English accent.

During the conversation that followed, I confirmed that he was indeed master of the *Karnak* and on my part, I let him know that not only was I a doctor from Richmond taking a sabbatical due to a family tragedy but also that I had years behind me on the sea and as an officer. He warmed toward me as we began to swap stories and when I mentioned the tale of the Spanish revenue schooner off Cuba, he became downright friendly, telling me he had heard of the incident. "Bloody mermaids is what I heard," he said, grinning broadly.

When his breakfast arrived, I took my leave rather than press my advantage and took the remainder of the morning and most of the afternoon strolling about the city seeing the sights. I returned about six to a vantage point in the Plum Point park just north of *Karnak's* quay where I could keep an eye on events as they unfolded. Pretty soon, the captain appeared with two other officers, through the sally port and down the plank they came, across the street and into the same restaurant where I had met with Captain Brownless earlier. I followed after, close to ten minutes, picking a seat close to the door and pretending not to notice the trio I was observing.

"Dr. Carlile!" Brownless bellowed out.

I jerked my head up and swiveled around. Catching his eye, I waved. "Come join us," he called while gesturing me over with one hand.

I made my way around the tables that separated us and shook the captain's hand. He introduced his fellows as Mr. Gibson, the mate, and Cookson, the engineer. I shook hands with both, making sure to make good eye contact then took a seat at the table. "Too bad our sawbones couldn't make it, he's been gone all day," Brownless remarked.

I smiled inwardly at this news but said, "He's likely holed up with one of our fine Virginia belles, providing expert medical advice."

This drew a laugh from all around. The talk then resumed around an incident that occurred three months earlier on their last voyage out. They had picked up a pilot, as was usual, to negotiate the entrance to Havana Harbor. Upon entering the anchorage, he was back over the side, down into his boat, when he fell into the sea. The *Karnak* had stopped to assist, picking him up, when a huge tiger shark, at least fifteen feet from nose to tail, appeared from behind the ship and grabbed the man, pulling him under. All they saw was blood afterward, and they theorized that the monster might have swallowed him whole.

Now all sailors have had their share of shark encounters, although this one was obviously of exceptional size, if maybe not quite as big as was being claimed. Still following the code, I theorized that sharks follow ships, hoping for a free meal of scraps and other garbage thrown over the side; and from my experience, the larger the ship, the larger the sharks that follow. *Karnak* was certainly a large vessel.

I followed this with, "Fat Spaniards are undoubtedly far tastier than lean English sailors, that fish just thought you were feeding him dessert!" The men at the table roared with laughter at this.

At this juncture, the waitress arrived with our plates and must have just heard the word dessert coupled with the uproarious laughter that followed. The girl eyed us suspiciously, no doubt thinking we were making fun of the board of fare.

"Our desserts are homemade!" she asserted indignantly which only caused us all to burst into new fits of laughter.

"Are they Spanish?" choked out Brownless through his laughter, causing us additional convulsions. I had tears running down my cheeks, I guess you had to have been there to appreciate it. The waitress did not, she turned and stomped away.

The following day was Sunday. At seven in the evening, I once again observed the captain head for the restaurant across from the wharf, and, once again, I followed him in. "Just the man I wanted to see," he greeted me. "My doctor has gone missing, and we sail at daybreak. I wanted to ask you if you would fill in, even just temporarily should he not make it back. A pleasant voyage on a grand ship, your duty would be primarily seeing to the passengers. We have ten staterooms, sixteen guests currently."

"I'd like nothing better!" I exclaimed. "I'll grab my bag and report aboard this evening."

On the way back to Mrs. O'Toole's, I stopped in the tavern to meet with Davvy. He was in his usual corner spot, so I pulled up the stool next to him. "Good job on your end," I told him, placing the second gold piece in his hand. "Don't let him go until after the ship sails tomorrow."

Davvy gave me a quizzical look as if looking to see if I was fooling with him then just said thanks. I bought him a beer then left the establishment.

The O'Toole house was dark and quiet when I returned, although Mrs. O'Toole had left me a small lamp on the entry table. She was always thoughtful like that, and I told her so in the note I left her, letting her know I had obtained gainful employment and appreciated her hospitality. I packed my belongings and, with seabag over my shoulder and medical bag in my hand, walked back down to the *Karnak* while allowing myself to revert to the rolling gait of a sailor.

I could hear eight bells ringing midnight as I approached the ship, along with some quiet conversation and a laugh. Changing the watch, I mused. "Ahoy," I called. "Dr. Carlile come aboard."

Mr. Gibson met me at the sally port to welcome me. They had obviously seen my approach and reported it—they were expecting me. I took note that communication was good on this vessel. Gibson detailed a crewman to show me to my berth.

"Apologize, sir," he said. "We haven't had time to clear Dr. Buchanan's baggage yet." He was watching me intently although appearing not to. Evaluating the cut of my jib as sailors like to say.

"Tomorrow's soon enough," I replied, getting the impression from his demeanor that Dr. Buchanan had been a respected member of the crew, and I was a Yank. I would have to prove my worth apparently. I was feeling pretty pleased with myself that for thirty dollars, I had managed not only decent employment with the opportunity of starting fresh in a new locality but continued pursuit of a new love interest. This was dampened somewhat thinking over Davvy's response to my praise and the crewman's obvious respect for the man I was replacing. I found myself with a twinge of guilt, hoping that my thirty dollars wasn't the cost of a good man's life.

17

I slept fitfully that night, no doubt partially due to my conscience but also because the coal fire was stoked up at 3:00 a.m. to bring the boiler pressure up for our departure. The hiss of steam and the creak of metal expanding, as it became heated, were something I would become used to but wasn't as yet. I couldn't quite go back to sleep, so by a little after four in the morning, I was dressed and on deck, noticing the distinct difference between the black darkness of my cabin and the gray of the predawn. The full watch was on deck in preparation for our departure and as they didn't know me as yet, I think they took me for a passenger as such were surprised by my presence on deck at that hour and left me to my own devices. I pulled out my pipe, and the smoke served to wake me further.

The captain came up at five, and as the tide had already turned, all hands were called. We warped away from the pier, and the captain used a cone-shaped voice pipe to communicate instructions with the engine room. The whole ship throbbed in time with the engine rotations propelling the screw, and *Karnak* began backing away from her berth. As soon as we had sufficient distance into the river channel, the engines were reversed and given additional power. The helm was thrown over, *Karnak* pivoted as she slowed her sternward progress then began moving forward in a smooth maneuver. I could see that piloting a steamboat had its own seamanship requirements and was pleased with the practiced manner with which the vessel got underway. No sooner had we began forward progress when topsails were loosed and set, we gained speed smoothly and rapidly.

The motion of the ship coincided with the arrival of some of the passengers on deck, arriving in ones and twos from the cabin amidships. Eight men and one woman came out, moving directly to the starboard rail to watch as the city slipped by to stern, the remaining passengers apparently preferring to sleep through our departure. I was pleased to see that Priscilla Sutherland was the woman who was up and about, that she was not just another pretty face. She had her arm around her husband's waist and her head on his shoulder as they watched the panorama of the shoreline slip past. Already we were leaving the Elizabeth River, land disappearing behind to port as we stood in close to the sparsely-wooded tidal marshes of Sewell's Point, bypassing the shallows of Craney Island Flats. Ahead was the open waters of Hampton Roads.

"Dr. Carlile," came the voice of Captain Brownless at my elbow. "Good to see you up and about."

"Aye, sir, wouldn't have missed it," I replied with enthusiasm. "She's quite the proper lady and well-handled," I said, referring to the *Karnak* but with my eyes still on Priscilla Sutherland.

"We've got a fine crew, been together for a while," he stated with some pride. "They do right by me."

"Speaks well for the master, sir, when you see a taut ship," I said, finally turning to give him a smile.

At this point, the knot of passengers at the starboard rail began to disperse back to the cabin to escape the cool morning air; that was when Priscilla spotted me standing with the captain. I saw her do a double-take as if she was unsure. Then a smile started around her mouth, froze, then turned to a frown as she disappeared into the cabin with her husband. I decided caution was in order and determined to let matters take their own course. We were, after all, together in a small place and bound to have further contact.

We wore ship hard to starboard, steaming at speed into the Chesapeake. Once clear of all hazards between Fort Calhoun and Point Comfort, all hands were piped to breakfast. I made my way aft to the wardroom and was introduced around. *Karnak* had a good number of officers as befit her size and function. Mr. Holmes, the second mate, had already eaten and was leaving when we met as he had the watch coming on. I had, of course, already met Mr. Gibson and Cookson, the engineer. In addition, there was Woolrich, the purser, a jovial portly fellow with the lightest of red hair fringed around a gleaming bald dome. Finally there was Mr. Smith, the third officer, who was not quite friendly. He was obviously an old-hand sailor who had been around. Medium height, medium build, medium-brown hair that was just slightly shaggy, he was probably the most useful man aboard but didn't take well to me. Perhaps with a sailor's sixth sense, he felt that my replacing Dr. Buchanan so conveniently was not quite right. I determined to avoid him as it could be possible.

The wardroom had their own steward, Arthur. He was a pimply-faced teen who tried desperately to serve our meals with a sense of decorum as if he were a waiter serving royalty. The crew to a man called him Arthur Wellesly, after the old Duke of Wellington. It was pronounced as one word, *artherwelesly*, and by the time I came aboard, it had ceased to even be amusing; it just was. Food was normal shipboard fare, although the officers ate better as everyone chipped in on fresh fruit and vegetables for the pantry. Passengers had their own dining room and their own menu. Cook had his work cut out, making this all work, but had three stewards to assist him.

After breakfast, I determined to get my space in order. My cabin was large for shipboard, eight by ten feet, but doubled as the dispensary. It consisted of my bed under which was a sea chest, an examination table, cabinet for surgical tools and various remedies, and a porthole which allowed good light in addition to the skylight over the companionway corridor to which my door opened upon. In fine weather, the porthole could be opened to allow air as well. I obtained a sturdy box from the cook and carefully packed Dr. Buchanan's belongings then organized mine. Mr. Holmes sent a man to collect the box I packed, and it was stored somewhere in the hold. I was pleased to note that Buchanan had a stock of ambiguaton along with ginger to chew as I imagined that my primary duty would likely involve seasickness among the passengers. By then, we were clearing the mouth of the Chesapeake and beginning to encounter the choppy ocean waves, so I decided it was about time to check on potential patients. I was always amazed at the consistent speed of the

Karnak, and she was a much more stable vessel than the little *Mary Eleanore*. All in all, I felt I was in for a pleasant voyage.

We took the outside passage to avoid the push of the gulf stream and by June 11 sighted the Abacas in the distance to starboard. I'd been busy making daily rounds with the passengers; two of the women persisted in misery with seasickness, but the others enjoyed the reading, strolling the deck, and the dining offered by cook. We had glorious weather all the way down, sunshine and fresh breeze. I had the usual bumps and bruises with the crew, lanced a boil, and petroleum salve for a rope burn. The morning of the eleventh, one man was cut by a splinter when a large fish took his line. He had a nasty gash on his forearm from being pulled along the cathead where he was perched. My professional manner and practiced whipstitch, witnessed by his mates, did much to bond me with the crew. When the news got around about my competence, the men became reverently friendly, my patient proudly showing off my tight and even work. "The doc shoulda been a sailmaker," he told his cronies.

That afternoon, I received a visit from Priscilla Sutherland at my infirmary. She started by telling me she was having some stomach discomfort but then asked me bluntly why, if we were friends, I had not come by to say hello when I had seen all the other women aboard. "You've been the healthy one," I answered, "and I didn't want to disturb you on your vacation with your husband."

"He's way too busy with his investments and profit percentages to pay any attention to li'l ol' me," she said while pouting very prettily. "Now he's locked into cards with some of the other gentlemen."

I took her hands to assist her sitting up on my examination table, the touch and eye contact was electric. I tried to remain professional, listening to her heart and lungs with my stethoscope, then probing her abdomen with two fingers to see if I could locate an obstruction. "You seem fine," I told her. "You might consider altering your diet, make blander choices."

She looked right at me then and asked, "What are you really doing here? I've heard of you in Richmond, you have a successful practice. You didn't say anything about the *Karnak* when we first met, but now here you are! Are you chasing after me?"

"Captain Brownless is an old friend," I lied. "When his surgeon left the ship suddenly, he asked me if I would fill in temporarily."

She hesitated, then lowered her chin and, while looking through her eyelashes, whispered, "I was hoping you were chasing after me."

"I'd rather die than disappoint you, ma'am," I responded gallantly then kissed her. It was a soft, slow kiss, to start, but escalated into a hard passionate kiss. I scooped her up in my arms and carried her to the cot, kicking the door closed as I did so. She seemed to hesitate once more then put her arms around my neck and pulled me in for more.

Priscilla had wonderfully perfect breasts, if just slightly pendulous. She had faint purple lines on her lower belly that let me know that she was a mother. She made love with her head turned to the side, eyes closed. I started being gentle with her; but when she whispered, "Again!" I lost the remainder of my composure and was a bit rougher with her than I intended. She responded by wrapping herself around me tightly and digging her fingernails into my back.

When we were finished, she looked at me with a grin and said, "I always heard medical men were good."

"We do study anatomy," I replied with a big smile. "Hope I was able to treat your malaise effectively."

For the next two days, we had a regular afternoon tryst—perfect by me. I was feeling like a new man. We were due to arrive at New Providence on Nassau early afternoon of the fourteenth. I was surprised that morning by an angry Priscilla Sutherland. She said, "I had a conversation with Captain Brownless last night at supper. He said you only met just before we departed from Norfolk. Wonderful bit of luck is what he said."

"I agree," I said. "Wonderful bit of luck."

"You lied to me!" she yelled. "I don't want to see you or even hear about you ever again, do you hear me?" All I could do was shrug as she turned and stomped off.

Samuel and Priscilla Sutherland left the *Karnak* that afternoon. I just hope that in looking back on it, Priscilla has fond memories of our encounter just like I do. After all, she was hoping I was chasing her. The only downside was that nothing remains secret aboard ship, and my reputation took a hit when rumors began to circulate. It is all good when a sailor can make something happen with a woman, but they hold their officers to a higher standard.

The remainder of our trip, Havana then back to New York by July 2, was uneventful. I half-expected Dr. Buchanan to show up in New York; when he did not, I agreed to staying on for another voyage. Like the captain said, a pleasant voyage on a grand ship.

On July 24, we hit a significant gale, not a hurricane but the precursor to the upcoming season. Being a steamer and sizable, we were able to plow right through but I had my hands full with sick passengers. The next day, the twenty-fifth, we had an odd event. We were off the Abacas chain once again when we sighted a small schooner of about ninety feet to starboard, closer in to the islands. Although she looked to be American-built, she was flying the Spanish flag. When she sighted us, she changed course and ran for the coast, perhaps mistaking us for an English warship. She was a bit worse for wear from the previous day's weather, and shortly after beginning her run, we saw her strike the reef off of Lynyard Cay. We steamed in closer to investigate and identified her as the *Peter Mowell*, named after a man familiar to me from Baltimore. The ship was a total loss as she began to break up on the rocks. We observed literally hundreds of black men, women, and children pour out of her and begin swimming for the cay.

Importing slaves to the Americas was illegal, enforced primarily by the English and United States Navies, and that explained why they had tried to run. Although I had heard there had been a resurgence of this trade, especially by Portuguese traders as they needed a constant supply of manpower for the mines in Brazil, the Spanish were guilty as well for their sugar cane plantations in Cuba. I had heard also that some of these slaves continued to be smuggled illegally into the United States, certain of a premium price. Origin of the term *black market*, I guess.

I implored the captain to launch boats and render assistance, volunteering to go myself, but he declined, not wanting to put his own ship and men at risk. I did convince him to report the incident to the authorities in Nassau when we arrived so that the welfare of the people involved could be checked into and appropriate legal action could be taken against the owner of the schooner.

Most of the remainder of our voyage was marred by intermittent stormy weather. When we were almost back to New York in August, I had a new tryst; she was pushy, and I must admit that I couldn't say no. I was at a point in my life when I was lacking moral conviction and just allowed it to happen. This led to my having an altercation with Mr. Smith who was apparently tallying up my indiscretions. He called me a cad and a bounder at supper in the wardroom, and the other gentlemen present had to pull us apart to prevent a brawl. I went to the captain when we docked, thanking him for the opportunity he had provided but thinking it best that I moved on. He had heard of the bad blood between Smith and I and agreed with regret. I packed my belongings (and some of Buchanan's equipment) and found myself ashore in New York City.

18

New York in the summer of 1860 was a place of turmoil. It had been the center of trade in the United States since the Revolutionary War, and the business and merchant elite were facing a dilemma. Traditionally their wealth had been generated by bringing in the raw materials coming out of the continental interior and the southern states then reselling these to manufacturers both outside and inside the country. Cotton was a key piece of this picture, and many were worried that a Republican/Lincoln victory in the upcoming elections would result in disruption of this flow of money should rebellion erupt. The Democrats controlled the city government and echoed this sympathy for the southern situation in spite of any moral feelings to the contrary about slavery. The general population included a huge percentage of immigrants, principally German and Irish, who just wanted work and the chance for improvement.

By then, the city had expanded dramatically to include the Long Island municipalities of Brooklyn in Kings County along with Williamsburg and Green Point in Queens County. Across the Hudson River were Jersey City and Hoboken providing an unbroken urban metropolis. There was an abundance of poverty and not a lot of sanitation which made things filthy with an overwhelming odor, especially in the August heat.

I determined not to stay and purchased a ticket the next morning at Penn Station. Once clear of the city, I had a pleasant ride south through the New Jersey countryside before crossing the Delaware River and easing into Philadelphia and Jefferson Station. We had an hour wait, so I decided to stretch my legs, taking a quick look at

Independence Hall, a short distance to the south. Although my family was from Philadelphia, I had never been there. The remainder of the ride was longer through Delaware and upstate Maryland. I was thoroughly sick of the heat and hardwood bench seats when I arrived in Baltimore that afternoon. I collected my bags and walked up the hill to my Uncle Thomas's house. I was greeted with a big hug from my Auntie Eleanore. When I explained my intentions of getting back aboard ship with my Uncle Thomas, she frowned but told me they were due to return in about two weeks. I decided to spend some time with my daughter in the interim. She was now nine months old.

I found my father (and all of Baltimore for that matter) a seething political quagmire. The initial Democratic convention had been held in Charleston back in April, but all the delegates from the Deep South had split with the rest of the party, not wanting a moderate like Stephen Douglas who was iffy on the slavery issue on the ballot. The result was no result, so a second convention had been held in Baltimore in June. The Deep South delegates held their own second convention in Baltimore as well, each nominating different candidates and each announcing themselves to be the true Democratic Party. The main body nominated Steven Douglas and Ben Fitzpatrick, although in an unprecedented act, Fitzpatrick refused the nomination for vice president. The southerners nominated John C. Breckenridge and Joe Lane from Oregon on a strictly proslavery platform. In addition to all this, the Know Nothings, with their traditional power base in Maryland, met in convention in Baltimore also and formed a new party—the Constitutional Unionists—in an attempt to incorporate the remnants of the Whigs into their numbers. Thus Baltimore found itself in the national political spotlight. Many felt the rift in the Democrats would ensure a Republican victory for William Seward, the front-runner. Therefore, it was a shock to everyone when Abraham Lincoln, who had the support of abolitionist factions, ended up winning the Republican nomination. Loose talk was everywhere about secession should Lincoln win the election.

My father griped endlessly that this divisiveness had wrecked Douglas's chance for the presidential run and predicted that

Baltimore, as a city, would be in ruins if the country split. Much of the wealth of the city was based on the import of raw materials from the southern states and the export to them of manufactured goods. He stated that New Orleans would become the principle exporter of cotton, especially since the majority production of this commodity was moving westward into Alabama, Mississippi, and Texas.

I spent much of my time visiting with my daughter, Nelly, as everyone called her. She was pretty and sweet, although I could already see the beginnings of a headstrong nature. She had a tendency toward tantrums if she didn't get what she wanted; I was suspecting Maddie and my stepmother of spoiling her.

I also managed to have a civil conversation with my father regarding investment strategies for my savings. I expected him to guide me in the purchase of property or real estate, but he was a smart old merchant and had me invest in stock in DuPont, a Delaware chemical company that manufactured most of the gunpowder made in the United States. After the panic of '57, companies had difficulty attracting new investors, so it was easy for me to purchase the securities. Although the economy had stabilized significantly, the memories of bank failures were fresh in everyone's minds, especially when it was publicized later that these were mostly due to "irregularities" committed by bank officers.

My father had always had little trust in banks and had only kept enough in accounts to manage his business affairs. He certainly had a thorough understanding regarding the outcome of honorable ideals, and the location of the majority of his wealth was kept a huge secret. I could easily see how my father became a wealthy man when he started out as a poor journeyman shoemaker making eight dollars a week. I then turned around and incurred his wrath briefly by hiring a lawyer and setting up a trust whereby the dividends from my new investment would go to my father for the ongoing care of Nelly. I trusted his old Quaker meticulously-honest accounting and knew that, at the very least, Nelly's education was going to cost him if I didn't make the proper arrangements.

When the *Mary Eleanore* put in to port on the twelfth of September, I went right aboard and asked Uncle Thomas to sign me on. We argued which was like having a debate with an angry bull. His point was that I could best serve myself and everyone else employed in the medical profession, not hiding out aboard a little merchant ship.

I said, "You too, sir." He just glared at me after that. I added, "Besides who is going to run this old scow when you're gone?"

"That's not for a long time yet," he replied then sighed. "Okay, I do need a competent second officer, report aboard before supper."

So it was, I resumed my nautical career. I found the captain to be especially hard on me, a level of supervision he had not employed previously. He also involved me more in the shipping business, checking inventories, payments, and evaluating what cargoes to purchase and which brokers to move products for. I had a lot more contact with the businessmen in our ports of call as a result. Clearly he was not only introducing me to the business end of the operation but also introducing his business partners to me as well.

Leaving Baltimore at the autumnal equinox, we carried mostly tobacco and shoes—the shoes to be offloaded in Charleston, South Carolina, the tobacco to move on the next leg to London, England, along with lumber and/or cotton, whichever we could negotiate the best price or be paid best to transport on consignment. We avoided going too far south, as always, this time of year to avoid the storm season.

We sailed up the Thames River in fog and drizzle which was exacerbated by the pall of coal smoke hanging over the city. After the fresh breeze of the open ocean, it was initially difficult to breathe the air. We unloaded, ensured the anchor watch was set, then the captain and I hired a hack to take us into town. We crossed a bridge into the south end, arrived at a building marked London Armoury Company, and Thomas asked to see a man, James Kerr. Mr. Kerr was apparently unavailable, so Uncle Thomas left a cashier's check and obtained a receipt, $500 drawn on the Bank of Maryland which I knew to be the financial institution favored by my father. We had greasy sausages and chips at a local eatery then returned to the ship as a wagon pulled up with five oblong boxes which the captain had stored immediately in our hidden compartment on the orlop deck.

Baltimore was awash with news on our return at Christmas. Lincoln had won the presidential election, although he had received less than 40 percent of the popular vote. South Carolina and Tennessee had assembled conventions to discuss secession, and Georgia had called for delegates from all the southern states for a debate on the subject. Several southern senators and representatives had resigned from congress. Many Marylanders were calling for similar measures, Baltimore in particular was a hotbed of southern sympathies. To add insult to injury, everyone was up in arms over Buchanan's Secretary of War, John Floyd, who was forced to resign over the disappearance of Bureau of Indian Affairs bonds and had compounded his treachery by ordering the transfer of quantities of cannon and ordinance from the Pittsburgh armory to locations in the South following the election results.

Uncle Thomas tried for a fast turnaround to get a cargo to Charleston before anything further developed, but we had to abruptly change plans when news came that South Carolina had voted to secede, federal troops had fallen back into Fort Sumter in the harbor and were likely to impede merchant traffic in and out of the port. We determined to head for Savannah, Georgia, instead, departing Baltimore on January 14, during a thaw in what otherwise had been a cold and snowy winter. When we arrived, we were surprised to see uniformed troops swarming over Fort Pulaski, Fort Jackson, further upriver and several new defensive structures being built along the river between the two. The state of Georgia flag had replaced the US banner flying above these installations. Following an uneventful voyage across the Atlantic and back, we had a new destination for our illegitimate cargo; this was delivered in Virginia to uniformed soldiers instead of the normal crew we were used to. They had the password, so we figured the drop to be correct.

When we returned to Baltimore in May, I found much had changed. Lincoln had passed through town on the way to his inauguration in February, changing his time and route to deter detection and any unpleasant confrontations he was advised by his Pinkerton security men to expect and avoid. Mrs. Lincoln had followed the route on his itinerary and had been accosted by ruffians. Following the April shelling of Fort Sumter in South Carolina, Massachusetts state troops marching through town on their way from the train station to Washington were attacked by citizens and in turn, fired on the crowd. In the ensuing fight, four soldiers and twelve civilians were killed.

The Maryland legislature voted not to secede but also issued a proclamation to the federal government not to allow troops to pass through Maryland on their way to attack the southern states. When this was denied, Governor Hicks took matters into his own hands and ordered railroad bridges between Baltimore and Washington to be destroyed by the Maryland state militia. Lieutenant Merryman of that force was captured by the federal troops, accused of treason and imprisoned at Fort McHenry without trial even though he was in uniform and following the governor's orders. A writ of habeas corpus was issued by the United States Supreme Court to secure him due process, but this was ignored by Lincoln and the military authorities. Yankee troops under General Ben Butler moved into Baltimore, taking over the park on Federal Hill and turning it into a fort overlooking the city. Their intent was obvious; they placed fifty cannon pointing toward the center of the city, instead of outward, to defend it from an invading army. In all, over forty forts and other troop encampments would be built in Baltimore during the war, along with about twenty hospitals or POW camps. Lincoln just went ahead and suspended civil rights in the city and had many governmental facets run by the military authorities.

My father's friend George Kane, the police commissioner, was accused of organizing the April riot and being in league with an assassination plot and was arrested. Soldiers came in the middle of the night and took him to Fort McHenry. Once again, he was held without trial and was transferred to a prison in New York to further impede any possible legal action to get him tried or released. The sad thing was that Kane and his men separated the crowd from the soldiers during the April riot at real risk of harm to themselves in order to prevent further loss of life. My cousin Bill Carlile, was an officer at the time, was there and told me it was truly a scary event. My father was also detained but was released when he just rambled on about everyone's firm loyalty to the government, telling them nothing about himself. He was especially questioned in depth about George Kane's activities; I think he told them they were barely acquainted. I did hear my father remark that being a Democrat was not good for your health in those days.

In June, I happened to meet my old friend Stephen Gardiner and was shocked and appalled to see the change that had happened with him. The smart, glib lawyer that he had been was replaced with a brain-damaged version. He was thin, dirty, and ragged with unkempt hair and a growth of matted beard, making a living begging or doing odd jobs. He could barely string words together to make a sentence. I was told that he had joined a group of worthies in Washington that had decided to protest Lincoln's presidency by walking up to him on the street and shaking his hand vigorously, trying to inflict a bit of pain. Ward Lamon, my old nemesis, was Lincoln's bodyguard and punched Stephen in the head, dropping him to the ground and causing the malady. Apparently Lincoln admonished Ward, saying, "Give the poor fellow a chance, next time hit him with an ax handle instead of using your fist!"

I was not amused and vowed revenge for the fate of my friend. It seems his stepfather would not provide him with any help, saying he got what he deserved. I took him to a tavern for a meal and a beer; when I left him, I gave him two silver dollars. Not much, but it was all I could afford at the time. I hoped it would tide him through until the next handout.

Many of the young men in the city began leaving for Virginia to join units in the new Confederate Army. Virginia was one of the last states to secede and join the Confederacy but once done, Richmond was made into the capitol of the new Confederate Republic. There was even loose talk around of a rallying point being designated for Marylanders to form their own regiments. All-out war was looming on the horizon, and I began to wonder if I should join up to get in on the action before it was over. Uncle Thomas was the smart one; he told me Lincoln would never allow the southern states to remain out of the union, that it would be a long and ugly fight. He told me that like America in the Revolutionary War, the South didn't possess the manpower or resources for success unless they could convince a foreign power like England or France to intervene on their behalf. I was not totally convinced but decided to bide my time.

I noted some strangers hanging out around the harbor area, men that I had not seen before buying drinks for sailors and engaging them in conversation. One in particular, a short skinny fellow with a beard and mustache, seemed out of place around the docks, an area worked mostly by burly thugs for longshoremen and sailors with their brown skin and easy rolling gait. He appeared to have an inordinate interest in the *Mary Eleanore.* I asked Uncle Thomas to be careful, that I suspected the ship was being watched, but he just chuckled at me with that twinkle in his eye and told me I worried too much. I explained my concerns to Maller, the bos'n, and hatched a plan where I walked right up to confront him and Maller came up from behind.

"Yo there, sir," I said to his face. "What's your business with my ship?"

The man eyed me while licking his lip nervously but puffed himself up and stated, "My business is none of yours!"

He turned to walk away and ran smack into Maller. Maller grabbed him with one massive hand by the front of his shirt, picked him clear off the ground, and placed him on the wall behind with a thud, hanging in his shirt by the armpits. Now Maller is a scary stump of a man who makes his living keeping real men under control. He has a thick German accent and biceps the size of my thighs.

While I pulled out my knife and began cleaning my fingernails, Maller told him, "Ven I kill you, der vil be no inquiry 'cause novon vill ever find you."

I almost felt sorry for the guy when I saw the wet stain start to spread in his groin area. Maller laughed an evil chuckle and tossed the man into the street. We linked arms and began to stroll down the wharf, singing a ditty, "Oh blow ye winds high-ho over the ocean, oh blow ye winds over the man on the moon." I can always admire a man who enjoys his work.

Our next voyage out proved to be my final journey aboard the *Mary Eleanore,* although I didn't know it at the time. We made for Nassau, as the southern ports were now all blockaded, then for England. Our contraband cargo for this trip were Robert Adams revolvers, but the agent we roughed up must have had no sense of humor because we had no sooner rounded Fisherman's Island inbound into the Chesapeake when we were accosted by the steam sloop USS *Seminole*, ordering us to heave to. We were boarded by a young naval lieutenant, accompanied by a burly bos'n's mate and five marines. After a cursory search of our papers and cargo revealed no anomalies, we were nonetheless ordered to proceed to Baltimore, with the prize crew aboard, over the strenuous objection of the captain. On our arrival, the crew were herded into an empty warehouse at gunpoint where we were interrogated and released, but the captain was whisked away under guard. The *Mary Eleanore* was tied up at the customs dock where some gentlemen in black suits boarded her and went below. For my part, I attempted to come across as stupid and ignorant, they didn't seem to get it that my last name was the same as the owner. As we departed the warehouse, I invited Maller to have a beer. We chose a dark corner of a favorite watering hole and decided we needed to take action to save Uncle Thomas and the *Mary Eleanore* from the hands of the federal authorities.

19

They were holding the *Mary Eleanore* under guard at the customs quay off Block Street with plans to search her in the morning, the cargo and ship's stores having already been unloaded and examined on the pier. That night, I slipped quietly below the Yankee fortifications on Federal Hill, their intentions made obvious with the majority of their cannon facing down toward the center of the city. I met Maller at the Montgomery Street Dock across the basin from the customs pier at 10:00 p.m. like we had previously arranged. Maller had obtained a small skiff from friends and was waiting for me when I arrived there. The night was perfect for our scheme, mostly overcast and just a crescent moon so the harbor was shrouded in darkness. The only real illumination came from the taverns and inns behind the ships across the water, although I could discern a single bright light coming from Fort McHenry out on Locust Point to the east and the intermittent swing of the lighthouse beacon on Seven Foot Knoll in the Patapsco River channel beyond the fort. There was little movement to the air, which hung stagnant, and I could just hear the lap of the waves against the pilings as I descended the ramp and climbed down into the small boat. There was a strong smell of fish mixed with urine and refuse in and around the lower dock.

There was very little chop to the water as we rowed across, Maller had wrapped cloth of some sort around the oars to muffle any splash. We aimed purposely for the stern of a side-wheel steamer docked two vessels away from the *Mary Eleanore* where we could appraise the situation, tying up to the rudder chain to keep from drifting. There were two Yankee guards clearly visible with the light of the buildings behind them, lounging by the gangway, seeming intent on their own conversation. Their rifles had bayonets fixed but were stacked against some barrels next to them on the pier. There appeared to be no one on the ship itself. Luckily the *Mary Eleanore* was tied off to the wharf on her starboard side as her smuggler's compartment was on the left. Still I figured that left only about thirty-five feet between the guards on the dock and the false wall I would need to disassemble to remove the crates inside. Even though the wall was designed to be removable, making some noise would be unavoidable. As I watched, one of the guards pulled a pipe and some makings from his pocket and began to fill the bowl generously. He paused briefly to laugh at something the other soldier said before lighting it with a match, the flare seeming to cut through the darkness of the night.

I removed my shirt and shoes, and, as I was preparing to go into the water, Maller pulled a bottle out from a sack at his feet. He whispered, "For varmth an' courage," as he uncorked it and held it out to me.

I took it, took a long swig, then passed it back. He wiped the lip of the bottle on his sleeve then took a pull on it himself. I grinned at him then said quietly, "Don't wait up for me, hon, I might be late!" Then I soundlessly rolled my body over the gunwale of the skiff and into the cold water of the basin.

I have always been a strong swimmer, and my body soon warmed to the chill of the water. I stroked the hundred yards to the *Mary Eleanore* with just my head above, leaving barely a ripple to denote my passing. When I reached the ship, I grabbed onto the main chains amidships, pausing to listen intently to see if I had been discovered. The soldiers were busy complaining about their sergeant who was, according to them, apparently both a thug and a bully. As they went on about the stench emanating from the new hospital being built adjacent to their barracks, I hoisted myself up out of the water behind the ratline deadeyes and swung my feet over the railing, noting, even in the darkness, that the main hatch covers had been left open after the cargo had been unloaded. I crab walked on my hands and feet over to the opening then crept silently down the ladder to the orlop deck.

It was pitch-black below decks, but the ship had been my home for a long time so I was able to make my way by feel. Our smuggler's hole was ingeniously made, two internal clasps held the false wall on one side to the aft bulkhead while the forward side was fastened to a stave with a spring-loaded bolt. A knot hole barely larger than the width my finger provided access to the mechanism used to slide open the bolt. The whole panel fit almost seamlessly into the side of the ship, leaving a compartment behind the false wall four feet long by just under two feet deep along the entire height of the deck or about four and three quarter feet. It was a spot just above the waterline and under the scuppers so remained remarkably dry except in the worst of weather.

I located the knothole by feel, pushed back the bolt, and slid the entire panel toward me, being careful to let the bolt slide back slowly and noiselessly. I unclipped the latches on the inside of the wall and quietly set the entire panel off to one side. Then lying on my back, I used my knife to carefully unscrew and remove the latch hardware from the aft bulkhead so there would be no further trace that the compartment had ever existed. I put the hardware pieces in my pocket, leaned the panel against the ladder, and began moving the four cases inside to the base of the ladder, putting them on my body so there would be no noise of them scraping along the deck. The cases were not too heavy, each containing ten revolvers that were, in turn, boxed with bullet mold and reloading equipment. It required a clean and jerk motion to heft them to my shoulder and place them on the upper deck. I then crept back up the ladder myself to the main deck, using my elbows to slither out of the hold.

The Yankee soldiers were still lounging against the barrels on the dock. I could now hear the rattle of dice in a box and the complaining sounds from one man accompanied by the triumphant chuckle from the other. I repeated the process of moving the crates on my belly to the railing, then lowering them gently into the water so they did not splash when I released them to sink slowly into the bay, leaving a trail of bubbles as they disappeared out of sight. This objective accomplished, I crawled back over to the hatch and paused to reassess the situation. The soldiers still seemed intent on their dice game, so I lay flat on my stomach, and, leaning down into the hatch-way, I gripped the panel on both sides, pulling it up hand over hand. When I had it over halfway out, I rolled over on my back to allow the panel to clear and come down on top of my body. It was heavy and ungainly in shape; just when I thought I was good, one corner struck down on the deck with a thump.

There was a pregnant silence for about two seconds, then I heard the larger soldier say, "You hear that?"

I saw both their heads silhouetted above the starboard rail as they stood to look. At that point, I balanced the panel on my left hand and used my right shoulder and arm to give the panel a mighty heave, it clattered on the larboard railing loudly before I heard it splash into the water below.

By now, the soldiers had their rifles up and were yelling, "Who goes there!" loudly and repeatedly. I could hear by their voices that they were spooked, so I lay very still, remaining flat on the deck. I heard the big one say, "Go check it out."

The other soldier laughed nervously and said flatly, "You go check it out."

I could see through the opening in the starboard railing that they had moved together to the gangplank, weapons at hip-level and pointing up but in my general direction. I fished one of the metal latches out of my pocket and threw it sidearm toward the bow. It was a great toss, considering I was laying flat on my back, it carried all the way forward where it smacked against the foremast, caromed off, and splashed further on into the water. This caused the guards to begin cursing and yelling again, but the gun barrels swiveled away from me toward the front of the ship. I took full advantage of the distraction and sprang to my feet. I hit the ship's railing in stride, diving into the water below. One of the soldiers had good reflexes, I heard the pop of his rifle firing while I was midair and the corresponding thwack of the ball striking wood close by before I hit the water.

I don't know how close I came to being shot, but I definitely stayed under water until I felt my lungs were bursting, rolling to my back before coming up so that just my mouth and nose broke the surface. I gulped in air then submerged and continued to put distance between myself and the *Mary Eleanore*. I was a couple of hundred yards away and had veered west into the harbor before I stopped to have a look. The alarm had been sounded and a dozen or more men were now aboard the *Mary Eleanore*, along with several lanterns that were bobbing about. I could hear authoritative voices giving orders from across the water.

I continued to swim for perhaps fifteen minutes more when I heard the splash of oars and Maller calling, "Psst, over here!

I swam to the skiff, and he pulled me in over the gunwale. I was always amazed at the strength of the man, he hefted me out of the water effortlessly. I began to shiver almost immediately even as I was pulling on my shirt. Maller pulled his bottle out of the bag at his feet and passed it over.

"You ver zapposed to be sneaky," he said with an impish smile.

"Can't have 'em thinking they're in charge," I said, looking back over my shoulder at the turmoil still going aboard the ship.

We had an uneventful row to the inner harbor. Maller dropped me at the Pratt Street bridge over Jones Falls before returning the skiff to its owner. The sky was just beginning to get light in the east by the time I had trekked up the hill to Baltimore Street. I turned in and slept until midmorning.

In spite of our efforts and there being no evidence against my Uncle Thomas, it was three months before he was finally released, and then only after the mayor raised a fuss due to repeated pressure from my father and his friends. Attempts filing a writ of habeas corpus were simply ignored by the military authorities who wouldn't even admit that they had him in custody. When he came home, his eyes were hollow and his cheeks sunken in. His clothes hung loose; he had lost about thirty pounds. My uncle would never talk about his treatment in prison, but he had an obvious abiding hatred for the federal authorities ever after. They kept the impound on the *Mary Eleanore* through September, after which we had to take on a completely new crew. Our cargo was gone by then, without a trace, nobody in the military or customs authority were even willing to consider compensating us for our property. Not all the new men could be trusted, so it was decided by the family to discontinue extracurricular activities at least for the time being.

I decided at that point to take a more active role in the conflict. So in October of '61, I set off across the Potomac for Richmond to see if I could swing an appointment with Stephen Mallory, the Confederate secretary of the navy.

I made it to Richmond on the evening of the fourth of October, having had to avoid noisy patrols of soldiers on both sides of the Potomac River. I found the city to be much busier than before. Richmond had not only become the capitol of the new nation just four months previously, but command and logistics for the Confederate Army just to the north occupied portions of the city. I finally found lodgings at an inn on the south side of the James River in Manchester after searching for a couple of hours and was appalled at having to pay about four times the prewar rate for what was clearly a dive establishment. The Richmond and Danville tracks, just a block away, added that little touch of ambiance that made the place special. Still beggars can't be choosers and having arrived on a Friday, I was obliged to sit through the weekend before getting any kind of appointment. I recall being frustrated; I clearly remember having an exaggerated sense of self-importance, being both a seagoing officer and doctor offering my services.

On Saturday, I visited some of my previous haunts, looking for old acquaintances and contacts, but the city was full of strangers. The streets were filled with soldiers on leave, mostly recovering wounded and sick, along with many young gentlemen like me in pursuit of prominent position or commission. I began to suspect correctly that I was not the guy the Confederacy couldn't do without.

I was therefore surprised when I presented myself on Monday morning at the naval department offices and was ushered straight in to see Stephen Mallory. Mallory was a short round baby-faced individual with a fringe of curly beard surrounding his face, but his manner belied his appearance. I guess I should have figured as much, after all, he was an ex-senator from Florida and had chaired the committee on naval affairs. He skipped all formalities and got straight to business.

"I'm told you're familiar with James Bulloch," he remarked. "Do you have his trust?"

"As far as I know," I answered. "We used to do business together, or at least, he and my family. But we have had several conversations."

"You are familiar with English ports?" he queried.

"And French," I answered.

He pushed back in his chair and eyeballed me. "I may have need for your services in the near future, but for now, I'm going to refer you over to Spotswood at OMS," he said, referring to Dr. William Spotswood, formerly of the US Navy but now running the office of medicine and surgery for the Confederate Navy. The man was a true Virginia aristocrat, related to George Washington, and descendant of old colonial Governor Spotswood.

He rapidly scribbled a note on a sheet of paper, folded and sealed it, then handed it across the desk.

"Thank you, sir," I chirped enthusiastically.

"Careful what you wish for," he cautioned as he came around the desk and ushered me out of the office.

I found OMS on Bank Street, down the hill, in an old brick building previously used to house state records. William Spotswood greeted me cordially but cautiously when I finally made it past the flurry of clerks and tradesmen vying for his attention. He was thin and grey, about midfifties and his unkempt beard did not speak to the navy man that he was. When I presented my letter of introduction from Mallory, he became more friendly and ushered me into an office that contained an old wood desk piled with papers, along with crates with still more papers piled in various stacks around the room. He removed two of the crates from a straight-backed chair which he then pulled up to the desk, motioning me to sit.

"What might I do for you, young sir?" he asked. "You appear to come to me highly recommended."

I explained my background as a ship's officer and my later practice as a doctor in Richmond. I then told him of my position aboard the *Karnak*. "I've come to offer my sword and my stethoscope to the cause."

"Two things in your way, son," he said. "First, surgery on battle casualties is fast and messy with shells exploding about for distraction. Not like treating seasick ladies." I tried at this point to sputter that I had seen my share of things, but he waved me silent then continued with, "Second, the congress, in their wisdom, have only authorized five surgeons and five assistant surgeons for the entire navy. These positions have long been taken, so I don't have a commission available to offer you."

My facial expression must have given away the feeling I had in my stomach at that point, and he took pity on me. "I am, however, badly in need of an assistant as you can see," he said with a wave around the room at the piles of documents. "Mallory does want you kept close in any case, and we don't want you running off to join the army," he said with a curious grin. "I could offer you $100 per month, and I could use your obvious abilities collecting and organizing supplies. If I know Mallory, he'll have something a little more active for you sooner rather than later."

I nodded my assent, but my mind was thinking that I didn't quite know what I was getting myself into, between the professor-like man in front of me running the department and the chaos of paper records all around.

"Settled then," he said. "I'm tasked by the Confederate Congress to accomplish four objectives. First is the establishment and operation of a naval hospital, second is the production and acquisition of medicines, third is obtaining or the fabrication of medical and surgical equipment and supplies. Last is the direction and assignment of naval medical personnel."

"Numbers two and three are where you come in, my boy. We will need kits set up to provide the necessary supplies to stock infirmaries aboard ships being commissioned by our navy, along with infirmary wards in the hospital we shall build."

"I've developed some plans based on my experience with the US Navy," he said, "but I expect that you will let me know if you think of anything different." Spotswood then also then scribbled a note on a piece of paper, folded and sealed it. "Report tomorrow morning to our warehouse at Twenty-Fifth and Franklin, know where that is?"

"Aye, sir," I replied. "East of the bridge."

"Give this to Mr. Bollingham, I suspect you'll get along. And oh," he added, "bring your gear, plenty of room for you to stay there, and lodging is at a premium in the city now."

The morning was gone when I left the office and my mind was full of thoughts as I crossed the bridge back over to Manchester, so I was taken unaware when my path was suddenly blocked by two youths of about fifteen years.

"Wait there, mister," said the larger youth, a beefy red-faced kid with dark-blond hair. I noted other bodies beginning to fill in behind me and realized I had walked right into their little trap. "I believe you owe us a toll, sir," said the large youth with a smile while pulling a nasty homemade looking knife from behind his waistband.

"Let's check my wallet," I said, twisting around a bit as I reached into my coat to have a look at the pack behind me. As I surmised, the four boys behind were younger and smaller. Instead of a wallet, I pulled out my Colt revolver from the hidden holster and in one smooth motion, pointed it right at the large boy's face, cocked the hammer back, and strode straight toward him. His eyes opened real wide, and he began to backpedal rapidly to escape me. It took just a few steps before he tripped on the uneven pavement and fell hard on his backside, his knife skittering into the gutter. I maintained the muzzle of my pistol about three inches from his nose so he could see the black hole at the end of my barrel clearly. The rest of the kids scattered and disappeared, the only smile now was the one on my face.

"Now let's have *your* money," I said.

"I don't ha—" he started, but I cut him off with a bellow.

"I'm not playing a game with you!"

He reached slowly into his pocket.

"Your next move better be a careful one," I hissed at him.

He slowly pulled out a small wad of bills, maybe ten dollars total. He gave me a hateful look when I snatched it from his hand, but I just uncocked my revolver and said, "You've only yourself to blame, the folly of youth is underestimating your opponent."

I knew I didn't get all his money, but the point was made. When I stepped around him, I stomped hard on his knife, right where the hilt met the blade. Pretty sure I bent it for him.

I spent my ill-gotten gains that night on a bottle and a girl. She was sweet and smelled pretty, so I let her do all the work 'cause I was feeling lazy. She drank most of the bottle anyway.

21

The warehouse on Franklin Street was a decent brick structure, although it still smelled pungently of the tobacco which previously had been stored there for export. Mr. Bollingham was an older ex-navy petty officer who still had the bulging forearms and big hands typical of his trade. He told me he had been a steward for Dr. Spotswood before the war. In any case, he was used to providing organization by any means necessary which is what I needed. He ran roughshod over the laborers who moved supplies both upstairs and down. Spotswood was right, we got along famously. Bollingham had taken over the entire second floor and had created a receiving area/ office in the center between where the staircase emerged from below and where a freight lift, rigged to a block and tackle, came up from the loading dock off the alley behind the building. He had cunningly constructed bulkheads from crates and old boards to create both enough width of passage to accommodate large objects yet everything going in or out had to go by the office counter to be checked. My only concern with the setup was that the naval ordinance was being accumulated and stored on the floor below; in the event of an errant spark, we might all be blown to smithereens.

I set myself up a space in the northeast corner where I had direct access to the fire escape as a personal backdoor. I had a window on both walls and so had good light. I kept my work space open to the warehouse area and only screened off a small section for a cot and my sea chest. Bollingham had somehow acquired a desk for me, a scarce commodity in a rapidly-expanding Richmond. That, a small table, and four chairs that had been a dining set completed the space, and I had an ideal setup for meetings or interviews.

The majority of my job then became combing the city and surrounding area locating providers who could manufacture complicated utensils to fill trepanning kits, amputation sets, postmortem sets, and stomach pump kits to name a few. This meant conveying a broad range of specifications on scalpels and specialty knives to the producers. Other items included ferrules, forceps, bone saws, trephines of various sizes, syringes, pumps, irrigators, and fleams. I even took a meeting with a telescope maker to see if an inexpensive ophthalmoscope could be manufactured for our efforts. In 1861, the new Confederacy was in a solid position, the federal blockade was not yet efficient and Confederate dollars bought almost 90 percent of the going rate for greenbacks. Specie could get huge discounts in an uncertain world, but in any case, my meager budget did not significantly impair my ability to do the job.

I enlisted the help of my old friend Andy Gibson, the apothecary, to act as a middleman for medications and supplies. He got a bit of profit from this lucrative government contract, and I soon began to amass quantities of quinine, laudanum, chloroform, ether, opium, iron, and tinctures like veratrum viride to induce vomiting and blue mass, a compound made from mercury and chalk which was a common cure all in those days. I invaded the lady's patriotic associations to obtain bandage rolls from old clothes and medical lint for packing wounds which they produced by scraping their blankets. My greatest success of all came from Sydney Nye, a family connection from the old days. He ran a still in the southeastern part of the state, and I bought for cheap all the brandy he could make. I shipped this by rail in cases marked "military supplies" through Petersburg and into the capitol. We stockpiled so much that I began relabeling and reselling the stuff to the local watering holes for a nice profit. I then used the cash source to pad my budget and, sorry to say, my income. We had enough surplus alcohol that sometimes at the end of a long day, Bollingham and I would "take a meeting" long into the evening, ensuring that the quality of the product was up to government specifications. With my previous experience in the family business, I made quite sure the books balanced.

The balmy fall weather continued through November and December; spirits were high in the city. The war had become a stalemate other than some skirmishing in the western portion of the state and over the mountains in Kentucky. Our victory at Bull Run had apparently taken the vigor out of the Union side, although, of course, there were rumors of them training a massive army in Washington. President Jeff Davis had left most foreign policy alone. Everyone figured the allure of cheap cotton to drive the British and French textile industries would naturally lead to their support and recognition; indeed the English declaration of neutrality was all but a tacit recognition that the Confederacy existed as a nation, and this was soon followed by similar declarations from France, Spain, the Netherlands, and Brazil. This meant that our ships were as welcome in foreign ports as any other.

Then in November came an event that we all thought would seal our chance for English recognition. Two Confederate diplomats, Slidell and Mason, were traveling aboard the British mail packet RMS *Trent* when she was fired on and boarded by the USS *San Jacinto*. Our men were abducted and imprisoned in Boston. Now I had met Charles Wilkes, captain of the *San Jacinto*, during my days of partying in Washington; and although he was being hailed as a hero in the north, I knew him as a man with a superabundance of ego and a little less quantities of judgment. While unsuccessfully trying to catch the CSS *Sumter* in the Bahamas, Wilkes had heard that the Confederate diplomats were leaving Havana aboard *Trent* and determined to make some headlines for himself, knowing the British ship would have to take the narrow Bahama Channel to make St. Thomas on a direct route.

Wilkes made a mistake though. If Slidell and Mason were contraband as he claimed, he should have taken the *Trent* as a prize to be adjudicated by a court. By removing the men against their will, he was in violation of international law and committing the same offense that had caused the United States to go to war with England in 1812. In effect, he was a hypocrite. In any case, England declared the incident illegal and unjustified and demanded reparations for the international insult, requiring the release of the men and an apology. France weighed in, agreeing to support British demands. England even began to send troops to Canada and start work upgrading the defensive works in their Caribbean colonies. We were all disappointed then when Lincoln backed down, apologized, and released the prisoners.

When January came, the weather turned brutally cold and it snowed. Bollingham and I suspended work for a couple of weeks and spent most of our waking hours in front of the woodstove on the first floor of the warehouse encased in coats, scarves, and extra blankets. I believe we exceeded our previous alcohol consumption during those weeks. By the end of the month, the weather broke, then my first mission was to scrub the campfire smell from my clothing and get a good bath in. Feeling I had returned to humanity, I decided to attend a function in the ballroom of the American Hotel, but it was a disappointing evening. All the belles doted on the young men in uniform while I chafed in my status as a mere civil servant.

When February arrived, the war began to ramp up again. The action initiated in the West, to everyone's disappointment, there were a series of reverses along the Tennessee River. Then some action closer to home when Union forces probed south to Bull Run, but Joe Johnston had already withdrawn behind the Rappahannock River to prevent any possible flanking movement by the Union forces.

At the beginning of March, an even more exciting event took place. When Virginia succeeded, state troops had taken over the Gosport Naval Yard in Norfolk. The Union commander destroyed the ships under repair, but the dry dock was unharmed. About one thousand naval cannon, gun carriages, gunpowder, and shot were captured. The USS *Merrimac* was burned but was raised with her hull, engines, and boilers intact. She had been converted into an ironclad warship, the CSS *Virginia*. On March 8, she steamed out, accompanied by the James River squadron, promptly destroying the USS *Cumberland* and USS *Congress* and drove aground three other US frigates, *Minnesota, Roanoke,* and *St. Lawrence.* The next day, the Union brought up their own ironclad, the USS *Monitor* and they fought to a standstill. Although this action didn't raise the blockade of the James River, it was an incredible victory for our navy.

On my end, two things happened as a result of this battle. First we finally had naval casualties, so arrangements for their care had to be made. The army had begun to develop a hospital on Chimborazo Hill. Dr. Spotswood decided that our first effort would be a ward to the side of that facility. I made several trips up the hill, ensuring our ward was properly set up and equipped. I was rather impressed at the setup going into place on the hill, wide avenues between the wards, facilities for feeding and clothing the men, along with workshops producing the equipment. The whole hospital was cleaner and airier than any other of its kind I'd seen previously. Our ward began to treat not only the wounded but also the sick from the James River squadron. When I was done there, Spotswood had me set up a smaller clinic at Gosport in Norfolk. These tasks at least kept me busy, and I believe I impressed with the speed and organization delivering these outcomes. I gave liberal credit to Bollingham for our successes.

Secondly I was called up the hill to report to Mallory at the navy department. When I arrived, I was immediately sworn in by his aide and commissioned as an assistant surgeon, CSN. I was given written notice to stand by as an aide to the secretary while awaiting further orders. I went right out and had a sharp new uniform tailored; the gray coat had thin black shoulder straps, collar, and black cuffs with three brass anchor buttons each. Nine double rows of buttons down the front made for a suitable dress coat, and I had the whole lined in black silk. I crunched the kepi down in front, as was the style, so that the laurel wreath emblem and gold band were barely visible. While I was in Mitchell & Tyler's outfitters on Main Street for the hat and gray trousers, I saw they stocked officer's swords made by Boyle & Gamble, a reputable Richmond firm. I could not resist as I had never owned one; even the basic model I purchased was beautiful with a leather scabbard and brass fittings. I was glad not to opt for something more gaudy, that way it worked for both dress and less formal occasions. I did have to order the black sash as only medical personal uniforms were faced in black, but they had it ready in less than a week. I noted that Mallory raised his eyebrows when I first reported for duty in uniform. I adapted by only wearing the coat and sword when I was out of the office on errands.

By the second week of April, we received news that Union General McClelland had landed a large army at Fort Monroe, down below Yorktown. Our army kept them bottled up there with strategies to deceive them into believing we had more men than we did and that, along with General Jackson tearing up and containing a large federal force in the Shenandoah Valley, kept the Union boys from moving until on into May. I, however, was gone by then. On April 12, I received orders and a sealed dispatch packet for now-Commander James Bulloch in Liverpool, England.

I left immediately per my instructions, grabbed a hack to pick up my chest and take me to the station, then caught the southbound train for Wilmington, North Carolina, arriving early in the evening. Wilmington was obviously thriving as a port city, even more so now that the Virginia ports had been closed pretty effectively. The bustling riverfront was established just where the Cape Fear River widened out in the lowlands. As per my instructions, I located and went aboard the sidewheel steam schooner, *Annie*, and met Captain Hansen who detailed an officer to get me established in the passenger cabin.

We got steam up at first light the next morning and were underway just as the tide was turning. I for one was thrilled to be back aboard ship and watched intently as the scenery passed us by. The middle of the river was a series of low wooded islands, broken by a very few farms. We kept to the east channel until about halfway down. We came to a significant gap between the islands and turned southwest across the river to the other side, the point of our turn marked by tumble-down buildings resembling an old-town site and a gang of black workers building gun emplacements on what must have once been an ideal landing place. There was an odd feel about the place and an ethereal shimmer in the air, so I asked one of the crew about the place.

"Roe Noakers,'" he said enigmatically.

"What happened to the town?" I asked.

"Brunswick Town," he stated flatly. "British burned it down during the Revolution, weird things there ever since."

"They never rebuilt?" I asked.

He just looked at me like I was crazy and walked away.

It was afternoon when we completed the twenty miles down the river to Fort Fisher on Federal Point, a new series of fortifications being constructed to augment defenses along with the existing Fort Caswell on Oak Island across the way. The area around Fort Fisher was flush with Carolina pines, a ladder to a signal station was built into the tallest tree. We anchored in the lee of Zeke's Island which was really a series of low swampy pieces of land. An artillery battery emplacement dominated the only high piece of ground I could see. That knoll was maybe ten feet above the water. In the channel were crews carefully mining the main river channel with torpedoes, explosive devices set so that enemy warships could not manage the way through up the river without the design of the defenses.

We sat there, anchored, until almost sunset but with the coal fires remaining lit. Finally there was a signal from the platform above, letting us know the position of the federal squadron off the coast and we got underway. I immediately could see *Annie* was built to be a blockade runner; she was fast. As we rounded into the channel, I could see the lighthouse ahead, known as Old Baldy, that marked the river entrance, and I was told also detailed the location of Frying Pan Shoals. Captain Hansen knew his business, and we skirted Smith Island without issue. I could see the Union ships frantically steaming north in attempt to intercept us, but we were already doing well over twelve knots when we hit the Atlantic swells. We turned east nor'east and they never stood a chance of catching us.

After supper was served, I noted the change in the feel of the ship when we turned southbound for Nassau and the Bahamas, making the trip in just over two days. I changed out of my uniform before departing *Annie*, made my compliments to Captain Hansen, and caught the British mail packet out the next morning for Liverpool.

After a fast passage, I arrived in Liverpool late afternoon on the fourteenth of May. I caught a bumboat for shore and as I knew the port well, after making arrangements to transport my belongings, I walked the half-mile or so up the hill with my dispatch bag to the house on Sydenham Street. I was greeted by the butler, Morgan, who ushered me into a sitting room but made a point of noticing the slight bulge of my holstered revolver under the left armpit of my coat. I opened it to show him, his expression didn't change, and he just said, "Very good, sir."

After perhaps ten minutes, I was taken to an office where I met with my old acquaintance James Bulloch. I passed over my satchel and after breaking the seal, he spent the next quarter hour reading the material. He looked rather disappointed but cheered up and congratulated me on my commission. I later found out that Secretary Mallory had promised him command of CSS *Alabama*, currently being constructed after he had successfully built and launched the *Manassas*, but the orders I brought specified that my uncle Raphael Semmes would get that appointment. Semmes had previously commanded CSS *Sumter* for the past year, but the English authorities had taken possession of her at Gibraltar in January after complaints from the United States that they were harboring a fugitive warship. They had let Semmes and his officers go, however, and they were en route to England.

We talked some of home, but I found I didn't need to update him much; he had just returned to Liverpool at the beginning of March in time to launch the CSS *Manassas* and get her tender off to meet her in the Bahamas with her armament and munitions. The past November, Bulloch had run the blockade into Savannah aboard the *Fingal* with a cargo of Enfield rifled muskets and Blakely rifled artillery pieces he had purchased for the Confederacy. He related how, unfortunately, the Savannah River was now closed. I told him of my experience coming out of Wilmington and expressed that I didn't see any way the Union could totally close the Cape Fear River estuary with the multiple exit points involved.

Bulloch dismissed me then, indicating we had a busy day ahead on the morrow. "Morgan should have a room ready for you by now, and there should be some leftover supper in the pantry. We're pretty informal around here, Mrs. Lloyd, the cook, comes in the morning and sets us up for the day."

When I stepped out of the office, Morgan was right there to show me upstairs to my room. I noticed that some things had been moved almost imperceptibly in my chest, although nothing was taken. Apparently some security measures were in place, and I would soon find out why.

After getting squared away, I went down to the kitchen and finished off a delightful meat pie from the pantry. In spite of my reservations regarding most English cooking, I found Mrs. Lloyd to be a wonderful chef. We always had something hot for breakfast, typically sausages, scones, or fresh eggs, and she left pies, sandwiches, puddings, and fresh bread for our other meals. The house was usually busy during the day but quiet at night.

The next morning, immediately after breakfast, we jumped into a carriage that had pulled up at the front door. Inside was a round-faced man, a bit older than myself with wild hair, bushy sideburns, and a goatee that would be the envy of any southern plantation owner. He was dressed impeccably, and his sharp blue eyes looked at us out from under his eyebrows.

"Dr. Carlile, CK Prioleau," Bulloch said by way of introduction. "CK, you're taking some risk driving right up to our door. We're under fairly constant surveillance here."

"It's hired," he said, gesturing around himself at the carriage in general with a gloved hand holding a silver-headed stick. "Besides I keep away from the windows." His hard drawl let me know he was a southerner as well. He banged the cane on the carriage wall, and we moved out down the street.

I was facing to the rear in the coach, and through the window, I saw a man emerge from a doorway, across from the house, run down the block and swing into a small, two-wheel trap which then pulled out behind us, but at a distance. The other two gents in the carriage with me didn't seem to notice or care. We made our way down the hill to the river then turned onto a stone pier. As we passed, a man pulled a heavy chain across the entrance. The trap pulled up at the chain and tried to gain entrance but to no avail. I clearly heard the man at the chain shout, "We're all full, you'll have to catch the next."

On our part, we continued down a short ramp to a floating dock then onto a sidewheel steam ferry which, almost immediately, pulled away from the shore. The men on the stone pier above continued to shout at each other.

Prioleau looked at me with a twinkle in his eye and said, "Worth every penny just making them squirm."

He was an easy man to like.

We debarked at Woodside, then back up another ramp to the road, the driver showing remarkable skill juggling whip and brake to manage a smooth ascent. We turned south on the Chester Road into Birkenhead, continuing until we came to a gate on the right with a large sign, "Laird & Sons." The guard admitted us, pulling back a fence piece that rolled on wheels, and we entered into a large open yard area with several yachts and other small vessels out of the water on blocks. As we climbed down from the carriage, we were met by a man who proved to be John Laird himself. He led us down a narrow stone roadway past large storage sheds until we emerged at an immense dry dock facility, dug back into the embankment and encased in stone and timbers. In the dry dock was a finished hull, copper-plated to the waterline, and with much of the decking completed as well. She was long and lean, 220 feet from stem to stern with a beam of 32 feet amidships. She was set for three masts, and the large propeller at her stern told me she was to be a steamship as well.

We took seats on a stage set up overlooking the facility while workmen still swarmed over the hull. Soon two men went to a capstan-looking device attached to the gate separating the river from the interior of the dry dock and began turning the wheel which in turn caused the gate to withdraw into the side of the embankment. Water swirled into the basin and quickly, the hull floated off the chalks which had been holding it in place. A woman in a white dress, decorated with a blue sash, stepped out on a ramp and broke a bottle over the prow, announcing, "I christen thee, *Enrica!*"

I looked over, askance, at Bulloch; but just then, a string band struck up the tune "Dixie," causing a little commotion until Laird got up and had a word with one of his men, shortly after which the tune changed to "Rule, Britannia." Bulloch then sighed and turned to me, saying, "When we launched the CSS *Manassas*, we originally named her *Oreto* to ward off suspicion. CSS *Alabama* shall be *Enrica* until we get her commissioned."

As we departed the stage, hawsers were attached from *Enrica* to a steam tug in the river, and she was towed slowly from the dry dock upriver within the Laird compound to Graving Dock #4 where her engines would be installed, masts stepped, she would be rigged and made ready for her maiden voyage.

On the return, we stopped by Prioleau's residence in Merseyside, Allerton Hall. More precisely, it belonged to his wife, but in England, it amounted to the same thing. Allerton Hall was a Palladian-style manor house of three stories, the center set back slightly from the two wings. A grand place, but I was soon-to-be more impressed with the townhouse he built at Abercromby Square off the East Lancashire Road. His main home there was a cross between southern-plantation-style and English lord's manor. The artwork and painted ceilings were spellbinding. I could see that his Savile Row suit was not just a trapping for effect.

While Prioleau was off collecting papers he needed, we were invited to tea by his wife, Mary Elizabeth, and we were shown into the library. She was stunningly beautiful in that English ivory-complexioned way. Her slender waist made her appear taller than she really was, and her dark hair offset bright-blue eyes. She must have been in her early twenties, but she had that comfortable presence of one who is born to authority. She maintained interest and eye contact during every phase of the conversation—I could have sworn she was flirting just a bit. When Prioleau returned to take us back to the house on Sydenham Street, Mary Elizabeth excused herself to attend to some matter with the children, but my eyes continued to follow her as she departed.

I soon became used to the routine at the house; my main occupation was to arrange for the armaments and supplies to outfit *Alabama* once she was commissioned. Since it would be a breach of neutrality for England to allow a warship to be built for us on her soil, the vessel herself would be built as if she were a merchantman, then all military hardware would be loaded as cargo on a separate ship to meet at a location in international waters, then arm her. English manufacturers were delighted to sell us arms and munitions. We had to use English merchantmen to transport them, but often, we bought these ships ourselves and they had an English owner on paper. To this end, I mainly liaised with Archibald Hamilton of the London Armory Co.; he had connections all over England in the armament industry. If he couldn't provide something himself, he did know just who to talk to. Confederate Major Caleb Huse was another master in the trade. On the surface, Huse was charged with purchasing arms and ammunition for the army but had his fingers in so many dubious operations that later on, the government had to send another officer, Edward Anderson, just to check up on his activities.

Our entire operation was financed through Fraser, Trenholm & Co. and their Liverpool offices of which C. K. Prioleau was the managing partner. Not only did Prioleau generate immense wealth for his company by brokering all cotton shipments to England from America (netting him personally 5 percent off the top), but funds could be deposited with the company by the Confederate government at their offices in Charleston, South Carolina. or even New York City, and the funds would be available for purchases anywhere the company representatives were available to provide checks. Naturally this gave the US Ambassador Charles Adams fits, and he launched continuous and vigorous complaints to Lord Russel, the English foreign minister, but little could be done as long as the law was not broken. Adams did employ many spies to see if he could root out our organization. These spies were generally easy to elude as they valued their pay above any hard work, but you didn't want to be caught out alone and cornered by these men; they were generally street trash who enjoyed thrashing a defenseless person, if they could manage getting the upper hand. My normal routine when leaving the house was to go into the bakery down the street, walk straight through to the alley in back, then reverse directions. I had an arrangement with the baker, and although I always suspected someone would be waiting for me back behind the store someday, nobody ever was.

I had an endless list of details to attend to because if we were to outfit *Alabama* at sea, there was no room to miss anything lest a gun or guns would become unusable. We heard later that this had actually happened with *Manassas*, renamed CSS *Florida*, when she was commissioned. Lack of rammers, sights, beds, locks, and quoins rendered her guns inoperable and she ended up having to run the federal blockade into Mobile Bay under a hail of shell fire she could not return in order to finally be fully equipped.

In the meantime, news of the war was grim that spring. We heard about the bloodbath that was the Battle of Shiloh and the death of Albert Sidney Johnston, a man widely acclaimed as the most able general in our army. This was closely followed by the fall of New Orleans, the Confederacy's largest city and major manufacturing center. This cut the flow of supplies down the Mississippi River. Things brightened into the summer months. We learned that Robert E. Lee had taken command of the forces in Virginia and had delivered a string of victories against McClellan who was trying to drive up to Richmond by way of the James River Peninsula, driving him all the way back to Fort Monroe with his tail between his legs. We heard the casualty statistics later; the war was getting to be a bloody affair.

In July, I made my final purchase, a ninety-seven-foot bark *Agrippina*. As with most purchases, I stopped first to visit C.K. Prioleau to obtain a check. The routine was normal; I was shown into the sitting room where I was entertained in conversation by Mary Elizabeth Prioleau until CK arrived with the funds. She was always elegant and friendly, and I was always willingly gallant. It was only later that I figured out that this was a game they played to determine how trustworthy their associates were. Certainly I was always left with a guilty feeling that I was betraying CK by being enamored with his wife. I'm very glad I never pushed my luck, although I would pay later by maintaining their trust.

I caught the train south through Stafford to Birmingham, then east across the uplands to London, crossing the Thames at Vauxhall before pulling into the Southwark Station. I could clearly see the new road bridge under construction as I crossed. I caught a hack through the lower south shore, wincing at the smell of the area, a mixture of hide tanning, wool processing, and the food cannery all mixed with the stench of many people packed in tight. I was glad when we passed the intersection of Tooley Street and the Old Jamaica Road, starting up the hill into Bermondsey and the London Armoury Company where I would deliver the check for £1,400 to finalize the deal with Archibald Hamilton who would be the ostensible owner of the *Agrippina*.

Bermondsey was a bustling place, once home to the manors and town houses of the aristocracy, it was now a center of commerce in the city. In addition, the International Exhibition of Science and Arts was in full swing in the gardens of the Royal Horticultural Society in South Kensington, very nearby. This event was sponsored by the late Prince Albert, the consort of Queen Victoria who had passed the year before, and literally millions of people from all over the world had come to view the exhibits and technological inventions.

The offices of the London Armoury Company were in a brick building that had once housed the Southeastern Railway Co. I was expected, admitted immediately, and escorted upstairs. Hamilton was a no-nonsense businessman, making his fortune supplying the Confederacy with arms and equipment. He had dossiers on three merchant captains; we needed an English registered skipper to command *Agrippina*, keeping things above board, legal and proper. We settled on Captain Alexander McQueen, an old hard-drinking Scot whose loyalties were easily bought to be her master, then I began to make arrangements to have her loaded. She was a brilliant choice, built stout to carry a maximum of cargo rather than having any sailing qualities for speed. *Agrippina* was barque-rigged, her lower masts taller than normal to hold maximum canvas at that level, but the effect made her look a bit stubby. She blended right in with thousands of merchantmen, plying their trade along the Atlantic and Mediterranean coasts, a grimy unlovely ship, painted black with a yellow bead along both sides.

If I had apprehensions about loading naval cannon, ordinance, supplies, and large amounts of men's uniform clothing in broad daylight, I needn't have worried. We might as well have loaded English wool for export as much as anyone noticed. I guess the Union spies were so focused on the impending departure of the *Alabama* in Liverpool that they missed us loading in London completely. We topped off our cargo with 350 tons of fine Welsh coal, and on August 2, with our papers all in order, we slipped down the Thames and set sail for Praia on the island of Terceira, in the Azores, for our rendezvous with the *Alabama*.

After entering the English Channel on a cold wet and windy day, we enjoyed the next six of fine weather before arriving on the evening of the ninth off Terceira and slipped into Praia harbor. Captain McQueen left an anchor watch and headed immediately, with the remainder of his crew, to shore to imbibe in whatever entertainment was to be had in this sleepy backwater town. The captain apparently knew this port well and was looking forward to our time there.

The next morning, *Alabama* came steaming into port, almost immediately displaying a British white ensign in her main backstays. Our skipper answered with his number, and *Alabama* came to anchor off our starboard bow. Fully fitted out, she was a beautiful vessel; at 220 feet in length and only 32 in beam, she looked like a racer. Her sticks were all of yellow pine, the best for being supple without breaking, and her standing rigging was iron wire, new in my experience. She was fore and aft rigged but carried square sails on the fore and mainmasts from topsails to royals. As she was almost empty, the line of her copper hull plates was clearly visible. McQueen and I put off in the jolly boat, rowing the short distance across to go aboard.

We were met at the rail by her interim captain, Matthew Butcher, another officer possessing the British Board of Trade Certificate necessary to sail legally from Liverpool as a merchant; although I heard later that *Alabama* had departed directly from her sea trials without reentering port as action by the government was impending to prevent her sailing. We made plans right there, on the quarterdeck, to transfer coal, stores, and supplies but to wait for Captain Semmes' arrival to move over any arms or ordinance.

What followed was an idyllic week of life in a small harbor town. The offshore breezes from the Atlantic kept the temperatures mild, sunny but not too hot during the day and cool but comfortable at night. The town of Praia was picturesque in the Portuguese style with red-tile roofs and a plethora of hydrangea still flowering into the late summer in bright cornflower blue and white. The backdrop of steep hills covered in green foliage made it surreal. There were stretches of wide sandy beaches adjacent to the town, the water was warm and crystal clear, almost as warm as the air. Fish were abundant, and although we saw several large sharks, they never came close to us when we were swimming. Every day, the playful porpoises would come up to the ship and greet us with their click-like calls; we routinely fed them the heads and tails from our daily fishing. Once one of the sailors caught a huge fish, in excess of a hundred pounds. We had to utilize the capstan to finally land the monster.

On the nineteenth, the ship *Bahama* arrived, carrying with her Raphael Semmes. He came over to *Alabama* and immediately took charge. Butcher told him what we had accomplished, and he seemed to grasp immediately what needed to be done. He assembled the English crews from the three ships, promised them signing bonuses and the lure of potential prize money in addition to their pay. Very quickly, he had more than eighty volunteers to fill able-bodied and petty officer positions. He had brought with him approximately twenty-five ship's officers and warrants from England, including fourteen who had served with him aboard the CSS *Sumter*.

The bos'n was sitting at a small table in the center of the quarterdeck, taking names and getting signatures from the newly-enlisted men. Semmes was standing to the left, a few paces off, with his arms folded. After the push of volunteers had cleared, I stepped up to report for duty but was interrupted by Semmes who recognized me instantly.

"John Carlile, what are *you* doing here?" he boomed out with just a shade of venom in his tone.

I came to attention in front of him and responded, "Reporting as ordered, sir," with just as much boom but far more cheer.

"By whose orders and in what capacity?" he asked in more of a conversational tone now that the surprise was over. He looked me over and as I was not in uniform, I could see the curiosity in his eyes.

"Commander Bulloch sent me in *Agrippina* to equip and join your ship, sir. I hold a commission as an assistant surgeon but thought it best, under the current circumstances, to remain incognito."

Semmes cleared his throat and his hand moved up to begin stroking his goatee, then he stopped and a brief smile came to his face.

"I already have a surgeon and so will have no use for your services," he said flatly. "Per regulations, you are a limited duty officer and I cannot use you in a line officer capacity."

"Am I dismissed then, sir?" I asked, beginning to hope I would not have to serve under his command.

But then, McQueen, who had been watching this show, chimed in, "E's the one that knows where everythin's at aboard *Agrippina*."

"I guess that makes you my ad hoc supply officer, Mr. Carlile, at least until I can get rid of you properly," said Semmes while turning away, the last part mused just loud enough for me to hear.

I realized I had been ad hoc dismissed, so I relaxed my shoulders and shot McQueen my best dirty look. He just grinned back at me, exposing brown broken teeth and stretching out the spider veins on his red cheeks and nose. Captain McQueen may have been a loud-mouthed boastful old drunk. but there was never a question of his intelligence.

The next morning, *Alabama*, *Bahama*, and *Agrippina* sailed south into international waters. In the calm waters leeward of the Azores archipelago, we began transferring guns, stores, and armament. Over the next three days of backbreaking work, *Alabama* was transformed into a warship, mounting six thirty-two-pound guns, three to a broadside, an eighty-six-pound eight-inch smoothbore amidships on a massive swivel mount, and a one-hundred-pound Blakeley rifled gun forward, also on a swivel mount. The *Bahama* departed quickly the night of the twenty-third, apparently fearing being caught by the British authorities engaged in this activity and headed north for England. I was supposed to have returned with her but was left behind in the rush. *Agrippina* sailed for Brazil with instructions to obtain coal and gunpowder to resupply *Alabama* at an appointed rendezvous in the Caribbean. Thus I was left aboard CSS *Alabama* when she was commissioned August 24, 1862, but without a defined position. All I could do was attempt to remain unnoticed by the captain or he would task me with odd duties, mostly to amuse himself. Once he sent me to check a gauge in the boiler room which just caused Mr. Freeman, our engineer, to rail at me in a torrent of brogue I could barely understand. I do have to say that between Captain Semmes and his executive officer, Lieutenant John Kell, they were the perfect duo to turn the *Alabama* into a commerce-raiding machine.

We spent the better part of two weeks in leisurely sailing and steaming, sorting the crew into their optimal assignments, then practicing sail and gun drill until a measure of proficiency was achieved. This was not only for the men, the captain and officers were keen to learn the ship's best sailing points along with the combinations of steam and sail that would achieve speed and maneuverability. *Alabama* had dual steam engines that drove a single shaft propeller, but that propeller was also retractable so as not to add drag should we just desire to use the wind for propulsion.

I was glad to find I had one acquaintance aboard, Irvine Bulloch, who I had met with several times before in both Georgia and in Liverpool. He had been appointed midshipman and assigned to the ship, but once Captain Semmes figured out he was adept mathematically and could navigate with proficiency, he was given the post of master's mate. I also quickly became friendly with the surgeon Semmes had brought along. Dr. Llewellyn was a Welshman who didn't talk much about his past, but I was always surprised by his ability to fit seamlessly into situations; he obviously had experience shipboard and was adept at modern medical procedure, including combat surgery which requires speed and a cool head. Rumors said that he had served in the Royal Navy during the Crimean conflict. For sure, I could see that he was dedicated to the men and willing to stand up to the captain over dangerous conditions aboard or dietary concerns. We pitched in together to set up the infirmary, and my prior experience in this task was invaluable.

I had few friends in the wardroom, most of the officers wished to remain in the captain's good graces so stayed clear of me unless duty required it. Lieutenant Kell, our exec, was the exception. Kell was very tall, well-made, and fearless. He had a bushy beard that, together with him starting to bald, made it appear that his face resided within a circle of hair. He always looked at you from beneath thick eyebrows, and the junior officers were afraid of him to the man. I found him intelligent and articulate and often after supper, we talked politics and theory when our duties weren't pressing. Kell had spent twenty years in the US Navy and was thoroughly good at his job. I often wondered why he had not been given a command of his own. He hailed from a Georgian family and was a staunch supporter of the South.

As the new crew began to gel and real operations loomed near, tensions began to mount. Although our officers were Confederate, our crew was almost entirely English, they had signed up for the prospect of prize money and were, in effect, mercenaries. I wondered how they would do if we got into a serious scrap, regardless of how well-commanded they were.

On the fourth of September, Mr. Kell declared our crew ready to commence business, Captain Semmes established a northwesterly course to see if we could locate the Yankee whaling fleet. In the evening, we watched the island of Faial dip below the horizon in an otherwise empty ocean. I decided to keep a concise record of our voyage since I was mostly unemployed aboard; so I involved myself in the navigation of the ship. Our midnight sextant recording that night put us right on the thirty-ninth parallel of north latitude.

The next morning dawned sunny but with a brisk wind out of the southeast. At about ten in the morning, the lookout announced a sail off the starboard bow. The captain ordered us to change course to intercept and to hoist an American flag. The other ship must have had a sixth sense, however, no sooner had we come around when she also changed course due north and ran. This piqued Captain Semmes's interest, and we packed on as much canvas as *Alabama* could hold. Still we only gained ground slowly, but by two in the afternoon, the mystery ship was hull up on the horizon or about four miles off. The ship was brig-rigged, and the step of her masts had seemed familiar, but now that we had closed, there was no doubt—she was the *Mary Eleanore.*

I made my way aft to the quarterdeck and the captain.

"By your leave, sir," I announced.

"Eh?" he responded, snapping his telescope shut against his hand.

"She's the *Mary Eleanore*, sir. She's been a friend to the Confederacy in the past."

"She'll be a friend again when her Yankee insurance company has to pay for her," he snapped at me with a slick smile playing on his lips. "And she'll keep us warm tonight when we burn her up."

Just then, a call came from the lookout at the masthead, "She's turning, sir!"

Semmes pulled up his telescope and put it to his eye. "Stand by to wear ship, Mr. Kell," he called to the lieutenant.

"Stand by to wear ship," the call went out.

Then from Semmes again, "Bring her around to three two five." This was followed by a, "Double damn!" as it became apparent that the *Mary Eleanore* had stolen some distance on us, having had time to better plan and execute the maneuver.

Not much more than a minute passed when another call came from the lookout, "Another sail, sir, bearing dead ahead and beyond the brig."

This caused an amount of concerned chatter among the officers present, and Semmes wrinkled up his forehead in thought for a second; but then, a smile broke out on his face and he turned to me, saying, "Your Uncle Thomas is a wily old scoundrel, he's going to give me something I can't refuse."

In a quarter hour, I understood what he meant as we could easily see the new ship, a whaling ship with her topsails backed, a huge sperm whale trailing from her tackle. We altered course slightly to head right for the whaler while the *Mary Eleanore* turned again to make her escape, this time to the north and east. We identified the new ship as *Ocmulgee,* out of Boston. Big surprise for her when we came up on her, ran out our guns, hauled down the American flag. and ran up the stars and bars of the Confederacy. Her crew members were still engaged in stripping great chunks of blubber from the creature she had in tow when Lieutenant Armstrong was sent with an armed party in the cutter to get her skipper, Captain Osborn.

We spent the remainder of the afternoon and into the evening first sequestering *Ocmulgee's* crew, then transferring her stores, barrels of beef, pork, and flour. Lieutenant Kell estimated her worth at $50,000; we waited until the next morning to set her on fire so as not to attract undue attention at night. The thirty-seven men of the crew were put into three of her whaleboats and pointed in the direction of Flores Island, some ten miles distant. Our crew grumbled a bit, thinking that if she could be sold instead of burned that there would be prize money; but first, the ship would have to run the blockade to access a Confederate prize court. Second, we were slightly undermanned and a prize crew would further diminish our numbers, and third, it was explained to the crew that the Confederate States legislature had passed a measure allotting 20 percent value of any destroyed Union property in lieu of prize money. This news quieted the grumbling, and our crew perked right up with the image of beer money in their pockets.

Later that morning, we sighted a schooner. When we came up to her, she ran up a British flag. She would not stop for our inspection; we were obliged to fire a round across her bow. She still would not heave to, and it wasn't until we scored a direct hit on her main mast, bringing her into the wind, that she hauled down her flag and ran up an American one. She was the *Starlight*, also out of Boston. Captain Semmes showed his temper with her master when we discovered *Starlight* had three women for passengers that had been put in danger needlessly. Dr. Llewellyn and I were called upon to treat two crewmen, slightly wounded in the fusillade, before they could be transported over to the *Alabama*. I could see Llewellyn was no lubber, the way he swung himself up onto *Starlight* from the *Alabama's* cutter, a move requiring skill and timing in the choppy water of the open ocean.

While we were dealing with *Starlight*, a whaling brig flying the Portuguese flag sailed up, thinking we were assisting a ship in distress. We checked their papers, found all in order, and allowed her to go on her way. She had no sooner disappeared over the horizon when yet another whaler, the *Ocean Rover*, sailed up. She also was fooled by our switching out of the stars and stripes for the stars and bars and was captured forthwith. Both *Starlight* and *Ocean Rover* were burned the next morning. *Ocean Rover* was homeward bound and had over a thousand barrels of rendered whale oil; when the flames reached her cargo, she burned ferociously. The crews were once again paroled, put into *Ocean Rover's* boats, and pointed toward Flores Island.

The next day was the seventh of September, and we repeated our performance, this time, flying the Union Jack as if we were an English warship. We overtook the bark *Alert*, a shot across her bow was required before she would surrender. While she was burning, another schooner, the *Weatherguage*, came up to find out what the commotion was about and fell right into our clutches. Once more, boats full of crew were bound for Flores while their ships burned. We had taken and destroyed five Yankee ships in three days and gotten in some gunnery practice; the whole ship was in a celebratory mood. Some tobacco had been taken from *Alert*, and each hand received a generous portion. We were all disappointed when Monday, the eight, dawned bright and beautiful but with an empty horizon all around. We saw nothing the entire day; the crew spent the time readjusting the stores we had plundered from our victims and making little changes to the trim of the spars under Mr. Kell's direction to elicit maximum speed under sail. The captain had voiced his displeasure with our failure to catch the *Mary Eleanore*.

On the ninth, we immediately sighted and overtook the small whaling brig *Altima*; she was almost worthless having been out six months without making a catch. She didn't even have stores remaining that amounted to anything but burned brightly nonetheless. In the late afternoon, we spotted a large whaling ship to the southwest. They had to tack into the wind to try to elude us. Our steam power made the difference in this contest. As it was getting dark, we overtook her. She was the *Benjamin Tucker* of 349 tons. As we were well away from land, her thirty-man-crew became our guests. Sighting nothing for the next couple of days, we decided to steer northeast, back toward the Azores; and the sixteenth dawned to the sight of another small whaling brig, the *Courser*. She stubbornly refused to submit until we fired several rounds into her. We used *Courser's* whaleboats to send both crews we had captured off to Flores Island, again distant on the horizon.

By the eighteenth, we had captured and burned our tenth ship and figured we had destroyed more worth of merchant shipping than had been the total cost to build and equip the *Alabama*. Whaling season in the Azores was coming to an end, and the weather had taken a turn for the worse, so Captain Semmes decided to head northwest for Newfoundland. American harvests would be nearing completion and grain ships would be heading for Europe. On October 3, we entered into the Gulf Stream and immediately began sighting sails. *Emily Farnum* was the first stopped but proved to be British-owned. She was a huge ship, well over a thousand tons. We put aboard our remaining prisoners and allowed her on her way to Liverpool; but once we cleared away, she turned around and headed back toward New England. The captain wasn't too worried, however. We had been routinely flying different flags, adding a second funnel, changing sail configuration, and other means of disguising our vessel.

Over the next week, we took seven more ships, all large with cargoes of flour and grain but also carrying passengers. *Alabama* was becoming crowded with prisoners, and some interesting events took place. First there was a crewman on the ship *Dunkirk* who was recognized by our officers that had served with Semmes on CSS *Sumter*. This man, George Forrest, had deserted while that ship was in harbor in Spain. A court martial was convened, and Forrest was found guilty. I was prepared, at that point, for a grisly outpouring of naval justice, but the captain commuted his sentence. He was dishonorably discharged from the navy and made to serve out the remainder of our cruise as a hand but without pay or prize money.

The ship *Tonawanda* had passengers in addition to her cargo, including women, children, and a seventeen-year-old slave named David White. We ended up bonding the *Tonawanda* and using her as transport for all our prisoners. Captain Semmes freed David White from his Yankee master and made him a paid crew member; he became our wardroom mess steward. The ship *Manchester* had aboard a stack of newspapers. We were thus able to read firsthand reports about the uproar we were creating along with reports of the movements of the Union Navy, including the dispatch of the USS *Tuscarora* to find us in the Azores.

On October 14, we were struck by the remainder of a hurricane and forced to steam into the direction of the weather for safety. The wind and sea were high, and visibility was poor. We endured these conditions for the best part of four days then a smaller storm that followed in its wake. We weathered both these storms fairly well but had our work cut out for us afterward, repairing and replacing some spars and rigging we had lost. In addition, the storms had cleared the seas of other ships. It wasn't until the twenty-third of October that we sighted another sail.

By this time, the Yankee ship owners were becoming pretty adept at crafting paperwork indicating that ship cargoes were property belonging to foreign nationals, neutrals in the war. If the ship was determined to be American-built or owned, Captain Semmes invariably found fault with the paperwork then destroyed the ship and cargo. By the end of October, we were running low on coal and food supplies in spite of our continual augmentation from the captures we had made. The captain used an almost worthless take, the *Baron de Castine*, to unload all our prisoners onto. He provided her captain with a description of all twenty of the ships we had taken and even provided a letter addressed to Mr. Low of the New York City Chamber of Commerce stating that our next hunting ground would just be off New York City harbor. We then turned south for Martinique where the *Agrippina* was waiting to resupply us. The US Navy responded by sending a task force headed by USS *Vanderbilt* to search the area we had just vacated.

We took two prizes on the way south, including, on November 8, just off of Bermuda, the *Thomas B. Waltzek*, a ship similar to ours in rigging. We were not only able to replace the spars we had lost in the hurricane, but eleven of her crew volunteered to sign on for our ship. Our compliment was finally getting up toward what we should have to fight her effectively.

Our stop in Martinique was problematic to say the least. On the sixteenth, we dropped anchor off Fort-de-France next to *Agrippina*. We landed our prisoners, but many of the crew were anxious for some shore leave. This was denied until we could be effectively resupplied; but as we could not prevent the men from having contact with the swarm of bumboats that descended on us rather immediately, quantities of liquor made their way aboard. An all-out brawl erupted among the crew with talk of mutiny if no shore leave was allowed. The mob, headed by George Forrest the deserter, came aft to present their demands; but the officers on deck, including myself, Irvine Bulloch, Art Sinclair the watch officer, Howell our marine lieutenant and midshipman Anderson, stood shoulder to shoulder with pistols drawn and obstructed their way. The leaders of the insurrection were loud and obnoxious, but we stood fast and none wanted to be brave enough to be in front. Lieutenant Kell arrived posthaste, took one look at the situation, and ordered general quarters. Reluctantly even the drunks turned to and went to stations. Besides no one wanted to argue with Kell. At all. Ever.

The captain had the pumps manned, and the hoses were turned on the drunks until they were gasping for breath. George Forrest was clapped in chains in the brig which brought the whole matter to an end. Dr. Llewellyn, who had bravely attempted to rescue an injured man when the brawl first erupted, had his leg broken just above the ankle. I set it for him and the bone mended well, but the injury was a compound fracture and the bone had pierced the skin. Infection set in and although we finally got control of the issue, there was a time when I thought I might need to amputate, and he had a painful limp ever after.

To top off our difficult situation, Captain McQueen of *Agrippina* had arrived in Fort-de-France more than a week before our arrival and, as was his custom, spent his time in the local taverns. His bragging of his association with and pending arrival of *Alabama* came to the attention of Yankee agents. Soon after our arrival, the steam frigate USS *San Jacinto* arrived and took station outside the harbor. Fighting her was not an option, we were seriously outgunned. Captain Semmes, with some not-so-kind words to McQueen, ordered *Agrippina* to sail for Blanquilla Island. Two nights later, after making a show of settling in for the night, we slipped our anchor chain and quietly made our escape without being observed. Fort-de-France was, after all, a large harbor in a wide bay and the *San Jacinto* apparently not too observant.

We resumed our activity unabated in the Caribbean, concentrating on the area between Cuba and Haiti. Although we had received coal and powder from *Agrippina*, we were still low on foodstuffs until the third of December when we took the bark *Parker Cook* with a cargo of beef, pork, cheeses, hardtack, and butter.

On December 7, we sighted a large passenger steamer, the *Ariel*. Our usual trick of flying the stars and stripes then changing out at the last minute for the stars and bars worked like always, although we had to fire a second round through her rigging when she wouldn't stop for the one across her bow. Lieutenant Low took over a boarding party, bringing back her captain and the news that there was a company of US Marines aboard *Ariel* that he had to disarm and that there were a large number of very frightened women and children aboard who were certain we were pirates. Captain Semmes ordered Lieutenants Armstrong and Sinclair to put on their dress uniforms and go to the *Ariel* to quell fears. Both men returned without a single button remaining on their coats, the ladies all being anxious for a keepsake of the event.

Now we had the problem of hundreds of prisoners; and then a machinery malfunction caused us to have to shut down the boilers to make the necessary repairs. We had to bond *Ariel,* parole the prisoners, and send her on her way because we had no good option to land all the prisoners in a civilized location. Our engineer, Lieutenant Freeman, showed his wizardry with the mechanics once again, and we had steam up inside forty-eight hours, to everyone's relief.

On the twenty-second of December, we made landfall at the Arcas Keys, a group of three tiny islands off the coast of Mexico. The next day, *Agrippina* joined us, and we spent the better part of two weeks leisurely loading the remainder of the coal, recaulking, rerigging, and scraping *Alabama's* copper plating which had become especially foul with seaweeds in the tropical waters. We had a decent Christmas and New Year's celebration, complete with fireworks—starburst shells from our eight-inch pivot gun amidships. The mood of the crew had returned to positive, that is, all but George Forrest who remained behind, stranded on the sand and grass atoll of Arcas, cursing us loudly as we sailed away.

W e sailed north from Arcas Keys on Thursday, January 8, 1863. Captain Semmes had learned from captured newspapers that Union General Nathaniel Banks had set out from New Orleans with an expeditionary force to take Galveston, Texas, in an amphibious assault. Semmes was determined that *Alabama* should provide an obstruction to this operation.

On the eleventh, at just after seven bells in the afternoon watch, we had just made Galveston light when the call from the lookout sounded, "Land ho!, Sail ho!"

A nod from the captain had Irvine Bulloch up to the foretop with glass in hand. He was back in a minute, breathing hard, and reported, "Five Yankee warships, all shelling the harbor. No sign of enemy transports, but one of the warships has turned our way to investigate."

"What do you make of her?" came the inquiry from Semmes.

"A side-wheeler, hard to tell what she is carrying but she looks to be one of their conversion jobs." Bulloch was referring to the plethora of ferries, transports, tugs, and other ships the Union had converted into warships in their quest to complete the blockade of the south. "She's on a bearing to intersect our course."

Captain Semmes ordered general quarters and the decks cleared for action. He set a westerly course, the Union Jack flown and t'gallants taken in to decrease our speed. The sun was already getting low on the horizon, being that it was winter, and Semmes was keeping us between the setting sun and the Yankee warship to make it more difficult for them to spy us out. The next report indicated that the

Yank seemed to have thirty-two-pounders in her broadside like us but only two per side. "Plus she's got something smaller on a pivot for a bow chaser."

What followed was an excruciatingly tense hour as the enemy ship closed on us but was pulled further away from the rest of the Yankee squadron. When the two ships were about two hundred yards apart, her bow about even with our sternpost, a call came from across the water, "What ship is that?" I could see they were struggling to get a make on us in the gathering dusk.

"Her Majesty's ship, *Spitfire!*" responded Semmes through his speaking trumpet.

A pause, then, "Stand by to receive an officer for verification!" from the Yank.

A boat was lowered, half-dozen or so men tumbled down into it and immediately started off in our direction. Our British flag came streaming down, replaced by our Confederate battle ensign, and Lieutenant Kell yelled across the water, "We're the CSS *Alabama*, damn you!"

"Run out the guns!" came the order from Captain Semmes, then, "Fire!"

There was a deafening blast as all five of our large guns erupted simultaneously, and *Alabama* rolled in recoil. I could see our shots strike home and at least one explosion. A pillar of steam erupted from her main hatch; her boiler must have been pierced, and this was followed by black smoke as a fire took hold.

She was game though and returned fire immediately, *Alabama* shuddering as an explosion went off below decks. We were turning now, across her bow as the Yank's speed fell off along with her boiler pressure. We were now only fifty yards apart when we fired again, and I saw chunks fly off as our shots slammed home. As I watched, spellbound with my ears ringing, I saw the crew of her bow chaser pivot their gun around to bear, the breath sticking in my throat when the muzzle was pointed directly at me. I was visualizing the flash that would spell my demise and was powerless to do anything about it. Then the black hole I was staring down swiveled further on before firing, the shot smashing through our railing amidships. A crewman at the eight-inch gun cried out and threw up his hands, a foot-long splinter of wood sticking out of his chest like a spear. He did a half-turn before his legs gave out, then sat heavily down on the deck, eyes bulging wide and looking at the impaling shard and bloodstain slowly spreading on his shirt.

I started forward to render assistance when the cannonball came rolling back to the base of the gun truck, fuse still spitting sparks from a hole in the top. I stopped dead in my tracks; in my mind's eye, I could imagine the blast that would decimate the crew there. Then there was a faint wisp of white smoke from the fuse hole before the next roll of the ship sent the ball skittering out of sight. I stood rooted to the spot, my gut not trusting that an explosion would not take place, when I heard a shout, "Mr. Carlile, close your mouth!"

I snapped shut my mouth and looked over to see Lieutenant Kell grinning at me, the look on his face letting me know that death was just the next big adventure. He must have been watching as my dilemma unfolded. I think he was actually amused by the drama. I smiled back at him, maybe a little foolishly, then took off running forward to assist the fallen crewman. I grabbed him roughly under the armpits and pulled him away from the rest of the crew who were trying to reload the gun around him. He let out a howl and left a red smear on the deck behind him as I dragged him away, the powder boy appearing and sprinkling sand to keep the others from slipping on the blood.

I tore his shirt away from the protruding splinter and noted that although I could see the skin and flesh pushing out from under the shoulder blade on his back, the shard had not gone all the way through. I could also see that his ribs had deflected the wood from piercing his chest cavity, although one or more was surely cracked. Blood was oozing slowly from the wound. I determined my best course was to get him to the operating table lest removing the object result in a hemorrhage I couldn't control on the deck. I lowered him, still hollering down the main hatch, then supporting him with his good arm over my shoulder and walked him back to where Dr. Llewellyn had an operating area set up, a single lantern swaying from the overhead beam providing light to work by. I plunked him down on the table, turned to Llewellyn, and reported, "It's superficial, he's just cryin' like a baby."

When I got back on deck, the gunfire had ceased, the whole battle had lasted less than twenty minutes. The Yankee ship was on fire and obviously sinking by the bow. They fired one final shot into the air from their forward gun, maybe as a sign of surrender, but I noticed that their flag was still flying at the masthead, it had not been struck. The enemy crewmen were abandoning ship, jumping into the water and swimming away or holding on to random flotsam to keep their heads above water. We immediately began launching our boats to perform rescue services. It was now almost fully dark, but we managed to get most of their men out of the water. Their captain reported about ten men not accounted for, but I know for a fact that the boat they launched to verify our identity had pulled clear and escaped in the darkness. It seemed the Yank ship was the USS *Hatteras*; she went under with a huge hiss as her fires were extinguished by contact with the sea water. She stayed afloat for about ten minutes longer, just her stern bobbing in the waves, before finally disappearing into the now-black water.

By then I was busy attending to the wounded. One more of our men was injured, apparently shot in the cheek. I extracted the bullet while Llewellyn was doing triage with the enemy wounded. The bullet was lodged under his cheekbone and against his upper jaw but not deep which was curious. When I removed it, I immediately figured out why. The nose of the thing was flattened and crimped, it must have ricocheted off a hard object before striking the crewman and reduced the momentum of the projectile as a result. I gave him an extra swig of medicinal brandy and told him he was just unlucky, the person who had shot at him had missed before the deflection.

One of the Yanks was hurt pretty badly, having been scalded by steam escaping from the ruptured boiler. Luckily he was past any pain, most of his chest, neck, and one side of his face were completely blistered. His left eye was fused in the socket, looking like a hard-boiled egg, and the eyelid was melted away. Llewellyn had to remove the eye to offset infection setting into the cranium. We doused the man in cold salt water then pulled off dead skin from around the blisters that had popped. Llewellyn covered all the affected area with flour while I soaked bandages in a carbolic acid and water solution. We repeated this several times during the time he was aboard, and although initially I thought he was a goner, he had a strong constitution and was recovering when we dropped off our prisoners.

Another of their wounded was a black man, he had a deep laceration but his immersion in the ocean had effectively stopped most of the bleeding. The area around the cut had swelled, causing the flesh to pull back away from the cut and making the stitching more difficult. He was built like a sinew, with almost no body fat, and I had to be careful not to include muscle in my stitching. I was shocked when I saw his back. It was crisscrossed with white scars, some covering other marks that were older. His wrists and ankles had like marks all around. He would not take anything for the pain, just stared at me silently with a look of hatred on his face. He must have misinterpreted the perplexed look on my face when I noted his scars. He drilled me with his eyes and said softly, "Yeah, my blood is red too." Funny, it was the Yankee ship's surgeon who came to assist us that was the one who refused to treat the black man.

On the twentieth, we arrived at Port Royal in Jamaica, gladly paroling our prisoners, over a hundred of them to the US Counsel there. The captain was sick and left the ship for four days to recover, leaving Mr. Kell to repair and reprovision the ship. We had taken seven hits of one sort or another during our battle with USS *Hatteras*, and although none causing serious damage, there was much work to be done by the carpenter and his mates making the *Alabama* pretty again. Shore leave had been granted all around outside of the ongoing work and victualing parties; but when the captain returned, many of the men were not to be found. We assembled a shore patrol, scouring the bars and brothels to recover most of our men but nine were never found. When we sailed out on the twenty-fifth, we had to list these men as deserters.

26

We set a course for our old hunting grounds off the coast of Haiti and in a single day, we already had our next victim, the barque *Golden Rule*. We continued our process of taking merchantmen, burning them up and landing their crews and passengers ashore. We had taken fourteen more ships by the beginning of April when, running low on fuel, we came across the *Louisa Hatch*, carrying a load of smokeless coal. Captain Semmes then decided to head for Fernando de Noronha in Brazilian territory where we transferred the load using open boats during the week of April 10. While we were there, we had two whalers sail right up to us and we added them to our list.

We next headed for Bahia, just below the eastern tip of Brazil, intending to take advantage of the trade rounding Cape Horn. While we were there, we met up with the CSS *Georgia* on May 13, and a party atmosphere prevailed. Many of *Georgia's* officers were acquaintances of ours and some time was spent swapping stories.

We spent the next month cruising in southern waters. Two events happened that directly affected me. On June 5, we ran down a large clipper ship, the *Talisman,* who happened to have aboard four brass 12-pounder rifled cannon which were taken aboard and stored. After that, Captain Semmes was on the lookout for a fast ship that could be converted into a secondary raider. Fifteen days later, we came across the *Conrad,* a 350-ton barque and we believed we had the necessary ship. We mounted two of the 12-pounders on her and commissioned her the CSS *Tuscaloosa*. Lieutenant Low was given the command, and fifteen crewmen came aboard, along with a good supply of small arms. I was assigned to her as well, the captain finally finding a good excuse to get rid of me. I assumed a dual role of surgeon and navigator; although I was given no authority, I was assigned to the larboard watch to keep our heading true. During my nine months' service in the *Alabama*, we took fifty-three merchant vessels, most of which were burned. Our role in creating financial havoc in the United States was well underway.

I for one was glad to be quit of the *Alabama*, and I think John Low was as well. Low was a Scotsman recently immigrated to Savannah, Georgia. He had been a mate in the British merchant service who had started up a shipping company in Savannah thus was an acquaintance of James Bulloch. Bulloch had requested him as an aide; he was commissioned and sent to Liverpool. Low was an officer aboard *Fingal* on her famous blockade run and was the temporary skipper of the CSS *Florida*, delivering her to John Moffitt at Nassau in 1862. He was instrumental in getting *Alabama* ready to sail but was not part of the *Sumter* clique which had made him the odd officer out. This had undoubtedly influenced Captain Semmes's choice in his selection to take command of the little *Tuscaloosa*. I had met Low several times in passing while in Liverpool; we were on equitable terms, although he had steered shy of me while aboard *Alabama* to stay off Captain Semmes's shit list.

We sailed southeast toward the South African coast, then established a bit of a grid to see if we could find an American ship engaged in the India trade. After an uneventful month, we sighted a large ship, the *Santee*, and overtook her quickly. Our brass cannon were rifled and proved to have good range. On inspection of her papers, we discovered that although *Santee* was Yankee-owned, her cargo of rice was English-owned. I'm very sure that Semmes would have burned her, but Low bonded her and sent her on her way. I think he was nervous about the number of prisoners we would have to guard—*Santee*'s crew was double our number.

Our crew almost mutinied when the *Santee* sailed off. A month with no prize was disappointing after the success of the *Alabama*; the crew knew the bond would not hold up, and their percentage would have been higher with just the sixteen of us aboard. I had a word with the bos'n's mate and advised patience, that the possibility of netting money for the *Santee* was still there and we would have more prizes to come. Better than a rope around the neck for mutiny. He made me promise the crewmen we would burn our next prize, and I told them I would prevail upon Lieutenant Low to do so. We set off in a grumbling mood for the Cape of Good Hope.

We dropped anchor in Simon's Bay, South Africa, on August 8, taking on food and water for a ninety-day cruise. We still had her previous cargo aboard. On a tip, we sailed north, up the coast, and stopped at the tiny harbor of Angra Pequena, selling the goatskins and wool we had been hauling about. The Boer trader paid us in gold dust; he showed me a rough diamond which didn't impress me. It looked dull and greasy, but he was pretty excited about it. While there, we received word that *Alabama* had gone on into the Indian Ocean, so Low decided to head back West for South America. After two months of scouring an empty ocean, we put in at Florianopolis on St. Catherine's, November 19, to purchase supplies. The political wind had apparently turned against us. First we were denied the ability to purchase food, then a government official arrived and told us point-blank that we were to leave Brazil before dark.

So back across the Atlantic we went, returning to Simon's Bay and Cape Town on Christmas Day. We obtained three chickens, fresh fruit, and some honey from shore and had a glorious supper supplemented by a little extra grog for the holiday. The next morning, the anchor watch called out an approaching boat and I scrambled up to the deck to see the launch from the neighboring ship, HMS *Narcissus*, completing its glide up to our chains with oars straight up. A young lieutenant bounded up the side, followed by a pair of marines in their red uniforms. Low came forward to meet him at the gangway and ask the meaning of the visit.

"Sir, I'm here to impound this ship," came the reply in a nasally voice. He produced what appeared to be a legal document from his coat pocket. "Her majesty's court finds this to be an uncondemned prize which makes you in violation of neutrality laws in an English port."

"Funny, nothing was said last time we were here!" said Low, now becoming agitated and raising his voice.

By now, six more armed sailors were on our deck, the glint in their eyes suggesting that a bit of action might liven up their day. They formed in a rough semicircle behind their officer with the two marines flanking the group on either side.

"You can take that up with the proper authorities," stated the English lieutenant with just a hint of a sneer. "In the meantime, you and your men need to get your personal belongings together for escort to shore."

Once again, I packed up the infirmary with my personal belongings; by now, I was especially well-equipped as a doctor and a surgeon. Lieutenant Low paid me off, along with the rest of the crew, so I had funds to survive ashore. Low decided his role was to fight the English court over the rights to the CSS *Tuscaloosa*, but I knew this to be a lost cause so I decided my duty was to report back to Bulloch in Liverpool.

To that end, I booked passage with the Castle Line which contracted to provide mail service from India. I boarded the *Warwick Castle*, a clipper ship, and had an idyllic time as a passenger rubbing elbows with the wealthy English merchants and their wives. Once they found me to be a Confederate naval officer, my stories were in high demand, especially the tale of CSS *Alabama* vs. USS *Hattaras*. We had perfect weather until the day before we reached the English coast; we ran into a wall of fog and rain with seas higher than should be expected in the light wind. I continued to spend most of my waking hours on deck during the final three days while the rest of the passengers were hunkered down in the cabin. I have to say, it didn't take too long to start smelling ripe in there.

After making my way back to Liverpool and the house on Sydenham Street, I went right back to work, making acquisitions for the cause. At my initial meeting with Bulloch, he agreed that dealing with the British authorities had become much more difficult for two reasons: first the success of *Alabama* and her cohorts was costing some Englishmen money in lost product, and the US Counsel was livid with the foreign office over allowing *Alabama* to get loose on the American merchant fleet. Insurers were being bankrupted, and no one wanted their cargo to be carried in an American ship due to the risk. Second, the war was looking gloomy for the Confederacy. The loss at Gettysburg even though the Yanks didn't follow it up, the loss of Vicksburg giving the Yanks total control of the Mississippi River, and finally the loss at Chattanooga giving the Yanks a toehold in Georgia.

Still I had free rein to operate, my objective was the same as before—getting together all the parts and armaments to outfit a new commerce raider to augment our slowly-growing little fleet. This time around, Bulloch was determined to buy the proper ship rather than have her built. Laird and Sons, our builder, was under constant surveillance from Yankee spies along with additional oversight from the British Foreign Office.

Lieutenant Low arrived in mid-February but took a leave after finding out his wife had died. I certainly knew how he felt but didn't have the time or inclination to provide him with guidance or counsel. In the beginning of April, two things happened. First I located and bought a tender for our raider-to-be. She was the *Laurel*, a stout little vessel, a lot like *Agrippina*, almost as wide as she was long. I began to fill her with all the product I had been buying to outfit our new project. Second was a promotion to lieutenant. Apparently my duties were incongruent with my position. As aide to Bulloch, I needed to have a line officer status or it looked too much like I was a spy.

Mary Prioleau was the big surprise; she seemed so happy to see me back yet a little sad and a bit vulnerable in her big townhouse. She was a classic English beauty, with her porcelain complexion, and she was my primary contact when I needed a check for the purchases I was making. I began using my visits to talk with her about things going on in my life. When Lieutenant Low found out about his wife, I talked with her about how it affected me and about Mary, my wife. She was so understanding and kissed me lightly on the cheek when I was leaving.

After that, I began flirting with her and she really got into our little verbal trysting. We became *very* friendly in a relatively short period of time, and I began to daydream of whisking her away to somewhere we would never be discovered. My promotion came through on Monday, April 4, and that Saturday, the Prioleaus threw a gala ball in my honor to celebrate. I had a brand-new uniform coat and pants tailored for the occasion and arrived looking dashing. The party was full of influential people, Liverpool City officials, wealthy merchants, and leaders of various organizations such as the Southern Independence Organization and the Organization for the Cessation of Hostilities in America, hoping to gain members or donations.

Of all the ladies present, Mary Prioleau was the most lovely in a pale-blue silk gown that, with dark-blue ribbons, set off her eyes and complexion perfectly. Toward the end of the evening, I finally made it onto her dance card, although we had exchanged pleasantries on a couple of occasions earlier. Charles Prioleau had retired to his study much earlier to conduct business with some of the other guests as was his custom.

We began a waltz, and Mary was a bit closer than necessary, spinning through our rotations. The fabric of her dress was thin and smooth; I could feel her hip with my fingertips through the material, and her perfume was something amazing. When I looked down at her, I could see quite far down the décolletage between her creamy white breasts, and the breath caught in my throat with a little hoarse gasp. I began to get aroused. I'm very sure my eyes were getting a glazed look, and she returned that with a look of amusement. I leaned in and whispered, "Run away with me," in a husky voice.

She stopped dancing but, in a smooth motion, took me by the hand and led me over to an empty corner by the crystal punchbowl. Once there, she looked at me angrily, and I immediately realized my mistake.

"John," she said in a scathing voice. "It's my job to be friendly with you, get your allegiance, and continue to assess whether or not you are capable of stealing from us. There is a lot of money involved. I do consider you a friend, however, to both my husband and I.

"And I know you are smart," she continued. "You couldn't possibly believe I would give all this up," she waved her arm around for emphasis, "and my millionaire husband for a jaunt to some nowhere hiding spot?"

"Of course not," I asserted, trying to hide my pout. So I gave her a wicked grin and said, "It would have been a tropical paradise, not just a nowhere hiding spot."

She gave me a speculative look like she didn't know whether to believe me or not, so I said, "Besides I'm not going to apologize. That perfume you're wearing, ma'am, is enough to make the devil himself pliable in your hands."

She assessed me, her expression lightening, and said, "Then it serves its purpose."

She walked away and left me standing there, so I did what any normal man would do—got drunk and staggered toward home. I woke the next morning on a doorstep to a lady beating me with a broom so she could get her children out of the house for church.

If I had hoped the incident with Mary Prioleau would be kept secret, I was sorely disappointed. On Tuesday, Bulloch called me into his office and informed me that I was being transferred to Montreal in British North America to work for Jacob Thompson.

I arrived at Montreal in May and as instructed, checked into the St. Lawrence Hall Hotel on Rue St. Jacques uptown. I initially thought I was being punished by being sent to a backwater station. I soon found it was a marvelous place, a five-story white brick facade with gabled roof, rotunda clock tower on top, and the equivalent or better of any of the New York City hotels in the finery of the décor, cuisine, and service. Montreal was not the size of New York or even Baltimore, but it was the center of business and industry in Canada. Rue St. Jacques was in the prime location of the uptown business district, and the hotel was situated directly across from the post office and the French Cathedral. Anyone who was somebody could be found having dinner or supper in the grand hall restaurant, and wedding receptions of the affluent were a consistent fixture of the banquet rooms on the main floor. In addition to the features of the hotel, upscale retail establishments occupied rental space on the ground floor with access both from the interior of the hotel and having frontage on the street.

When checking in, I left a note to be delivered to Jacob Thompson, then adjourned to my fourth-floor room to settle in and wait for further instructions. It would be useful to digress at this point and describe how things worked. In British North America, the Confederate Secret Service achieved its true form with a constant stream of schemes being plotted and carried out by many operatives.

Jacob Thompson, the ostensible head of things, worked directly for and reported directly to Judah Benjamin, the Confederate Secretary of State and, by proxy, Jefferson Davis. Thompson was an intellectual and controlling personality, his background was in economics, journalism, and law—or government in general. He had been a congressman in the past. Nothing that happened in the Canadian area of operations escaped his attention or happened without his approval, no matter what evidence (or lack thereof) came to light later. He was assisted by an enigmatic man, George Sanders. Saunders was a cold and ruthless character, skilled in anarchy and the ideology of terror warfare, organizing bombings, assassination, and destructive raids. These two men insulated themselves using a set of operatives who were called handlers. These handlers were selected specifically to not be directly associated with command at the top and were assigned specific operations, running them only through one team leader on the ground. That way, the connection could be severed at either of two levels in the event of awkward legal ramifications. At times, the handlers met each other but no information was shared between them; only Thompson and Saunders saw the bigger picture. Looking back, these men already knew, by the time I started working for them, that the war could not be won, that only a fortuitous series of events could salvage a peace that would allow the Confederacy to have a continued existence. I worked first as a courier, then as a handler.

Laterally providing logistical support was Clement Clay. Technically Clay worked for Secretary of War, James Seddon, but he was an ex-judge, legal expert, and a whiz at supply logistics. Clay's clerk, Bill Cleary, assisted with legal research but more importantly was the man who could grease the wheels of the British legal system in Canada. I once heard that there were two million dollars in gold deposited in a Canadian account for operational expenses, and I know from experience they were drawing from the Frasier, Trenholm & Co. accounts as well. Gives one a decent idea of the importance the Confederacy placed on our operations. It is also important to know that Thompson and Clay detested each other, even when cooperating on projects to achieve like goals.

About an hour later, I was beginning to doze off when there was a sharp rap on my door. I answered to see a man in hotel uniform who told me, "Compliments, sir, Mr. Thompson sends his regards and asks if you would join him in the dining room."

I quickly combed my hair and brushed my suit, grabbed my dispatch bag, and skipped down the stairs to the ground floor. At the entrance to the dining area, I was met by the maître d' asking for my reservation. He pretty much looked down his nose at me, although I was decently dressed. Or so I thought. "I'm meeting with Mr. Jacob Thompson," I declared.

"Hmmm," he said as if not amused. "Follow me."

He led me through the diners to a table by the wall where a well-dressed man waited. He was short, balding, and bearded. I had expected Thompson to be taller and a little older, so I said, "I'm afraid there's been some mistake, if you'll excuse me!" I turned to walk away when a hard-looking man jumped up from a nearby table and blocked my way.

"It's Carlile, I'd know him anywhere," he said.

I instinctively pulled a chair out between us, then recognized the man. "Patrick Martin," I said cautiously. He was a competitor from the old days in Baltimore.

Then a third man stood from the table to my left, held out his hand, and said in an authoritative voice, "Dr. Carlile, I'm Jacob Thompson. Pleasure to make your acquaintance." He turned to the other two men and said, "Beverley, Patrick, thanks for your assistance." Then back to me again as the other two men walked away. "Sorry about the shenanigans, but one must always be careful. Won't you sit down?"

This was the man I was expecting. Taller, fifty-five-ish, impeccably dressed in a dinner jacket with a trim goatee. I sat opposite him, he turned to a hovering waiter and said, "Two scotches, my usual." The man left to do his bidding, and he leaned forward and told me, "Under the table, you'll see another bag. Put yours next to it, then take mine when you leave."

Our drinks came, the scotch was quite good and I said so. He was all business and said, "You'll be leaving tomorrow morning on *Sea Star*, do you know her?" He was referring to Patrick Martin's barque-rigged ship.

"Yes, sir," was my reply.

"Good, he'll have more information on your route for you. Deliver the bag only to Judah Benjamin, do you understand?"

Once again, I felt that just a, "Yes, sir" was appropriate.

Thompson picked up a newspaper that he had set off to his left and resumed reading. I took this to be my dismissal, so I made the bag switch and stood to go.

Thompson looked at me over the top of the paper and added, "Oh and by the way, Dr. Carlile. Next time, proper dinner attire would be more appropriate in this venue."

*****

We remained well out to sea past Cape Henry as we sailed south in *Sea Star* to avoid any contact with the Union naval patrols. I had asked Captain Martin how he was planning to get me past the Yankee blockade into Virginia. He told me, "I'm not. I'm sailing with a cargo for Nassau." All said with a smirk. Any further questions I had for him were stonewalled. He finally told me, "Look, when you were in the trade, you had your secrets, well, I have mine."

On the evening of the eighteenth, I was told to make ready for departure; and shortly after dark, we began to exchange lantern flashes with another vessel. Soon thereafter, we hove to and were approached by a small racing schooner of something like twenty-five feet. I swung down into her, settling down into the cockpit with my bags, and a case of something unknown landed at my feet as well. My astonishment at seeing such a small craft so far out was followed by a crazy ride, full sails set in the pitch-black with each wave crashing over the bow. I swear we topped fifteen knots at one point, and a couple of the bigger crests almost caused us to founder. I was definitely cold, wet, and a little scared—the fear that happens when you have absolutely no control over your surroundings. In addition, in spite of having my sea legs, the crazy spinning, raising, and dropping caused that feeling to start back in my throat, telling me my last meal would soon be regurgitated. I kept swallowing, hoping that would help.

About then though, the sea began to calm and the wind to die off as we approached the coastline and I began to get a sense of the horizon around me. The turmoil in my stomach started to ease off as well, but it was replaced by a feeling of exhaustion, I was only just able to start taking in the current scheme of things. I was glad to be spared the embarrassment of looking like the sea had any effect at all on me, so I set about looking amused at the circumstances aboard the boat. The skipper was at the stern post, a firm grip on the tiller. I could not make out his features, the hood on his tarpaulin coat was pulled down, but he was slightly built, almost like a girl. His crewman was a different matter. He was loosely tied off, just forward of the mast, and was a big square-faced fellow with a shock of blond hair blowing loose in the wind. This pair must have been sailing together for a while, words were not necessary to get the job done.

The horizon was getting light behind us when we rounded Grommet Island into the lake behind it. We made our way south into Owls Creek. We were almost at the west shore on a back channel, in the middle of a marsh, before I saw an old stone pier sticking out into the water; at a slightly-deeper place, we glided right up and tied off. As I stepped off, a black man appeared holding a fine-looking chestnut horse, saddled and ready to go.

"Suh," he said. "Take the trail to the top of the hill, you'll see the Kempsville road."

I turned and thanked the skipper; now that his coat was down, I could see he was just a kid of about sixteen. "Quite the location you have here, hard to find."

He grinned in amusement and said, "It was built by Blackbeard, the pirate, a hundert an' fifty years ago, it was meant to be hard to find."

I mounted and made my way cautiously up the hill, turning right onto the road, then let the animal have its head. He obliged me by breaking immediately into a trot.

28

Richmond was depressing, so many hungry and ragged-looking people in the streets. Everywhere you looked there were wounded soldiers in stages of recovery, but many of these were on crutches, missing limbs. I knew from experience that arm and leg wounds made up the majority of battlefield causalities and if a bone was damaged, amputation was really the only safe recourse. Most were also just boys; their disabilities would wreck their chances at a useful future.

Returning to Montreal was so much simpler than my sea voyage to Virginia. I was paired with another courier, John Surratt, and we took the old road through Bowling Green to Port Royal to avoid the clash ongoing between Lee and Grant at Spotsylvania Courthouse in the wilderness. I had an itch to visit my wife's grave when we rode through but decided better of it. We passed several Confederate cavalry check points before crossing the Rappahannock, after which we saw nothing of either army. We rowed across the Potomac narrows into Maryland. At Morgantown, Surratt introduced me to a group of men who routinely made the boat crossing on behalf of our service. We picked up new horses on the Maryland side and finished the night at my old friend Sam Mudd's house in Carroll County. He laughed out loud when he saw it was me. After breakfast and a nap, we rode north, I parted with Surratt at his mother's tavern, south of Washington City, then I pushed hard and made it to Baltimore about sunset.

My father was actually glad to see me. We had supper, and I regaled the family with tales of my war activities, especially my duty aboard *Alabama*. She was a household word such was her fame. After the meal, my father and I adjourned to his office, and, over brandy and cigars, he became serious.

"So then, what are you doing here really?"

"On my way to Canada," I replied enigmatically.

"Montreal," he said flatly. My eyes narrowed and I sat up straight, this reaction just confirming it for him.

"They have you working for Thompson then," he said with just a hint of disapproval. "Be careful with him."

I hadn't realized my father was so well-informed, but I guess I shouldn't have been surprised.

"Been okay so far," I remarked. "I'm just a courier."

"Jacob Thompson is an old school politician, he would gut you and wear your skin if it suited him. He wouldn't even blink." He went on to say, "Look, son, I admire your position, but you have to look out for yourself too." Right now, you are a reb officer, not in uniform, behind enemy lines. That, to some people, makes you a traitor and a spy, lots of actions can be tolerated when made by a man in a uniform but not without it."

"Guess I have trouble swallowing having my rights taken away," I remarked in return.

He grunted at me then and said, "You always had trouble being told what to do."

We smoked in silence for a while, then he said, "Let me tell you about my Great-Uncle Abraham. He was an influential man in Philadelphia, helped to fund and build the Carpenter's Hall. He was a man of principles, a Quaker and a pacifist who refused to fight for either side. When the British took the town during the Revolution, they imposed on him to vet and issue passes through the lines, trusting that he knew the townspeople. He helped many of the poor get out of the city when they couldn't feed themselves and their children."

He took a last draw on his cigar at that point, then crushed it out and exhaled the smoke.

"When the British finally left and the Americans returned, there were some who coveted Abraham Carlile's property, so they accused him of being a traitor working for the Brits, and he was hanged in the public square." Many upright people objected to the hanging, but the fire-eaters had their way." A pause, then, "Even now, the fire-eaters always seem to get their way."

After our talk, I spent some time with my daughter in the drawing room until it was her bedtime. She was four now with dark hair and a gleam of mischief in her eye. She was an adorable walking talking bundle of questions in a little calico dress. I almost cried when she kissed me on the cheek goodnight before bouncing up the stairs.

The next morning, I bought a train ticket for Montreal without even a question asked. The hardest part of the remainder of my journey was having to rush my supper in Albany during the hour between connections. When I met with Thompson, I described how easy it was to travel around the country once I was behind the enemy lines. He told me to stand by, that he would have a new job for me on the morrow.

The following afternoon, there was a knock at my door and I opened it to admit Thompson and another man—intense, short and stout with wild hair and a forked beard that was streaked with white. Thompson introduced him as George Sanders, then sat back and let Sanders handle my briefing.

"To begin with," said Sanders, "I have some documents for you."

He opened his bag on my little hotel writing desk and began to look at some documents.

"You are now Dr. William Lierly, surgeon general's office with the War Department." He pulled out a paper with an official seal, detailing the commission. He then pulled out a single sheet, folded twice, and handed it to me. "Your orders."

I scanned the letter which ordered me to make an inspection of conditions at Camp Douglas, a prisoner of war facility in Chicago, to compile a report complete with recommendations. It was signed Joseph K. Barnes, Col., Asst. Adj. General.

"Is this real?" I asked.

"Real enough for your purposes," replied Sanders. "While there, I expect that you'll be able to draw a plan of the camp, figure out the security procedures, and locate any potential escape routes. Do you know Richard Semmes?"

"I have an uncle by that name, but I've never met him," I answered. "My Aunt Mary Eleanore's brother, I hear he lives in Chicago."

Sanders pulled out another letter, this one sealed.

"A letter of introduction. Your uncle belongs to an organization called the Sons of Liberty, the chapter in Chicago is run by a circuit court judge named Buckner Morris. You're to let Morris know we can provide him with arms and ammunition, but I expect you to make an assessment of his organization's ability to assist you with a large-scale prison break."

I grunted my assent that I understood the instructions, but Sanders waived that off and continued.

"After that, your Uncle Richard will provide you with a wagon and some basic supplies."

At this point, he pulled another document from his bag; this proved to be a sutler's license issued by the Military Department of the Ohio.

"This is issued to Gilbert Sawtell which is who you will become for the next leg of your trip. Your cover is you are heading south, taking a new load of goods to sell to the troops in Chattanooga. You must make it to Hillsborough on the twelfth of July and check in at the livery there. You'll be expected and will be taken to meet with Captain Clingman, a cavalry officer. You will coerce him to use his command to assist you at Camp Douglas, after which you will break the prisoners out, or, if not expedient, you will set a fortuitous date for the completion of this mission."

I pondered this for a second and couldn't help thinking about what my father had said but just asked the first question that came to mind. "How many prisoners?"

Sanders gave me that weasely little smile that I came to know so well and said, "About six thousand, but some of them won't be in any shape to leave." Even Thompson showed a little smile around his eyes. "Any questions?"

"Nope," I answered. "I'm sure I'll have to figure things out as I go."

I started to wrap my head around what it would look like, marching thousands of men across the Illinois countryside, escorted by a handful of cavalrymen. I wondered if these two had thought through some of the little things like how I was going to feed these men, not to mention organizing them for mobility or how we were going to handle any local militia. I had heard that there were no officers interred at Camp Douglas, but that was probably better. At least there would be no wrangling over who was in command, and the senior NCOs would actually be helpful. I finally decided that becoming boggled by logistics was not helpful either.

"One last thing," said Sanders. "Deal only with the leaders of your groups. Don't even let the others see you or as few and as little as possible. The fewer people that can identify you, the safer you'll be and the better chance of success you'll have."

In my mind, I was saying, *No, the safer* you'll *be.* But I kept my mouth shut.

I had a couple of days to kill before my ferry departed, so I determined that some prearranging needed doing if I were to succeed. First I configured some hiding places for my various papers, assuming I would look very guilty if I was stopped carrying documents in more than one name. To this end, I did two things: First I took my left boot and cut out a slot on the inside of the heel facing the arch. Thus hollowed, I tapped in a small shim so the entry was covered snugly but I could still pry it open with the tip of my knife. I covered the shim with boot black so it would pass any cursory inspection. In there, I secreted everything that would reveal my true identity. Second I altered my medical bag. Originally it was made with soft leather covering, a rectangle of hard thick hide on the bottom to provide shape and solidify the whole. This hard piece was doubled over on itself, then stitched through to have the softer finished fabric cover it both top and bottom. I opened the inside stitching and placed the identity papers for Gilbert Sawtell inside, along with the letter of introduction for Richard Semmes. I resewed this, figuring that although it would take a little time to retrieve these papers, that was the least of my worries, considering I carried a stitching kit in my bag anyway.

I then went out and bought a suit coat that was a bit too large in the middle. This did a much better job concealing my shoulder holster and, with a spare shirt folded around my stomach, made me appear somewhat overweight. I coupled this with a pair of round spectacles that were just regular glass and an out-of-style derby hat. The whole effect made me look like I'd spent far too much time in an office.

The ferry to Sainte-Catharines took almost three days, up the St. Lawrence River, then across the entire length of Lake Ontario. The train would have been faster, but I was told not to take the chance of traveling through Toronto; apparently the police there were run by something called the Orange Council, a group of affluent rabidly British loyalists intent on running the show in Upper Canada. The authorities were on a fairly constant state of alert due to rebellious workers who had a reform movement going and were above any ramifications regarding the level of force they were able to use. Pacification of the poor and the Catholics.

At Sainte-Catharines, I was met at the wharf by my contact, Jacques Bolanger, a small and slightly-built man with dark hair and dark features who had to have been part-native. He spoke just enough English to get by and that with a thick French accent. He led me to a stable where he had two horses already saddled. We mounted and rode south out of town. At first, Bolanger looked at me as if he was worried he would have to do a fair amount of babysitting. When he saw me mount and ride, he did a second appraisal and his mood lightened considerably.

It was getting toward dusk and we were approaching the village of Fort Erie when we turned right, off the good road, onto a track or, more accurately, a trail down the hill into the forest. This opened up onto a gravelly beach occupied by a tumble-down shack on a short pier that proved to be a boathouse. We tied the horses off on a log made for the purpose and headed for the structure. After opening a well-oiled padlock on a door that was much sturdier than appearances suggested, Jacques lit a lantern hung to a rafter as we were going through the entry. He closed the door behind us. I could see a small skiff moored in the water and a canoe upside down on the plank dock. The whole place smelled of fish and burnt metal. There was a workbench on the far side with a fair collection of woodworking tools and a couple of small boxes that I recognized as containing Colt sidearms. He gestured for me to help him get the canoe into the water, it was lightweight and seemed to be made from thick strips of bark fastened to a branch work frame, then tarred to make it waterproof. Once we had it in the water, I climbed into the front while

Jacques grabbed a pair of home-carved paddles then extinguished the light.

We pushed out into what was more of a lake than a river, it didn't take me long to figure out the rhythm of paddling the craft, and I was surprised at how fast we could make it move across the water. In less than an hour, we made it across to a large town. Jacques pulled us right up to a dock in the main harbor. I stepped up onto the pier, inside the river entry, and found myself in downtown Buffalo, New York, right in front of a building with a simple sign that read "WAREHOUSE." Bolanger tossed my bags up by my feet and, with a nod, pushed off and disappeared into the night. Not a soul was there to witness my arrival so far as I could tell.

Bolanger had left me right where Main Street meets the harbor, a dingy spot, but by following Main into the downtown area, I was soon out of the rough neighborhoods; and it was just over a half-mile to my destination—the American Hotel up by Lafayette Square. The hotel was a big square brick fortress-looking five-story building occupying the center of the block but once inside was far less forbidding with tapestries and plush carpeting. I got a room for the night then settled in for a good night's sleep.

In the morning, I went down to Erie Station and purchased a ticket for Chicago. I also bought a newspaper. I was pleased to see that the editorials were unsympathetic to the Yankee war effort. General Grant's Virginia campaign seemed to be meeting the same fate as the other Union generals' efforts had. He had been thwarted by Lee in the Wilderness, had shifted to the east, but once again, Lee had anticipated his move and had beat him to Spotsylvania Courthouse. The casualty lists were seemingly endless, but still, Grant had not retired as the other generals had before him and was apparently shifting east again toward the area around Gaines Mill which had been fought over in 1862. This was, of course, very near to where I had lived with my wife in the good old days. There was a lot of grumbling about the slaughter in the eastern theater and the lack of progress in the West.

I returned to my hotel and had dinner before checking out, returned to the train station, and caught the afternoon westbound for Chicago. I should have known better and spent the money to get a room in the sleeper car for a two-day trip with stops. As it was, I felt pretty disheveled by the time we transferred over to the Illinois Central Rail line that took us into the city. Sleeping on the hard wooden bench seat didn't help. It was the afternoon of Friday, the tenth of June, when I arrived. I had planned this so that it would be difficult for them to get any answers or confirmation of my mission from the War Department. Two o'clock in Chicago was three o'clock in Washington, and anyone in the upper echelon would be leaving the office for their weekend. I knew I would still have to think fast on my feet to make things work.

I was amazed to find that Camp Douglas had its own train station across the street on the north side of the compound. Stepping down off the train car, my senses were immediately assaulted by the place. Whereas there had been a bit of a foul smell when we were approaching, the second I stepped through the train car door, there was an overpowering stench of sewer, rotting garbage, and death that made it difficult to breathe. I pulled out my handkerchief and held it to my face to make it more palatable and was lucky I did so, for when I stepped down from the car, I was hit by a swirling stiff breeze that contained sand particles which stung the skin and got into my eyes in spite of my fake glasses.

I gingerly crossed the street which still contained slick almost-hardened mud and approached the post gate which was manned by two sentries with faces wrapped and wearing goggles. There was a small guardhouse just behind the gate that I assumed was used for relief from the elements. I believe that my appearance and demeanor—mussed up, hat pulled low, handkerchief over my face, tears streaming down my cheeks, and generally in a foul mood— actually went a long way toward supporting my cover story.

I went up to the closest soldier, a thin pimply-faced youth who was slouching against the gate post. I assumed he was state militia; he didn't even make a pretense of coming to attention when I approached.

"Dr. Lierly from the surgeon general's office, I'm here for a camp inspection," I announced, not bothering to pull out any documents as yet.

The boy soldier didn't move, just looked at me through his goggles which made his eyes look buggy. In a nasally voice, he called out, "Sarge!" It would have been funny if I wasn't already grouchy.

There was some rustling and bumping from inside the guardhouse, a scraping of a chair against a floor, then after a pause of maybe twenty seconds, the door to the building flew open, a somewhat unshaven face poked out and growled, "What!"

"Guy from th' gov'mnt here," the kid responded. I was waiting for him to pull out a straw to chew on.

The face looked me over and sighed. "Send him in," he said resignedly.

The sergeant proved to be a talkative fellow. While he examined my orders and identification, he let me know a few crucial details. He told me that there had just been an inspection from a Colonel Marsh of the inspector general's office in April and that they had been working on correcting identified deficiencies. After dispatching a runner to the camp headquarters, he also informed me that although his militia regiment provided general security for the camp, a battalion from the Invalid Corps were the detail that actually guarded the prisoners. I started adding numbers in my head.

The runner came back, and I headed south with him as an escort, then around the corner into a parade ground area. It wasn't too difficult to make out the functions of the buildings surrounding the square, the headquarters offices, post office on the east side, officers' quarters to the west and some kind of guardhouse to the south, beyond which was another square surrounded by rows of barracks, and a small hospital further south. To the southeast were barracks buildings that were to house the prisoners.

I climbed the steps and was glad to be inside once more. I was shown into an office directly across the central hall, an officer with captain's bars on his shoulders stood and came around the desk, supported by a cane. He held out his other hand to shake mine and announced himself as Captain Thomas, then inquired about my business. I could see immediately he was not a militia officer and his cane was no doubt due to some combat service. I determined to make an ally of him.

"Dr. Lierly with the surgeon general's office on behalf of the inspector general," I announced while shaking, then pulled out my orders and identification and set them on his desk. "I'm here to follow up on the recommendations made by Colonel Marsh from his April visit, could you direct me to Colonel Sweet, the commandant of this facility so I can get this ball rolling?"

From behind me, I heard a voice boom out, "Colonel Sweet is not here right now and doesn't need to see you. *Lieutenant* Colonel Marsh provided us with *recommendations.* Furthermore, doctor, we've made all the changes necessary and don't require your services."

I saw Captain Thomas roll his eyes, so I smiled at him with my eyes then spun directly around to face another army captain, this one of medium height, dark hair, and sporting a bushy black beard and mustache thick enough to cover the majority of his mouth. Softly, but with venom, I said, "I'm a doctor in this role, but if you bother to look, you'll find that I also hold a commission as a commander in the United States Navy which is roughly equivalent to a major in the army. In the future, I would prefer to be addressed as sir, *captain.*"

He did not like that, but it did cause him to back up a step.

I continued, "If Colonel Sweet is unfortunately away, does that mean that you are commanding this little post in his absence?"

"No...sir," he admitted, adding the sir after a slight pause. He looked over my shoulder, at Thomas, who apparently silently confirmed that my documents were in order.

"Then," I said, "If you would run along and fetch whoever is currently in charge, *captain.*"

He gave me a look as if he suddenly found he had a turd in his mouth, started to say something but changed his mind, then spun on his heel and stomped down the hall, yelling for an orderly. I turned back to Captain Thomas who told me, "That's Sponable, he's the colonel's pet and in charge of the camp patrols. Used to be with the Thirty-Fourth New York and has some stories about his combat experience, but mostly, I think his unit was once run off by some Virginia home guard unit when they were stealing horses."

I chuckled at that, but Thomas added, "Do be careful around him, he can be a problem and he does have Colonel Sweet's ear."

"Captain Thomas, you are the officer of the day?" I asked.

He nodded in the affirmative, so I continued, "Could you arrange an escort tomorrow for me to check out the hospital, prisoner barracks, and solitary confinement areas? I'd like to be done by Monday afternoon, so I can complete a report on my observations on the return train to Washington."

"Certainly, sir," he responded. "I'll have you ready to go at 0800 hours, will that do?"

My turn to nod in the affirmative.

He offered to set me up with a room in the officer's quarters on the post, but I declined, stating a desire not to put anyone out. Silently I wondered how anyone could stand being posted there.

As we were finishing, an older man, with oak leaves on his shoulder boards, walked in and introduced himself as Major Joiner, told me something like 122nd Michigan. I shook his hand, commended Captain Thomas for his problem-solving skill, then left the post on my own without waiting for an escort. I took a commuter train from the Camp Douglas uptown to Central Station, then got a hack to the Tremont House Hotel on the corner of Lake and Dearborn Streets. After checking in, I went out and located a newspaper stand, purchasing a copy of the *1863 Chicago Directory*. It was pushing seven in the evening by then, and I figured Richard Semmes would be home from work, so I hired another hack to take me to the address I got from the directory, being careful to have him let me off at the corner market down the street.

I walked up to the door of a small house in a pleasant neighborhood and knocked on the door. The man who answered was undoubtedly the one I was looking for—he had the same sharp features as his siblings that I knew and had the same goatee and mustaches as Raphael Semmes although going gray as he was a little older. When I presented the letter of introduction, he even stroked his goatee, just like his brother, as he was reading.

He looked at me and inquired, "You are Mary Eleanore's..."

"Nephew," I finished his sentence.

He invited me in and told me I had come on an admirable evening, that the Sons of Liberty were holding a meeting that night. We had soup and fresh bread while we talked.

"They even included a hundred dollars to get you set up with horse and wagon," he said in an amazed tone. "You must be here for something important."

I explained that my superiors wanted a feasibility study for a prison break from Camp Douglas and that being a doctor, I was the best candidate for the job. I also told him that in my opinion, moving a couple of thousand released prisoners cross-country was a monumentally far-fetched scheme.

"Ah, Buckner Morris's idea," he replied.

"The judge?" I asked.

"He's not a judge anymore, just a post office supervisor. He was mayor of Chicago for a couple of years a while back before his stint as a circuit court judge, and I think he wants to be back in the limelight. Son, you'll find that most of us just want an end to the war with reunification of the country. The abolitionists and President Lincoln's administration make that scenario impossible."

I mused on that thought for a second then remarked, "Lincoln's policies are surely contrary to the freedoms we get in the constitution, and that is a big piece of the issue. But I'm doubtful that the Confederacy will consider rejoining the Union of its own volition. Too much water under that bridge and specifically too many casualties."

"I hope you're wrong on that account," he said. "But speaking of casualties, have you seen the latest from Cold Harbor?"

I knew of Cold Harbor from having lived close by. It was not a river port or anything like that, just a crossroads with an inn that did not serve hot meals—hence Cold Harbor. It started out as kind of a joke, but the name stuck.

"What happened there?" I queried.

"General Grant tried to plow through Lee's defensive positions again," he said. "They are saying that in one assault, he lost seven thousand men in less than a half-hour. To top it off, he would not arrange a truce to retrieve his wounded, many of them died as a result. Rumor is that soldiers were pinning their names on their uniforms before charging so their corpses could be identified. I think that you'll be well-received by the Sons of Liberty tonight, even though Illinois regiments are all in Sherman's army, none with Grant."

He locked up, and we walked the mile or so to the Masonic Hall where the meeting was to take place. A beefy-looking man at the door was screening visitors, and he questioned my identity.

"My nephew, Dr. Lierly from Washington, who is interested in our cause," Semmes said.

The man gave me a doubtful look but admitted me on Semmes's say-so. We proceeded up the stairs and to a door on the left which opened to a banquet room that was set up like a lecture hall. In the front was a podium, flanked on both sides by tables with chairs behind them, all of this decked out in flag-style bunting. A dozen rows of chairs faced this with an aisle in the center, in the back were more tables with punch bowls and bakery goods set out. There were about a hundred people in the room, almost entirely men but one woman who stood out and appeared to have some status with the others, judging by the knot of men standing around trying to get a word in with her.

Richard Semmes introduced me to two men, Wilbur Storey, who was the editor of the *Chicago Times*, and Charles Walsh, the leader of the chapter, although I didn't catch his occupation. The meeting was brought to order by Walsh, and we took a seat toward the back. After chapter business and some impassioned speeches, mostly regarding getting a favorable candidate to run against Lincoln in the upcoming election, the meeting began to wind down. At that point, Semmes stood and introduced me to the group.

"William Lierly with the surgeon general's office," I announced. "I'm visiting to look at conditions at Camp Douglas."

I saw the woman turn her head sharply to get a look at me before I sat back down, a stir of sidebar conversation erupted from the rest of the audience before Walsh brought the meeting back to order. When the meeting ended, several members went out of their way to shake my hand, most letting me know what an abysmal place Camp Douglas was and citing that thousands of prisoners had died there over the past two years due to the unsanitary conditions.

Then the woman came up to me and grabbed my hand. She brought what was undoubtedly her husband with her. Semmes introduced them as Judge Morris and his wife, Maribeth. The judge was older, thin and gangling with a shock of white hair and a protruding chin. Maribeth, from afar, had looked to be about midthirties and seemed familiar. Up close, she looked to be a little older than that, although still a striking-looking woman with curly blond hair and blue eyes that contrasted with her black formal dress. She had an interesting pin made from a midfifties copper large cent, just the liberty head cut out. I also realized what seemed so familiar, she bore a resemblance to Eugene Parrish, my old roommate from school. At least her face did. The rest of her proportions were quite different.

We spoke of trivia until the other members began to thin out, and once we were somewhat alone, Semmes prompted me that I could speak more freely with these people. I looked at Buckner Morris and said, "Your plan to free the prisoners at Camp Douglas came to the attention of my superiors."

"Your superiors being...." Morris responded.

"I'm really an officer in the Confederate States Navy," I stated.

Now this information made Maribeth Morris excited, she could barely contain herself. "You must come to supper at our home tomorrow night, Dr. Lierly!" she exclaimed.

"Now, Maribeth," the judge started.

"No, Buckner," Maribeth said. "Something needs to be done about our situation, you've made no progress."

"We must be careful," the judge began again.

At this point, I broke in and said, "I'll be there at six. In the meantime, you can decide if I can be helpful to whatever situation you find yourselves in."

After a pause, Buckner Morris said, "Seems fair enough. Some of our country's best men are imprisoned at Camp Douglas. Were they to escape, they would send the Michigan militia to hell in a handbasket."

I asked Maribeth Morris about her unique pin to which she replied, "The Republicans call us Copperheads to be nasty, but we've embraced the term. We cut out the heads of copper pennies and make pins out of them to make the point."

The crowd continued to thin out, so Semmes and I took our leave. At the door downstairs, I asked him how quickly he could have the horse and wagon ready. He told me, "Monday morning."

We said our goodbyes there, and I slipped out, heading back to my hotel with my coat collar up. There were too many people hanging out in the shadows around the hall for my taste, and I didn't necessarily want to become associated with the group.

When I returned to the hotel, I found my precautions useless. There was already a man sitting in the lobby, reading a newspaper, who eyed me when I entered, then checked his watch. He might as well have had a placard in his hand that read, "Watching Dr. Lierly."

30

The next morning, I returned to Camp Douglas at eight, as promised, and sure enough, Captain Thomas had a guide arranged. This turned out to be a corporal named Gillespie; no one ever told me his first name and no one ever said it. He was just Corporal Gillespie. I had a strict itinerary to fit my schedule best, hospital and solitary facilities on Saturday, then prisoner barracks on Sunday. That way, if there were any snitches among prisoners that got wind of what I was up to, I would be gone before the news got relayed to the guards. In any case, they would be expecting me back to finish up on Monday and I would be on the road south in a different identity.

Corporal Gillespie turned out to be a quick study and knowledgeable about how the camp functioned. We donned face wraps and goggles and set off for the hospitals. It turned out, there were now two of them. I got a good deal of instruction from Gillespie; he told me that they never should have built the camp where it was. The location was low-laying and boggy to begin with, so the ground couldn't absorb the sewage from thousands of men and horses. They had installed two sewer lines, but there were no seals on the pipe connections so the waste ran as much out as in. Many of the prisoners didn't practice good hygiene and, especially during the cold season, didn't want to leave the relative warmth of the barracks in order to urinate. That, coupled with the sheer number of sick prisoners, left the whole place reeking of filth. Any high ground in the camp had been denuded of topsoil, and the underlying sand was then whipped up by the constant wind that Chicago was known for until the swirling air currents, laced with sand particles, raced through the facility.

The first hospital was the old one, and I could see it was the worse for wear. It contained seventy beds, all in an open format, with two aisles. I could see that the original attempt was to allow air flow, but now, that just meant that the smell of the camp added to the smell of the sick. This ward was reserved for the contagious sick including cholera, typhoid fever, smallpox, and dysentery. A check of their medical supplies showed them to be woefully inadequate in medicines and surgical utensils. What kits they had were rusty and caked in crusty blood. Gillespie told me the Confederate government had offered to send medicine to help but this offer had been refused. For me, this brought to mind all the supplies I had amassed for the Confederate OMS early in the war.

The second hospital was new, completed at the end of April, I was told. It contained two wards of 75 beds each, one ward for the guards and one for the prisoners. This facility was far better equipped, and I made a show of being more thorough in my inspection of the guards' ward than the prisoner wing. Once again, Gillespie, my tour guide, filled me in on the numbers. Seventy-five was adequate for the soldiers, the total detachment being about six hundred on the average. About two thousand prisoners were in need of medical care at any given time, a 125 beds were available. In my mind, the important fact was that if an escape was made, easily a couple of hundred armed soldiers would be available to give chase, even if they were militia that still made this a desperate venture that would require a decent-sized armed rear guard to keep the Yanks at bay long enough for the others to get away. I also noted that at least a quarter of the men would have to be left behind, too sick to move. In my notes, I was including a detailed map of the camp as I went.

We had a midday meal of hard meat and harder bread, but at least, the coffee was palatable. We visited the two punishment cells immediately after. The first cell was in the same square as the old hospital, located in a hole underneath the guardroom there. I looked in; it was about twelve by fifteen feet with one small window. The stench was so bad I couldn't bring myself to go down the ladder. There were about twenty men inside. When I questioned why so many, I was told there had been an escape attempt just over a week previously—the prisoners trying to rush the wall. The ringleaders had been identified and been given sixty days' confinement.

The second punishment cell was similar, only it was within the prisoner square. There was no structure on top and was completely covered, with the exception of two three-inch holes to allow air. Once again, I declined the opportunity to go in. Outside were some interesting punishment contraptions. In addition to the normal array of ball-and-chains, there was a bar suspended eight feet off the ground. I was told this was for suspending offenders by the thumbs so they had to stand on their toes. There were also contraptions that looked like sawhorses, only they were some four feet tall and the top board was honed to a sharp edge. These were affectionately known as mules, and I witnessed one man being made to ride one, he was trying hard to have his hands take the weight rather than his privates.

I checked the prisoners' water supply before leaving the area; there were twelve sinks which appeared adequate. Gillespie said this had been increased from one after Colonel Marsh had visited in April. When we returned to the headquarters building, I turned my goggles in to Gillespie and left, once again, without escort. I figured that Gillespie would need to report to Captain Thomas about the extent of my activities anyway and as I turned the corner toward the gate, I saw him run up the steps and enter the headquarters building. Word of my supposed identity and that I might just have a bad temper must have gotten around, the guards at the gate came to a clumsy present arms as a salute when I was walking through.

The intercity train got me back to Central Station at five in the afternoon. Instead of returning to my hotel, I walked past it then turned north across the river on the Rush Street bridge and into an older part of town. It wasn't too far to the Morris residence, and a maid answered my knock. She indicated that the judge was not home as yet but let me into the sitting room to wait. It wasn't two minutes before Maribeth Morris came in, this time, in a flower-embroidered calico dress which, I had to admit, suited her better than the black formal from the previous night.

"You are early, Dr. Lierly," she admonished me, her dress making a whooshing sound as she slipped into the chair across the table from me. "Supper isn't for another hour yet." Her tone was scolding, but the twinkle in her eye said otherwise.

"I got off work early," I replied. "And the mystery you alluded to last night had me wondering about it all day, ma'am." I guess I was wondering quite a bit more about her mystery than I alluded to.

"We must wait for my husband to bring you into that," she stated. "But tell me about you, Dick Semmes said you are a Confederate officer?"

"A lieutenant in the navy, ma'am, an aide to the secretary of the navy on special assignment," I said, rather exaggerating my status. I could see she was impressed. She began to lean in toward me.

"Have you seen any action?" She was positively purring.

"I was aboard the *Alabama*, then the *Tuscaloosa*." I could tell she had never heard of the *Tuscaloosa* but was definitely familiar with the *Alabama*.

I embarked on a sailor's yarn about the battle between *Alabama* and the USS *Hatteras* with myself in the leading role. I was up standing on the railing, directing the gun crews' fire without concern to my own safety when knocked off my feet by an exploding shell, luckily suffering only a minor wound. I called for us to cease firing when I saw their sailors abandoning ship, then in spite of my wound, I personally went out in the longboat, pulling Yankee sailors from the water, smacking marauding sharks away from them with just an oar. It was such a fun story by then that I included a tug-of-war with a shark on the end of my paddle and gave her just a small peek at the scar on my chest. I went on about the perils of war by describing, in graphic detail, treating the wounded sailors from the fight. By the time I was done, Maribeth Morris didn't need her whole chair, just the edge of the seat.

Then the front door opened and Buckner Morris came in with a bounce in his step. He was obviously spry in spite of his age. I glanced over at Maribeth, her reverie had been broken by his arrival and she was now back in her chair, but her cheeks were still a bit flushed. When Buckner saw us in the room, he came right in and extended his hand. I stood and took it, he didn't appear to notice his wife's agitation.

"Dr. Lierly," he exclaimed. "Didn't mean to keep you waiting!"

"Just arrived, sir," I replied. "And Mrs. Morris has been a most gracious hostess."

I gave a short bow in Maribeth's direction, she in turn gave me a curious little look that I couldn't quite decipher. Buckner Morris remained oblivious.

"I'll leave you gentlemen to talk," Maribeth announced. "I must check on Olivia and supper." She stood and sashayed out of the room in a rustle of calico.

"Please pardon my wife," said Buckner with a smile. "Olivia, our girl, is fully capable of running the entire household, but Mary insists on providing supervision.

"No apology necessary. Judge Morris, you were rather enigmatic last night regarding a matter I might be of assistance with—"

"After supper," he cut me off. "That can wait. Now, son, tell me how you came to hear of my scheme regarding the prisoners at Camp Douglas."

"I'm a naval officer, an aide to Secretary Mallory. But I'm also a doctor, so I was asked by Jacob Thompson to look into your plan to free the prisoners here, my cover is following up on a report to the US Adjutant General's Office."

"Ah yes, Thompson, that makes more sense," he said. "But, son, you're taking a huge risk."

"As are you, sir," was my answer.

"Hmmm, yes."

At that point, Olivia appeared and announced that supper was ready. We stood and I followed down the main hall then left into the dining room. It was set for just three; we waited while Maribeth came around the table to my right and sat demurely, then we both took our seats as well. What followed was a sumptuous meal of roast pork and new potatoes with a tart white wine. Even with my recent meals in fine hotels, this one was outstanding, and I remarked as such.

"Olivia is a great chef," said Maribeth, and we all toasted her abilities as she came in to clear the plates.

"You'll find Chicago is famous for meat, much of the country's supply is slaughtered and packed right here," added Buckner.

We followed the meal with a delightful apple pie and even if the apples had to have been canned, the exotic taste of cinnamon reminded me of childhood and home.

Once done, I saw Maribeth give Buckner a significant hard look; he sighed, pushed his chair back and stood.

"As much as I have a great bottle of French cognac that has need of some exploration, we should have our wits about us on this next part of our venture," he said. "If you would follow me, please."

I followed him into the kitchen, with Maribeth behind me, to a door with stairs beyond leading down to a basement. Although the house was gaslit, the basement was not, but I could see that the space was lit by a lantern and as soon as I started down the staircase, the unmistakable smell of human habitation hit my senses. When my eyes got below the level of the basement ceiling, I saw a group of men arrayed in defensive posture.

Maribeth pointed past me at the man in front and said into my ear, "Dr. Lierly, meet my cousin Corporal Henry Anderson of the First Kentucky Cavalry, Confederate. Henry, this is Dr. Lierly, a Confederate officer."

"What unit, sir?" Anderson asked suspiciously.

"Naval officer," I said. "Most recently aide to Secretary Mallory. Before that, aboard the CSS *Alabama*. I'm on a special assignment to evaluate springing prisoners from Camp Douglas." I counted that there were seven men there. "How did you men end up here?"

"We tunneled out a week ago," Anderson replied. "A bunch of other guys charged the fence for us as a diversion while we escaped through a tunnel we dug under the barracks."

"My brother George brought them here to me," Buckner added.

"Okay," I said, trying to think this turn of events through. "I've an errand to run, starting Monday, to see what support I can get for my mission, but then I'll be back." I turned to Buckner and asked, "Can you keep them safe for another week and does your group possess any arms and ammunition?"

Buckner hemmed and hawed for a couple of seconds but after a bump from his wife admitted that they had a small cache of rifles. He also said a member of the Sons of Liberty had offered a barn outside of town as a temporary refuge.

"What's your plan, sir?" Anderson asked me.

"From what I've seen so far, our best plan is to go east to Detroit, something just under three hundred miles. We could cross the river there into Canada or, worst case scenario, go further north above Lake St. Claire where it is more rural."

I gave Anderson a cursory once-over examination, looking at eyes, ears, throat, and chest, then started on the others.

"You men look pretty good, although a little malnourished, do you think you would be up for a trip like that?"

"They cut our rations last January," Anderson responded. "They said it was due to our government cutting rations for their POWs. But we'll make it," he said after a pause. "We've been well-treated since we got here, but Camp Douglas was a hellhole."

"Good," I said. "In the meantime, follow orders from Judge Morris until I return and try to keep in shape."

"Yes, sir," they all chimed in unison.

"How long were you at Camp Douglas?" I asked Henry Anderson.

"Eight months," he answered. "Me an' a couple of my boys were with some Tennessee cavalry at a place in Georgia called Leet's Tan Yard when we were attacked by Wilder's Brigade. It was right after we won at Chickamauga, we got pinned down right away, our Tennessee guys pulled out and left us there. Both my boys died in that camp. You know, every day, some of our boys die there," he said sadly.

"Get the men together," I said. "I want you to draw a map of the camp with as much detail as possible. That way, if we were to mount a raid to release the prisoners, we'll be as ready as we can be."

The formulation of my plan to save face on an ill-conceived mission was starting to take shape. When I left the Morris residence, it was already fully dark. I walked back to the river before I hailed a hack to drive me the short distance back to my hotel. I didn't want stray eyes connecting me back to the Morris home, and I didn't want anybody at the hotel wondering why I was walking around the city at night. As I went up the main staircase toward my room, I saw the same man with the newspaper from the previous day. He was running out the door to catch the hack driver before he left.

My first observation at the camp the next morning was the headcount, and this, in spite of looking at a sad rag-tag bunch of humanity, was an amusing affair. There were forty-two prisoner barracks, each housing approximately 175 prisoners but some 40 to 50 remained sick in bed in each barracks. The able men lined up outside in their assigned places, then the games began. While they were being counted, the prisoners used a number of gambits to fool the guards, switching places, leaving open places in the middle of their ranks or falling out of formation in desperate need of the latrine. Inside the barracks, among the sick, it was the same with healthy prisoners claiming sick then switching beds to alter the count. This did not appear to be random but rather a carefully scripted plan as when caught at it, punishment would follow. It was truly a lot like herding cats.

Just a rough calculation on my part put the prisoner population at well over seven thousand. My tour of several of the barracks showed them to be full of vermin: mice, rats, fleas, ticks, bedbugs, and other varmints. Even as early as June, swarms of flies covered the kitchen space and cooking utensils as well as any unfortunate sick man in his bed. Universally there were sections of floorboards rotten or missing, providing easy entry for rodents and most likely egress for those prisoners inclined toward extracurricular nighttime activities. I also noted that the northeast portion of the fence was not yet complete, the guards resorted to roughly-constructed chevaux de frise, along with an increased eyes-on guard presence to prevent escapes. There was a deadline painted on the dirt beyond which a prisoner would be shot, but the guards were nervous about this. Apparently there had been so many incidents in the past that orders had been put in place that any shooting event was subject to review by a board of officers.

Viewing these prisoners and the conditions they were forced to endure was heartbreaking, but I could not allow this to show on the surface of my demeanor. In fact, the best I could do was see if there was any possibility of feasibly breaking them out without having them be slaughtered in the attempt. General Grant was the person who insisted on cessation of prisoner exchanges. He knew that even if this meant his own soldiers would face even worse treatment, he could replace them where the Confederates could not. Grant was making statements like he would reinstate exchanges if the Confederates would exchange captured black soldiers, but the result was the same. Boys languished in prisoner of war camps being mistreated and dying. There was no chance in anyone's mind of the Confederate government allowing the exchange of escaped slaves back to the north. It violated every tenet of their belief system.

I toured fifteen of the forty-two barracks and even had Corporal Gillespie write down some names of those in particular need of medical care but generally refrained from conversation with the prisoners unless it came to methods of food preparation or hygiene. Then I proceeded on to view the camp latrine sinks and the water supply. The twelve pump heads were possibly the only feature of Camp Douglas that was adequate to supply the needs of the men, even if the water came in unfiltered from the lake.

On my return to the headquarters building in the afternoon, I thanked Gillespie and told him he had been a superior guide. I visited Major Joiner and let him know I would return in the morning to provide Colonel Sweet with a synopsis of my findings, but he would have to wait for my full report after it was submitted to the inspector general.

"Any hints for me, sir?" he inquired.

"Good news is that it would seem that most of your men treat the prisoners humanely which keeps the bad situation you find yourself in from being a whole lot worse. I will make every attempt to focus on the positives." If there is a positive aspect to hell, I completed the sentence in my thoughts.

"Certainly appreciate that," the major responded.

I told him that Corporal Gillespie did a great job as a guide but that just resulted in a "Hmmm" from Joiner; that in turn told me that Gillespie worked for Captain Thomas, not Joiner. I got a bit of a chill from that knowledge. Thomas was an experienced and capable officer. There was no way, if he was in charge of my visit, that he would not have sent a query to verify my identity and have the man I saw in my hotel follow me around. That's what I would have done, trust nobody. There was, after all, a war being fought.

I caught the intercity train back to Central Station and walked immediately back to the Tremont Hotel, not caring further for their opinion of my arrival in style. Opinions change with circumstance in any case. There was the man in the lobby, hat pulled low, and reading a newspaper that partially covered his face. So to get control of things, I went to the desk and checked for messages. There were none of course, but I made a loud show of my disappointment and quickly made for the front door, exiting, then about four shop windows down, I turned abruptly to the left and slipped into the alcove of a clothing shop door, pulled out my pipe, and waited. In less than thirty seconds, the man with the newspaper poked his head out of the hotel entrance and looked around but, being unable to locate me, started to walk in my direction. I tensed, preparing to confront him, but he stopped, apparently thought better of it, turned around, and went back inside. The shop I was in front of occupied space on the ground floor of the hotel, so I went inside.

No customers, perfect for my situation. The clerk at the counter was scrawny and balding, wearing thick glasses. I went directly up to him, pulling a silver dollar out of my pocket which I placed on the counter in front of him.

"I need a favor," I announced.

He looked at me warily but had trouble not looking at the dollar in front of him.

"There is a lady waiting for me in the hotel lobby that I would prefer not to meet. Her husband suspects we have been together, and

I think he has a pistol. Could you let me through into the hotel from your back entrance?"

Now his wary look had turned conspiratorial, he was seeing himself earning an extra dollar today.

"Of course, sir," he said, leading me toward the rear of the shop where a closed door occupied a spot on the back wall. He pulled a key out of his pocket, winked at me, and said, "This opens on the service corridor. If you go to the right, you'll find a staircase the maids use to change out the linen."

He unlocked the door and let me through, then started giving me some advice about women, but I just put my finger to my lips and made a shushing sound. I thanked him for saving my skin and slid through the door, turning right as he had suggested. I heard the door shut and the lock turn behind me as I made my way to the stairs.

I packed up my belongings then went out the backdoor into the alley behind without even checking out. I emerged onto the street around the corner from the main entrance and hailed a hack who seemed glad to get the fare. I had noticed a corner grocery two blocks from Richard Semmes's home during our walk on Friday night. I had the driver take me there. He looked curiously at my destination, but I said nothing when I paid and tipped him.

In the daylight, I could see the sign on the store said "Spezio's." I walked in and bought some hard peppermint candies for a penny to give the driver time to move along before I re-emerged on the street to make my way to Semmes's home. He was surprised to see me so early but said he had things moving along. We once again took a long stroll to our destination, this time, to the southwest until we were approaching the outskirts of town. The further we went in that direction, the stronger the smell of livestock. We finally emerged into an area full of pens, chutes, and barns with a smattering of fat cattle, pigs, horses, and freshly-sheared sheep to be seen in some of the enclosures.

We made our way to a barn about a quarter of a mile further down, knocked, and entered a side door. The structure was pretty normal as these things go—dim inside, a central aisle with stalls on either side, and stray hay everywhere—until we reached the center. Parked right there, in front of the open double doors, was a medium-sized wagon, the kind used more for a mobile kitchen. The front half, or more like three quarters, was covered, but the back section was made like a built-in cupboard. I was liking what I saw so far. There were voices echoing in the barn and as we went around the wagon, we came upon two men dressed in working clothes and Maribeth Morris, dressed in a riding habit, her blond hair tucked up into a small top hat adorned with a green ribbon. She was holding the reins of a tall black mare. A few stray hairs emphasized the line of her neck.

"Good afternoon, Mrs. Morris," I greeted her.

I think she was noticing the way I was noticing her athletic build, all tucked into the tight-fitting outfit.

She smiled and said, "Please, Dr. Lierly, it's Maribeth."

"And I am just Bill," I responded, holding her hand in mine by just the fingertips.

She handed the reins of her mount to one of the workmen.

"Come see what we have for you here," she said, getting a better grip on my hand and leading me over to one of the stalls.

Inside were two beautiful stocky gray mules.

"They are named Bobby and Suzy."

"You have a great eye for animals," I said then added "They are perfect for my purpose. I even think I can tell which one is Bobby and which is Suzy." Anyone who knows mules understands that the males are exceptionally well-endowed.

She laughed at that and said, "I'm from Kentucky, we pride ourselves on knowing good stock." She accompanied this with a look that included a twinkle of amusement in her eye. "I wish you success in your venture and return to us safely. I would love to hear more of your seagoing adventures."

"I'm in your debt, ma'am," I said gallantly.

"Maribeth," she reminded me, retrieved the reins from the workman, then swung right up into her saddle. She turned the horse to go then, looking over her shoulder, said, "Yes, you are." She dug her heels in and her horse took off at a run.

Richard Semmes gave me an appraising look and asked if I was good with the harness. I let him know that I was.

"Looks like I'll need to cultivate a relationship with the mules though."

He chuckled and said, "Yup, kinda like a marriage. Good luck!"

"I'll see you when I return," I said.

He left and the workmen went about their business, so I took stock of the provisions in the wagon. Semmes had thought of everything: there were provisions for about two weeks and plenty of water in a keg. In the cupboard, I found chewing and smoking tobacco, belt leather, whiskey, and other trade goods to support my cover, even a small bag of sutler's coins. He had included a straw mattress and a pile of blankets. I was going to be comfortable at least.

I added a bale of hay from the loft to my supplies, then turned to my new companions. I found some grain and a bowl, then slipped into their stall, putting the bowl down to occupy their attention. I brushed them both down and rubbed their ears and noses so they could get used to me but all the while watching carefully because mules are sneaky and like to bite. Seems we started things out friendly.

I removed the documents for Gilbert Sawtell from my medical bag and placed the ones for Dr. Lierly back in there, carefully res-titching it, then hiding the bag under the seat of the wagon in the toolbox before crawling into the back of the wagon and sleeping on the mattress. It was not bad, but I made a note to see if I could rig a hammock later. I was up before dawn, but at that time of the year, it started getting light enough to see well before the sun broke the horizon. It was cloudy and cool, good weather for a trip. I brought Suzy out first and got her into harness, then brought Bobby over. He was a little agitated and gave me a death-stare like I was trying to steal his girl. Still he was glad to assume his place even if he did keep tossing his head when I was trying to get the yoke on.

I got moving and took the Bloomington Road south. Bobby and Suzy had obviously been together for a while and worked well together as a team. We made fast progress, the road was wide and well-traveled. Most of the traffic at that time of the day was head-ing into the city instead of going out. In any case, nobody took any notice of me. As the miles rolled by, the prairie farmland gave way to green and rolling hills, just the hint of uplands in the haze of the distance. I made the town of Pontiac by sunset but continued through for an additional couple of miles before I found a nice turnout by a grove of trees. It had obviously been used previously as a stopover by travelers such as me. I unharnessed and hobbled my team, gave them grain before allowing them to graze on their own, and put out a bucket of water for them. I made a campfire stew and spent some useful time with two thick branches, a blanket, and some rope, rigging a nice hammock. I slept very nicely.

Tuesday dawned clear and looked to be hot later. I blew right on through Bloomington and continued on the road toward Springfield. We didn't make quite as good of time due to more frequent stops to rest and water the team, but Bobby and Suzy were troopers; they seemed to be restless to get to where we were going. At dusk, I called a halt at an inn on a slight rise overlooking a small town. It had turned cold and begun to spit rain. I was looking at the sky, and it seemed like a thunderstorm was moving in. I got the mules unharnessed and into the barn before the weather broke. I paid the boy there to feed and rub them down. I was soaked just running from the barn to the house but had a decent meal in front of the fire. It seemed the town was Lincoln, Illinois, and was named for the president who was a founder. The proprietress was a war widow, made a point of saying so; she kept up the conversation, telling me that President Lincoln had advised against naming the town for him, saying nothing good ever came from a place called Lincoln. I laughed but didn't give my opinion. I drastically revised that opinion later that evening when she came to visit me in my wagon. Far be it for me to deny a woman in need of comfort. Besides the hammock made the whole thing an interesting adventure. I was really glad I used sturdy rope to construct the thing. And had a sturdy wagon to attach it to. We spooned for a little while after, then she got up, planted a big kiss on my forehead, and left me to my thoughts. I have fond memories of the event, although I did notice I was missing some of my supply of chewing tobacco later on.

The next day, I was up early as usual. The boy helped me to harness my team. Before leaving, I pressed a quarter eagle gold coin into his hand. I was feeling some largesse lingering from the night before and figured the kid, who was eight or nine at the time, would have a tough road ahead if his dad wasn't coming home. The weather had resumed being mild, and I made excellent progress even though Springfield was a busy town. The road turned more due south after Woodside and became rougher as the surrounding terrain became hillier. Crossing creeks became more frequent and the bridges worse the further I went. Just before Shop Creek, my map indicated a road to the left that would be a short cut to Hillsborough and indeed I found it, but it looked pretty rough so I decided to stay on the main road and stopped for the night several miles north of Litchfield. I figured that I was less than twenty miles from my rendezvous in Hillsborough and ought to be able to make it there by midmorning with an early start.

The spot was nice and grassy with a copse of trees for shade and shelter. I got Bobby and Suzy unharnessed and hobbled, then built a fire, starting coffee and some supper. It was approaching fully dark when a wagon and team came rattling up the hill on the road. The driver seemed to hesitate, then seeing my campfire, turned off the road and pulled up next to my rig. He jumped down, stomped his feet to get the circulation going, and came on over to my fire and sat right down without asking. He held his hands out in front to appreciate the warmth of the flames.

"Coffee'll be done in a couple a minutes," I said with raised eyebrows. He was an older man with wild curly white hair but still looked solidly built. This was confirmed by his grip when he reached around the fire to offer his hand.

"Mordecai Morgan," he announced.

"Gilbert Sawtell," I responded.

That caught his attention, and he gave me a curious look.

"You don't look like any Sawtell I ever met. Where you from?"

"New York," I answered warily.

"City?"

"No, Buffalo." I gave him a death stare to make him shut up. "You want some coffee you'd best bring a cup."

That gave him pause for a second, then he laughed, jumped up, and went over to his wagon to retrieve a tin cup hanging from it. When he came back, I poured coffee and we both stared into the fire.

"Sorry for grilling you," he said. "But there's a load of Sawtells where I'm from, and Gilbert Sawtell runs a mercantile in town. Besides your accent's off, sounds mid-Atlantic."

"Where are you from," I asked him instead of listening to my inner voice and letting it drop.

"Wheeling."

"Want some supper?" I asked, trying to head off his suspicions.

"Had some in Litchfield on the way through," he said. "Got to get to my chores anyway," he said while standing and flicking the grounds from his cup into the fire.

I ate quickly while he was gone, then crawled into my wagon to keep from having to deal with the man further. Besides I hadn't slept a whole lot the night before.

I got up before daylight the next morning to try to avoid further conversation with the man but was out of luck. He came up from behind me while I was harnessing the team and again started questioning me. When I turned around to look at him, Bobby bit me in the back of my arm, right in the middle of the triceps. I jumped about a foot and yelled out a curse in frustration and pain. Mordecai Morgan busted out laughing and slapped his leg repeatedly. I was sorely tempted to pull out my pistol and aim right between his eyes. Instead I started yelling at him.

"What's your damned problem, mister! I'm not bothering you, why are you bothering me?"

He appraised me for a second before responding.

"There's been a bunch of trouble in the hills around here lately, and you're sure not what you appear to be. Makes me wonder who or what you really are. Your clothes aren't right, your wagon isn't right, you've got a real expensive team of mules there. Hell, you're sleepin' in a hammock like a sailor. Are you stealin' stuff or are you a carpetbagger headin' south to buy up cotton or confiscated property for cheap?"

Well, at that point I let my coat open far enough so he could see the butt of my pistol. He laughed and opened his own coat to display a sawed-off shotgun converted into a pistol.

I spun around to Bobby and Suzy, who were starting to get agitated with just standing there in harness, and said, "Mind your own damned business, if you have a problem take it up with the sheriff."

"Oh, I intend to," he snarled.

I stepped up onto the wagon box and smacked the reins, we jolted off to a start then turned onto the road heading south. The sun was just peeking over the hills in the east, and the countryside looked surreal in the light.

"I intend to!" I heard him yell after me.

"Tell him he can find me in St. Louis!" I yelled back at him and broke the mules into a trot down the hill toward Litchfield. I didn't let up on the animals until we had covered a mile or so. Besides I was still irate with Bobby for nipping me.

I made it to Litchfield while constantly looking over my shoulder, expecting any minute for a cavalry troop to appear to apprehend me. When I took the turn east toward Hillsborough, I held my breath, expecting every second for an alarm to be sounded. I was thinking I was in a fix and stood out like a sore thumb, but the truth was there was a fair amount of traffic and nobody even took notice of me except a skinny stray dog that felt an urge to harass Bobby. In my current mood, I was rooting for the dog.

Hillsborough was not far, and I rolled into town just after eleven. I sighted the livery two doors down from the general store and pulled over in front. A boy came out immediately and asked if I needed my team and wagon put up. I thanked him and told him not yet, that I was here to see a man about a horse, the code I had been given.

"Okay, mister," he said and disappeared inside.

Immediately a man stepped out and looked me over.

"Sawtell?" he asked.

"Yup."

"I'll take you where you're going."

He disappeared inside but reappeared mounted in a matter of seconds. We moved out of town to the north and east, it was only a few miles before we started into the hills, the farms around looking less prosperous the farther out we went. In the uplands, the road narrowed and entered the woods, a fact I was glad of since the day was becoming hot and the shade was appreciated. I tried a couple of times to initiate some conversation with my guide, but if I got an answer at all, it was one word. We were following the west side of a waterway called Shoal Creek; but after about two hours, we came to a side road which we took to the right that immediately went down to a ford in the stream. I was a little nervous about the crossing as I was a less-than-experienced driver, but Bobby and Suzy were old hands, doing the work with little assistance from me. After we were safely across, Bobby turned his head all the way around to look at me. I swear he called me an idiot.

After several miles up this rough road, we took another right turn onto a side road in the middle of a small prairie, an old broken-down shack marked the spot. We entered what looked at first to be a canyon but turned out to be an abandoned limestone quarry, three or four tumble-down buildings on a wide ledge, and a pond that had filled up the old stone workings. Close to a dozen horses were sequestered in a makeshift corral behind the buildings. When coming through the entrance, my guide nodded to a man with a carbine lounging against a tree. As I rolled to a stop in front of the first building, a man emerged while putting a hat on his head.

I was startled by his appearance, gray coat with yellow cuffs and collar, gold single-sleeve piping of a junior officer. Three gold collar stripes identified his rank. Gray trousers with yellow side stripe, saber and pistol in a holster, along with cavalry gloves on his belt that almost covered his CSA embossed buckle. But the most amazing thing was the hat, wide-brimmed and adorned with a large white ostrich feather. It made him look like a cavalier from bygone days. He nodded to my guide as he stepped down from the porch and said, "Thank you, sheriff."

My guide touched two fingers to his hat and abruptly turned and rode off in the direction we had come from.

The captain turned back to me and said, "Mr. Sawtell, I presume."

He held out his hand, forcing me to jump down from my seat to shake it.

"Captain Thomas Clingman, I presume," I responded.

Clingman looked back over his shoulder and called out, "Gillette!"

A rough-looking man, with a revolver in his hand, appeared from the door onto the porch.

"Yes, sir," he responded.

"Please take Mr. Sawtell into custody while we search his wagon."

I started to protest, but the man, Gillette, stepped up, pointed his pistol at my head, and cocked back the hammer.

Clingman poked around the outside while yet another man, this one skinny and bearded, began rifling through my wagon and belongings. I watched, fuming, while he filled his pockets with my tobacco then handed my whiskey bottles down to Clingman who stacked them by the porch.

"We got us our very own supply wagon, cap'n," he said, gloating.

Then he pulled my doctor bag from underneath the box, turned it over, and dumped my instruments and medicines on the ground. That was it for me; I walked up to the man Gillette who was holding me at gun point. He got real nervous and started to order me to stop, but I smacked his gun hand to the side with the back of my left hand. It exploded with a deafening roar, but I kept coming and hit him with my right fist dead center in the face, knocking him to the ground. I stepped on his wrist while simultaneously drawing my own revolver from inside my coat, cocking it with my thumb and pivoting, bringing it to bear on Captain Clingman. He was fast though and already had his own weapon drawn on me.

I kicked the hand of the man under my feet, heard him yell and his gun go skittering away under the porch, so I stepped away from him and kept moving sideways, never taking my eyes or aim off of Clingman.

"I'm not kind-hearted like my men," he said with a hint of amusement. "And I will end you, sir."

"Not if I end you first, pretty boy," I answered impolitely, having had enough of his gentlemanly shit. My left ear was ringing, and I could feel the skin beginning to blister, the shot must not have missed by much.

That made him frown. He raised his weapon straight up and cocked the hammer back down in a practiced manner.

"No sense in further gunplay," he said. "It would only attract unnecessary attention."

I saw, out of the corner of my eye, that the man with the carbine had come up behind me and was now only perhaps twenty yards away, so I maneuvered so as to have them both in my view but still kept my aim directly on Clingman.

"I came here to offer you a chance to assist with an important mission," I said.

"Respectfully declined," Clingman said with the smile returning to his face. "Stand down," he told the man with the rifle. "If he wanted to shoot he would have done so already."

"This is important," I insisted.

"You want our help with the prisoners at Camp Douglas, Dr. Lierly," he said with a mischievous look.

This took the wind out of my sails a bit.

"How did you know?" I asked.

"I put two and two together when I saw the doctor tools," he said. "The news came down into town yesterday, and I'm well-connected hereabouts. This town here is named after Hillsborough, North Carolina, where I'm from and many of my kin around here are from there. You met the sheriff, he's my cousin. You sure stirred up a hornet's nest in Chicago, doc. The Yanks are combing the whole area trying to find you."

I finally holstered my pistol and asked, "You can't provide assistance at all?"

"Nope," he responded. "We're perfectly fine right here, disrupting Yankee commerce."

"You mean robbing and plundering from innocent civilians," I said trying to insert a barb.

"Now that's just hurtful," he said with a pout. "First off, there are only five of us here. Second, if you haven't noticed, the front line we have to return to is around Atlanta, a thousand miles away. Third, I can see you're no fool, and you have to know you're on a fool's errand, orders be damned. Bustin' those boys out would just get them all killed."

We climbed up the steps and sat in chairs on the porch while Clingman's men went back to whatever duties the were performing, although Gillette was cradling his hand and giving me the stink eye.

I called over to him, "I really am a doctor, I'll look at your hand when I'm done here."

I turned back to Clingman and lowered my voice. "I already broke some prisoners out and want to get some more, but I need horses and arms to get them to Detroit, then to Canada." This secret agent thing sure left me exaggerating my accomplishments on a consistent basis. This prompted an incredulous look from Clingman.

"How many did you get out?"

"Just seven so far, but I'd like to get at least that many more before I'm done."

"No wonder they're looking for you."

He paused and stroked his chin while he thought about that.

"I'll tell you what I *can* do," he said slowly. "I'll trade you two horses for some of your supplies. I'll also get you some different clothes, damn if you don't look like a snake oil salesman driving a chuck wagon."

"Already had one teamster call me a carpetbagger," I admitted. "Could I get some of my tobacco back though? The whiskey I don't need, but I do like to smoke sometimes."

He laughed and said, "Done."

After making these arrangements, I called Gillette over, sat him down on the edge of the porch, and examined his hand. The middle two knuckles were turning black, and his hand was swelling up. I tested his phalanges, both in the hand and in the fingers, and found no evidence of a break or dislocation. I suspected my kick caught him direct into the two long fingers. Served him right, even if he was just following orders. I wrapped his hand to immobilize the injury, then told him, "Next time, pull the trigger or you'll end up dead."

"Sorry, doc, you didn't look like no kinda fighter."

"Underestimate your opponent, end up dead," I persisted. "Go back to farmin', it's safer."

I walked over to the stack of whiskey bottles that had been removed from my wagon, picked up two, and handed one to Gillette. As I took the other bottle back to my wagon, I told him, "Drink one of those and you'll be fine in the morning, doctor's orders."

"You're a funny guy, doc," he said sarcastically, but I noticed he tucked the bottle inside his coat as he walked away.

It was getting long into the afternoon by the time we got the supplies unloaded and the horses tied off. Captain Clingman was unhappy with me because his man Gillette was in no shape to help by then.

I just gave him a nasty smirk and repeated, "Doctor's orders." I declined their offer to stay for the night, thinking that these men would steal anything not tied down in the middle of the night.

The sun was setting by the time I was back out of the hills and forest, they had given me directions for a side road that would take me to the Illinois Central Railroad and the access road that paralleled it to the northeast. Clingman had told me not to go anywhere near Litchfield or the horses might be recognized. *Great*, I thought. Hung for a spy or hung for a horse thief, take your pick.

The road northeast through Rosamond was in great shape. I could see that it had been graded and improved by the railroad gang. I was slower returning north though as it was a longer route and I had twice as many animals to take care of. In addition, the mules were not as fresh and getting a little grumpier getting started every day. I turned east, and one unusual thing happened. On Saturday, I pulled off for the night, just outside the town of Shelbyville. I was just settling in when I heard the hoof beats pounding of what sounded like a cavalry detachment coming toward me on the road from the east. They were coming fast, and I was paranoid, thinking they were coming for me. The hair was standing up on the back of my neck, and my animals were getting agitated, whinnying and stomping. I grabbed my gun and jumped out of the wagon, running for a copse of trees in just my stocking feet. I slid in behind a log that afforded a good view of the road, lit up clearly in the full moon. By now, I could hear the rattle of their equipment and the blow of the hard-breathing horses, the thundering noise of the hoof beats reaching a crescendo as they swept up the hill. A hard gust of wind swept through the copse and along the road, but the horsemen did not pass. I could hear them, the clatter and hoof-beats of the riders fading off to the west. Thinking there must be a trick of the terrain that hid them from my view, I walked out into the road, but all was silent and nothing stirred.

Then out of the corner of my eye, I saw a little girl in a white dress standing in the road, looking at me. In that instant, I thought that it was my daughter, I turned to admonish her for being out so late and in the road where she might be trampled, but there was no one there. That scared me, I got the uneasy feeling that the apparition was my little girl and that something dreadfully wrong must have happened. I was a thousand miles away and unable to do a thing about it. I barely slept that night, but the next day was as sunny and warm as the previous one.

I can't say what happened that night, but there are still times when I'm dreaming that I'll see that little girl's eyes staring at me.

At Madison, I turned due north and onto the long road through Champaign back to Chicago. Interesting that I completed a ten-day trip, covering over five hundred miles in a country at war yet didn't see a single Yankee soldier the whole time. And they were actively looking for me.

33

When I returned, the wagon and team to the barn things were not at all good. The seven escaped Confederate prisoners were now housed there, and although Vince Marmaduke, the owner of the barn and surrounding stockyard, was initially glad to have the free labor, there were questions being asked around the city following my visit to Camp Douglas, and the Yanks had apparently discovered I had attended the Sons of Liberty meeting. Loose talk was that the authorities were pushing for the military to authorize searching homes and businesses without cause or obtaining a warrant. Marmaduke was known to be a member of the Sons of Liberty and was scared, figuring he was close to the top of the suspect list. In any case, he started right in on me to get the escaped prisoners off his property. I told him that I needed an immediate meeting with Charles Walsh, Buckner Morris, and my uncle Richard Semmes then would make this happen.

After he departed on this errand, I met with Corporal Anderson and the rest of the escapees. I told them we would not be getting assistance from Captain Clingman, that I was devising a concise plan to get them to Canada, but we would not be breaking out others from the camp. They were disappointed but not too much. More than anything else, they seemed to trust my ability to get them away safely which is more trust than I had in myself.

The first to arrive at the barn was Maribeth Morris. She came galloping up on her black mare, positively launched from the saddle and surprised me by wrapping me up in a solid hug. A huge part of me wanted to add a kiss to the squeeze but to my credit, I refrained. I was in enough hot water without adding more problems.

"Oh," she said breathlessly. "I was so afraid for you, the army is searching for you everywhere. They have had the whole city in an uproar since you left."

Then she noticed my ear which, by now, looked like someone had hit me with a hot poker.

"Bill, what happened to you?" she asked, reaching up to touch it with just the tip of her finger.

That sent an electric shock through me, but I said simply, "He missed."

She went over to sit on a hay bale while we talked further.

"My contact that was supposed to provide support for this mission is unable to do so, although I managed to obtain two horses. I'm going to have to get these men out first, then return for more later on. At least I know that I'll have to bring the support I'll need with me next time, and the reconnaissance is already completed."

That made her a little angry, her eyes flashed when she added, "The Sons of Liberty can provide support."

I took her hands in mine, looked in her eyes, and said, "No one is doubting your commitment, but the support I would need is a twenty-to-thirty-man-trained-cavalry detachment to fight a running rearguard action against the soldiers based at Camp Douglas. You are brave to stand up for your rights, but you have no military training. It is likely that men will be killed in an attack on the camp, I'd like it very much if there were as few casualties as possible."

"What are you in need of right now?" she asked.

"My funds are pretty depleted and I need six horses, but I no longer need the guns I asked about last time. I've got about a hundred dollars to make that happen, although I could sign a document saying the Confederate States government owes for the remainder."

Now it was Maribeth Morris's turn to look amused.

"You silly man, just steal them. What are they going to do, hang you?"

At six in the afternoon, we had a meeting in the barn. Present were Buckner Morris, Maribeth Morris, Richard Semmes, Vincent Marmaduke, Charles Walsh, Corporal Anderson, and myself. I announced at the outset that I would be leaving that night with the escaped soldiers which prompted a joyous reaction from some, not so much from others. When I told them I would be back to get more men out, the reaction went the other way. We worked out a rough map of the area. I mentioned that I had returned to the barn by a main road a little to the south. We all agreed that this would be a great way to completely avoid Camp Douglas as it skirted the entire area south of Oakwood Cemetery. However, I was told it turned south at the heights above the Calumet River; we concluded it best at that point to access the Illinois Central Rail Line to cross the river using their bridge at the village of Tolleston.

I asked Richard Semmes to wait after the others had left, I asked him if he knew exactly who I really was.

"In this business," he said, "you have to know if you can trust someone. My sister Mary Eleanore confirmed you are my nephew John Carlile."

"Please do not tell anyone," I asked him.

"Maribeth Morris?"

"Especially not her," I answered. "She could get herself in big trouble trying to save me."

We said our goodbyes, and I went to brief the men on the upcoming plan. Marmaduke had told me of a livery run by a man he detested; this man also rented out rides so was guaranteed to have a quantity of horses on hand. As soon as it was dark, we set out to cover the half-mile to the livery. When the men were in position, Corporal Anderson and I came riding up and dismounted in front of the livery. As expected, the night person was a boy of about ten years, skinny and scraggly. He came running out to meet us.

"Can I take your horses?" he asked.

We dismounted, and he took the reins; we followed the boy and the horses inside. A lantern hung from the ceiling rafters by a rope through a pulley. It illuminated the inside of the building nicely. I could see clearly that there was no one else inside. Quietly I pulled my pistol from under my coat so that when the lad turned around, it was pointed right at him.

"Mister," he started to say.

I interrupted, "Don't move and don't make a sound and you won't get hurt."

I thought the poor kid might cry for a second, but his eyes got real big when Anderson got the other six men inside and closed the place up. We tied the boy to a chair and saddled six more horses.

We left the place two by two, every ten minutes, with Corporal Anderson leading off with one other man. We were not disturbed in the half-hour it took to get us all out the door. I was last to leave. Before I went, I left a voucher on the desk next to the boy for the cost of six horses.

I looked the kid straight in the eye and said, "Listen up, boy, this is important. My name is Captain Thomas Clingman, I'm requisitioning these horses in the name of the Confederate States Army to further my campaign to capture Springfield." I'd learned well the value of misdirection from Rafael Semmes. "Your boss can redeem the cost of the horses from the Confederate government when we've won the war."

I signed the paper Thos. Clingman, Captain, CSA.

Then I gagged the boy, mounted, and rode off into the night. It took just over an hour to be completely clear of the city and another hour after that to find the railroad bridge, get across, and make it to our rendezvous at the Tolleston post office which was right on the rail line. Everyone had made it without a hitch, and it was just about midnight. I decided it best that we put in as much distance as possible from Chicago, so we put a couple more hours riding under our belts out into the Indiana countryside.

It took five full days riding to make it to Detroit, but we didn't push too hard to make sure we didn't break down any of the horses. Luckily all but one of the men were experienced horsemen and the other not half-bad. Sitting around campfires at night, we all told stories, the men were amazed to hear I was a naval officer as they had seen firsthand my skill on horseback.

"My dad sent me to military school," I said, and they all nodded as if they understood.

Once in Detroit, we just took the ferry across the river to Canada. I used my identification as Gilbert Sawtell and put the story out that we were a construction crew heading for a job in Sainte-Catharines. Worked like a charm, but by the time we got into town, we were out of supplies and I was out of funds. I hunted down my old contact Jacques Bolanger and he arranged to put us all up in a local hotel and send a telegraph to Jacob Thompson in Montreal. Jacques told me I wasn't expected back, much less with released prisoners in tow. He said he heard my mission was supposed to be a diversion for a different operation, to release captured officers in Ohio using a riverboat across the lake. The other news I heard, while in Sainte-Catharines, was of the sinking of the *Alabama* by the USS *Kearsarge* on the nineteenth, more than a week earlier. There weren't too many details, but I did hear that David Llewellyn had perished while caring for the wounded aboard until the ship went down. A heroic move for a brave man who didn't know how to swim.

34

It was not Jacob Thompson who came to Sainte-Catharines to debrief me but George Sanders instead. He had another man in tow who he introduced as Captain Thomas Hines. A small thin man with a sandy mustache that looked like a brush sticking out of his lip. When Hines spoke, his voice was that of a mature woman. I initially suspected he might like boys better than girls.

I showed Sanders the scale map of the camp that I had drawn and the map drawn by the escaped prisoners, my estimations of prisoner numbers, health, garrison numbers, my thoughts on what kind of pursuit force the Yanks might muster for a chase, and the quality of that force. I briefed him that Captain Clingman's force was no more than a band of highwaymen content to remain where they were and rob civilians for personal gain. I told him that the Sons of Liberty were mostly old men who were word-warriors, that at the first hint of trouble, they were likely to turn on our cause if they could see personal benefit or save their own skin. I concluded by reporting that the men who had arrived with me had broken out of their own accord and that successfully releasing a body of prisoners would require a mounted rearguard of at least twenty to thirty experienced cavalrymen to hold the pursuit force at bay while the main body of prisoners was marched across the countryside. I did put to words a thought that had been going through my mind on the way to Detroit, that if a train could be stolen, that could provide a solution. I didn't put to words my misgivings about the reaction of the Canadian authorities to the presence of five thousand escaped prisoners of war crossing the border into their country.

I did reiterate that moving around the countryside appeared not to be problematic.

When Hines asked if having a couple of thousand Copperheads present for the Democratic convention in August might change the situation on the ground, I asked him, "You ever have any dealings with them?"

"Unfortunately, yes," he answered.

That made me give him a closer look. I said, "The Sons of Liberty have a stash of about two dozen rifles, I doubt if many of the Copperheads coming for the convention are bringing guns with them."

That's when Sanders chimed in, "Thank you, Dr. Carlile. You are obviously better suited to planning operations than carrying them out in the field. Turn your men and your intelligence over to Captain Hines, he will be taking over the operation from this point. Please report to Thompson in Montreal, we have a new operation for you to assist in planning."

He abruptly turned and walked out the door.

I could feel my face turning red, and I thought, *You are better suited to blowing up defenseless women and children than fighting a war like a gentleman.*

Hines turned to me and said, "Well, that was a bit unfair. Seems you took significant risks and accomplished much with very little support."

I thanked him for his observation and took him to meet the men.

Several days traveling together had started forming a bond between myself and these men, so I had misgivings about turning them over to a new commander who didn't look like much to me. But the men knew him instantly, he was a cult hero with General Morgan's cavalry raiders. Seems he had been an aide to the general, conducted his own operations behind enemy lines, and had been instrumental in the escape of the officer group after they were captured. His escapades were stuff of legend, to hear the men talk.

In any case, I had received funds again, so I bade the men goodbye, packed up, and checked out. I bought a ferry ticket for

Montreal and was on my way once again. I had some hope that Jacob Thompson had a better opinion of my endeavors than George Sanders obviously did. I took the opportunity to relax in the beautiful early July weather on the ride back east.

On arrival, I resumed residence at the St. Lawrence Hall Hotel, a different room had been reserved for me but again on the fourth floor, and my baggage had been transferred there. The day after my arrival, I met with Thompson and his usual cadre for a midday dinner. Thompson was angrier yet more businesslike than I had seen him in the past, dismissive of Clement Clay's stream of legal advice. I heard later that his home in Mississippi had been burned down by Yankee soldiers as was becoming the trend. George Sanders sat through the meeting with a slimy smile on his face, barely even touching his food.

When it came to my turn, I was told Judah Benjamin had sent a newly-commissioned lieutenant named Bennett Young who had a scheme to cause disruption by invading from Canada with a small force, taking over a community and wreaking havoc there, potentially causing the Yanks to have to deploy troops badly needed on the front lines to the Canadian border. Clay indicated that England would be incensed if this came about. Thompson countered that Quebec would be pleased as punch and would prevent any consequences to the Confederacy or the operators perpetrating the raid. Since Canada lacked a strong central government, it looked to be an interesting dilemma. I was ordered to meet with Lieutenant Young, assist him in identification of a target community, help him put together a unit to conduct the raid, then provide all necessary logistical assistance to pull it off.

Bennett Young was not really what I expected, he was just a twenty-one-year-old kid, but I was pleased to see him demonstrate intelligence and common sense. I heard through sources that he had been captured, escaped through Canada, returned to Richmond, then pitched this raid scheme to Judah Benjamin. He had been impressive enough to merit a commission as a first lieutenant and sent back to us to carry out the mission.

While Lieutenant Young began assembling men, mostly assorted escaped prisoners of war from various camps, I began collecting supplies and maps of the surrounding area. Very quickly, we decided that our target would be St. Albans, Vermont. Several reasons stood out: It was a significant town and county seat of about four thousand inhabitants close to the Canadian border, only fourteen miles. There was no military presence in the town, and three major banks. My primary goal was to have an economic effect on the enemy to get their attention. The town had an arterial roadway, a turnpike once across into the US that led from Montreal to the north and to Burlington, Vermont, to the south along with a rail connection to both yet was geographically isolated having Lake Champlain to the west and the Green Mountains to the east, making it difficult for a relief force to converge there. An added bonus was that J. Gregory Smith, the state governor, had his residence in St. Albans, virtually guaranteeing us national focus on the raid.

Lieutenant Young managed to put together a force of twenty-four cavalrymen, in addition to himself and myself. We shifted our base of operations to Sainte-Jean, Quebec, further down the pike toward the US border. I obtained fifty .36 caliber Colt Navy revolvers, two for each man in the unit, and a bag for each called a Morocco satchel, so-called because of the material it was made of. Any shoemaker can tell you that Morocco is kidskin, light yet strong and typically, this is used for ladies' shoes. We planned the operation with the men in meticulous detail so it would go off without a hitch. Our target date was set for October 18.

Young and I had several shared experiences that we discussed while we were in the planning stages. He had been in Camp Douglas after having been captured with General John Hunt Morgan at the end of the great raid. His first escape attempt had failed, and he had spent thirty days in confinement, in the hole that I had not been willing to venture into. He then told me that he had escaped by bribing a guard with the assistance of a judge's wife.

"Maribeth Morris?" I asked. He must have noticed a hint of amusement in my tone; he tensed up and blushed just a tinge. That caused the nasty side of me to come out just a bit, and I asked him, "Did you spend any time in her cellar?"

He blushed hard and started to get angry. "Now just wait a minute," he started, stammering.

"No dispersions intended," I told him. "She is a fine lady who is putting herself on the line for the cause."

His reaction told all, however. I calculated she was easily old enough to be his mother, I also figured that the cause was not the only thing she was putting herself on the line for, but I didn't want to alienate Bennett Young, so I let the matter drop. I told myself I was glad I hadn't become part of her distractions, but the truth was she would have equally just been a distraction for me as well. Of course at the time, I had been thinking I would be returning for more intrigue in Chicago.

Lieutenant Young and I also compared notes on running the blockade in Wilmington, North Carolina. That is, when he was around to make our planning sessions. Much of August and early September he spent doing errands behind the lines for Captain Hines. Most of this was apparently carrying dispatches and moving funds.

The plan we developed was for Young and his men to arrive in the town in twos and threes, citing a hunting convention in the mountains. St. Albans business district was arranged mostly along Main Street, the north/south arterial roadway where it met Lake Street which teed off to the west toward Lake Champlain. On the east side of Main Street, across from this tee, was an old-fashioned New England-style town commons bordered by Bank Street to the north and Fairfield Street to the south. One long block to the west was the town foundry and the rail shops for the Central Vermont line, important because among the businesses, they employed as many as seven hundred physically-fit men who could be used against us if things went badly. The railroad tracks themselves were just to the west of the shops. At the end of September, I completed a personal reconnaissance of the town to finalize the details.

Lieutenant Young was to ride in with the first few men on October 10, and check into the Tremont Hotel on Main, then the others were to arrive in twos and threes, checking into the Tremont, the American House Hotel on the corner of Main and Lake, the St. Albans House Hotel on Lake and Catherine Streets across from the foundry, and at the Willard, a boarding house further down Lake

Street. Some men would arrive by coach, some by rail, and some would take the train further south before arriving at St. Albans from that direction. At the appointed time, the men would divide into six teams of four, one team to take the St. Albans Bank, then the Franklin County Bank, both on Main on the north side. The second team would take First National Bank on Fairfield Street to the south. Team 3 would scatter out and begin assembling horses at the north end of the commons while team 4 would hit two liveries and the harness shop for saddles and bridles. Team 5 would provide cover to the west in case of a response from the rail workers, and team 6, with Lieutenant Young, would gather any stray citizens that happened along in the commons to prevent an alarm from being sounded. This would also allow Lieutenant Young to maintain a central position for command and control. His group would also become the rearguard for the rest as they would not be burdened with any of the loot.

The second part of the plan more directly involved me. On the escape route to the north of St. Albans was the smaller town of Swanton which also had a bank. We decided to rob that bank during the escape back across the Canadian border. I would accompany the last man to hold up that business when our riders began to come through so they didn't have to waste any time dismounting. We would simply hand them the plunder and be on our way. The other aspect of this was that if, for some reason, the main road was cut off, we could ride south to warn our escaping friends so they could utilize the set of secondary roads that branched off to the northeast. What I didn't know was that there was a third part of the plan. While I was gone reconnoitering before we deployed, George Sanders had come down to Sainte-Jean and distributed vials of a flammable liquid, Greek fire, among the men. He told them that because the Yankee Armies were pillaging the Shenandoah Valley and the area around Atlanta, Georgia, they were ordered to burn down the town of St. Albans. Young and his men began to jokingly refer to themselves as the Fifth Company of Confederate Retributors, although I'm not sure where they thought the first through the fourth companies were deployed.

By the fifteenth of October, all of the men had departed for their appointed rendezvous; so on Sunday morning, the sixteenth, I set out for Swanton, accompanied by Oliver Perry, a young Kentuckian whom I suspected could handle himself in a rumble just fine. He never said a lot, but when he did, it was usually some observation that would provoke at least some thought and, most of the time, a chuckle to go with it. The weather had been warm into the beginning of the month but was cloudy that morning and before we even made the border, it started to drizzle. In addition, our mounts were problematic. Both were stallions, mine a black and Perry's a chestnut. It was really obvious that the two horses didn't like each other and as time went on, I suspected that they didn't like us much either. Still we were both capable of keeping them controlled in spite of their constant attempts to get in front of each other.

The border crossing was nothing more than a toll booth with a pole for a gate. We paid our nickels and moved on down the road to Swanton which we reached by two in the afternoon. Now Swanton exists at a bend in the Missisquoi River where it turns north before emptying into Lake Champlain and leaving a sediment marsh for a delta in its wake. The turnpike crosses an old stone bridge over the river just south of town. A second newer bridge crosses the river to the west just below an old ferry landing, providing access to the lake and the railroad depot, plus a secondary small collection of businesses just beginning to flourish there. The main downtown area is dominated by two churches, a bank, and the post office, the rest of the businesses being small. Starting a block to the east, a few dozen residences sprawl up the hill, mostly situated on two side streets. It is a beautiful New England village, especially at that time of year when the leaves are beginning to turn color. The wide variety of deciduous trees ensure that every shade of red, orange, and yellow are represented in the panorama.

We put the horses up at the livery and took a room at the inn, then walked the town and took a closer look at the bridge to the south, figuring that to be a choke point to the escape of our main force and likewise a place where pursuit could be delayed in the event we needed to mount a rearguard action. The bridge was placed at a narrow point where there were a number of spots in the rocks and trees along the river that a gunman could make for an uncomfortable crossing yet provide that ambusher enough distance from the road to easily escape to the northeast. We returned to the inn for the evening meal then quiet tankards of local beer while keeping an ear open for news and gossip tidbits that might provide additional intelligence to aid our mission.

Monday, the seventeenth, we spent quietly other than making a trip to the bank to get the layout of the interior. I managed a talk with the manager on the pretext of thinking I might open a business line of credit. My ruse worked splendidly, he was most neighborly and invited me back of the house to his office to confer. Either that or he really wanted a piece of my money. I did note that the safe was modest and was left standing open. It was out of sight from the cashier cage, and the backdoor was heavily barred. A simple wood half-door separated the front from the back area, jumping over would not even slow me down.

The eighteenth was our day of reckoning, we got our horses from the stables and took off south toward St. Albans. After a few miles, we found what we were looking for—the road crested a small rise that gave us a clear view of the road for over a mile, across open farmland, until it disappeared into the forest in the distance. It was cool and cloudy, threatening rain but none falling. We had to tie our mounts off separately because they continued to fight. We sat there for over three hours, waiting, but nothing happened. There was no traffic on the road and no sound or movement except for the birds, and, at one point, we saw a farmer's wife come out and hang some washing on the clothesline. We amused ourselves, making untoward comments about her physical attributes while she was bending over to get a new clothing article, then stretching up to hang it on the line. It turned out Perry knew about indecent things I hadn't heard of, even with my experience as a sailor. I pitched it back pretty well though and soon, we were rolling on the ground, laughing until it hurt. It's a guy thing, a bonding experience.

At three o'clock, we decided to head to St. Albans to see what was delaying Lieutenant Young's assault on the town. We were close enough that we thought for sure we could hear gunshots if they happened, but it remained quiet. As we neared the town, we detoured up the hill to the east, trying to find a vantage point from which to view what was going on. The town commons was full of people, wagons, and makeshift stalls selling produce and crafts. Literally hundreds of people were milling around, men in groups, conversing, and women with their baskets, purchasing ingredients for upcoming meals. The answer struck me like a brick—it was market day in St. Albans. Young must have decided to postpone the raid due to the circumstances. We mounted up and returned to the road back to Swanton.

We had just entered some woods, the light dimmed and the road narrowed just a bit when Perry's horse decided to get into the lead. My mount saw it coming and bit the other horse on the flank. Perry's horse screamed in rage, made a jump to the side away from us, then did a toe hop and a kick. Perry managed to keep his seat initially, but when his animal slid into the gully on the side of the road, there was a sickening snap of a bone breaking, and both horse and rider went down.

I jumped from my mount instantly to render assistance. I swear my animal had a I'm-pretty-pleased-with-myself look. If he had been able to, he would have been smiling. Perry had been thrown clear and was now sitting up, but his horse was in a bad way. He made two valiant attempts to get back on his feet, but his left shin bone was completely snapped and he went back down on his side both times. He just lay there, looking at me with big eyes, looking scared.

I went over to Perry who was insisting he was all right, although I could see a purple goose egg beginning to form on his temple. He was going to have a nice headache once the shock of the thing wore off.

"Led with your head, I see," I said, trying to lighten the mood. "Good plan!"

"It's nothin'," he responded. "What about my horse?"

"A goner," I said while pulling him to his feet. "Why don't you lead mine down the road a little ways so I can take care of it."

He led my horse away and as soon as they were out of sight, around a turn, I pulled out my pistol; and, while talking gently to the poor beast, I pressed the barrel to his head behind his ear and pulled the trigger. He jumped then twitched then was still. I couldn't help but have a tear in my eye. Even though he was mean and arrogant, he was a beautiful creature and it was sad he had to come to an end like that.

Because we had to alternately walk or ride double, it was after dark by the time we returned to Swanton. Perry was feeling nauseous, so I took a closer look at him. In the light, his pupils dilated unevenly, indicating a concussion. I put him to bed then asked the innkeeper's wife to take him up some broth from the stew on the fire while I went out to stable my horse. I didn't perceive that his injury was serious, but it was likely to throw a crimp in our plans. I was going to have to communicate this to our main party and still remain above suspicion to keep Perry from being captured by his association with me.

After getting a message to a local man, who took care of dead animals and like noxious tasks, I checked on Perry then went straight to bed. It had been a taxing day, and I was just exhausted.

35

The next morning, I was up early and woke Perry to check him out. The swelling on his head had begun to subside, leaving a nice purple bruise in its wake. He admitted to a significant headache and some dizziness when he sat up. It didn't appear that we were going to be robbing any banks today. I went down for breakfast and made arrangements for Perry to be fed as well. While I was eating, I saw the gluemaker go past southbound with his cart. At least, the mess from the previous day was being cleaned up.

I went out and got my horse from the stable; he was mean-spirited once again that morning. When I mounted, he had his ears back, then took me over to the wall of the barn and smashed my knee up against it. It hurt like hell, and I wondered if I would be able to stand up if I dismounted. It was really obvious that he did it on purpose and equally obvious that he had perpetrated that trick before. Now I realize that an animal's behavior is the product of his trainer, but that man was not present in that moment, so I leaned forward and punched that horse hard on the side of the head. He was more cooperative after that.

The stable boy said, "Geez, mister, that is one mule-headed animal. He raised hell all night, and he did everything he could to keep from being saddled this morning."

"Yeah, he's my favorite," I said sarcastically, then told the kid about what happened the previous day and added, "He busted up my partner pretty good."

"Was wonderin' why that other horse didn't come back, he was almost as mean as this one an' just as hard-headed."

I rode out and soon returned to the vantage point from the day before. The day was partly cloudy, but there were sun breaks that made it nice. It wasn't quite as quiet as the day before. A group of men were haying in a field on the far side, and two wagons passed, heading toward Swanton. When the glueman came out of the woods, hauling the chestnut stallion on his cart, I retreated down a farm lane between hedges to keep him from noticing my vigil. Early in the afternoon, that same farmer's wife came out to pick vegetables from the garden behind the house, making me miss Oliver Perry, my companion. Then it got real quiet for a couple of hours.

By three o'clock, I could no longer stand wondering what could have happened to Lieutenant Young and his boys so I mounted up and started off toward St. Albans. I crossed the valley and was deep in the woods, just past a turnoff with a battered wooden signpost that said "Skeet's Corner," when I heard the rumble and clatter of many horses approaching fast, accompanied by an occasional gunshot. I dismounted, holding my horse as far to the side of the road as I could manage. The first batch of about ten riders came rocketing around a corner into my view, bent over the necks of their horses and obviously in high spirits.

When they saw me, they pulled up abruptly, and my mount reared up as the mass of horsemen spilled around me. I recognized Tom Collins, Lieutenant Young's second-in-command, among them, yelling to him to keep his men moving.

"It was glorious, doc!" he yelled back to me. "But they are right on our tail!"

"Forget the bank at Swanton and split your men up at every right turn, that will make them pause,"

"Yes, sir!" he yelled, digging in his spurs, and the group raced away, followed in intervals by more riders in groups of two or three.

Finally Bennett Young came up on his big black charger with Charles Higbee, riding double behind him. Two others were with him, providing occasional cover fire to slow down some pursuers, out of sight, down the road. Higbee was obviously wounded and holding on for his life, so I dashed up and assisted him onto my own mount, helping to get his feet firmly in the stirrups. I could see that Higbee had been shot in the back and was in obvious distress.

"What about you, doc?" Young asked, all the while pivoting his horse in a full circle and waving his pistol shoulder height, muzzle pointed up in the air.

"I'll be fine," I answered. "Get going. and I'll buy you some time."

They also galloped off down the road, Lieutenant Young looking back and taking one final shot at the pursuing forces before dashing away. The Yankees were hesitant to follow until they saw the road was clear other than just me, dismounted, apparently unarmed and standing in the middle of the road. Then they came charging up, led by a man that, although in civilian clothes, had the bearing of a military officer. There were perhaps fifty of them, I don't know why they were so tentative. They could have overwhelmed Young's bunch at any point. I guess nobody wants to be the first to get shot.

In any case, I was suddenly surrounded by a large number of horsemen, all armed with pistols, shotguns, and carbines of various sizes, types, and calibers, all pointing them directly at my head.

"Hands in the air!" their leader yelled.

I did a great impression of being lividly angry, jumping up and down, and hollering, "Don't just stand there, go and get them! They stole my horse and right out from under your noses!"

Well, that caused them to mill about and generally get in each other's way. The gun muzzles were wavering now, not quite pointed at me anymore. No one wanted to have to explain shooting one of their own.

Their leader recovered his senses, however, and asked, "Who the hell are *you*?"

"Dr. Carlile," I answered. "I was visiting up in Swanton, and I'm on my way home to Albany."

I could see that he was suspicious and was not convinced by my story, but a well-dressed man behind him tugged at his sleeve and said, "He's nobody, let's get going!"

By the time they were reformed into a proper column and back on the chase, I figured I had provided Young and his men with an extra fifteen minutes easily.

"Get my horse back for me!" I called after them.

A man in the back of the group waved half-heartedly as the column moved out.

I turned and walked after them, back toward Swanton. I was still limping somewhat due to the thrashing inflicted on my knee by the horse; but perversely, I was glad to be rid of that animal. After clearing the woods, a second group of riders came up from behind and passed without even taking notice of me. I just waved as they rode past. I grinned, figuring there were probably a hundred men chasing us with possibly militia soldiers to follow. This would get a nice splash in the newspapers.

The next morning, Oliver Perry and I went to the Swanton train station and purchased tickets for Montreal. No problem, business as usual. George Sanders was wrong about a couple of things but correctly gaged the reaction of the Canadian authorities. The pursuit from the citizens of St. Albans didn't stop at the Canadian border. They captured eighteen of our men, after they had stopped for the night, including Bennett Young. The Canadian Police stepped in and held them on a warrant for extradition, however, which made the pursuers furious that they couldn't just bring them back to Vermont for trial. Then, since our men were heroes in Quebec and as they had broken no law in Canada, they were released. A dozen or so of them were rearrested later at the behest of the United States government, but Jacob Thompson hired competent lawyers and they were released again on the technicality that only the Governor General of Canada, not the provincial authorities in Quebec, could issue a warrant for extradition. Bennett Young and a few others were again arrested much later but were treated as celebrities until the whole thing was dismissed nine months later.

The Greek fire Sanders provided didn't ignite, so nothing burned down in St. Albans. Probably that was a lucky break for those of our men who were caught. Our guys made off with about $210,000 from the three banks. The pursuit party claimed to have recovered $88,000 of the stolen money, and $40,000 was turned over to Thompson who spent it all on lawyers for the men. That meant that roughly $80,000 went to line the pockets of individuals, both among our men and in the Yankee pursuit party. I know Bennett

Young came off with a little bit, he sent the Tremont Hotel some bank notes from the St. Albans Bank to settle his unpaid bill for his stay there during the time he was in Canadian custody (he also asked for copies of the newspapers that had his name in them). And I found a ten-dollar US greenback alongside the road during my walk back to Swanton. That still leaves $79,985 unaccounted for.

I followed the story for months in the newspapers, but all the aftermath above happened long after I was already dispatched on my next mission for the Confederate government.

36

I first met John Wilkes Booth on October 22, after my return from St. Albans. It was a chance meeting. I had seen George Kane in the lobby of the St. Lawrence Hall Hotel and had made plans to have coffee and talk. Booth showed up as well; he was an old acquaintance of Kane's, and so we were introduced. I had heard of him, of course. He and his brothers were noted actors that performed the American circuit up and down the Eastern seaboard. Booth dominated the conversation, even talking over any attempt Kane and I made to converse with each other. Booth bragged about coming to Montreal to meet with Jacob Thompson, telling us that he had a scheme that would win the war for the Confederacy. He said he was highly placed in the organization of the Knights of the Golden Circle, along with connections in the highest circles of the federal government. I winked at Kane and told him I had heard of the Knights of the Golden Circle before.

I figured, if there was a Yankee spy anywhere within a mile of us, that Booth would be spending time in prison just as soon as he returned to the states. I almost choked when George Kane told him who my father was. I got out of there as quickly as I could manage an excuse, but before that, I made a point of having Kane describe what it was like at Almira prison where he had spent over a year without having a solid charge or any court hearing just because Lincoln believed he was a threat. Even if Booth was an ass, he deserved some warning about the game he was planning to play.

Imagine my shock and dismay when the very next day, following my debrief of the St. Albans affair with Thompson and Sanders, that I was assigned as handler to Booth's project. I argued vehemently that Booth had no experience and even less affinity for running a secret mission, that he was bound to get himself and anyone associated with his project killed. I also made the point that the existing connections I would have to utilize to support his plan could also very well be compromised which could be disastrous for a number of operations already in place. Sanders had that slick smile on his face and told me that the project had merit, that it was my job to make sure it came off without a hitch. He had already made a point during the debrief of the St. Albans affair to note that I had not robbed the Swanton bank as originally planned and that in fact, I had not been engaged with the enemy at all during the raid. And I had thought that secrecy was important, silly me.

I had to admit that Booth's was a bold plan and badly needed. Atlanta had fallen to Sherman in September, and his men were busy sacking the city as well as every other major community in the area. Grant had General Lee pinned down in siege works around Petersburg and was gradually working his way to the South and West to cut the railroads and supplies to Lee's army. The war in Virginia had taken on the feel of slow attrition after the initial Yankee assaults had failed. These events appeared to have sealed Lincoln's victory in the upcoming election which was just a couple of weeks away. We still had hope for a McClellan presidency, but those hopes were fading fast.

Booth was surprised to find me as his contact with the organization. I knew, at the time, he initially dismissed me as an inconsequential contact and possibly believed he would be dealing directly with Jacob Thompson. Because he was extremely important. He told me so himself. I went over the plan with him before he departed for Washington on the twenty-seventh, it was simple yet audacious. Booth was a regular performer at Ford's Theater in Washington, and Lincoln attended plays there fairly often. There was typically advanced notice when Lincoln was to be present so special arrangements could be made to facilitate his arrival, comfort, and departure without his being disturbed. Booth said he usually had this information at least three days in advance from the manager. He planned to enter the presidential box with an armed party, tie Lincoln up, then lower him directly to the stage from the box. Waiting armed men would then hold off any rescue attempt from the crowd, and the president would be taken out the stage door in the rear to a waiting carriage. Fast horses would have him out of the city before an alarm could be sounded. Lincoln could then be exchanged for thousands of Confederate prisoners of war that could, in turn, effect the tide of the war. In addition, this should have a paralyzing effect on the Yankee government and be an embarrassment to Lincoln himself.

My first two moves were straightforward, or so I thought. I took Booth to meet with Clement Clay as I was curious about the line of succession should we successfully abduct Lincoln. Obviously Hannibal Hamlin, the vice president, would succeed and that was problematic in my mind. Hamlin was an ex-Democrat from Maine who, in the past, had supported conciliatory measures such as the Wilmot Provisio. In 1856, he had joined the Republicans and had become progressively antislavery ever since. I figured he would be glad to be out from under Lincoln's shadow and even escalate the war effort. He was not on the re-election ticket with Lincoln and winning the war on his own would be huge political capital. Andrew Johnson, the current vice presidential candidate with Lincoln, was a hard-head as well, possibly worse than Hamlin. So what needed solving was the question of, what if they wouldn't negotiate for Lincoln's return, what next? I wanted to make sure we had every obstacle identified, so I took Booth to Clay for some legal instruction on the order of succession.

Clement Clay, unlike Jacob Thompson, was always friendly toward me and seemed to like my appeal to his expertise in the matter. He informed us that per the constitution, succession to the presidency went through the cabinet, after the vice president, in the order of which department was formed first. That meant state, treasury, war, attorney general, postmaster, navy, then finally interior. Looking at the names, Secretary of State Seward was Lincoln's man but fully capable of operating the government independently. He would continue to support the war if the job came to him. Secretary of the Treasury William Fessenden was a different story entirely. He was fairly new to the cabinet but had been a senator from Maine. He came from a long-standing prominent Whig family, and although he was an early-on antislavery organizer, his policies had moderated during the course of the war. He and Hamlin, the vice president, were allies; but on his own, he was likely to be lost and want Lincoln rescued. If things got Secretary of War Edwin Stanton into a position of power, he would do his damnedest to burn the entire South to the ground. Probably Maryland too. In my opinion.

Anyway I attempted to explain this reasoning to Booth around his endless theatrical quoting and finally got him to realize that he should incorporate a secondary strike to take out Hamlin and Seward simultaneous to the Lincoln abduction if the full measure of paralysis was to be inflicted on the Yankee government. I told him that at a minimum, ten operatives needed to be recruited and trained. If I was hoping to put him off with this information, I failed miserably. I could see the gleam in his eye and his fingers begin to move as he counted out his possible cohorts. He told me he had four associates already at his disposal, "All good men and true."

Booth intimated that he was shy of funds for the project and although I suspected that he was a spendthrift, I did manage to get $1,500 out of Thompson to give to Booth for expenses. I think he felt sorry for me somewhat.

The presidential election was held on the eighth of November, so I left Montreal on Monday, the seventh. Although I was an officer in the Confederate Navy, I took the opportunity to be in Baltimore and visit the polls to vote. I figured it couldn't hurt. Although McClellan, the Democrat, got 45 percent of the popular vote, he only carried three states and none of those from the northwest where he had the majority of his support. I didn't dare to stop and see my family for fear that I might have been followed or might be looked for there; I didn't want any nasty consequences to befall them. I took the train on down to Washington City on the morning of the ninth to make my prearranged meeting with Booth in the lobby of the National Hotel where I gave him the dispatch bag containing his money. Once again, the drop was made with identical bags, him dropping his empty one and picking up mine and vice versa. I had to reiterate to him not to have his men witness exchanges between us as he had two men who were obviously watching—I assumed they were his. We made arrangements for a spot to drop notes for follow-up correspondence. A chalk mark would alert the other party when a note was waiting. Later I would discontinue these drops because inevitably, every time I would check the drop, there was some inconsequential note or another waiting for me and I began to fear for my safety.

Next I went to a livery and hired a horse and tack, starting off southeast to Charles County and the home of my friend Sam Mudd some thirty miles away. It was cool and rained off and on, the weather coming in from the northwest in intermittent squalls. I was thoroughly drenched by the time I arrived, and Sam sat me down by the fire.

"Sorry I can't offer you a hot supper," he told me. "Frank's having a new cook stove delivered and installed, we tore out the old brick stove but the new one hasn't arrived yet. Damn the war anyway!"

By Frank, he was referring to his wife, Sarah Francis. He had a sister, Francis, so he had always called his wife by the masculine diminutive in the most loving way, of course.

"I have a man I need you to meet," I told him. "But I want you to keep your distance from him as best you can. Do you know Wilkes Booth?"

"Know of him," Mudd answered.

"He's doing some work for us," I said. "If the plan works, I'd like to bring some horses to you for, ah, like a coach stop kinda thing."

"By us, you mean the cause," he said a little sarcastically.

"Of course," I answered. "But I'm sure you have somewhere on the farm, away from the house, so you don't have to know what is going on. Believe it, keep your distance."

"Tomorrow morning, I'll show you a place." he asserted.

That night, we sat around the fire in the living room, telling stories about the old college days, fellow students and professors and their quirks. Sam had four young kids who sat around wide-eyed at the tales we wove, obtaining unclaimed corpses and the like for medical experiments, along with some of the unusual afflictions we had to treat while practicing and perfecting our art on the poor who couldn't afford a real doctor. Frank sat in her rocker, knitting and voicing occasional displeasure when our descriptions became a little too graphic. It was all very domestic and for a moment, the worries of a nation at war were held at bay. Looking at his beautiful family, I felt guilty about involving Sam in something with the potential to destroy all the happiness in their world, especially considering the cast of characters likely to be involved.

The next morning, Sam showed me a spot where there was a tobacco drying shed, together with a penned-in area to hold the teams when they were harvesting that part of the farm. An ideal spot and far enough from the house for plausible denial of events if necessary On the walk back up to the house, I told him, "Next time John Surratt comes through, ask him to meet with me in Washington, he'll know where."

"He's due in a couple of days and always stops in, I'll let him know. Mondays I do rounds in the village," he said, referring to the town of Waldorf. Have Booth meet me at the inn, if he can't make it this Monday, I'll look for him on the twenty-first. I'll show him the lay of the land. Besides," he added while giving me a wink. "Frank has always wanted to meet him!"

I had another wet, rainy ride back to the city. I successfully hooked Booth up with Sam Mudd, then met with John Surratt. His mother had moved up from the country and opened a boarding house on H Street. This became Booth's headquarters for the plot at hand. Surratt also introduced me to Colonel Samuel Cox who had a home in Bel Alton, close to the Potomac River on the Maryland side, in fact, quite close to my previous crossing at Morganville. I was told that if a crossing needed to be made, Sam Cox was the man to get it done.

Abraham Lincoln declared November 24, to be a national day of Thanksgiving and the last Thursday in November to be the same in perpetuity. I think he was just thankful he had won the election.

37

I arrived back at Montreal on the twenty-sixth of November, accompanying John Surratt and his dispatch bag. John informed me the news was that a Yankee cavalry raid on Richmond had been stopped and a copy of their orders discovered. They were to kill Jeff Davis and any of his cabinet members, if at all practicable. Davis was incensed by this information and was ordering Thompson to move forward with all efforts to eliminate Abraham Lincoln if he could not be captured. Surratt didn't confirm it, but I took that to mean that Booth's plot was not the only plan to get the president and that the perimeters of my mission were changed as well. Surratt also gave me the news from Georgia—General Sherman had burned Atlanta to the ground, along with the towns of Cassville, Rome, and Marietta. Sherman then turned east and marched on Savannah, leaving a sixty-mile swath of destruction across Georgia. There were many sad tales of civilians left homeless, starving, and destitute in addition to the atrocities committed by the Yankee soldiers. When criticized for the actions of his men, Sherman had replied, "War is hell."

I reported to Thompson and Sanders that our operation was planned to come about just after the start of the new year. I asked for funds for a carriage and two teams, along with several riding horses, so we didn't have to depend on rented steeds, a lesson I learned well from the St. Albans adventure. I also asked to have several carbines and pistols shipped to me in Baltimore so that we would have some measure of firepower in case we were pursued. The usual for a mission that was risky from the start—we needed lawyers, guns, and money. I also asked for an assistant, a man experienced and level-headed whom

I could count upon to accomplish tasks independently. They told me to stand by and they would work on my requests. That was after Sanders asked me why it would take so long to pull off the operation.

Interestingly, while I was waiting to go in and present my report, I heard some snippets of the conversation ongoing inside the room. First it was, "That will leave them no choice in the matter…"

Then I heard, "Don't give Carlile that, he doesn't have the stomach…"

Nice to know you're appreciated, but I already knew they considered me expendable. I was determined to carry out my part in a respectable manner. It seemed to me that as much as I despised Mr. Lincoln, the fallout of retribution for causing his death would be tremendous. No United States president had ever been assassinated in spite of the whispers regarding Zach Taylor's death.

The next day. I was sent for and given a round trip steamship ticket and dispatch bag for James Bulloch in Liverpool. I was told that by the time I returned, they should have arranged for the requests I had made. I caught the coach for Quebec City, an interesting ride as it started to snow that day. Canadian coachmen are practiced on the snow and ice, and this driver was no exception. What seemed, to me, to be uncontrolled skidding was actually planned maneuvers or maybe the man was just having too much fun.

I boarded the RMS *Melita*, a smaller vessel of the Montreal Steamship Company, and settled in for the trip. The weather was quite cold on the crossing, and we had to divert to the south somewhat as significant quantities of icebergs had been reported in the sea lanes, but still steamers were being built constantly better and faster. Even with the slightly-longer route, we made Liverpool in twelve days. For my part, it was nice to be clear of the land once more, and I spent the days prowling the deck and talking to the captain. Like any such man, he was proud of his ship and eager to point out her best qualities. Due to the rough weather, the other passengers were, for the most part, sequestered in their cabins, dealing with seasickness. In any case, I appreciated some time alone with my thoughts and the sea dashing around the ship.

On arrival in Liverpool, I found James Bulloch basking in his latest success. He had bought a thousand-ton steamer, the *Sea King*, which he had converted into a new commerce raider renamed the CSS *Shenandoah*. Reports of her success were coming in, she was now in the Indian Ocean and bound for the Pacific to destroy the Yankee whaling fleet there.

I received my instructions from Bulloch. I was to collect a check from Charles Prioleau and deliver it in person to Jacob Thompson in Montreal. This was a large sum and was for the purchase of a new ship in Canada. Just like old times but with a new twist. We spoke at length of my recent exploits, and I was glad to see his approval of my decisions. I valued his opinion as a mentor and as an intelligent man. Finally Bulloch warned me to be careful with Jacob Thompson; when I told him my father had said the same thing, he said, "Well your father is a smart man!"

He then asked if it would be problematic for me to meet with Prioleau, and I assured him it was not.

On leaving Bulloch's residence, I once again had to ditch the man who started following me down the street. I stepped into a storefront, counted to five, then walked back out, turning and walking directly toward him. The look of consternation on his face amused me to no end; he turned around and retreated rapidly back the way he had come. I turned the corner and disappeared before he realized I was no longer coming after him.

I caught a hack that took me to the Prioleau town house in Abercromby Square in the east end of the city. I was shown into the drawing room, and there was Mary Prioleau, beautiful as ever, in a green silk dress. The room itself was a power play of splendor with painted ceilings, gilded trim, and priceless artwork in the form of oil portrait paintings on the wall and oriental porcelain vases on the side tables. A large intricately-woven Persian rug dominated the floor space but only seemed to accentuate the rich gloss of the oak floorboards.

"Very nice to see you again, John. CK will be home shortly, he is expecting you," she said with a twinkle in her eye and a pleasant smile on her face. "Come sit and tell me of your recent exploits, I do hear that you have been busy."

All as if there was no water under the bridge between us. So I told her about Chicago and the St. Albans raid, all of which seemed to amuse her immensely.

"Last time we spoke, you told me of a paradise you knew of, but you never divulged the details," she said with just a trace of a wicked little grin, touching the edges of her otherwise cool exterior. Almost flirting. She was amazing, she should have been a diplomat. She had the ability to put me at ease then change it up and pull me in again. I decided to pay her back just a little.

"Pyrate Caye, ma'am. So-called because it was the lair of the red-headed Irish pirate princess Anne Bonney a hundred and fifty years ago."

"Sounds dangerous," she said dubiously.

"Not at all. A thousand acres of white sand beaches, warm clear ocean, vegetation of the most vibrant green and clear cold artesian springs of crystal water bubbling out of the ground. Blue sky and sunshine every day, and at night, there are so many stars that you can't tell the constellations apart. A paradise on earth, but of course, you would miss the social circles here in England. Pyrate Caye is an English possession but is uninhabited."

"And you've been to this place?" Once again with suspicion.

But now I had her, sucked right into my whopper of a sea story.

"I had the good fortune to spend over a month there once, although at the time, it seemed like misfortune. I know where it is exactly, having calculated the latitude and longitude almost daily during my stay."

She could not know that I would require a sextant and chronograph to perform these tasks.

I launched into a tale of shipwreck, barely surviving the mountainous waves that dashed my vessel on the rocks, with every moment seeming like an hour. After almost drowning, I desperately clung to a piece of flotsam and ended up washing ashore on the beach, all alone and having to survive on just my wits. I described long lonely days spent building shelter, eluding hostile headhunting natives, and acquiring sustenance until the British mail packet finally rescued me after noticing my signal bonfire that I lit with a friction device I'd created. By then, she was hanging on my every word, so I concluded, "That was when I decided to get my life together and go to medical school."

She must not have read Daniel Defoe's *Robinson Crusoe* or she would have noticed that I plagiarized extensively.

CK Prioleau came in at that point, rescuing his wife from me. Poor girl, her husband would be chiding her later for listening to sailor stories when she mentioned my adventure. I was wondering how nice she would be the next time we met. That would be unfortunate, but right then, it was well worth the cost.

"Hello, my boy," said Prioleau, seemingly unaware of any tension present in the air. Mary Prioleau excused herself as always, saying the children needed attending to. The check was large, in excess of fifteen thousand pounds. I got the distinct feeling that Prioleau didn't really want to part with it.

An English pound is based on the value of a pound of sterling silver which is 92.5 percent pure. A US dollar is less than one troy ounce of silver; after the California Gold Rush of '49 devaluated the price of gold pretty much around the world, the value of silver went up accordingly. The United States had a policy back then called free silver which basically meant that if you mined silver or possessed silver bullion, you could take it to a US mint and have it assayed and struck into the coin denominations of your choice for free. But when the price of silver was more than the face value of the coinage being struck for you, silver flooded out of the country to be sold in foreign markets. As a result, very few coins were minted and what coins that were in circulation were hoarded. That made it difficult to conduct cash transactions inside the country and, in turn, constricted the economic growth of the nation. The United States government compensated by changing the composition and weight of their coinage, altering values a bit more than 20 percent. Twelve troy ounces to the pound, with the additional percentage off the top, left the base exchange rate at 14.5–1. In addition, the United States had accumulated so much debt in their prosecution of the war that their currency was suspect on the world market.

At the current rate of exchange, I was now holding a piece of paper worth approximately a quarter of a million dollars. Easy to see the reason for his reluctance. We exchanged pleasantries for a few minutes, but as it became increasingly apparent that he had other pressing duties, I took my leave.

Traffic in Liverpool was intense on the way back in. It was after dark when I returned to the *Melita*. Not wishing to take any risks, I once again opened the seam of my medical bag, secreting the check inside before restitching it. I needn't have worried; my belongings were not molested. It was three days before we departed back for Quebec, arriving in that fair city on the twenty-second of December. It always amazed me how much steam-powered ships sped the trip across the Atlantic, especially on the westbound passage.

I left Montreal the day after Christmas. It was a cold and over-cast day, fit to be labeled dreary. I was a little depressed that Jacob Thompson had not allowed me to pick up the firearms I had requested to be delivered to Baltimore. I had hoped to sneak in a visit with my daughter and family for the holiday. Instead another agent had been assigned to make the delivery directly to the tavern in Surrattsville. Once again, proof that I was not trusted.

I was a little appalled at the ship purchased by Captain Martin for the purpose of our voyage. She was the schooner *Marie Victoria*, old and decrepit, and certainly not worth anywhere near the amount that I had brought over for the purpose of her purchase. She also seemed light in the water for a merchantman departing port. We were immediately off down the St. Lawrence River channel before I had the opportunity to stow my belongings, much less voice my displeasure.

When I came back on deck, I approached Patrick Martin and made this observation. I was abruptly informed that he was the god-damned captain and that I needed to mind my own goddamned business. I was fuming, but I determined to mind my tongue. Martin was holding all the cards, and I didn't trust that he would not have his men just toss me overboard. I returned to my cabin but walked past forward to investigate further. The hold contained only ballast stones and about twenty crates that seemed to contain papers, bal-ance sheets, and the like. Further forward were some trunks with personal belongings but no ship stores and no cargo. I determined to tread very carefully.

By sunset, we cleared the river proper and entered the outer islands. In spite of the cold, I remained on deck, even after it was fully dark, interested to see what would happen next. Eight bells in the evening watch came and instead of supper, as would be the norm, the captain came on deck, called all hands, and we hove to into the brisk wind. I walked over to him from the rail and stood silently a few feet off to his right side, the whole scene lit only dimly by the swaying lantern on the stern post.

Captain Martin looked over at me, seemed to consider for just a second, then said, "Dr. Carlile, would you be so good as to bring your belongings up on deck?"

"Aye, sir," I responded, making haste to accomplish the directive. Whatever was going down, I didn't want to appear uncooperative.

I was back on deck in less than a minute, with my seabag and trunk. I remained forward of the cockpit to stay out of the way. The captain had his glass to his eye, looking to the southeast. All hands were also looking in that direction, expectantly, so I did so as well. Suddenly I saw it too from behind a nearby island. A lantern and the glimmer of light reflecting off a sail; another ship approaching.

The order was given to get the ship's boat away; this was done with a minimum of fuss. I had to admit that in spite of my dislike for Martin, he ran a tight ship. I was one of the first into the boat, I sat in the bow, on top of my belongings. Last to go were the captain and his bos'n, swinging down into the waiting hands of the men. As we pulled away, I saw what they had done, the *Marie Victoria* began a slow turn, away from the wind, then gathered way slowly toward the surf breaking on the rocks of the nearby island. I could also see the other ship more clearly now in spite of the dark, she was the *Sea Star*, Martin's personal ship. After boarding, we were underway immediately, then the hands were piped for a late supper.

As things settled, I turned to Patrick Martin and asked, "Am I entitled to my curiosity?"

He gave me a speculative look and after a pause, stated, "We are rebels in a lost cause. Furthermore, we are known to be spies acting against the United States." He waved his arm toward the poor *Marie Victoria*, now in distress among the rocks. "We now no longer exist."

"And me?" I asked.

That put him aback for a second, then he busted out laughing. When he finished, he wiped a tear from his eye and said, "Doc, I could have had you thrown over the side any time!" Then more calmly, "You should disappear as well, there are more untrustworthy people in Canada than you think, and you will be hanged if they can catch you."

I know my eyebrows furrowed at this, and I said, "I have a mission in progress."

"Wilkes Booth is one of those who will get you killed."

"Yes, but others are depending on my part."

"You think too highly of yourself," he said flatly. "Your funeral."

We stood in silence for a minute or so, then I couldn't help myself. It was my turn to wave my arm back toward the stricken *Marie Victoria*, now completely out of sight in the darkness. "What about the rest of the money?"

Martin didn't even flinch. He said, "I received enough to resettle myself and my men, the rest Thompson and Sanders kept to help close up their operations."

Over supper, we discussed the situation. Martin was firm that he would not approach a port or go anywhere near any military presence, either Yankee or Confederate. I needed to get to Washington just after the New Year to coordinate the kidnapping scheme. We agreed that he would drop me in the spare boat from the *Marie Victoria* off of Cape May, at the old town so I would not have to fight the ocean surf. The lighthouse on the point would provide a great navigational beacon, and the nearest coastal fortification was far north, Fort Delaware on Pea Pod Island, guarding the Philadelphia harbor. We would have to worry about a random naval vessel coming out of the Philadelphia naval yard, but our intelligence was that the Yankees were collecting a huge assault flotilla of warships and transports down in Hampton Roads. Most likely, their target would be Fort Fisher and Wilmington since that was the only major port still open to the Confederacy. On my part, I agreed to keeping Martin's confidence regarding his continued existence. I really had no choice but to be enthusiastic about this, I figured the alternative was a December swim in the Atlantic Ocean.

In any case, it went off as planned. During my half-mile pull to the wharf at Town Bank, I watched with some nostalgia as the *Sea Star* disappeared into the dark and mist. It was a cold cloudy night, all indicators pointing to a nor'easter coming in; but I caught the ferry in the morning and beat the subsequent rain, wind, and snow to Philadelphia. By then, I was in my alternate identity as Dr. William Lierly. And if the seat on the train to Washington City was hard, the car was warm and dry. On my arrival, I caught a hack to the Surratt boarding house just off Mount Vernon Square. My knock was answered by Mrs. Surratt herself, a taller plain-faced woman with hair pulled back severely into a bun in back.

She seemed suspicious until I told her I was an acquaintance of her son, John, and was just looking for accommodations for two or three days. I noted that there was a hard-looking man with wild hair in the parlor. This gent never took his eyes off me while I was downstairs. Mrs. Surratt gathered some bedding from a closet by the stairs, then showed me to a room on the third floor with a window overlooking the street. It was only after she was showing the room that I asked her if she could put me in touch with Wilkes Booth.

"Does he know you, Dr. Lierly?" she asked.

"He knows me as Carlile," I answered.

"He comes by time to time, I'll see what can be done."

"Sure appreciate that," I responded with my best grin.

That finally got a smile out of her as she turned to leave. I watched the window and, sure enough, after a minute, the wild-haired man walked out the door, put on a battered top hat, turned his collar up against the rain, and walked off downtown.

That evening after supper, Booth arrived with two gentlemen in tow. They couldn't have been more different, the first being a short, weasely-looking man who looked to be a clerk. The second was younger and strongly built, he looked to me to be a thug. Booth called him Payne, said he was his second-in-command and that he was a Confederate soldier. Mrs. Surratt directed us into the empty drawing room and, at Booth's request, provided a bottle and glasses.

She then answered a knock at the door and after a few seconds, we were joined by John Surratt, then finally the wild-haired man in his rumpled suit entered, went immediately for the bottle, poured a generous portion, then sat at the entrance to the drawing room. Now that I had a closer look, the red eyes and broken veins in his nose gave him away as a heavy drinker.

Now Booth was in his element and completely animated, pacing the room like he was on stage. With dramatic effect, he informed us that President Lincoln was confirmed to attend a play at Ford's Theater in a week, on the evening of Wednesday, January 18. The guard for the presidential box was notoriously lax and prone to regular refreshment breaks in the lobby. Booth and three of his crew, heavily armed, would enter the box from the rear at their first opportunity, tie him up, and lower him directly onto the stage to men waiting below, then follow themselves down the rope. As the play was a comedy, this action would hopefully just get laughter from the audience. Lincoln would be carried out the stage door to a waiting carriage, then whisked away out of the city over the Eleventh Street bridge into Maryland, security of the city being not as tight over the East Branch into Maryland as it was across to Virginia. Typically there was one watchman over this bridge after dark.

In the meantime, Booth's men, Azerodt, the man at the door, and Arnold, would be at the house of Vice President Hamlin while Payne and Herold would go for Seward. On confirmation of Lincoln's abduction, these men would pretend to summon Hamlin and Seward to an emergency meeting at the White House; but instead, they would be taken north on the Bladensburg Turnpike and held in the cellar of a safe house near Clark's Mills. I spoke up regarding two issues: First that Ward Lamon would likely accompany Lincoln to the theater and would surely intervene physically. Second that Seward was known to be bedridden and might be hard to move. Booth assured me that he would be glad to shoot Lamon if necessary, and Payne showed off some bad teeth when he said, "Oh, Seward'll move all right!"

I pulled two documents out, finished one, then passed them both to John Surratt. "These are for General Hampton who is currently in Bowling Green. The first is asking him to provide a cavalry troop to meet me at Colonel Sam Cox's home at Rich Hill on the evening of January 17, just after dark. Then he is to prepare a unit to meet us upon our crossing into Virginia to escort us to Richmond. The second is a letter from Jacob Thompson, countersigned by Judah Benjamin, ordering the good general to assist you in your endeavors to the best of his ability."

John Surratt and I locked eyes following this statement. I think he was communicating thanks for getting him out of town. He simply said, "I'll leave first thing in the morning."

I continued, "I will collect the carriage at Dr. Mudd's farm and bring them up to John Lloyd in Surrattsville." "Mr. Booth, you can pick it up there and at the same time, bring the weapons we have secreted there to facilitate your efforts."

I paused, and Booth nodded.

"I will then guide the escort from Rich Hill to Dr. Mudd's farm to meet you, you should be able to make it there with Lincoln before daylight. At that point, you and your men can choose to either accompany us to Richmond or fade into the countryside."

I scanned the room and saw that the men were suitably subdued by my assertion of authority. Except Wilkes Booth. But I expected that. He was not about to let some person from the government steal his glory.

"Of course, we will be accompanying you to Richmond!" he asserted. "Wouldn't have it any other way!"

Booth was excited now; his scheme was finally being set into motion. I stood up at that point, trying to bring the meeting to a close. I raised my voice slightly to get their attention.

"Gentlemen! I don't need to remind you that if anything untoward happens to Abraham Lincoln, it will be viewed by the United States as a war crime. Not only will they be coming for our blood, but they will seek retribution against the Confederacy itself. Whatever kind of villain Lincoln may be, innocent civilians will be made to suffer if he comes to harm."

I walked out of the meeting and up the stairs. As I went up, I heard Booth say to Payne, "Fucking bureaucrats."

George Atzerodt poured himself another generous helping from the bottle on the table. As I closed the door to my room, I was hoping John Surratt would find Wade Hampton quickly. If I were the cavalry corps commander of the Army of Northern Virginia, I would definitely be seeking verification of the dispatches and that would take some time. I was also mulling over how glad I was to be leaving Washington myself in the morning. Booth's crew didn't overwhelm me with confidence.

39

My initial part in the scheme went off without a hitch other than Sam Mudd causing me qualms. He was increasingly nervous about the whole thing, enough so that his wife, Frankie, took me aside after supper and asked me what was wrong. Funny, Sam specialized in dysentery at school and here he was, shitting himself over a minor passive role in a plan that could benefit him directly. Maryland had declared emancipation of slaves in November, and Sam would not be able to pay wages to farm his land. I did my best to laugh and joke to ease the tension. Privately before I left for the tobacco shed, I reassured Sam that I was making very sure I was not seen coming or going to his place, and this seemed to calm him.

I got the carriage up to Surrattsville and stored it in the garage next to the tavern. John Lloyd, the proprietor of the tavern, tried his best to get money out of me for his participation, I had heard that he was an ex-Washington policeman, and I could see clearly that he had no moral center. I speculated on what caused him to lose that job and how he had come by enough money to rent and stock the tavern on a policeman's salary. In any case, I had provided all the tools for Booth to accomplish his mission; he would have to work with his own men.

The weather had held fine, dry and warm for a week with the breeze out of the southeast; and even if the temperature dropped almost to freezing at night, there was no precipitation to make things uncomfortable. I spent the sixteenth and seventeenth of January going over the route carefully to eliminate any chance of getting lost in the dark and noting any possible problem or minor obstruction along with alternatives to the main road. The road was alternately called the Mattawoman Road as it followed the stream of the same name, or the Baltimore Road, because it was the main road into the southern Maryland farmland.

The morning of the eighteenth, I noted that the wind had shifted more to the southwest with ominous gray cloud masses forming on the horizon, so I determined to make it to my destination in a more direct fashion. I made the crossroads at Bel Alton around five thirty. The drizzle had started, and it was already getting dark. I continued south out of the village to see if anyone was following, then doubled back before turning west. I carefully skirted the boggy terrain in the rain and fading daylight before finding the road up to Rich Hill.

I untied my blanket roll before tying my horse off to the rail, then knocked on the door, glad to be under the porch roof as it was raining much harder by now. Samuel Cox himself answered the door, although a boy came out of the darkness behind me to lead my horse away.

"Colonel," I announced. "I trust you are well." Sam Cox was a medium height thin man with a droopy eye and iron-gray beard. He had a persistent cough and cleared his throat pretty often.

"Well enough," he answered, leading me to the kitchen in back.

Entering through a narrow arch, I saw three men sitting at a table having coffee. As I was looking around the room, hoping to find more men, Cox introduced the ones at the table.

"Dr. Carlile, this is Sergeant Taylor and his men from the First Maryland Cavalry." The largest of them, with three yellow stripes on a gray jacket that looked suspiciously like my old one from the Maymont Academy, stood and fixed my eyes with his while shaking my hand rather firmly.

"Drew Taylor," he said. "These boys are Cady and Haskins." Both men at the table nodded but didn't get up.

"Sergeant, do you have more men?" I asked.

"Nope," he said. "We're all that could be spared."

I attempted to hide my disappointment by turning to my host and asking for a place to change clothes. Seemed obvious that by the time orders got down to some captain, he didn't want to lose any significant portion of his command to a wild goose chase. I think I surprised everyone when I returned dressed in my uniform.

"You're an officer?" Taylor asked me.

"Lieutenant in the navy," I responded.

All three soldiers exchanged nervous looks, and Taylor started in. "But—"

I cut him off with a laugh and said, "Don't worry, sergeant, you command the detail. I simply require your assistance to complete my mission."

That relieved the tension, but Taylor came right back with, "Which is?"

"Providing an armed escort for a carriage from Waldorf back to here, then getting the occupant across the river and eventually to Richmond."

Taylor stroked his chin, thinking. "Only what? Twenty-five miles."

A statement, not a question. Taylor was a Marylander and knew the area.

"We'd best get moving if we're going to make our rendezvous," I said to put a stop to his excess thinking.

What followed should have been a terrible journey, temperature dipping to about forty, pouring rain wetting us through in spite of our cloaks, and the road turning to mud. GW Haskins was the saving grace. He had missed his mark and should have had a bright career trodding the boards as a comedian. Nobody appeared to know his first name, he was just GW. I learned he was not from Maryland, but all three men started the war in Turner Ashbey's Seventh Virginia Cavalry, Drew Taylor and Henry Cady in Company G which, in turn, originated as Gilmore's Baltimore Guards. There were no Maryland regiments in the Confederate Army until later in the war. Although GW came from the hills of Western Virginia, he had somehow gotten transferred to G Company, then continued on with them when they formed the nucleus of the First Maryland. GW was equally irreverent of everyone, and as we slogged on north along the road, he did imitations of both Jeff Davis and Abe Lincoln, then launched into a long rendition of how their current company commander had come by his hat. This was apparently fit to crown an English cavalier from a couple of centuries previous, complete with wide brim and ostrich feather. On a patrol into the hills, this officer had traded with a Guinea and this had cost him a half-pound of Maryland pipe blend tobacco.

I had heard of these Guinea folks, hill people who were mixed breed of whites who had escaped indenture or otherwise didn't play well with others, free blacks, Cherokee and Choctaw natives who had disappeared into the hills rather than take the trail of tears west and even some Portuguese adventurers, or so it was rumored. The norm for these folk was a triracial mix over the past five or six generations and living in seclusion as they had even developed their own particular language. In any case, GW concluded the story, saying the Guinea man had gotten the better deal as the hat was not useful but the tobacco surely was. He punctuated this by squirting out a huge amount of brown spit from his chew, some of which dribbled down his chin hairs, and disappeared into the rest of the rain water coming down off his hood onto the front of his cloak. This story in particular, and his other antics, caused us all to laugh merrily.

We started out using a pattern of cantering for a quarter hour, walking for an equal amount of time, then dismounting and walking the horses. It seemed this was normal for patrol operations as the three men did this without any orders given; it was a well-practiced routine. Soon, however, it was obvious that making speed through the mud was ineffective as was our walking in it; we just let the horses walk and manage their own pace. Sergeant Taylor led the way with Cady and Haskins riding abreast behind him. I brought up the rear. They kept looking back to make sure I was still there for a few minutes until they realized I was fully capable of keeping up.

We made the tobacco shed on the Mudd plantation before midnight by my reckoning. Our four horses filled the place, so we sat above on the loft platform. Sergeant Taylor had GW take the first watch, "'Cause he talks too much!"

After two hours, I volunteered to take the second watch, so I sat out in the wind, cold, and rain, sheltering myself as best as possible against a wall and under the eaves with my back to the breeze.

Around four, Cady came out to relieve me. Although I was getting worried, Booth should have made it by then if everything had gone smoothly. I was also bone-tired, so I went inside to get some sleep.

It didn't start getting light until a little after seven which was when Taylor gave me a shake to talk about things. The rain had died off to a drizzle, but it was still cold, and I worried further that it might actually snow. I had to figure that something had not gone right, but I did not want to give up so quickly in case there had just been a delay. In discussing strategy with Taylor, we both concluded that it would attract too much attention to try to make it back south in the daylight, but I cautioned that if our mission was blown, the enemy could know where to look for us. We took a walk and found a spot not too far from the shed that had a good view of the road to a distance of a half-mile or so. I was really thankful that Sam Mudd had obeyed my orders and had not come down to see what was going on at the shed. In fact, nothing was stirring at all, even the wildlife were hunkered down from the wet and cold.

We dared not start a fire, even though there was a pit by the shed; so I chewed some jerky and attempted a biscuit that was mushy before napping fitfully until about noon when I took my turn on watch. The drizzle had died off, and it had warmed up some, but the ground was still wet. I gathered some heftier branches and made myself a rude platform so I could sit without getting soaked through again. When I was relieved, I returned to the shed, took my horse out, and gave him a good rub down. He had proved to be a splendid animal, unusual for those times when the army had sapped much of the available horseflesh. We talked among ourselves in low tones, in low spirits, since we had apparently wasted our time on this venture. Toward six in the evening, the light was beginning to fade so we saddled up and started on our trek south.

The Mattawoman Road was a good thoroughfare and didn't retain the mud except in the deeper ruts, so we resumed the canter, walk, dismount routine, eating up the miles. The moon was full and although it remained cloudy, the ambient light provided good visibility except when traveling through the densest parts of the forested areas. We saw a couple of travelers, but as soon as they saw our uniforms, they left the road and disappeared quickly. It was close to eight, and we were making good time. It was fully dark, and we had just dismounted to lead our horses, emerging from a wooded section into the moonlight when all of a sudden, the road was full of blue-clad horsemen, horses snorting, the rattle of equipment, and stamp of hooves in the puddles.

A sharp command rang out, "Git them hands in the air!"

In front of me, I watched the drama unfold. Sergeant Taylor emitted an audible growl and started to bring up his carbine, but several shots boomed loudly, along with bright flashes from the offending muzzles. Taylor dropped like he had been struck with an ax handle. Cady stood stock still, just letting go of his reins, but GW dropped flat to the ground and began rolling off the edge of the road which I think was confusing to the attackers and their horses, not wanting to have him underfoot.

I took advantage of the distractions. I pulled my horses head down hard and toward me, causing the animal to turn sideways in the road. I hit the stirrup on the run and turned back in the direction we had come, digging my spurs in at the same time. My horse bolted straight into the mount of one of the two men on the road behind me His rifle fired harmlessly into the air, and his animal shied right into the second man who was trying hard to draw a bead on me. His horse then lost its footing on the berm and went down with a shriek. My horse took off like a shot up the road, achieving a full gallop in the wink of an eye. I heard shots from behind, and at least one bullet whizzed by my head; but then I was off, the woods closing in on both sides, helping to increase the gloom and my ability to hide in it.

I heard another gunshot close behind me and became aware that I had at least one Yankee in pursuit. I pulled my pistol and turned, firing off a round behind me. Seemed like a foolish waste of ammunition when I couldn't see what I was shooting at, so I resumed my position low over my steed's neck and urged him to go faster. Another shot, and the bullet went by close. I felt it tug on my coat. That's when I realized these men had Sharps repeaters, they could reload on the fly. In panic, I turned my mount into the woods, thinking to ambush my pursuer as he came by me, but that was a mistake.

The next shot hit my horse with a thud, right in the base of the neck. He was a champ though and bounded twice further into the trees before his legs gave out and he collapsed.

That was just enough time for me to see it coming and kick my feet out of the stirrups before he fell. I hit the ground on my left forearm then shoulder, rolling to the edge of an embankment, then sliding down the hill about ten feet before I got one foot underneath me and came to a stop. I still had a firm grip on my revolver, but my gun hand was on the ground balancing me. I looked up to the crest of the hill and saw the Yankee cavalryman appear, distinct against the moonlit sky, even in the dark and with the backdrop of the trees. He could obviously see me; he was pointing his carbine right at me. His face was pale, eyes shining in the darkness, and I could see the contrast of his yellow sergeant's stripes looking white against the dark color of his tunic.

I saw his teeth gleam when he broke into a triumphant smile. "Dr. Carlile, I presume," he said.

For a half-second, I was stunned, then a hot flash of anger washed over me, and everything was clear. I started to rise up, my thumb cocking back the hammer of my pistol as I did so. In slow motion, I could see him recognize the ratchet sound of my hammer cocking and before I could point my gun in his direction, he pulled his own trigger. I slipped on some wet downed leaves on the steep hillside, and that must have spoiled his aim but not by much. I felt the bullet slam into my shoulder and twist me around. The thought crossed my mind that my arm was ripped off, but I was hopping mad. I steadied myself for just long enough to point and fire my own weapon.

The recoil from my shot caused me to slip and lose my balance once again; but before I fell, I distinctly saw a look of surprise on the Yankee's face. Then I was tumbling head over heels down the slope, pistol flying from my hand, and powerless to impede my fall until I splashed backward and headfirst into the creek at the bottom.

The shock of the icy water pushed the air from my lungs, and I struggled desperately to get to the surface. My boots filled with water, dragging me down, and my arm hurt like hell, almost useless.

I grabbed for a sapling sticking out from the bank with my good hand, but as soon as I started to haul myself out of the water, it pulled out by the roots and back into the stream I went. Luckily there was not much of a current, so I got my footing and steadied myself, then painfully crawled out of the water and lay there on the ground, shivering.

I wanted to just lay there on my stomach and go to sleep, but I knew that if I did, I would never get up. I scanned the area along the top of the embankment; seeing no one, I rolled over and sat up, cradling my left arm in my lap. I could feel the blood running down my arm, so I pulled out my handkerchief and tied it as tight as possible around my arm under my armpit, using my teeth to hold one end of the cloth while I pulled on the other end with my hand. This done, I rested. But soon, my teeth started chattering, so I staggered to my feet and slowly climbed back to the top of the hill. On the way, I lucked on my pistol and felt a little better for being armed.

The Yank sergeant was lying on his back, dead, the look of surprise still etched on his face. I could clearly see the bullet wound in his neck, just above the *pomum Adami*, the upward angle of my shot must have put the round directly into his brain. In the dark, a dead man looks ethereal; I was expecting any second for him to jump up and come after me. My horse was also dead, having bled out, lying on his side. I retrieved my blanket roll, but my shoulder was getting really painful and I was getting light-headed. The Yank's horse was standing about twenty yards off, eying me suspiciously. I made some clicking noises and held out my hand, but he was having none of it. Perhaps he smelled the blood on me or had worked it out that I was the cause of his master's demise. In any case, he turned, went back to the road, and trotted away toward the south and the Yankee patrol that had jumped us.

I reasoned that it wouldn't be long before I was hip deep in Yankee soldiers, especially after the sergeant's horse came back without him. They knew who I was and would be scouring the countryside for me. I also figured that anyone I asked for help could be scared or coerced into giving me up. I recalled having passed the old stagecoach road that branched off for Port Tobacco a mile or so back, so I crossed the Mattawoman Road and stumbled off through the woods in a general northwesterly direction, trying my best to leave no trace of my passing. After about ten minutes, I heard riders go by fast up the road behind me, but they must have missed the signs of my recent fight as they kept going on by.

The woods were dark and the undergrowth thick in places, so I was chafing at the poor progress I was making, but the difficult hike warmed me some. I was zigzagging through the forest, having to turn every time I came up to a large downed tree, thick patch of brush, or any other terrain obstacle. The blood-soaked sleeve of my coat began to stiffen, so I stopped to rest and fashioned a rude sling from the spare shirt in my blanket roll. I tied the rest over my good shoulder, making walking easier. Still every misstep jarred my wound and caused almost unbearable pain. At least, the forest I was in was mostly flat upland country so I didn't have to climb any steep hills.

Then behind me, I heard what I had feared. More horsemen, this time moving more slowly, then a shout of discovery. No doubt, they had found their comrade and my dead horse and would now know that I was on foot. I could hear the sound of more men arriving and shouted orders as a search was organized. It did seem like they first began looking on the other side of the road where there was evidence of the fight, and I thanked myself for the decision to cross the thoroughfare; but too soon, it became obvious that they had corrected their error and were on my trail.

That brought home the fact that I was leaving a clear trail for them to follow across the wet forest floor, and I became more careful and attentive about where I was stepping. I found a large old downed tree and pulled myself up onto it, walking along its length as to leave no trace. It came to a point where it had fallen on a rock outcropping, so I took advantage and made further progress across this formation.

I became aware of a crevasse in the rock just as I stepped into it. My balance was already shaky, so I tried to sit to prevent falling into the pit, but I was too far forward and ended catching myself by my armpits, causing excruciating pain in my wounded shoulder. I was barely holding myself and dreading a fall into the dark chasm. I scrabbled with my feet to find a toehold, but the side of the rock was sheer and slippery damp. It was no use, and I lost my hold, bracing myself for the fall when my feet found a ledge. I found I had been holding my breath and exhaled, then tried to explore my situation. The ledge turned out to be the bottom of the crack which was less than three feet across and six wide. One side narrowed to just a crack, but the wide side disappeared under a laurel shrub which formed a bit of a hedge-like barrier at the side of the outcrop formation. I was able to push aside the overhanging branches and crawl in behind them to create a hiding place.

I could hear my pursuers struggling through the bushes as they approached on both sides. Someone in charge had formed them into a skirmish line to cover a wide swath of territory. They were calling back-and-forth, I was relieved to note that they had lost my trail. I hunched down in a squat, on my toes and with my boot knife drawn, ready to strike swiftly and silently if I were to be discovered. A soldier came stomping through the hedge, just next to my head. I could hear him quietly cursing at the obstruction before moving further along.

Gradually I could hear the whole group moving away to the west, then veering southward, and I began to relax somewhat. I had no notion of remaining where I was. Clearly they would be back in the daylight for a more thorough search, and that might involve dogs. While I was waiting for my way forward to clear, I plucked a handful of leaves from the laurel, pulping them on the rock floor of the niche with the hilt of my knife. Carefully I loosened the bandage on my arm and applied the laurel mush to the wound inside my shirt. The relief from the pain was almost instantaneous, I was glad I remembered the analgesic properties of the plant from my studies. I attempted to do the same on the back of my arm, but that was beyond my ability in the condition I was in. When I could no longer hear the pursuit, I decided to break cover and continue my getaway.

After several hours, I began to think I was wandering in circles; but then I came upon a game trail which made my progress easier and the ground began to slope gradually down, giving me the impression I was approaching another stream bed. The path seemed parallel to this creek, keeping to the upland, when I came to the remains of a broken-down rail fence. Beyond, I could see there was a clearing, or at least a lack of trees, but between was completely over-grown to a height taller than myself. Moving along it, I found a deer trail going through, but that required me to bend over double to get through the overhead bramble. I emerged into an open field, it must have once been a cultivated area but now overgrown in grass stubble.

There was a bit of a structure, just a tumble-down shed really. It was off to the right in what appeared to be a corner of the field. I went to investigate. The roof had collapsed on one side, but that left an area underneath that was like a lean-to. I knelt to enter, it smelled strongly like an animal burrow. I moved slowly and carefully, hop-ing not to confront something that would harm me further. If the night was dark, it was pitch-black inside. I located a couple of small rocks and threw them into the enclosure, but nothing stirred. I gath-ered up my courage, pulled out my revolver, and moved resolutely in underneath.

The ground inside was dry, at least. I took off my blanket roll and sat with my back to the wall, cradling my bad arm. All I could do further was to wrap my blanket around me and hope not to be found by either the Yanks or the critter whose home I had invaded. With my arm and my pistol in my lap, I finally let myself relax and soon drifted off into a fitful sleep.

40

I woke with a start; something large was scrabbling around in my borrowed shelter and growling. My eyes opened, it was fully morning and although the light was dim inside my lair, I was looking directly into the black face and white fangs of a large dog. I froze, and just that small movement caused my shoulder to throb unmercifully. Scenarios began running through my brain, thinking that my gun was on my lap but my hand would not move to grab it. His breath was terrible, like rotten vegetables and fish. I thought that any second, either the animal would go for my throat or his Yankee handlers would arrive to take me into custody. Then the beast made his move. Panting, he slathered my face with his tongue, somehow getting his saliva inside my lips, nostril, and eye.

I sputtered and jerked my head away, seeing his tail wagging at the same time as being overwhelmed by the pain of my wound. My shoulder had completely stiffened and swelled up while I slept, my coat also had crusted solid with dried blood. I heard what sounded like the voice of a young boy, and the dog left me in a flash. I felt the structure shudder as the animal bumped it on his way back outside. I struggled to get up but was too weak, and this just caused me further discomfort. I could barely feel my feet, they were freezing cold and still soaking wet inside my boots. I was in bad shape and I knew it. To top it off, I had a strong need to urinate.

I heard the boy, closer now. "Watcha got, Bob," he said in his youthful voice.

The dog scrambled back in under the shelter once more, jumping around with excesses of energy and tail wagging at high speed.

He was a huge beast, black face, but body a silver-brown color, easily over two hundred pounds. He sniffed at my blood-soaked coat sleeve, then slurped my face again with his tongue. I held out my good hand, open palm for him to sniff, and he obliged.

"Bob, no lickin,'" came the youthful voice again.

The shape of the boy filled the entrance. He couldn't have been more than six or seven, round brimmed hat and jacket and a piece of rope tied to his pants to hold them up like a makeshift suspender. He had a small caliber rifle that was pointed in toward me until he recognized my shape, then he raised the muzzle.

"You okay, mister?" he asked.

The boy came in and stood there, looking at me. I noted that he remained out of my reach, a smart boy. The dog went over and sat next to him, their heads on an even elevation with each other. I saw that the boy had a pair of rabbits on a strap that was slung over his shoulder.

"What's your name, son?" I asked gently. I resigned myself to having been discovered and determined to befriend the boy in an effort to manage the situation.

"I'm Pete, and this is Bob," he said while simultaneously patting the animal on the head and eyeballing my uniform. I could see him evaluating my condition, and this was confirmed when he said, "Geez, mister, you look like hell." A pause, then, "My pa's a Confed'rate, you don't need to worry." He grinned and added, "You must be the reason cav'rys been runnin' up an' down the road all day."

I attempted a conspiratorial grin, but it was probably more like a grimace. "Yup, I'm the reason."

I began to think more clearly and knew I needed to take a closer look at my wound, so I determined to get the kid to assist me.

"Hey, grab onto my sleeve and help me get this coat off," I requested.

I lifted my left arm with my right hand for him to grab onto; and if this wasn't painful enough, when he grabbed on and pulled, it forced my shoulder back and I almost passed out, the pain actually forcing the air from my lungs in a grunt. Still the boy was strong for his age and persisted, the fabric broke loose from the shirt underneath, and the coat sleeve cleared my elbow. The wound opened and I could feel the blood begin to trickle down my arm again.

"You been shot," he said, stating the obvious. The whole side of my white shirt was reddish brown with dried blood and had completely soaked the makeshift bandage I had applied. When I pulled this away, I could see my shirt was ripped at the outside of the shoulder where the bullet had struck. I slowly unbuttoned my shirt and leaned forward while the youth pulled on my collar to expose the wound.

In spite of the blood, I could see the purplish-black puncture in my lateral deltoid muscle where the projectile had entered. The Yank had been above me, so although I could not see or feel exactly where the exit wound was, I was thinking somewhere around where the deltoid met the teres and the triceps. When I looked up at the boy, he was white as a sheet and I knew it must look terrible. A .56 caliber round is a large soft lead cone and carves a significant channel through flesh. It didn't seem to have struck the bone on the way through, and I was thankful for that.

"I'm gonna go get my mom," he said flatly.

"Give me a hand with a new bandage first," I asked of him.

I had him cut a large piece from the remainder of my shirt, fold it twice, then run it under my armpit and around my shoulder. After he tied it tight, I had him use a piece of stick to take an extra turn on the bandage to ensure the bleeding stopped. Then he left me on the run with that burst of energy that all children seem to possess. I recall thinking that at least the wound was below the rotator cuff before I wrapped my blanket back around me and drifted off back to sleep.

When I woke, it was to a feeling of déjà vu, as if the first time the dog licked my face had been in a dream. But then, Pete bounced in, followed by a woman who had to stoop to enter the shelter. She was dressed in an over-sized coat, so all I could see was mouse-brown hair pulled back and tied in a ponytail.

"Sorry we took so long," she said. "Soldiers were searching the house when Petey got home."

"Bob made 'em real nervous though," the boy added.

The woman continued suspiciously, "Who are you and what am I getting myself into if I'm going to help you? You stirred up quite a fuss."

"I'm nobody, really," I replied. "Just a navy officer, but I killed the man who shot me first, that may have made them mad."

She crouched over me, her expression clearly trying to decide whether or not she could trust me, then finally seemed to come to a decision.

"Well, you can't stay here, you'll freeze to death," she said. "Bridget Scott," she said by way of introduction. "My husband is also a Confederate officer." I think she added this husband part to immediately establish boundaries.

"Dr. William Lierly," I responded. "I'm a naval surgeon but finding it hard to fix *myself* up," I said with an attempt at a smile.

I was too weak to stand for long without getting dizzy and too large for them to carry but not too big for Bob the dog to drag me. They used my coat to fashion a travois of sorts by inserting two stout poles through the coat sleeves, then lashing a branch toward the bottom of the contraption to complete the frame. It was a rough ride and my feet drug on the ground, but we made it to the house.

"Sorry about the accommodations, but we no longer have horses," she told me. "When it became known that my husband had joined the reb army, the government came and pretty much confiscated everything. We've been living on what we can hunt and what we can grow in the garden."

"I can pay you—" I started to say.

"It may come to that, but for now, it would just look suspicious, me having money," she cut me off to answer.

I found myself constantly amazed, during my stay, at Bridget Scott's strength and energy. She immediately cleaned up my wound, even though I saw her wince when she saw the exit wound. I had her make sure there were no clothing fibers remaining in the hole in the front of my shoulder, douse it with whiskey, then stitch it up. The back was more difficult. The bullet had shredded skin and tissue on the way out. Bridget had to cauterize the area with a hot knife. I did my best to hold on, sitting backward over the back of a chair. But it was too much for me and I lost consciousness.

When I woke, it was almost dark, just a glimmer of twilight could be seen through a window. There was just enough light to discern that I was in a bed, in a room, with the door closed. I rapidly discovered that I was dressed in a nightshirt that was slightly too small, and it appeared I had been bathed before being dressed. In spite of all previous experience, I believe I blushed at the thought. I lay there for a few minutes, collecting my thoughts, then noticed that it seemed to be getting lighter instead of darker outside.

Thinking this to be a fluke, I sat up and moved my legs off the bed to stand. Although this motion made me feel light-headed, I persevered, getting up on my feet. Well, my legs would not support my weight, and I crashed to the floor in a heap, my head hitting the sideboard of the bed. Embarrassed again at having caused such a ruckus, I used my good arm to pull my upper body back up onto the mattress.

The door burst open, and there was Bridget Scott. Her look of concern quickly changed to merriment at the sight of me draped over the bed, the nightshirt failing to completely cover my buttocks. She burst out laughing at my plight until I was able to roll over and get myself situated, even then she could not help allowing a giggle to escape. I gave her a pleading look and said, "Stop!"

But then I could not help myself either and started laughing myself. Her giggle was that infectious.

By the time we got our wits about us, I noticed that it was getting fully light outside and figured out that it was morning, not evening as I had previously assumed.

In the growing light, I got a better look at Bridget as she fussed about, getting me back into bed. She was a little shorter, but not overly so, and roundish but in all the right places. My fall must have woken her, she was in a housecoat and her hair was astray. Obviously she had not had the time to put herself together.

"I want to thank you for your hospitality and kindness, I shall be out of your hair shortly," I told her.

This caused her hand to move to her hair reflexively. "You're welcome, doctor," she answered. "I would hope for the same courtesy should my husband be in your circumstances."

On that note, she bustled out, Petey was back in about fifteen minutes with a bowl of soup and a chunk of bread.

"Lef'overs," he announced.

It was rabbit.

41

I spent the next week recuperating. Initially I was weak as a kitten, but Bridget Scott was an admirable nurse and by the third day, I was on my feet again. After that, I tried my best to make myself useful around the place, splitting wood for the fire, some repair on the roof shingles, and shoring up the outhouse—things that had been neglected when the man of the house had been gone for over three years. The house itself was in great shape; Peter Scott was an engineer and had literally built the place like a fort. The foundation was bricked and good quality, unlike much in Maryland made from the native clay. The wings of the home angled away from the central living area, providing fields of fire on any approach with the whole resting atop a small hill on the property. Just like a fort.

I had to take it easy; I ran low on energy rather quickly which was not at all like me and I was bothered by a persistent cough. Still Bridget seemed to appreciate the help. Little Petey idolized me, followed me around like a puppy, asking never-ending questions; and my wound began to heal nicely with no sign of infection setting in. Evenings after supper were spent around the fire and after Petey went to bed, Bridget opened up talking with me while knitting or mending. I learned much about her husband. Easy to see she had been lacking in adult conversation for a very long time.

Unable to restrain my curiosity, I sent Petey into Port Tobacco to fetch me a newspaper, but there was no mention of any attempt on the president or any mention of John Wilkes Booth. I began to wonder if Booth had sold me out, perhaps to divert attention from himself or maybe so he didn't have to share any credit if his scheme succeeded. There was not even any mention in the paper of the authorities looking for me which left me doubly suspicious.

During our nighttime chats, Bridget told me that Pete Scott Sr. had been a sergeant in the Maryland militia before the war in the sapper company as per his engineering experience. He had been involved in destroying railroad bridges on the order of Thomas Hicks, the state governor in 1861 to prevent Union troops access through Maryland to attack the Southern states. He then found himself with a federal warrant for his arrest for following orders. Given that others in his unit had been arrested and imprisoned with no recourse to trial or lawyer, he spooked and accompanied General Steuart to Virginia, offering his services to the Confederacy. He had served in the First Maryland Regiment until their enlistments had expired but then found he still couldn't return home or be arrested for treason. He had reupped when the Second Maryland was formed, receiving a commission as a lieutenant in charge of their sapper detail. Most recently, he had been assigned to the engineer battalion in the army of the Shenandoah under Jubal Early. Bridget had received no correspondence from him since the defeat of that force at Cedar Creek in October, more than three months previously. She feared the worst which was painful to watch. She obviously loved her husband deeply.

I tried to console her, telling her that it was more difficult than ever to get letters through the Union lines; but inside, I was thinking that his promotion to officer sealed his doom. The culture in the Confederate Army was that officers lead from the front. That is how they managed to win so many fights when they had less men, less equipment, and less resources. It's also why so many of their best leaders were now dead. I read somewhere, after the war, that almost 20 percent of all Confederate generals were killed in battle or died of wounds received in combat.

In any case, the blissful domesticity of the Scott household made me start to question returning to my duty. Especially with the knowledge that someone in my circle had informed on me to the enemy. The question of how soon I was going to be able to depart was taken out of my hands because then, I became sick. It started with a fever and my persistent cough got worse, then progressed from there. I have only vague recollections of events. I do remember the grain of the wood on the bedroom door resembling a face. It was a veritable death mask, and it scared me. I was thinking it was calling for me to pass over into the realm of the dead. I recall another incident where I was trying to swat insects that, I was certain in my delirium, were covering the wall of the room.

Lastly, I remember waking up locked in the arms of a beautiful woman, stark naked, and covered in sweat. I'm not sure what transpired during that event, but it broke my fever and I was able to sleep deeply after that. If it was real, it must have been Bridget Scott, but she never spoke of it after and as she was such a decent woman, I never brought the matter up either. She did tell me afterward that I was responsible for my own recovery, that I had given her explicit instructions on an herbal remedy made from lung wort and oregano, along with feeding me red-dye salts from her paint set ground and mixed with vegetable grease and vinegar (which she suspected would just poison me). I had told her to make sure I was getting plenty of water and to mix in some apple cider. She told me I had requested limes, but there was no way to acquire those. Sam Mudd and I had experimented with the red azo dye back in college. I made a mental note to pass on this field test result to Sam when I saw him next. My urine was bright red for a week.

Toward the end of February, I could no longer tolerate my own inaction; my shoulder and arm, although still sore, had recovered some small range of motion without causing me considerable pain, and the war news was grim. John Hood had destroyed his Army of Tennessee at Franklin and Nashville, leaving no effective fighting force west of the Appalachians. Sherman had taken and destroyed Savannah, Charleston, and Columbia, South Carolina and was moving into North Carolina. Joe Johnston was powerless to even slow him down. Grant's pivot westward to cut off Lee's supplies via the Plank Road and the Richmond and Danville Railroad had been stymied at Hatcher's Run, but it had forced General Lee to have to spread his forces very thin in his defenses. Desertion was rampant in the Confederate Army, and it seemed only a matter of time before Yankee General Sheridan sent part of his force from the Shenandoah

Valley to slam any backdoor escape route closed on Lee. I determined that now was the time, if I was to make any difference to the outcome of the war. In addition, I was nursing a seething grudge against whomever it was that set me up. Getting shot has a way of making one desire a little payback for the experience.

The weather that month had been terrible with repeated massive storms, wind, rain, snow, and hail to the point that a rumor had circulated that there had been no full moon during the month. I, however, knew differently; my escapade with the Yankee cavalry had occurred just past the January moon, else wandering around in the forest at night would have been impossible, even in spite of the clouds. The weather kept us inside for the most part, and perhaps cabin fever also played a role in my decision to depart.

Before leaving, I showed Petey how to grease the well pump and also the foot pump in the kitchen. Pete Scott had rigged an ingenious invention that allowed Bridget to draw water directly to her kitchen sink simply by pushing up and down on a pedal on the floor. I also gave Bridget fifty dollars for providing me shelter. She tried to refuse, but I was insistent. Besides she had altered one of Pete Scott's suits to fit me as my uniform and clothes were completely destroyed. Bridget was blinking back tears when I left, I think she had come to the conclusion that her husband was dead and was hoping I might stay on. I told her I was forever in her debt and that I would come back to check on her.

I picked Monday, the twenty-seventh of February, to leave. The skies had finally cleared, and the sun was warm. Good thing because it took me four hours to walk to Port Tobacco. I passed a Yankee cavalry patrol on the way into town, and there was an infantry detail guarding the port facility itself; although normally, this was just a fishing harbor. In the past, they used to ship consignments of tobacco, hence the name of the town; but big firms, like my father's, had drawn the product from the countryside to ship quantity through the big port facility in Baltimore. The rail system had changed everything in rural Maryland.

Nobody paid any attention to me. I was just a busted-up fellow in an out-of-date suit. There were so many casualties from the war that cripples were the norm rather than the exception. I was able to buy a horse at the livery, and he directed me to the harness shop down the street for saddle and tackle. Both proprietors did take notice that I had money. Apparently there was not much of that going on in Port Tobacco.

I was hoping to make Dr. Mudd's farm before dark, but I was to be disappointed. I hadn't figured the horse I'd bought to be anything special, but he still looked passable when I'd checked him over. By the time I was a mile or two down the road, I realized he was elderly. It seemed I'd been duped by an expert. His teeth had been capped and whitened, hooves shaved, and even his mane and tail had been treated with boot-black to make them shiny. He'd then been fed oats for a burst of energy.

Too late to turn back when I discovered I'd been taken and by then, the steed's energy had dissipated as well. Pretty much the same speed when I was dismounted walking him as when I was riding. We spent the remainder of the day slowly plodding on up the road, and it was well after dark before I reached the turn at Waldorf. I'd had time to think on the way and remap my strategy. The enemy had found out who I was and likely what I was up to, and I had no idea who in my network had given them that information. On the positive side, no one had seen me in over five weeks; they would possibly be thinking I was dead or, at least, had given up. My adjusted plan was to avoid any familiar contacts and meet with Wilkes Booth in Washington without any witness to the event. If the enemy was alerted to my presence, I would know who was responsible. In the meantime, I had enough money to get by and I figured I would turn the tables by watching the members of Booth's gang. It was obviously a dangerous gambit but limiting my exposure limited my risk.

Instead of going to the house at the Mudd farm, I bypassed and went directly down to the tobacco shed. I pulled down some hay for my horse and gave him a good rubdown. He may have been old and slow, but he was also compliant, especially when he saw that I was determined to take good care of him. Just the sort of animal that would not attract any attention. I crawled up into the loft, a bit sore, having not pushed things with my wound until then. I did get a good night's sleep, but it took some fortitude to crawl out the next morning, especially when I looked out and saw it was gray and drizzling in the predawn light.

42

Even with an early start, it took me all day in the drizzling rain to make it into Washington, although I did happen upon a great location to headquarter out of. On I Street, just above Massachusetts Avenue, between second and third, there was a boarding house run by a Mrs. Pipes, an older home that was once nice; but the neighborhood had succumbed to the ravages of time, especially after the train tracks came through just to the east. Mrs. Pipes' house still stood out like a gem in comparison to those around it. The lot was larger and included a stable behind the house where I could house and feed my noble steed for a few pennies more.

My first order of business was to augment my wardrobe; for that, I knew just the place. I visited a second-hand store down by the navy yard. I purchased duck pants that fit tight in the seat but loose in the legs, a checkered shirt, and round tarpaulin hat, complete with ribbon. Then I stunned the skinny man behind the counter by selecting a very nice suit with a derby hat, perfect because the jacket was a half-size larger than I needed and would disguise my shoulder holster. It did smell a little musty like someone had died in it. I think the clerk was expecting me to run from the store without paying after viewing my crazy selections; he kept his hand on something under the counter that was most likely a club.

The next day was the second of March, and I made a trip to Baltimore. I took the train because I needed to be fast. Saturday, the fourth, was Inauguration Day, and I knew Wilkes Booth would not miss the spectacle. His hate for Lincoln was palpable. The Camden Yard station in Baltimore is a short distance from the waterfront where I found my father in his office. He didn't seem too surprised to see me.

"There's a rumor going around that the Yankees killed you," he said. "But when the Pinkertons came snooping around, I figured you'd gotten away. Besides you're too hard-headed to die that easy."

"It was a nearer thing than I wanted it to be," I admitted. "You have to know that if they came here looking for me that somebody snitched."

He laughed at that and said, "Yeah, I told them I'd disowned you." Then he sobered and added, "I hope the lesson made you more careful."

"The guy who almost got me called me by name. That was a bit disconcerting."

"But then you took the risk coming here to see me, it must be important," he mused.

My turn to laugh. "Don't worry, it's not lawyers, guns, or money."

I explained what I needed and gave him the address of the boarding house where I was staying.

"I'm going by Arthur Welch."

That made his head jerk up; it was my maternal grandfather's name. Although it was John Arthur, like me, he went by Art.

"Well, it's a good name," he said. "The rest won't be a problem. I'll send Gayle down with it."

At that point, an assistant knocked and came in with a document for my father's signature, so I got up to take my leave.

He looked at me a little wistfully and asked, "Can't you just walk away from this? At this point in the game, there is nothing you can change."

"Someone decided that I needed to be killed," I responded, now getting a little angry. "One of my men, a decent guy, was shot dead, another was captured, and they would have hanged me if they caught me, even though I was in uniform at the time. As it was, I was shot in the shoulder and barely escaped. This isn't about a mission any longer."

He looked me in the eye then and thought for a second before replying, "You have time then so be careful. Remember that revenge is a dish best served cold."

Where I was impetuous, I could always count on my father to be level-headed and thoughtful. Until you made him angry. Then not so much, as I had learned in my childhood.

I caught the afternoon train back to Washington, then walked to the boarding house. On a whim, I decided to turn south and make my way to Mary Surratt's house just to see if I could find a spot to watch the place without being seen. As it was getting dark and turning colder, I took advantage and turned my collar up which further obscured my face. On the surface, it would appear that H Street and I Street would be a block apart. But Washington has wide diagonal avenues that bisect the city and themselves, typically intersecting at public squares and parks. Really a marvelous design for a small city, but Washington had grown rapidly during wartime. Traffic norms were not always adhered to and crossing a diagonal avenue from a parallel north-south or east-west street could be a perilous venture when the thoroughfares were busy. In any case, I had to cross Massachusetts Avenue on foot, in the mud, at six in the evening which required a zigzag dodge of horses, carts, and wagons, all going in various directions and all in a hurry to get where they were going in the rain. And I thought spying was dangerous work.

I moved down H Street from the east, remaining across from the Surratt house. There was a grocery on the corner of sixth and H which had a four-step parallel walk-up from the Sixth Street side. I took advantage by parking myself behind the steps in the shadows where I had a good view of the front entrance to the Surratt boarding house. The gaslight pole was across the street, creating a perfect shadow to hide myself in.

I pulled out my pipe and settled in to see what might transpire. After nearly an hour with no activity, I was getting ready to go; just waiting was cold wet work. Rain water was trickling down the back of my neck, and I had not yet had my supper so my stomach was growling when the door opened and two men stepped out. The entrance to the house was on the second floor with stairs leading down to the sidewalk; the men remained on the small landing just outside the door, talking and laughing. In the light streaming out the open door, I instantly recognized John Surratt, the other man was smaller, dark-complexioned, and sported a thin mustache. I remembered him vaguely from my previous meeting there but did not recall his name; one of those men who does not stand out among others. As I watched, the men shook hands, then Surratt went down the stairs and walked briskly down the street away from me. The other man shivered and crossed his arms, not wearing a coat, then he turned and went back inside the house. I remained at my post for another half-hour, then decided to call it quits and returned to my digs and my supper.

The following day, I was up early, put on my old suit, saddled my horse, and rode down to the National Hotel on Sixth and Pennsylvania Avenue. The day was just gray and cloudy at first, then resumed the drizzle that had been ongoing over the past four days. It was only just over a half-mile but I as I was planning to see what Wilkes Booth's day was like, I wanted to be able to follow him if he caught a hack. It was well-known (especially among the wayward ladies of the city) that Booth kept room number 228 at the hotel and lived there when he was in town. That area of Pennsylvania Avenue was centrally located; the White House was not far and Ford's Theater, where Booth often performed, was equidistant in the other direction. As long as you remained on the avenue, it was relatively safe. The center market was a block down, and many commercial enterprises lined the way, along with what were called federal row houses. Back a block, however, the area was known as murder bay. It was not safe for the average citizen at night. Brothels had even spilled over into the row houses. Soldiers on leave were cautioned to stay in groups when frequenting the partying establishments. Squad strength was recommended.

I tied off my horse on the north side of the avenue in front of a commercial bakery known as St. James Millers, a busy location where I would not attract undue attention. I parked myself on a bench toward the corner, under the eaves of the building, where I had a clear view of the front entrance of the hotel, then started my waiting game. My patience paid off, and sure enough, at about 10:45 a.m., Booth emerged from the entrance in a hurry and hailed a cabby, the buggy pulling forward from the front of a line gathered there for that purpose. I jumped up and hurried to untie my horse, ready to mount and follow.

Just then, a second man appeared at the hotel entrance, it was George Sanders. I decided there was no way it could be a coincidence—they must have just met for some purpose. I kept concealed behind my horse to see what would transpire, watching from over the top of the saddle. Booth took off east, then Sanders caught the next hack in line and jumped inside. I made a quick decision to follow Sanders to see what he was up to. I followed him across town until he pulled up at the train station. I tailed him in on foot and was disappointed when he just boarded the northbound for New York City. I confirmed at the ticket counter that he had purchased fare only to New York. I received no other clues as to his plans.

I departed feeling like the distraction had wasted my morning. I decided to return to the Surratt house on Sixth and H Street to see if anything was happening there, but all was quiet. My horse made me stand out more than the night before. When the proprietor of the store started to give me the evil eye, I went up into the store to make a purchase. I was cold and damp, in any case. I got some fresh sweet bread and dried pork for a midday meal, avoiding the questions the man kept asking me the whole time. I came to the conclusion that my approach to the problem needed to be more direct, so I mounted up and returned to Mrs. Pipes' house. Even my horse was giving me the glare for dragging him back and forth across town when he would have preferred to be chomping hay at the stable behind the boarding house.

Saturday, the fourth, was Inauguration Day. I was up and out the door early to make sure I could reconnoiter the area in order to effectively scan the crowd. I wore my newly-acquired nice black suit, and I went armed with my revolver. Just in case. I went down Second Street then used Constitution Avenue to skirt around the capitol building to the east. It was raining again that morning, and a blustery wind had come up overnight. The roads were muddy in spite of the paving stones. After a month solid of rain, the drainage system couldn't keep up. I arrived about two hours before events were to begin and with the weather, there were few bystanders gathered as yet.

The dome of the capitol building had just been completed with the bronze Statue of Freedom on top. Brand-new, it glinted with reflections even in the weak light of the cloudy morning. The new white of the dome contrasted just slightly with the older construction below it. It was a magnificent structure with the Greek columns guarding the main entrance and the two large wings designated for each of the two houses of congress. The whole was set up on a small hill so it could be seen from many vantage points around the city.

I chose the south side raised lawn to plant myself by the railing, the wall beneath providing some relief from the wind. I was across from the entrance to the House of Representatives with a good view of the east entrance steps to the capitol, perhaps just over fifty yards away. As I waited, the crowd began to fill in, it looked like most of the city population were going to arrive. A photographer came elbowing his way through until he got to the vantage point of the wall. He tried to tell me the importance of his mission to get me to move, but I just laughed. He grumbled but was obliged to try with the group to my left and was more successful after launching into a speech about how his equipment worked and even enlisted their help setting up. They say a sucker is born every minute.

About that time, I caught sight of Wilkes Booth. He had drawn on his notoriety to make his way to the front, just below the capitol steps. I recognized his companion as well, Lucy Hale, the daughter of a New Hampshire senator. She was acknowledged as a belle of the city. During my days attending soirees in Washington, prior to the war, she had cut a wide swath with the upper-class eligible bachelors. It was even said that she had dated Bob Lincoln, the president's son before that young man had joined the army and left town to be a staff officer with Ulysses Grant down in Virginia. Why she would trade that for Booth, I couldn't fathom, but women somehow didn't seem to notice that Wilkes Booth was so full of shit that his eyes were brown. Funny, Lucy's dad was a hard-core abolitionist. I couldn't see

John Parker Hale approving of Booth and his rabid proslavery politics. Maybe that was the draw.

I determined that my best plan would be to wait and trump up a chance encounter with Booth after the event; easier than trying to get to him in a crowd of ten thousand people or more. Just then, the dignitaries at the top of the steps started motioning and yelling for quiet. An announcement was made that due to the weather, the inauguration proceedings were to be done in the senate chambers but that the president would come back out and say some words following. That caused a lot of grumbling; only a couple of hundred would be able to fit in the gallery inside. The rest of us were left miserable in the wind, rain, and mud. I noticed that mostly it was members of the press that were allowed in, but to my dismay, Wilkes Booth and Lucy Hale made it in as well.

I read in the newspaper later that Andy Johnson was drunk during his swearing in, that he gave the Bible a slurping kiss instead of placing his hand upon it. He then launched into a long rambling speech that nobody could understand until Hannibal Hamlin had to tug on his sleeve to make him stop. Johnson's next task should have been to swear in the newly-elected senators, but a clerk was brought in to accomplish this instead.

Meanwhile outside, the wind had died. It stopped raining, and the sun began to break through the clouds intermittently, warming things up a bit. The dignitaries running the show decided to return to the capitol steps outside to swear in Lincoln. After Solomon Chase completed this task, Lincoln turned toward the audience to speak. He started by saying that since this was his second term and since everyone knew what he stood for and about the progress of the war, that he would keep it brief. At that, some chowder heads in a group in the audience began to clap loudly, causing a ripple of laughter to run through the crowd. The remainder of the speech took less than ten minutes. In spite of my dislike for the man, I had to admit that he could speak. He had those people in the palm of his hand, speechless. Even when he was done and turned to go inside, there was only a smattering of applause, everyone silently going over his message of reconciliation and to remember that both sides thought their cause righteous in the eyes of God.

Lincoln, at least, seemed to be staying on message. In the past year, he had been proposing that states in rebellion should be readmitted when 10 percent of their population had signed an oath of allegiance; but congress wouldn't support that, preferring a harder line. When the congress came back, passing the Wade-Davis bill, insisting on 50 percent minimum, Lincoln had pocket vetoed that measure.

The crowd began to thin, most heading north to Constitution Avenue where the parade was beginning to form up. I made my move, keeping Booth and Lucy Hale in sight. They were slow, being in front meant they were in the back of the crowd when it came to exiting. They tried to skirt the crowd by heading east, directly on to Capitol Street which brought them directly toward me. I diagonaled to intersect their path and pulled in right beside them.

"Well, if it isn't John Wilkes Booth!" I announced innocently. Then with just a trace of sarcasm, "Imagine finding you here."

He looked at me, then I saw the recognition come over his face, and his mouth hung open. But it was Lucy Hale that took me by surprise.

"Why, Johnny Carlile!" she said, giving me that marvelous smile that had slain so many men. "It's been an age!"

Now I never realized she knew of my existence. I didn't think I even knew anyone who had even made it onto her dance card. But my reactions were fast, so I gave her a short bow, looked surprised to see her, and said in my best southern drawl, "Lucy Hale, and looking as lovely as you ever were."

That at least drew a friendly smile, but the distraction had allowed Wilkes Booth time to recover his composure.

I turned back to Booth and said, "I missed you at that President Lincoln thing, I thought you were supposed to perform for him."

He gave me a bored look and replied, "The president changed his mind at the last minute and canceled. But I never saw you afterward?" It was a question.

"I caught a sickness from being out in the weather, it turned into pneumonia."

Lucy Hale's turn to break in again, "So glad you have recovered, so many people never do."

"I'm a doctor, ma'am," I replied.

"That's right, you were attending the university when we last spoke!" She was very nice, but I still didn't think we had ever talked before.

I returned my attention to Booth. "Let's talk, say Sunday dinner tomorrow. Noon at the National dining room?"

He looked nervous but agreed. I took my leave then, forcing Booth to shake my hand and bowing to Lucy Hale.

"So nice to see you again, *Ms.* Hale." I put the emphasis on the miss.

43

Midday dinner at the National Hotel was a sumptuous affair, even if it cost a quarter. Although the National had been surpassed in some estimations by newer establishments such as The Willard, they still employed a fine chef to keep up on appearances. The onion consume was topped with bread and baked cheese. I went with the fresh oysters instead of the steak. I found, at that time of year, beef was universally cooked to shoe leather to get rid of the taint of severe aging.

Booth was already there when I arrived. He was quick to note that he no longer worked under my supervision.

"I know Sanders took you over personally when I was out sick, but I also wanted to make sure you aren't in the way of my other operation in the city."

That got him going, he had no doubt been told that I was out of the picture.

"Sanders told me you were dead, that's why I was so surprised to see you yesterday," he blurted out. "I was not informed about any other operation!"

"Hmm," I mused. "He didn't tell you about the tunneling..." There was a popular rumor that Confederate agents, coal miners from the Appalachians, were digging under the White House to plant explosives and blow up the president. Personally I thought that was hilarious. The city had been built on a swamp, and the streets didn't even drain when the rains came. It would be an issue keeping any tunnels from filling with water.

"They don't tell me anything," Booth complained.

I decided that pushing him was going to get me information, so while finagling an oyster into my mouth in as gentlemanly manner as could be achieved, I said, "It's just a question of *trust*." With emphasis on the word *trust*.

Booth just exploded at that. He pushed back his half-eaten plate of food and raised his voice. "*I am a patriot*."

"Hush," I cautioned. Everyone was staring over at us, many of them recognizing Booth. In my head, I was thinking that scoundrels often claimed patriotism when justifying their deeds.

"Sanders advised me to just kill Lincoln and have done with it," he said more quietly. "I should have done it yesterday. I had my pistol, and I was about ten feet from him."

"George Sanders thinks nothing can be accomplished without murder, destruction, and acts of terror," I responded. "He would be very pleased with himself while he watched you swinging on the gallows."

"Abraham Lincoln needs to die. Didn't you hear his speech yesterday?" This time, Booth was leaning in, whispering to me. "He doesn't just want to free the niggers, he wants them to vote and to run for office. To bring their ignorance into running my country!"

I had to think about how to answer that without causing a scene and bringing attention to myself. It also came to mind that the Confederate States was his country of choice but so many inconsistencies, so little time. "I heard him talk about reconciliation, that's all. Besides there's already plenty of ignorance in the government."

"You have some funny sympathies," he said, voice dripping with sarcasm. "What kind of patriot are *you*?"

"The kind that believes that citizens should not be imprisoned without legal process. The kind that believes that taxes shouldn't be leveed on some for the benefit of others or that influence shouldn't be bought. Governments are instituted among men, deriving their just powers from the consent of the governed. Whenever any form of government becomes destructive of these ends, it is the right of the people to alter or to abolish it and to institute new government. I guess that makes me a Jeffersonian."

My reference to the Declaration of Independence quieted him some. He pulled a coin from his pocket and placed it on the table, then pushed his chair back and stood.

"If you want in, we have an opportunity coming up to finish the original plan," he said. "Ms. Hale has told me that Lincoln is due for a visit to a military hospital in about a week to coincide with a performance being held for the invalids, and she has an invitation. My men will be ready to grab him on the road going there."

My face must have given away my interest because he gave me a sly look.

"Be glad to help out," I told him.

"Can I drop you a note at The Willard or should I use our usual cipher and drop?" The bland look on his face told me he had already checked The Willard and found out I wasn't registered there, at least under my own name.

So I told him, "Not using my real name there so go ahead and use the drop."

"Being careful?" he asked. "That's smart."

"Yup," I answered while standing and pulling a coin of my own out to cover the fare.

On leaving, I stopped to look in the shop windows, checking out my surroundings in the reflection off the glass. It took three windows before I spotted him, the small man with the thin mustache that I had seen at the Surratt house. I was expecting to be followed and had planned for it. I strolled slowly west on Pennsylvania Avenue, making sure he had no difficulty keeping up. As I passed the White House, I even stopped to stare at the building like a tourist. When I came to The Willard, I didn't even hesitate; I walked straight into the lobby then up the grand staircase as if going to a room. On the second floor, I went down the hall to the rear of the building, down the fire stairs, and into the alley behind. The whole thing took less than a minute, and I was heading on my way. Just in case, I stopped in a shoe store, positioning myself so that as I was looking over the wares on display, I could see the street through the shop window. In less than five minutes, the proprietor got nervous and asked if he could help me try anything on. I told him I was just looking and left the establishment. It wasn't much time, but nobody seemed to be watching me when I left.

The following day was Monday and thinking I could learn more about Thin-Mustache Man, I set up watching the Surratt house when it was just getting light. It was another gray drizzly day, but fortunately, I didn't have long to wait. He emerged from the house just before 8:00 a.m. with a satchel over his shoulder, turned west on H Street, then the next left on seventh. He was completely unaware that I was there, apparently intent on his destination. When he turned right onto Pennsylvania Avenue and headed up toward the White House, I began to suspect that his goal was to stake out The Willard to continue surveillance on me; but to my surprise, when he was just past the White House, he turned and walked down the drive toward the War Department building, joining the queue of others entering the place to start work.

I slipped into the line and went in behind him. The structure was narrow and deep with the Greek revival architecture so common to the public buildings in Washington. The inside was carpeted, and the walls were decorated with oil paintings depicting historical battle scenes. How they managed to keep the carpeting in such satisfactory shape in a muddy city like Washington, I do not know, but the place was kept tidy. I watched while Thin-Mustache Man went down a first floor hall to a suite of offices on the left marked "Charles Dana, Assistant Secretary." He did not enter the main office but a subsidiary door off to the side.

I went to the receptionist window and stood in a line that was growing quickly, seems Secretary of War Stanton took appointments en masse in the morning, and anyone trying to get appointment or promotion, curry favor, or provide supply for the army needed to be on his list before he arrived. When my turn came, I simply asked if the offices to the right of Secretary Dana were for his assistants. The man behind the counter snorted at that, grinned, and said, "Suppose so, in a way!"

He clarified by telling me that the assistant secretary was responsible for rooting out fraud, along with other intelligence operations, that the offices I was asking about housed what was known as the Secret Service. I thanked him and turned to leave. Just then, a man at the door stepped inside and announced loudly that Secretary Stanton's carriage had just pulled into the drive. Watching all the employees launch into busily doing their jobs after hearing the news gave me some indication of what Stanton must be like as a boss. I slipped out the door before he exited his carriage and went back down the drive to Pennsylvania Avenue. I noted as I left that Stanton entered the War Department building at precisely nine o'clock.

I walked the mile or so back to the Surratt house, deep in thought, plotting strategy. When I arrived, I went straight up the stairs and rapped on the door. My knock was answered by Mary Surratt. She said, "Why, Dr. Carlile, this is a surprise. What might I help you with?"

I gave her a short bow and replied, "Ma'am, I'm looking to have a word with your son, John, if he is at home."

"Why, yes, he is, although he is just packing for a trip. If you would sit in the drawing room, I'll let him know you are here. Can I get you anything?"

"Thank you, no, ma'am," I replied. "But I appreciate your hospitality."

Mary Surratt disappeared up the stairs and thirty seconds later, John Surratt bounded down them.

"How are you, doc?" he asked. "Mother said you needed a word."

"There's a man living here, part of Booth's team," I said slowly, trying to carefully pick my words. "I saw him at the War Department this morning."

"That would be Louis Weichmann," he said breaking into a grin. "He works there. We went to the seminary together before the war."

"He works for the Yankee military intelligence?" I asked incredulously.

"No," responded Surratt, his grin getting wider. "He's a clerk for Peter Watson, supply stuff. He does exaggerate his importance in the scheme of things. Booth and George Sanders both use him to get information, but I don't believe there's ever very much that's useful."

"This morning, I saw him take a satchel into the offices of Colonel Dana's Secret Service boys," I told him. "Any reason for that?"

"Hmm, don't know." This time, without the smile. "You should ask Booth."

"Booth and I don't play well together," I said. "That's why I came to you."

John Surratt became serious. "Listen, doc," he said. "When you disappeared, Booth wasn't surprised. But George Sanders was the one who looked like the cat who ate the canary. If I were you, I'd run, it's already well-known that you finish your missions your own way. Many of us admire you for that, but Sanders hates you. His boy died as a prisoner of war at Fort Warren, I think he is bent on retribution while you have a more refined approach."

That gave me something to think about for sure. I thanked John Surratt for seeing me and departed for my boarding house, detouring down Massachusetts Avenue to a leather maker I had seen there. I ordered a new medical bag to my own specifications, my belongings, for the most part, had been lost or were in storage in Montreal. I was promised it would be ready before the end of the week.

On the afternoon of Thursday, the ninth, Mrs. Pipes knocked on my door and let me know I had a visitor. By the little shade of apprehension in her voice, I figured it had to be Gayle. There was nobody waiting at the bottom of the stairs, so I turned to ask Mrs. Pipes as she was trailing me. I saw her eyes widen fearfully. Before I had time to react, I was grabbed roughly from behind, right around my middle, pinning my arms to my sides. I was picked up bodily, suspended in the air, and held there, helpless, with no opportunity for any leverage.

"Okay, Gayle, you can put me down now," I grunted out. I reassured Mrs. Pipes that he was an old friend and far less scary than he looked. She gave me a "harrumph" as she went by me toward the kitchen, but I could see the look in her eye had turned from terror to amusement. Gayle, on his part, spun me around and gave me a squeeze that nearly broke me in half.

Once free of Gayle's grip, I gave him a slap on the back and offered to take him out for supper. We left the package he had brought in my room, then walked over to the Ebbitt House Hotel on the corner of Fourteenth and F Streets as they served the best home-style food in the city. Using the term *hotel* for the Ebitt House was a little bit of a misnomer. It was actually a boarding house. Since it was owned by Caleb Willard, the brother of Henry, who owned The Willard Hotel, they did often take in any overflow from that establishment. The place had been known as Frenchman's Hotel in my college days, back then a real hotel, so the restaurant and bar inside had continued to operate unabated. There was one interesting feature—Caleb Willard had bought four buildings on the block and had enclosed the old alley that had run between them, turning it into bathrooms. These had wonderful oval windows, but that just meant that people going by could watch while the facilities were being used.

It turned out to be a mistake taking Gayle to the Ebbitt House. He knew Washington well, and we had no sooner finished our meal when he grabbed me by the arm and propelled me around the block to the Bull's Head. Whereas the remainder of the structures on the street Ebbitt House was on were occupied by satellite newspaper offices from various northern publications, behind the hotel lay the Bull's Head. This establishment marked the northern boundary of Murder Row and was infamous as a saloon where anything goes, copious amounts of beer and liquor flowing unchecked, gambling tables both public and private, and girls. Girls that performed bur-lesque on a stage that occupied one whole wall of the interior. Girls that wrestled in a mud pit in the center of the place, dressed only in camisole and bloomers, the wet fabric leaving little to the imagina-tion. Serving girls scraping for tips by delivering drinks, mostly hover-ing around the gambling areas where the money was right out on the tables. And of course, the regular professional girls who worked out of the upstairs brothel. There was even a gift shop where fine cigars, jewelry, or other expensive gifts could be purchased, although it was rumored that the main function of the shop was to pawn belongings or grant credit to the patrons, if suitable collateral could be provided.

The Bull's Head also employed a small private army of thugs to maintain order, protect the girls from being mauled, and relieve unsuspecting customers of hard-won gains at the tables. It was also said that the owner kept extensive records on the activities of the patrons, and the girls were expected to pass on any tidbit of insider information that might then be forwarded in turn for a reward. Gayle propelled me ahead of him through the doorway and past the bouncers; we went straight for the bar and started on pints of beer. Although it was a weekday and the place was not too busy, we luck-ily didn't stand out much among the soldiers on leave, government clerks having an after-work drink, and other working-class types. I could immediately see why. There was a significant game of chance happening in one corner, congressmen supported by their aides and what appeared to be successful businessmen, no doubt footing the bill for this excursion while hoping to get or maintain lucrative contracts. The majority of the waitstaff was hovering around this group like a cloud of mosquitoes hoping for a meal.

I was determined to go slow and barely sipped when Gayle encouraged me to drink or when a toast to old times was proposed. It wasn't too long before he was up and about, seeking livelier entertainment than I was turning out to be. I didn't worry much. Gayle could take care of himself and was pretty level-headed, even when drinking. After a couple of hours, I steered him away from a sketchy-looking prostitute and got him to the door, telling him to remember his sweet wife at home. Then we were away, down the street toward my lodgings, laughing and singing. I noted, soon after leaving the Bull's Head, that a man started out of a doorway to accost us, but one look at Gayle changed his mind and he faded back into the shadows.

Gayle slept that night on the floor of my room but was up and going first thing in the morning, none the worse for wear. He shoved his hat on his head on the way out the door and with another mind-numbing squeeze of a hug and some vague threats about how we were going to party next time he came to see me, he started out the door. All of a sudden, he stopped, turned back toward me, and said, "Oh, almost forgot. Your papa said to tell you that they came lookin' for you again."

Then he was off, down the street, toward the train station. I guess I shouldn't have been surprised by that statement, but I felt a chill go down my spine nonetheless.

I checked the package he had brought me and was pleased with the results. A sheepskin diploma from the Genesee Wesleyan College Medical School in the name of Arthur Welch. It had been folded and washed a couple of times, looking to be at least ten years old. There was a commission, making me a lieutenant in the New York State Militia, Medical Corps Staff, signed by the ex-Governor Horatio Seymore. Then there was the one I really wanted. An official letter ordering me to travel to Washington City in order to investigate a plot to assassinate President Lincoln. This order was addressed to Dr. Arthur Welch, Lieutenant, New York State Militia, and was signed Lafayette C. Baker, Colonel, commanding United States Secret Services. All these documents were wrapped in the dark-blue single-breasted uniform jacket of a Yankee junior officer, single bar on each side of the shoulder board and a silver embroidered MS on each, indicating that I was a medical staff officer. Detail was complete down to the brass buttons depicting an eagle clutching a globe with the inscription "New York" at the bottom. A pair of light-blue trousers and green sash completed the outfit. As I was hanging the uniform, I discovered a package of pipe tobacco in the inside pocket. My father was thorough to the last detail.

The first two documents went into the jacket pocket, but I emptied out my new medical bag onto the bed and inserted the orders into the space in the bottom of the bag as I had done on my previous adventures. The difference was that I did not sew it closed as I wanted fast access if necessary. I then resumed my reconnaissance of Wilkes Booth's operation. If I was hoping to get more on George Sanders, I was disappointed, but I was able to identify several of the other men.

In addition to Louis Weichmann, two others rented from Mary Surratt, the two who had attended the planning meeting previous to our abduction attempt in January. The dark-featured man was George Atzerodt. I found he spent a great deal of time in the bars or just drinking by himself. He struck me as a follower and not a particularly good one. The beefy kid was alternately known as Payne or Powell. Although he was introducing himself as a minister, I saw that he always carried weapons and knew how to use them. He was mean-tempered and perhaps had done some soldiering. I made a mental note to keep him where I could see him in a group situation. I also figured if things went wrong that he would be a good scapegoat; he was vocal about his politics, especially when it came to slavery. Made him feel good about himself if he could find others to beat down or think unkindly of.

As to Louis Weichmann, whom I had already identified, he seemed to be a timid little man, easily pushed around by others. When not working or running errands for Booth, he was usually hanging out with his friend and coworker Gleason from the War Department. Gleason didn't appear to be trading on information as Weichmann surely was, he seemed just to be a guy who didn't mind listening to Weichmann bragging about his exploits in the developing conspiracy.

David Herold was a mystery. He appeared to be in his midtwenties, but I found out later that he was younger than that. He was a fastidious dresser, always in a pressed suit. He was obviously smart and educated yet worked in a pharmacy filling orders. He lived with his parents down by the navy yard in a nice home. In a city full of single women, he was a confirmed bachelor. He operated in the group as Booth's aide, writing and delivering orders to the others, coordinating meetings, and the like. If Booth needed a companion for a trip, Herold was always there. I began to suspect that Herold was in love with Booth.

Three other men I was about to meet were Sam Arnold, Mike O'Laughlen, and Ned Spangler. Sam and Mike were both ex-Confederate soldiers, both discharged for unknown reasons although both younger men. Ned Spangler was a stagehand at Ford's Theater, in awe of Booth, and cared for his horses when he was away. One thing I was to notice about Booth's crew was that they were all from Baltimore in one way or another, and, with the exception of Ned Spangler, they were all young men.

On Tuesday evening, the fourteenth of March, I found a note in our prearranged drop. This was the first time I had collected anything there since my return to Washington; the hair on the back of my neck was up. It was in the standard Confederate service cypher, so I had to wait to decode it until I returned to my lodgings. I had the feeling I was being followed, so I resorted to a few maneuvers on the way but even after I got back, I couldn't shake the feeling. I kept looking out my window half the night to see if anyone was watching the house.

The note set a meeting for the next evening, the fifteenth, at Gauthier's Restaurant on Pennsylvania Avenue. I of course knew of the place but had never been there. Charles Gauthier was a master chef and confectioner, his restaurant on Capitol Hill had been the most high-class establishment in the whole city for many years. In addition to the restaurant and confectioner's shop, Gauthier's catered many of the better parties and events around town, most notably the last three presidential inauguration balls. I was alternately impressed with the apparent importance of the meeting and angry that Booth would waste funds on such an expensive rendezvous. The haute cuisine menu featured there was ala carte; with drinks, a couple could easily spend fifteen dollars on a nice supper. Even the waiter would be expecting a two-dollar tip.

I wore my nice suit for the event, arriving five minutes early for the eight o'clock meet. As I came up to the door, I almost ran into Lucy Hale who was exiting. Her eyes twinkled when we made eye contact. I gave her hand a kiss and asked how supper had been.

"Perfectly spectacular, John," she answered. Then with a sigh, "And the chocolate ice cream is to die for!"

I handed her up into a cab and saw her on her way, relaying the address instructions to the driver. I now understood that our meeting was just an afterthought to Booth's date with Lucy.

Just entering the establishment, I could see what all the fuss was about. The confectionery and comestible store was in the front, white marble counters encased in glass piled with sliced cakes and chocolates formed artistically into the shape of flowers, animals, and other intricate designs. The floor was of chequerware tiles, and the walls featured gilt trim in a helix shape. But what was most amazing was the huge crystal chandelier that was gaslit instead of the usual candles. It emphasized the fastidious cleanliness of the shop. Passing to the rear, I went up two marble steps into the restaurant itself, arriving at the maître d's podium. The floors were carpeted wall-to-wall and the walls beautifully papered. The tables themselves were of the same white marble as the shelves in the store, the chairs ornately carved from a dark-stained hardwood. It cost me a dime just to get to Booth's table, secluded in the back corner of the room.

I was the second to arrive. David Herold was already there and conferring with Booth. There was a bottle in the center of the table with several glasses, I took advantage and poured myself a drop. It was a rather good bourbon. We were soon joined by three others,

John Surratt, of course, I knew, and I was introduced to Sam Arnold and Mike O'Laughlin. We spent twenty minutes or so drinking and talking before getting down to business.

Booth announced that on the evening of Friday, the seventeenth, Lincoln would be attending a performance of a comedy, *Still Waters Run Deep*, at the Campbell Military Hospital. We would waylay his carriage as it came up Sixth Street, on the way to the destination. Campbell Hospital was in the north end of the city, an area known as Uptown. It was located on Boundary Street at the corner of seventh, but Sixth Street was the main thoroughfare north, and there was no doubt this would be utilized as it was the only paved street that far up. There was a small patch of woods on sixth, just south of the intersection of Boundary, providing an ideal spot for our ambush. North of Boundary Street were the freed slave camps and the Ecclesiastical School built for their children; the whole area being a chaos, not even patrolled by the army, it would be easy to head east, then south, to pick up the main road down through Maryland, the same route we had previously planned on using during our January attempt. It was an ideal setup, perhaps the only route in or out of Washington not guarded by armed soldiers.

We discussed having to take our chances getting Lincoln across the Potomac River as our contacts and resources there would not be prepared at such short notice, but it was well worth the risk. When I explained the elderly condition of my mount, I elicited an embarrassing round of laughter from the others and a quizzical look from John Surratt who was familiar with my horsemanship. I was assigned as lookout and would carry a shuttered lantern. I would flash it once if the presidential carriage went by without an escort, twice if there were guards to contend with. I could then make my getaway on my own schedule and not worry about holding up the progress of the group.

On leaving the restaurant, I immediately noticed a man in work clothes begin to follow me, but he was easy to get rid of, obviously an amateur because he did not know what to do when I entered a laundry and went straight through and out the back in spite of the protests of the girls working there. When I came back around the

301

block from the alley, he was still just standing there pondering what to do, just staring at the shop door.

We met Friday evening in the small triangle of grass and scrub brush between where Rhode Island Avenue ends at Sixth Street and the unnamed dirt track crosses perpendicular, north of which was swampy and wooded land, undoubtedly an unusable section of farm-land. We had an additional member, Lewis Powell or Payne or who-ever he really was, the man who hung out at the Surratt boarding house and pretended to be a preacher.

We rode north a hundred yards or so, then I broke off from the group with my lantern, just shy of the wooded area that encroached to line the street further up. The rest of the group continued on the road until they disappeared from my view in the dark and gathering mist. I dismounted, tied my horse off, and pulled up the collar of my coat to begin my wait. My horse was looking longingly at a patch of high weeds just out of his reach, then back at me with a look like I was a traitor. I ignored him and pulled my pistol out of the shoulder holster, double-checking the load and the caps. Just in case.

I waited a long time, not a soul passed by. Nothing. I was think-ing that certainly, we must have somehow missed the carriage when I heard a single horseman approaching from the north. I stood and put my right hand inside my coat, on the butt of my revolver, when out of the mist came John Surratt.

"Nothing yet?" he asked the obvious question. At my grunt in response, he added, "Booth is sending Herold to the hospital to see if we missed him. If so, we'll make an attempt when he starts back for town."

I started to reply but just then, we could hear the unmistakable sound of a carriage approaching on the pavement. Not fast but not slow, so it took a minute for the headlamps to emerge from the dark. Both Surratt and I went expectedly to the edge of the road, and I readied my lantern to send the signal. It was indeed a black-lacquered coach, drawn by a pair of black horses as we expected. As it went by, I saw the man inside clearly, he was short and stout. Not Lincoln. As it passed, the man inside turned to look at us, idle curiosity no doubt.

"Solomon Chase!" said Surratt who recognized him.

"Damnation!" was my reply, letting out my breath that until then, I hadn't realized I was holding.

We remained there, talking quietly. I let Surratt know that I had been followed repeatedly, each time after meeting with Booth. He laughed but not a pleasant laugh. He told me he was leaving in a few days on a new assignment to scope out Elmira prisoner of war camp in New York. I told him the circumstances of my sojourn to Camp Douglas in Chicago and the condition of the prisoners there.

Then the clatter of horsemen coming from the woods. Our group appeared with Booth at the head of the party.

"He wasn't there," said Booth, the disappointment dripping from his words. "Herold went up to the hospital, and Lincoln never showed." They had a spot roped off for him, but he never came."

45

In the Monday morning newspaper, I read that Lincoln had changed his plans. He had delivered a speech to some Yankee soldiers from the balcony of the National Hotel instead of attending the performance at the Campbell Hospital on Friday night. It was a little amusing that it was the National where Wilkes Booth lived, yet Booth was across town, waiting in ambush. Once again, Lincoln was one step ahead.

I had come to the conclusion that the man I wanted was George Sanders, even if it was Booth's men trying to pin down the location of my lodgings. I actually had a vivid dream one night where I had Booth by the front of his shirt with my revolver pointed at his face, demanding to know who gave the order to have me set upon and arrested. Of course, I woke before he could answer, in a sweat. The look of fear on his face, in my dream, was pretty satisfying though.

There was no longer any doubt that the fall of the Confederacy was only a matter of time. I decided that getting to Sanders before he disappeared was a priority, and Washington was not the place I was going to find him. I also knew that the authorities were no longer convinced of my demise, so Canada might be a good place to be for a while. I did figure that I had enough time to check for Sanders at his Brooklyn, New York, residence before having to get out of the country. That night, I thanked Mrs. Pipes for her hospitality, paid her in full, and donated my horse to her, telling her I wouldn't need him further. I packed up, ready for an early morning start.

Tuesday, the twenty-first, dawned clear and cool. I was up early and ready to go. Mrs. Pipes gave me some honey cakes wrapped in a napkin to tide me over on my way; she was always thoughtful like that. I was no sooner out the front door and down to the street when I heard a shout, "That's him!"

I was grabbed roughly by men on each arm and an army officer stepped in front of me.

"John Carlile," he said right into my face.

"That's not me!" I hollered, but he continued to talk over the top of my objections.

"You are under arrest for treason and spying."

I wrenched my shoulders to get out of the grasp of the men who had me and almost did, but then, something slammed into the back of my head. My eyes felt like they were on fire, spots danced in front of me, then things turned black around the periphery of my vision, and my knees gave out. They dropped me, and I landed hard on my backside, rolling onto my side. Then I was picked up under the armpits and dragged off down the road. Even in my dazed condition, I saw Mrs. Pipes on her doorstep, her mouth a big O.

They tossed me bodily onto the floor of a wagon with a canvas cover, five soldiers climbed in behind me and occupied benches on the sides. Getting my wits about me as the wagon started bumping into motion along down the street, I noticed that one of the men had stripes on his sleeves.

"Corporal, this is a mistake—" I started to say.

But he interrupted, "Shut up, Reb, I don't want to hear nothin' you have to say."

I figured that a good attack was my best defense, so I sat up and replied in as cold of a voice as I could manage, "Soldier, I am an officer in the United States Army, you will address me as sir."

The corporal snorted at that, but I could see it started him thinking and a couple of his men looked over at him nervously. I got to my knees and started to brush myself off, then pulled myself up onto the bench forward and away from the soldiers. I'd made enough of an impression that they didn't stop me.

"If you don't believe me, check my bag." They had tossed my duffel and my medical bag into the rear of the wagon. He reached down and undid the drawstring on the bag. Right on top was my uniform coat. That caused him some consternation, but he was no dummy and asked, "How come you're out of uniform? Sir?" Added after a second of thought.

"Special assignment," I said enigmatically. "Why did you men come for me?" Quizzically, conversationally. Building alliances. I wrinkled my forehead for effect, but the effort brought on a sharp pain in the back of my head. I reached my hand back to feel the lump, winced, and said, "What'd you hit me with, a tree?"

That brought on a nervous chuckle from several of the men and one, looking sheepish, said, "Gun butt. You were strugglin'…"

I waved my hand and said, "I understand doin' your duty but did you have to do it so well?" Now they were all chuckling, the tension gone from the back of the wagon.

The corporal then said, "Weren't told the whys, some guy pointed you out an' the cap'n said to grab you up."

"Hmmm," I answered.

Just then, the wagon pulled up to a stop. There was the sound outside of something heavy being moved, then the vehicle pulled forward again for just a few seconds more before coming to a stop again. This time, I could feel the motion of the springs as a man in front climbed down. The corporal also climbed over the tailgate and dropped to the ground. He glared back in at his men and growled, "Watch him." Then he disappeared from view.

About a minute passed, then the corporal was back. He pulled back the canvas flaps covering the rear of the wagon then dropped the tailgate which came down with a significant thud. The four soldiers, still inside, piled out and scrambled to the right to form a line. I stood, bent over, then made my way to the rear before jumping to the brick-paved ground. The landing made my head throb more.

I looked up, blinking in the sunlight. I saw the gate we had just passed through, next to which was a one-story stone building. Occupying the skyline over the roof was the dome of the capitol, shining in the morning sun. With the sun behind me, I knew exactly where I was—the yard of the Old Capitol Prison. The corporal was in front of me, coming around the corner of the wagon was the officer who had accosted me at Mrs. Pipes' house. I saw by the twin bars on his shoulder boards that he was a captain.

I went straight into my act. I came crisply to attention and announced, "Lieutenant Art Welch, sir!"

I could see by his lack of surprise that the corporal had filled him in on this information, but he still looked skeptical.

"You have identification, I take it?" He looked as if he was hoping I did not.

"Left inside coat pocket, sir." I turned around to get my bag, still inside the wagon.

"*Stop!*" he bellowed, making me freeze. I turned back toward him.

"Corporal, if you would be so kind as to get his coat," he ordered.

With a crisp yessir, the man undid the drawstring on my bag and pulled out the uniform coat. Fishing through the pockets, he pulled out first the folded diploma, then the commission, handing the documents to the captain as he pulled them out. The corporal then found my tobacco, he gave that a longing look as he passed the pouch to the captain also. The captain noted the "MS" on my rank insignia as he was looking at my diploma, then examined my commission.

"Why are you here, lieutenant?" he asked.

"Special assignment, sir," I said flatly, hoping to convey reluctance regarding the details.

He seemed to get the hint but then looked me directly in the eyes and asked, "Who is John Carlile?"

I held his gaze while I answered, "No one of my acquaintance."

He thought that over silently for a little while, so I opted to break his concentration.

"Sir, might I request a favor?" I asked. Now he looked put out, if not quite hostile. "Sir," I continued, "I'm likely to lose everything I own just entering a place like this. You appear to be a gentleman, could you hold my belongings until I get this sorted out?"

He broke into a smile of relief at the simple request and said, "Of course, lieutenant." He held out his hand and stated, "Jack Hebert."

We shook, then I reached into my suit jacket and pulled my revolver from the shoulder holster. I almost laughed at the consternation I caused, Hebert and his corporal starting to back pedal, the other soldiers frantically bringing up their rifles. I flipped it around to hold the butt toward Hebert, saying "I'm especially fond of this."

Got their hearts beating fast, served them right for bashing me over the head. Captain Hebert took the pistol from my hand, flashing the corporal a hateful look. He had the men form up around me, telling me finally that my fate was out of his hands.

"Above my pay grade," his exact words.

They formed up around me and marched me into the main First Street entrance. The prison itself was a brick three-story rectangular structure, the bottom floor with high ceilings. They had whitewashed the first floor exterior, possibly to match the two-story wing that had been added and ran the entire length of the south side of the compound and backing on a series of row houses on Capitol Avenue. We entered into a broad hallway that also functioned as a guardroom for the soldiers that were off duty. Immediately my nostrils were assaulted by the smell of filth and human waste. There was also the unmistakable smell that only rats have with their nests full of urine and feces. Once through this, we entered the offices where I was searched, shackled, and read the rules by the captain of the guard. Things like no singing, no communicating with other prisoners, no lights allowed at night, and other things read to me rapid fire. They took my documents and my money. I was then taken to a chair along the wall where a canvas hood was put over my head from behind before they forced me roughly into the seat.

I was just sitting there for about a half-hour when I heard a man's voice say, "John?"

I didn't respond, just tipping my head back until it touched the wall.

"John Carlile?" This time, a little more insistent.

"I wish everyone would just stop," I said wearily.

"Just trying to help."

"If you want to help me, just get someone from the War Department over here to sort this out," I said firmly.

The man just laughed. "This *is* the War Department sorting things out. They run this place. Nobody gets in or out of here without Secretary Stanton's say so. We'll get a panel of officers together for your court martial, then we'll hang you."

I could hear him walk away. They left me there, sitting for at least an hour, before a couple of men came up, yanked me to my feet and two rough blankets were piled into my arms. They had a whole lot of fun walking me down the hall, alternately pushing me or pulling me back. Walking in shackles is not fun to start with without having a bag over your head, so you can't see the obstacles in the way. Luckily my hands were chained in front of me when we reached the staircase because I got a big shove and tripped. I would have landed on my face if I had not caught myself with my hands. When I finally made it to the top of the staircase, I thanked the men for allowing me to be their play toy.

They pushed me along another hall until we came to a door, once through my shackles were removed, although a single new metal cuff was added around my left ankle. A ball and chain. For the duration of my stay there, I would have to carry an eighteen-pound cannon ball if I wanted to move anywhere. The bag was removed from my head, and my captors backed out of the room, the door locking with a loud clank when the lock bolt shot home. The cell was roughly sixteen by fourteen feet with eight bunk beds for furniture; opposite the door was a single-barred window that looked out to the north, overlooking A Street. Thirteen fellow occupants to keep me company, they were all dressed in dirty-blue uniforms. At least they believed me enough to house me with the Yankee miscreants.

Given the choice, men will typically pick the upper bunk, the exception being when they are accompanied by an iron ball. I got the top bunk closest to the door and settled in to my new abode. The other men already had connections among themselves, so I was the odd man out and dressed in civilian clothes. Ignoring me became the formal state of affairs when they found out I was an officer. That was perfectly fine by me; better if the bedbugs, fleas, and other vermin would have followed suit.

The routine was pretty simple: we were allowed downstairs for meals three times per day, the normal fare was either gruel, turnip soup, or salt beef, always accompanied by a hardtack cracker. It was a special day when you actually got a chunk of turnip in your soup. Bowl in one hand, cannon ball in the other. The water was especially bad, worse even than some I had seen at sea after months in the cask. Every two or three days, I was allowed an hour outside in the yard, but only two men at a time were ever allowed outside together. There was a community bucket that was a sink or latrine. This was emptied daily by one of us, taking turns when we went down to breakfast. But dysentery was prevalent due to our diet. By the middle of the night, this bucket could become oppressive. I heard that the largest cell contained twenty-one men; how they managed, I do not know.

I was there nine days, repeatedly asking the guards to have me questioned and brought to trial before I got any response. And then, it came from an unexpected direction. One of the men in my cell smuggled his bread back to the room. That night, he lost a fight over it with a large rodent and came away with a nasty bite. I cut a piece from his shirt for a bandage. I had a small pocket knife I had secreted in my sock on the way in. I kept it hidden, sharp, and let all my cell mates know I had it. I did my best to scrub out the wound on his hand then bandaged it up. I made a pest of myself with the guards until they allowed him to see the doctor.

After that, the men were friendlier; they told me which guards could be bribed to make things easier or make extra rations available. I told them that the guards had already stolen my money on intake and that my pay was being held for me by my CO Colonel Baker in New York, that he was not aware of my current circumstances.

"Lafayette Baker?" one of the men asked incredulously. Everyone was familiar with the saga of Lafayette Baker, part of the reason I had picked him as the signatory for my orders. He was a rogue and a bully who had engaged in questionable detective work before the war. He had found the ear of General Winfield Scott at the beginning of the conflict. He was sent on a mission behind Confederate lines that he completely botched but came back with a whopper of a story, starring himself as the hero and ace intelligence gatherer.

Secretary of War Stanton himself had promoted Baker to colonel and had made him chief of intelligence for the Union Army, replacing Alan Pinkerton. Baker continued to heap praise upon himself while accomplishing nothing other than torture, murder, and false imprisonment and hiring massive numbers of operatives to do that dirty work (the other reason I used Baker's signature). Stanton had finally caught on but, to keep his embarrassment under wraps, had quietly relegated Colonel Baker to managing the civil unrest in New York City.

In any case, the communication between prisoners and guards, then up the chain to the prison managers, must have been better than I thought. The very next afternoon, Friday, the thirty-first by my calculations, I was pulled from my cell. I was marched downstairs and into the prison yard by an armed party. I was beginning to worry that it was a firing squad until they told me to strip off my clothes, then they threw a bucket of cold water over me. They took me into the stone building that housed the guard post by the gate. I also found that the building contained the washroom and kitchen for the guards. I was allowed to scrub down; even if it was cold, it was luxurious, and I was shaved by the post barber. They even provided a cup of real coffee and fresh undergarments, then I dressed in my Yankee uniform which had been hung and brushed.

Still nobody filled me in on the reason for any of this. But after a short few minutes, a carriage pulled up and I was loaded inside where Captain Hebert was waiting for me.

"Seems you got someone's attention, lieutenant," he said, smiling at me.

"Took a while, I thought they were going to neglect me to death." That got a laugh out of him.

It was not far up Pennsylvania Avenue, just past the White House, when we pulled into the drive for the War Department. Captain Hebert may have been the only one in the carriage with me, but I definitely noticed that both the driver and his mate on the box in front were armed. Things were looking up, but I was obviously not quite out of the woods yet.

Hebert escorted me inside the building and down the hall to the office suite I had seen Weichmann enter previously, the one with Charles Dana's name on the door. We went to the right, as Weichmann had, and entered an anteroom consisting of a desk and a line of chairs along one wall. On one side of the desk was the entry to a hall with offices along both sides. I could see this was busy with individuals, both military and civilian, going back and forth, everyone in a big hurry. It was Friday afternoon, and I was sure they were anxious to wrap up assignments before the weekend. On the other side of the desk was a plain, unmarked closed door. When we entered, the clerk behind the desk nodded to Captain Hebert, eyeballed me, then slipped partway through the unmarked door and said something in a low voice that I could not discern.

After a short conversation, the man turned to us and said, "The major will see you now."

The man held the door for us as we entered, closing it quietly behind us. We both stood to attention and saluted the red-haired, red-bearded officer getting up from his chair behind a large oak desk. Hebert said, "Reporting as ordered, sir."

The major waved us to a pair of comfortable leather chairs then sat back down himself. He immediately turned his full attention to me.

"It has come to my attention that you work for Colonel Lafayette Baker."

"Yes, sir," I answered. *Keep it simple, don't volunteer anything*, I told myself. Let them answer their own questions.

"What do you do for Colonel Baker, lieutenant?" was the next question.

I paused, hoping to look uncomfortable. "Begging your pardon, sir, but my orders are not to divulge details except to Colonel Baker or Secretary Stanton." I had thought this scenario through previously, just in case.

The major got rather red in the face and in my peripheral vision, I saw Captain Hebert's eyebrows go up. Then I got lucky. The door opened behind me, and a man stepped in. The other two men jumped up to attention, so I followed suit.

"Sit down, gentlemen," the man commanded, then proceeded to occupy the third leather chair in the room. He sported a black bushy beard and had the silver eagles of a full colonel on his shoulder boards.

"You are Lieutenant Welch," he said. Not a question. "I am Colonel Dana. Do you know who I am?"

I nodded in the affirmative and said, "Yes, sir."

He continued right on, "I overheard you say you have orders from Colonel Baker, might I see those?"

I half turned to include Captain Hebert in my response and said, "In my medical bag."

Hebert rose from his chair and left, telling the other two he would return with the item in question as quickly as possible. Colonel Dana then asked the major if he would check with the secretary to see if he could have a moment of his time. After the major also left, Colonel Dana began to question me intently. I could see he was well-informed about many things but not about things behind his lines. So I spent some time creating a backstory for myself with him, using details from my past experiences to add realism. I told him my initial assignment had been to conduct physical examinations for draft surrogates in New York City. With the federal government instituting a draft to supplement their army, a selected citizen of means could pay another man to serve in his stead, but many of those surrogates were unfit for the service. Then drawing on my experience at Camp Douglas, I told him that I had assisted with an inspection of the prisoner of war camp at Elmira. The major rejoined us during this, and both men listened attentively while I described hospital and barracks conditions.

Dana asked me about my investigation. I repeated that I had been told not to divulge detail and added that I had been told by Colonel Baker not to trust anyone as there were traitors in high places. He also asked me if I had used the alias Dr. John Carlile. I told him, "No, but that is the fourth time I was asked that since I was arrested. Does he resemble me to some degree?"

Dana laughed at that and replied, "We don't know what he looks like, but we do know that he is a Confederate assassin."

Reverse interrogation is an art form, and he had unwittingly provided me with vital information. The hard question I had been waiting for never came up. When cleaning me up for the meeting, the prison guards had to have seen my gunshot wound. Although healed, it was pretty fresh, just about eleven weeks old; and there was no doubt about what might cause such a scar. Seems like after four years of war, these kinds of things were so common as to not draw any notice.

It was well over an hour before Captain Hebert returned with my medical bag. They watched in amusement as I carefully emptied it out on the desk and pulled up the false bottom. All three men crowded around the desk, examining the document. I overheard Colonel Dana indicate that he "would know that signature anywhere." I believe I was thanking my father in no uncertain terms for his attention to detail. The major was sent off, once again, to check in with Stanton, returning with the news that he had time for us.

We trooped out of the office and down the hall, now only dimly-lit and empty, the clerks and other workers and supplicants now long gone for the night. The place was just a little spooky after hours with all the oil paintings on the wall, scenes of conflict and carnage. We entered Secretary Edwin Stanton's office, an unusual arrangement. He stood behind a large table that substituted for a desk, and he made everyone else stand on the other side as well. The room was almost bare of furniture with the exception of a settee, or sofa, on the left wall.

The man himself reminded me instantly of my father. It wasn't his face or the forked beard, it was more the attitude. He had that Quaker bullying, self-righteous, blessed-by-the-Lord certainty that his opinion was the only one that mattered that my father also possessed in excess. At least I was experienced in handling that. Besides it was high-time I unleashed some payback.

"Well, lieutenant, what information do you have?" he blurted out savagely, in an attempt to make me feel insignificant.

I held his gaze, then held up my hand toward the other men in the office as if to indicate that I wasn't prepared to speak in front of just anyone. Stanton sighed, apparently feeling he was indulging my overactive sense of self-importance.

"These gentlemen are in my inner circle of trust, lieutenant. You may speak freely in front of them."

It was time for a good yarn.

A sailor story has to have enough fact to rope in the listener before you lead them down the garden path to amazing events that they didn't think possible, so I started with the basics.

"Colonel Baker sent me to uncover what he believes is an assassination plot against President Lincoln. There is a man named George Sanders who is from New York, he works for Jacob Thompson who is currently in Montreal."

Now I had their attention. Of course they knew Sanders and Thompson.

"I followed Sanders from New York City on the train four weeks ago, that is how I came to be in Washington. Sanders had several meetings while he was here, all in the dining room of the National Hotel."

Time to take them to the promised land.

"His first meeting was with the vice president, Andrew Johnson."

46

There was stunned silence for about three ticks of the clock, then the three men behind me erupted in excited conversation. Edwin Stanton just looked at me silently, appraising.

"You are absolutely certain," he said softly.

"I followed George Sanders from New York," I started out. "He spent two nights at The Willard, I believe he used an assumed name. I staked out the premises, then followed him. He had supper that evening in the National Hotel dining room. I was sitting in the lobby, trying to keep tabs on him, when Vice President Johnson came downstairs and went into the dining room. Of course, this was before the inauguration, so he wasn't the vice president yet. I trumped up an excuse to speak with the maître d' and saw them talking together. A small package changed hands from Johnson to Sanders before Johnson went to his own table."

Now the major had paper and pen out on the corner of the table, scribbling frantically.

"You'll swear to this, lieutenant?" Now Stanton had a hard tone to his voice.

"Of course, sir."

"Go on, son."

I'm not your son, I thought. *Even if you're trying to make me feel like a prodigal one.*

"The next morning, I followed Sanders back to the National Hotel where he had breakfast with two men, one looked to be a thug, the other a preacher. Didn't seem correct to me, so I followed them. They went to a boarding house on Sixth and H Street. I later identified these two men as Powell and Atzerodt. Powell was masquerading as a priest but moves and acts like a soldier. Those men are in cahoots with another man who lives at that boarding house—Louis Weichmann who works here in the War Department."

I was watching the officers to my side carefully out of the corner of my eye when I made this last statement. Colonel Dana maintained a neutral expression, but the major looked up from his scribbling and made eye contact with Captain Hebert.

"George Sanders went to the train station the next day and caught the express for New York City. I confirmed with the ticket agent who indicated that was the final destination. I didn't continue to follow Sanders because I was worried the others might make an attempt on the president at the inauguration, so I began trying to work out the members of the conspiracy here in Washington."

Now I was even receiving smiles and nods of affirmation.

I moved on. "I surveilled the boarding house on H Street, but neither of the men I was watching went to see the inauguration. I spent several days by the grocery on the opposite corner. I think the shopkeeper must have blown my cover, my continued presence there was making him nervous. There was very little activity after that, or at least. as far as I could tell. The woman who owns the boarding house seems to have kicked out Powell and Atzerodt. although Weichmann continues to reside there."

"Oh," I added as an afterthought. "The conspirators had a big meeting at Gauthier's Restaurant on the fifteenth. There were eight or nine of them there. My funds were dwindling, and I couldn't afford the bill of fare. I was on my way back to New York to report my findings to Colonel Baker when I was arrested by Captain Hebert."

"Lieutenant, it seems you've been most active and attentive to your duty," said Stanton. "I'll be sure to let Colonel Baker know."

"Thank you, sir," I responded. "But this kind of thing isn't really my cup of tea, and I couldn't have done too well or I wouldn't have been arrested by you."

Then Colonel Dana broke in with a question. I could see that he was the one person in the room not entirely convinced.

"Lieutenant, have you ever been to Baltimore?"

It was a trap, and I knew it. Something about my accent must have piqued his curiosity, careful as I was to sound like a Yankee. Now anyone from Baltimore would insist that the correct pronunciation for that city is Bahdah-more.

So I answered, "No, sir, never been to Baltimore, but I did spend some years growing up here in Washington. I think that's part of the reason Colonel Baker selected me for this assignment."

That seemed to satisfy him, at least for now. He was clearly a difficult man to dupe.

They asked me to step out into the anteroom while they discussed the matter. I looked at the clock as I left the room. It was quarter past midnight. Saturday, April the first. I grinned at that thought. April fool's day. That whopper of a story should have them running around in circles for a while. With a decent run of luck, they should be able to pick up George Sanders and do my work for me. Now I just had to figure out how to extricate myself from this whole mess. I had some thoughts about that. In the meantime, it appeared that they trusted me enough to wait for them by myself, but I probably had only just the weekend before they started finding holes in my story. I was very sure there was already a telegraph waiting for Lafayette Baker on his desk.

Captain Hebert was the first to emerge. He went directly out front and ordered the carriage brought around. I heard a grumpy response, but he got prompt results, the mark of a respected officer. He waved for me to follow and as we climbed into the coach, he asked, "Hungry?"

"Enough to eat a horse."

We went to a tavern up the avenue, about three blocks, and had a decent meal in spite of the noise of the revelers and the drunks, a typical Friday night on the town. Many people at play after a week of work, others looking on and watching for opportunity. After the meal, Hebert took me to the Ebbitt House and checked me in. He had brought the rest of my belongings when he had gone to pick up my medical bag. Nice to get a room and a meal at government expense. Captain Hebert told me to be ready to be picked up Monday morning, first thing.

It was after three in the morning by the time I got settled in. I had a warm clean bed for a change and slept in until almost noon, needing the recharge. I only had sixty dollars but was glad for that. It was a bit of money but wouldn't last long, so I had to be frugal. I opted for a large meal at dinner prices rather than pay for an additional expensive supper later on. I assumed someone was watching, so I went straight back to my room to relax and nap.

After dark, about seven in the evening, I dressed in my uniform and left my room, went down to the lobby, then out the front door. I couldn't tell if I was followed, and I didn't want to try anything diversionary that would create suspicion. Besides, being followed would play right into my plan; I was counting on it. I went around the corner and entered the Bull's Head where the action was in full swing. I took a vacant seat at the end of the bar, ordered a beer, and began nursing it while I watched the place.

After about two hours of waiting, I saw a scenario developing that I liked and took action. There was a young girl, a little pale and a little thin, who was working the floor without much success. A clique of other working girls were actively blocking her from having access to any of the more affluent men at the gaming tables or other groups of nicely-dressed men drinking and carousing. At one point, this girl was actually given a shove by another girl at which point, three others started laughing at her.

I ordered a bottle of cheap whiskey and two glasses from the bartender, walked right up to her, gave a crisp little bow, and, while looking her directly in the eyes, said, "Okay if I buy a very pretty girl a drink?" I didn't think it was possible to make a prostitute blush, but I think she almost did. I took her arm in mine and steered toward an open table in the back. Another of the girls tried to coax me away, but I gave her a very cold stare and said, "Do you mind? I'm rather too busy for your little games." That backed her up.

I sat with my selected young lady, uncorked the bottle, and poured her a generous amount. I gave her a closer look while she sipped the whiskey. I wanted a smart girl who needed the work, and she looked like she would fill the bill. Her hair was rather long but mouse-brown so she didn't really stand out. She had rouge on her cheeks, but that only accentuated her pale skin. She was actually kind of pretty in a plain farm-girl way. She looked like she could use a good meal. When she was almost finished with her first drink, I refilled her glass. That just made her appreciative look turn suspicious. She looked at me and said, "Mister, if you want to take me upstairs, it'll be two dollars."

I laughed which caused her further consternation and said, "How'd you like to make twenty dollars instead?"

Now she looked straight at me but didn't make eye contact. "I don't do nothin' peculiar or dangerous."

I laughed again and said, "Nothing like that. What is your name, young lady?"

After a pause, "Rachel."

Probably not her real name, but hey, me neither. "Well, Rachel, suppose you finish that drink, I'll give you two dollars and we can go upstairs where we can discuss my business proposition privately." Which is exactly what we did. I brought the bottle along to maintain the image.

Her room was small—just a bed, nightstand, and cheap armoire. She lit a small lamp on the nightstand, further accentuating the dinginess of her lodgings. The walls were likely to be paper-thin. She sat on the bed, but I remained standing.

"Here's the deal," I said. "I'm working for the War Department, but I need to disappear for a short time to complete my mission. You will probably discover that there is a man following me."

"Oh," she said in a breathy gasp. "You are a spy!"

Apparently that was way better than being a soldier or a politician these days.

"Lieutenant Welch, at your service, ma'am," I said with a big smile. "I want you to let me out the backdoor, then after an hour, I want you to go downstairs and raise a fuss. Tell the bouncers that as I was leaving your room, three men knocked me over the head and dragged me out the backdoor."

I paused to let that sink in. I'm going to give you ten dollars now, and I'll leave an envelope for you with ten dollars at the bar when I find out this was reported to the police."

She lay back on the bed and assumed a posture that reminded me vaguely of a cat and said, "Sure I can't give you your money's worth?" She rubbed the palm of her hand over the blanket to encourage me.

I bent over her, putting my hands on the bed on either side of her and kissed her lightly on the forehead.

"As lovely as that sounds, I don't have the time."

I took both her hands in mine and pulled her to her feet. She was even prettier when she pouted.

She guided me down the back stairs and opened the door for me. Standing there, in the dark doorway, I gave her a little kiss on the lips and whispered, "Remember—"

She cut me off with a hard kiss of her own, pressing herself up against me and whispered back, "Don't worry. Lieutenant Welch and three men clobbering you."

Then she smiled brightly up at me, gave me another squeeze, and said, "Just so you know what you're missin'!"

"Maybe when I get back, you could arrange a freebie for me," I answered, leaving the statement open-ended.

Looking just like the young girl she was, she replied, "Not a chance, mister. You're cute and all but not as handsome as Johnnie Wilkes Booth." Then she closed the door in my face. She had no idea of how that statement cut me.

I re-entered the Ebbitt House through the bathrooms but still had to scurry through the edge of the lobby to get up the stairs. I removed my uniform coat, just in case, although anyone seeing the light-blue trousers would recognize them as army. Once in my room, I changed quickly into duck pants, checked shirt, and pea coat and, setting my tarpaulin hat at a jaunty angle, slipped downstairs and out the side door. I had left both suits hanging in the closet and the medical bag with my papers visibly sitting on the bed. I was taking no chances when they came to search the room. My revolver and holster I took with me, rolled up in the bottom of my bag. The Yankee uniform was once again folded up on top.

I went two blocks south before returning to the Bull's Head, finding a convenient crevice on the way to stash my seabag. I walked back in, bellied up to the bar, and started in on a beer. It was encouraging that the bartender didn't recognize me at all; he was busy and being all manly for the serving girls. Right on schedule, I saw Rachel appear at the top of the stairs. I noticed her hand go up to her face—I swear I saw her pluck a hair from her nose before she came running down the stairs with tears streaming down her cheeks. She was yelling out for the bully boys that provided security for the bar. I had to hand it to her, she was very good and created quite a disturbance.

Immediately Rachel had three or four of the bouncers around her asking questions. She was sobbing, pointing up the stairs, and talking in disjointed sentences. The men started shouting at each other, then one took charge. He sent one man out the front door while the other three went racing up the stairs. I was about to consider the act successful when another man stepped up to Rachel and grabbed her roughly by the arm. He was black-haired and dark-complexioned, dressed plainly but neatly. I could see Rachel was scared when he started to question her, and when he let her go and followed the other men up the stairs, she collapsed into a chair. I got the impression that this time, the tears were real.

After a few minutes watching the drama unfold, I exited the bar, assuming the rolling walk of a sailor, weaving a bit back-and-forth and singing a song as I made my way through the beehive of activity and men with lanterns out on the sidewalk. The black-haired man in the neat suit was standing there, looking very frustrated. So as I walked right by him, I started up on a new verse of my song.

"Oh, I wish that the girls were like fish in the ocean…"

I made sure to bump him with my elbow as I went by.

It took me a week of hanging out in the southeast sector of the city, down by the commercial docks, before I landed a berth as an able-bodied seaman on a steam barque bound for Quebec. In the meantime, the city throbbed with the news of the fall and burning of Richmond, then Lee's surrender at Appomattox Court House. We warped out before dawn on Thursday, the thirteenth, just in time as it turned out. I didn't find out that Booth had actually assassinated Lincoln until we arrived in Quebec. The Yankee uniform had gone into the Potomac River that first night, wrapped around a large rock.

I never did give the girl Rachel her other ten dollars, but times were hard and money tight. I hope she just figured that I ended up a casualty.

My initial destination was St. Catharines. It had seemed like such a nice quiet town when I had visited there previously. Of course, that had been in the summer, not in the winter.

EPILOGUE

After forty years, I can see signs that the South is beginning to recover economically. Although nobody there will even admit they lost the war. It was seven long years before most of the rebellious states were admitted back into the Union. Until then, the people of those states weren't even allowed to elect their own officials. Instead the federal government appointed everyone in power. It was enforced by the military occupation. Sometimes the government appointed black folk to be in charge of things, just to punish the genteel white people some more. Since there was no money, work, or opportunity left in the South, there was a mass migration of blacks to the cities, especially to the north. They would work harder for less pay than even the Irish. Racism was already there in the United States before the war, but those with power in government had a great time ramping up the hatred. I find people in general to be like that. It's not any fun to be rich and powerful if you can't keep it exclusive. The more "others" you can trod on the backs of, the better off you feel; and if that person looks different, so much the better. Some folks even have a true talent for it.

Everyone is familiar with the fate of Wilkes Booth—he got what he asked for. Not only infamy but all the credit for the assassination of President Lincoln. Being the narcissist that he was, he took with him everyone else around him. The only surprise was that it took twelve days to find him when nobody wanted to hide him. Even Sergeant Corbett, the Yankee soldier who shot Booth in Richard Garrett's barn, ended up trying to be a preacher, went insane, castrated himself, then disappeared into the wilds of Minnesota.

Four of Booth's conspirators were hanged publicly, including Mary Surratt, her crime being that she hosted meetings in her

Washington boarding house. More of the meetings were held at the National Hotel but no blame was placed on those proprietors. Mary Surratt went to her end still protesting her innocence. Powell the thug just took his end without a word, Atzerodt the drunk mumbled some encouragement to the others, and Herold refused to sit for the reading of the death warrant. I believe the whole country lost a sense of what is civilized behavior when they allowed the public hanging of a woman.

My friend and colleague, Sam Mudd, was found guilty of conspiracy, although he was not involved in the assassination, just the plan to kidnap the president. Wilkes Booth stopping at Sam's farm to have his broken leg set doomed him; Sam couldn't get his story straight. I'm told that the testimony of that weasel Louis Weichmann was instrumental to the finding. Sam, along with three of the others, were sent to Fort Jefferson in the Dry Tortugas—hell on earth if there is one. He spent four years there before he was released, contracting yellow fever in the process while attempting to save the other sick men on the post. He was released but never pardoned, health broken and died young.

George Sanders fled to Europe after the war; his last act of terrorism was to have a bomb shaped like a lump of coal placed in the bin on a Yankee riverboat, the *Sultana*. The ship was carrying over 2,000 people, including 1,961 who had been prisoners of war and were returning home to be discharged. The ship exploded, burned, and sank rapidly, taking 1,100 of those poor men with her. They had survived the prison at Andersonville only to die in a terrorist attack after the war was over. I always thought it suspicious that the government tracked down John Surratt and brought him back to stand trial, yet they never bothered with George Sanders. George returned to New York in 1873 and was never tried for his crimes, even though Wilkes Booth still had a bank draft from Sanders in his pocket when he was caught. But his fate is the stuff of a different story.

Jacob Thompson initially fled to England but then returned to Tennessee. Somehow he was wealthy beyond imagination and developed a horde of investment strategies. He did very well for himself with all the influential friends that money could buy.

Clement Clay was the opposite. He surrendered himself in Georgia and was imprisoned. I heard that only an impassioned plea from his wife, directly to President Johnson, got him released. The specter of the plot continued to hang over his head; nothing he tried got him anywhere, and he died a pauper.

The young officers Bennett Young and Thomas Hines both returned to Kentucky after the war and became prominent businessmen. Both gave generously to public works. I never met Lieutenant Peter Scott, but I had my father check on Bridget, his wife, after the war. Seems Pete Scott survived after all; he surrendered with General Lee at Appomattox, was paroled, and returned home. My father probably sent his man Gayle down to do the checking. That would have scared Bridget some, but Gayle and Bob the dog would have got on famously. My hope is that the Scotts have a great life, complete with many fat and successful children.

James Bulloch, my esteemed mentor, was never allowed to return to the United States, a wanted man for the rest of his life. Apparently causing financial havoc is way worse than having soldiers die for you. The three ships that Bulloch had built for the Confederacy almost forced the insurance companies into bankruptcy, and the American whaling fleet never fully recovered. They filed a lawsuit against the English government for their role in allowing it to happen, however, and won. They recouped some of their losses eventually. One of the few incidents in history where foreign governments didn't just ignore an American lawsuit. James Bulloch had the last laugh in the end. His nephew is now the president of the United States.

Colonel Lafayette Baker swept back into Washington to head the chase for Booth following the assassination, claiming it was his man Lieutenant Welch who had initially uncovered the scheme. Due to my report to Stanton, Andy Johnson was investigated for his presumed part in the plot to murder Lincoln. This almost led to his impeachment later for his policies on not allowing blacks' citizenship or the vote and trying to get rid of Stanton in 1868. I followed those developments as they unfolded with interest. After Lieutenant Welch's uniform coat was pulled out of the Potomac River, Colonel Baker put him in for a posthumous Medal of Honor.

Congress forwarded the matter, but President Johnson refused to sign off on it. I did find a family in Steuben County, New York, who liked having a hero cousin, and they keep petitioning their congressman for the medal. Maybe someday. A grand hero's funeral was had, and the uniform coat was buried in the soldier's cemetery at Arlington, Virginia.

My family didn't prosper in the long-term. My half-sister, Caroline, didn't survive the war; she died trying to rescue the other children at her boarding school in Carlisle, Pennsylvania, when that city was destroyed by Confederate raiders. She was just fifteen years old. I did always wonder how my stepmother allowed my father to name her after his first wife, but that was their issue. Then in August of 1865, the *Mary Eleanore* disappeared with all hands in a hurricane. I heard they were trying to make it into Wilmington, North Carolina, just ahead of the storm, an odd one that tracked in from the east out of the Atlantic rather than the normal weather from out of the Gulf of Mexico. The lighthouse marking the shoals at the river entrance had been damaged in the attack on Fort Fisher, and nothing in the South was getting repaired very quickly.

I have to say, it was not like my Uncle Thomas to make a mistake like that, even in the dark and in a hurricane, but there were rumors that he had to make a rendezvous to land a portion of his cargo at the Brunswick ghost town after dark. My Aunt Eleanore never believed that he was dead. Even when she passed a couple of years ago, she bought a dual plot in the cemetery with his headstone next to hers, no death date.

My father died in 1877. There was a nice ceremony as befitted a pillar of the Baltimore community. My stepmother ensured that his estate passed to Thomas, her son. Thomas was always interested in women's fashions, shoes, handbags, and accessories. Perhaps Baltimore was not the town for that; he invested all his money in a line of high-quality handmade shoes and went broke. He couldn't compete with the assembly line processes being perfected in places like Boston and Philadelphia. Thomas finally married when he was older but never had children. Better than my half-brother, Alfred. I think he is still in prison for his proclivities with other men.

My daughter, Nellie, took advantage of her lack of supervision when my father passed; she was only seventeen when she eloped with a Pennsylvania Yankee. She always was a bit headstrong like that. She is, after all, the only child in her generation in our family. She made a good life of it though. I believe I'm to be a great-grandfather any time, if not already. I try to make it up to Lockhaven before Christmas every year to see her and her kids when things are slow, to keep connections intact. She is the only one I trust to keep the secret of my true identity. Although it's been forty years, I still do not trust the government.

As for my doings since the war, well, that's another sailor story.

ABOUT THE AUTHOR

Kurt Burke is an avid historian and researcher. Originally from Pennsylvania, he now resides in Washington State. After serving in the United States Marine Corps then a twenty-five year career in social work and mental health counseling, Kurt is now semi-retired. He currently does technical work for the local county sheriff's office and is exploring his capacity as an author of historical fiction.

CPSIA information can be obtained
at www.ICGtesting.com
Printed in the USA
FSHW022206080620
70733FS

9 781098 010027